Mute

A.W. Wilson

Copyright © 2021 A.W. Wilson

All rights reserved.

The moral right of the copyright holder has been asserted

This book is a work of fiction. Names, characters, businesses, organisations, places and events are either the product of the author's imagination or are used fictitiously. Any resemblance to actual persons, living or dead, events or locales is entirely coincidental.

awwilson.com

Printed and bound by Amazon

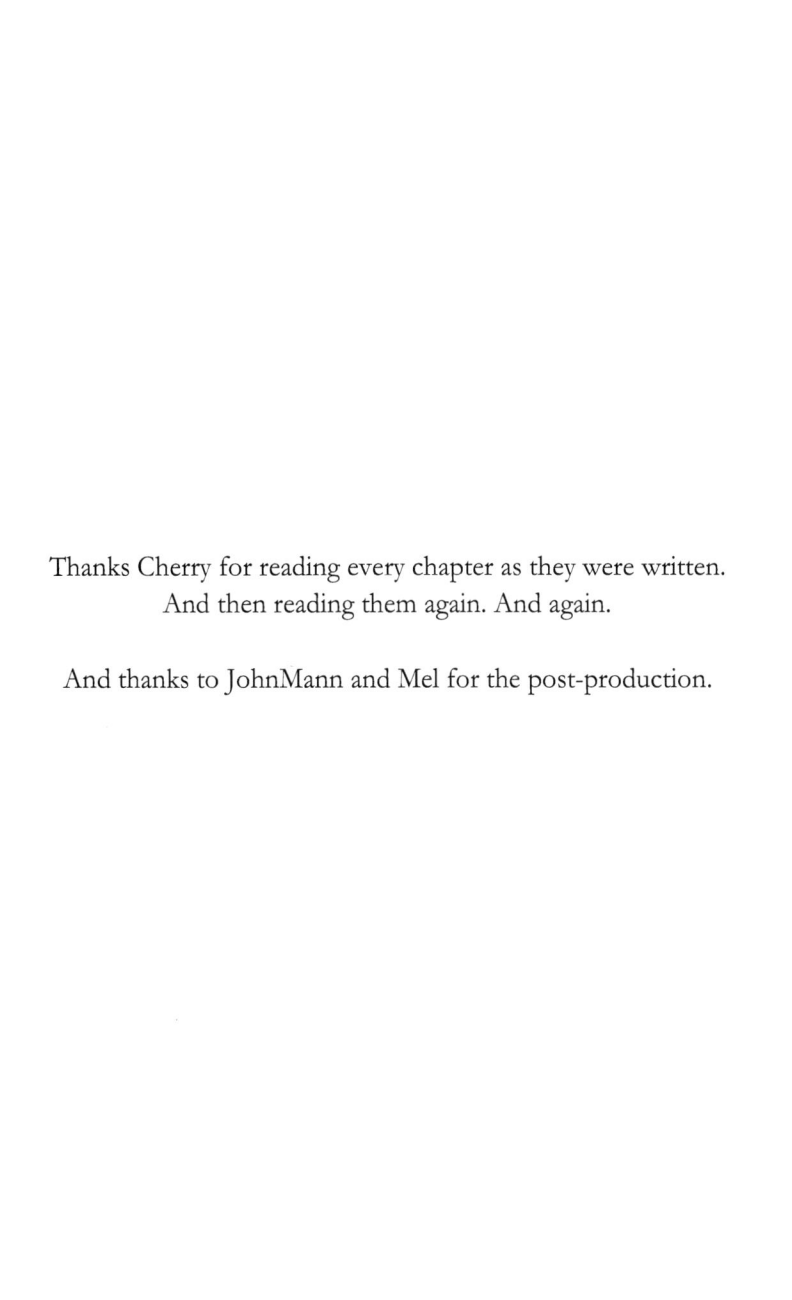

Thanks Cherry for reading every chapter as they were written.
And then reading them again. And again.

And thanks to JohnMann and Mel for the post-production.

Chapter 1. Apocalypse Soup Kitchen

The apocalypse came and went and I missed it. It's a shame. I mean it's a shame about the apocalypse, not that I missed it.

Could I be the last human alive? I don't have enough information to answer that. It's definitely possible that I'm the last man on earth, the last man standing, but it's just as possible that other people survived whatever it was that ended the world. There could be what they call in those post-apocalyptic movies, pockets of humanity, ramshackle bands fighting to keep the species alive, to rebuild, all that malarkey.

Or maybe it only happened on my patch. Maybe it was a purely local catastrophe. If that's true then I'm going to look a right muppet when I'm found, what with me living like *I Am Legend*.

I'd better explain how I got here. I'm not sure who I'm explaining this to though, there might not be anyone to hear it. I know I shouldn't think like that but I can't pretend I'm feeling at all positive right now.

Here's what happened.

It was a big night. A big session. There were three of us, Rachel and Pete and me. We all called in sick from work on the Friday and went out for a late breakfast. Then we started on the beer and the shots. We really hammered it all afternoon. Then afternoon became evening and evening became night and we carried on hammering it. The drugs came out at some point, they had to or we wouldn't have lasted. It was properly messy.

We ended up back at Pete's. I don't remember much apart from feeling really up for it with Rachel and realising pretty quickly that she was feeling really up for it with Pete. I think I might have toyed with the idea of trying to get all of us involved in something but that would have been too weird, and more to the point, why would Pete have wanted me involved if he was on course to get Rachel all to himself anyway? And besides, I don't think Rachel wanted me involved at all.

So I left them to it. I remember that part. I remember the walk home. It was stupid o'clock, maybe eight am, full-on daylight and people from the real world starting to go about their business. I just kept my head down. I was in a right old state and just needed to get home. My pride was hurt because of the Rachel and Pete thing and I was coming down like a sledgehammer on a rock.

When I got home I made a decision, a necessary decision. There was no way I was going to spend one of those horrible sleepless comedowns lying in my bed, sweating and twitching, tossing and turning - starting to doze off then coming back round again because of all the chemicals still racing around in my mind, making it buzz and whirr and spin and not stop not stop not stop. I've been through enough of those awful times. So I hit my stash: Temazipam, Diazepam, mazzies, dizzies, jellies, downers, whatever you want to call them. I hammered a load, I was taking no chances, I dosed up good and proper.

Then I had a big gin and a fat joint and that was that.

I woke up a long time later. At least a day later. I knew I'd been properly knocked out. It took me a while to shake the fug of sleep from my head, it seemed to take hours, then I realised I was in a different kind of fug. A fever. I was proper hot and proper ill. I started shivering like crazy so I wrapped myself in the duvet and tried to sweat it out. I was burning up but I was freezing too. I was a human Baked Alaska. I held the duvet really tight around me but I was still cold. I jumped out of bed to get a jumper from a drawer and in the few seconds I was out of bed the chill hit me double hard and I started shivering like I've never known before. It was like I was drilling a road. I thought my teeth were going to fall out from all the rattling. I grabbed not just the jumper but all the clothes I could hold at once and bundled myself back into bed. I put the clothes under the duvet and just lay there, burning and shaking. I was hallucinating, the delirium from the fever spiced up by whatever leftovers from Friday's session were still loose in my system.

I lay in that sweaty pit for days and it was more than a bit shit. I'd put a pint glass of water on the bedside table when I'd first gone to bed and that's all I had to drink the whole time. I didn't go to the toilet once. Every bit of liquid in me was sweated out. I thought I was going to die.

But I didn't die.

I was, as they say in books, slipping in and out of consciousness. I have no idea how long this went on for, this loop, in and out, in and out, but I remember finally slipping back into consciousness and this time it felt different. Something had changed. The loop had broken and I didn't fall into that crazy fevered dreamworld again. The fug and the fever and the shivering had gone. I still felt awful obviously, after all I was dangerously dehydrated and starved of food. And all from a starting base of eighteen hours of drink and drug abuse. It's not really abuse though is it? That's how drink and drugs are meant to be used.

But the point is that I was back in the land of the living, as they say. But I wasn't as it turned out, not amongst the living, I was just back.

The first thing I had to do was drink. I shuffled to the kitchen sink and filled a glass, downed it and refilled it, downed it and refilled it. Downed it.

I was gutted to find that the electricity was off. I assumed it had to be because of something I'd done in my stupor but I couldn't remember anything. I looked at the flip-switches in the hallway cupboard but they all seemed to be pointing the right way. That was as far as my electrician skills went so I decided to worry about it later, eating something was a much higher priority.

I fried up some sausages and started eating while they were still far too hot. My mouth burned but I swear I could hear my stomach thanking me, even though its voice was all muffled by the food I was shovelling down.

I got back into the sweat-bed and slept again. A different sleep this time, a normal sleep, more of a nap really. I was out for about an hour and when I woke up I felt much better than before. Going to the toilet was a bit of a mission. It took ages for things to start moving, like there was a blockage somewhere in the plumbing, but once it got going it really got going. I took a long shower, working hard to get rid of the stench of sweat that was ingrained in my skin. I got dressed and decided to go out for the staples: bread, milk, eggs and the like. I thought about turning on my phone but didn't feel in the right state of mind to trawl through what I thought had to be millions of messages left over the last, how many days? I wasn't ready to find out just yet.

Before I could do anything there was a knock at the door. I didn't open it straight away, I called out instead with a *who-is-it* or something similar.

"Good afternoon sir. I have been carrying out regular sweeps of this area and had previously marked your residence as inactive. I did this, sir, because I was unable to observe any activity. However, in my most recent sweep, which is the one I am carrying out now, sir, I have observed activity. I have updated my records accordingly. Your residence is now marked as active."

I responded with a *what-the-hell-are-you-talking-about* or something similar.

"This is my area, sir, my *sector* if you will. It is my assumption, sir, that activity in a residence indicates the availability of flesh and sinew. Flesh and sinew and blood, oh my."

It was typical Pete. He was always on a wind-up. He loved doing voices, pulling pranks. I opened the door.

It wasn't Pete. It was a zombie.

It was an awful-looking thing, human but all melted and lumpy. Its skin was this dirty purple colour and its eyes were bulging like in that bit at the end of Total Recall where Arnie gets sucked out onto the surface of Mars and his head's going to burst because of the thin atmosphere. The zombie was wearing a white short-sleeved shirt, open at the collar and tucked into high-waisted brown cords. Its shoes were black and chunky, like the ones the square kids at school wore, by choice or because their parents forced them. There were more lumpy welts on its forearms and it was wearing a plastic digital watch. On the other wrist it had one of those copper bracelets, the ones you used to see advertised in the back of Sunday supplements that are meant to ward off cancer and heart disease. It didn't seem to have done this guy much good.

It was obvious from its clothes that this thing had been human until very recently, and now it was a zombie.

It was holding a clipboard.

I tried to shut the door but it blocked it with its knee. "You need to allow me access to your meat, sir. This is my area, my *sector*."

I had no replies, just violence. I used the door as a weapon, slamming it against the thing a few times and then knocking it to the ground with a well-placed kick, although not so well-placed that I didn't get stinky discharge on my socked foot. I ran past it, up the steps and into the street.

The place wasn't teeming with zombies but there were more than enough to scare the bejesus out of me. It was weird seeing all the torn human clothes hanging off their lumpy, purple bodies. I saw one that was wearing a stupid hat. He must have been a prick while he was alive if he wore that hat. He's a zombie prick now.

Moving as quickly as I could, I took some shoes off a corpse in the street. All the flesh had been sucked clean off the bones. There were corpses in a similar state all over the place. It was like the zombies' mums had brought them up not to waste any food. I ran around like an avatar in a video game, picking up useful stuff while trying to avoid getting killed. I eventually found a secure place to hunker down.

I'm sure there's an irony to this but my secure spot is a morgue. It's a nice morgue, minimalist design, clean lines, low roof, and in terms of security its perfect. The door's made of layered steel. It was open when I got here and when I pulled it closed behind me it felt like I was shutting myself into a bank vault. It doesn't have proper windows, just a thin strip of meshed glass running along the top edge of each wall, like you used to get in public toilets. The only way in or out apart from the Fort Knox door is a three-foot wide hatch at the front. It must have been where the bodies were dropped off because there's this metal chute underneath. I guess the corpses would have slid down that onto one of the trolleys that's in here, then been rolled off into the cold storage drawers. The hatch is made of the same stuff as the door, it only has a handle on my side and it's got a hefty bolt keeping it shut. Next to that and a bit lower down there's this smaller hatch like they have in post offices where the cashier's behind a glass screen. It's a drawer and when the cashier pulls it open on their side it closes on yours.

Because the place was so secure already I didn't need to take all the extra precautions that you see in the movies - nailing boards across windows, sticking mops through double door handles, that sort of caper. Nothing's getting in here anytime soon.

I've got plenty of food, not nice food but edible food, a mix of dry and tinned. There's no power but I've got all the water I need. I picked up some books and crossword puzzles from my travels around town and they kill a bit of time when there's enough daylight coming through the little slits of window, that's if I can manage to get my mind to stay focused. It's not much fun in here but the one thing in my favour is that I'm not dead. And you'd be surprised how important staying alive is. Even when life seems like no existence at all, something makes you hang on. Maybe it's the hope of rescue. I do hope I get rescued. But I know I'm not going to be. Help's clearly not on the way.

This would have been a perfect bolthole if it wasn't for one thing: they know I'm in here. There are five of them camped outside.

They're a funny bunch. I've seen plenty of zombie movies and they can't normally speak. Usually the most you can expect is for them to howl the word 'brains' over and over. This lot are different, they're very talkative, extremely chatty. I should qualify that: they're not chatty in a *how-was-your-weekend* way, they're chatty in a *can-I-eat-your-liver-and-drink-your-blood* way. They're always polite, but very assertive, very clear. I respect that about them. You know where you stand with these zombies. Admittedly, that first one was a bit slippery, trying to fool me into thinking he was some kind of official and all, but fair play to him for using what was left of his imagination.

I'd like to know their back-story. In the movies the rules are very clearly defined: The zombies come into being because of something specific. A military weapon – biological or chemical - a plague, an alien invasion, something along those lines. With this lot I've got no idea what the premise is, I slept through whatever kicked it all off. It's frustrating. I've tried asking them but they can't tell me, they don't seem to remember what happened. And even if they did, it's almost impossible to get them away from the subject of how much they want to eat me.

Another thing I'm none the wiser about is if there's an ongoing process of zombification. In the movies, a scratch or a bite turns you, or sometimes you have to be killed by one, then you come round a few hours later with a lopsided gait and a hankering for brains. I don't know if I'd get zombified if I got scratched by one of this lot, but I don't suppose it matters. They don't want to scratch me, they just want to eat me, they've made that abundantly clear.

I was surprised that more didn't turn up, but they seem pretty discreet. In the movies they make a right old noise whatever they're doing, like when they're ripping someone's guts out, uncoiling the intestine like a floppy garden hose, it always attracts loads of other zombies. Before you know it the place is crawling with them and none of them gets a fair share. But these ones, these real ones, they're more careful. I think they realise that if they keep it quiet about how there's a live human being in here then there'll be more of me to go around. I respect their discretion.

Another thing I respect is their ability to reason. They're a bit stubborn and will go on a bit about the stuff that's important to them, namely the fact that they want to eat me, but once I get their attention they do listen to what I'm saying. And that means I've been able to manage them. Up to a point.

Mute

I've got everything any good morgue attendant might need in here. There are plenty of things to cut with, it's a proper Aladdin's cave of blades. There are scalpels, saws, tongs, clamps and pokey things. There are tools that are like ice-cream scoops, but sharper and with a longer handle. It's properly well-stocked, this place.

There were six bodies in the drawers set into the back wall.

I held my breath and got busy, slicing and dicing and jabbing and tugging at the first cold storage corpse. Because the power's off it wasn't cold anymore and it didn't smell too good. I went for a leg first, the least gooey bit, thought I'd ease in slowly.

I tried to tell myself I was just slicing the meat for a kebab but that didn't seem to help much. I puked all the way through and gagged and coughed and puked again. I sliced the shin and the calf and the ankle, and even through all the sick and all the snot - and even through all the tears - I couldn't help but marvel at the quality of the tools I had at my disposal. So sharp, so sleek. The choice of the professional.

I put the meat into stainless-steel trays that I found stacked in a cupboard. And then I was ready to serve.

And that's how I've been managing them.

I had to make an announcement. I had to tell them that there's no point in them making a big fuss outside, I wasn't going to let them come in and eat me. But I told them I can give them a daily meal, and after a lot of whingeing and griping they finally agreed.

That post office drawer I mentioned? Well that's the serving hatch for my canteen.

Welcome to the Apocalypse Soup Kitchen.

I make them take turns so they get a portion each. I don't want one getting starved and going nuts. I want them all under control. They moaned a lot at first, insisting they were used to bigger meals, but I had to take a hard line to make the supplies last.

Very occasionally they'll get a treat, like the other day I surprised them with a handful of toes. They liked that. Very appreciative they were.

I've been doing what I can to eke this out for as long as possible. I found some blood bags and syringes and all that transfusion paraphernalia and I've been storing up a pint of my blood at a time. I've started giving it to them every few days to save on the corpse meat. They don't seem to mind it but they're always a little more restless on the liquid lunch days. There are only half a dozen bags so I have to get them to throw them back through the hatch so I can refill them. They seem happy to recycle. They're friends of the earth zombies.

It's getting harder to keep the bags topped up - my blood is literally running thin.

I asked them this morning what will happen when I run out of stuff to give them. I kept it vague of course, I didn't let on how low on supplies this soup kitchen actually is. I didn't want to stir them up. They're polite, as I've said, but they're determined, and extremely bloodthirsty. Properly thirsty for blood, they are. I asked them what they'll do when it runs out and the leader one, he told me. "We will decide that there is no longer any reason for discretion. We will bang on the metal door with sticks and bars to make as much noise as possible. This will bring many others of our kind. We will make sure we are at the front, for purely selfish reasons, but we will use the strength in numbers - the actual physical strength of the large numbers - to break into this facility. Then we will tear the sinew and muscle and fat from your bones. And we will drink your blood."

I've got one and a half bodies left, not counting my own.

Chapter 2. Romance is undead

Iqbal was excited, he'd clocked up enough airtime to take a passenger, and his choice of maiden flight was a no-brainer: he would whisk Georgie, his girlfriend of three months, to Paris for the weekend. When Georgie heard Iqbal's breathlessly delivered news, she rejected the French capital and opted instead for the Northern Isles of Scotland. At first Iqbal felt that his romantic bonfire had been royally pissed on, but he quickly saw the attraction of spending several days in total isolation with the girl he still couldn't quite believe had agreed to sleep with him on a regular basis.

So the Northern Isles of Scotland it was.

When Georgie was seventeen, her then-boyfriend, a lad called Mark who worked in his parents' fish and chip shop in the evenings, had passed his driving test and taken her out for a spin. Georgie had found it so strange sitting in the passenger seat and watching Mark doing such a grown-up activity as driving, that she had spent the entire journey laughing hysterically. Mark's look of concentration as he monitored the road ahead, the gear-changes, the careful placement of his hands on the wheel, it was all too much for her. It was as if the boy she'd had her first awkward fumble with had been replaced with a grown-up imposter.

Ten years on and a different guy but a similar experience ten times magnified: Iqbal nosing around the outside of the plane, carrying out the safety checks, noting things on a clipboard with a serious face on, and Georgie not knowing where to look or what to say. The whole thing was just too bizarre.

Side by side in the cockpit, their headsets on and Iqbal, still wearing that earnest look, turned the key in the ignition just as Mark had done in his mum's Ford Fiesta all those years ago. Georgie's innate curiosity and eagerness to learn won over her almost Tourettic urge to laugh and she listened intently as Iqbal talked her through everything he was doing as they rumbled towards the runway. She was impressed by how much he sounded like all the airline pilots she had ever heard making their announcements on the countless flights she had taken.

Impressed, and more than a little bit aroused.

Georgie was fascinated by every word, every action as Iqbal worked the controls to power them down the runway and hoist them into the sky. It was only when they had levelled out and were cruising, the engine still rumbling away not unlike that old Ford Fiesta, that she got the giggles again.

Iqbal feigned offence at Georgie's hysteria but in truth he loved it. He was doing something he knew very few other guys could do and he enjoyed being *the man*. He was treated to the best blow job of his life that evening, and eagerly returned the favour once his windsock had filled out again.

They had a fine old time on the island, not that they saw much of it. The cottage was so idyllic it was a cliché. The weather was terrible but they didn't care. They saw almost nobody but each other. Their phones were off and they felt changed, rebooted.

The storm that raged all through the first full day and into the second night kept them confined to the cottage and would have kept them awake had they been trying to sleep. The rain made a percussion section of their windows, windows that afforded them ringside views of the bleak beauty of lightning flashes over open sea. If Iqbal had had a ring on him he would have proposed, and Georgie would have accepted. They both said the 'L' word repeatedly and it felt perfectly natural on their tongues. They had missed Valentine's Day by two weeks, but that didn't matter in the slightest. This wasn't the version of romance sold in greetings cards, this was the real thing.

Home time on Sunday afternoon came far too soon. To their disappointment the storm had passed and despite a rather strange three-minute downpour earlier on, the skies were clear, robbing them of the excuse of being grounded by the weather and forced to stay longer. They didn't want to leave their romantic bubble and the flight back to real-life, to work, was dreary. Iqbal followed the coastline and the view of clifftops and empty beaches, whilst striking at first, soon lost its appeal. They both became lost in thoughts of what this newly turbo-charged relationship meant for their short- and long-term futures; when they had left home they had been just a few notches up from 'casual', now they were in love.

As they cut inland and approached their home airfield Iqbal stole glances at the woman he knew he could no longer live without, at the flawless dark skin and magical green eyes that solemnly watched him as he prepared to land. He thought she was the most beautiful thing he had ever seen.

He should have been happy, deliriously so, but his main emotion was fear. Something was wrong, very wrong indeed. There had been no response from air traffic control, nothing on the radio at all and the airfield was devoid of life. He didn't want to worry Georgie so he told her this wasn't necessarily a problem, which would have been true had they been landing out of hours. But this wasn't out of hours and it had just dawned on Iqbal that he hadn't seen another aircraft for the entire flight.

Iqbal knew he had to take them down anyway; there wasn't enough fuel to linger. Both in an attempt to stifle his nerves and because Georgie had seemed to like it, he talked through each of the landing procedures as he brought the plane down, executing a perfect landing and bringing them to a gentle stop. As he opened the door he told Georgie to stay put, that he would come around to her side and help her get off the plane, although he didn't say 'get off', he said 'disembark', the pilot vernacular.

Despite Iqbal's efforts Georgie knew that things weren't right and her belly was an industrial paint-mixer of tension as her now loved-one walked around the front of the aircraft. The tension upgraded to full-scale horror when Iqbal reappeared from the still slowly rotating propeller and she saw his face. She had never seen anybody so terrified. His wide eyes were fixed on something behind the plane and Georgie couldn't see what it was but the sight of Iqbal's fear was enough to make her more scared than she had ever been in her life.

Iqbal looked up at the cockpit and locked eyes with Georgie. He was hurling words in her direction, screaming at her to go go go, to move, to get the fuck out of there.

And he turned and he ran.

Figures emerged from behind the plane, ten, maybe a dozen, each one a ghoulish parody of a human-being. Their skin was a deep purple, tightly drawn back from eyes that bulged like cartoon goldfish. They stampeded past; a pack of two-legged greyhounds after Iqbal the hare. Iqbal ran for his life, or so it seemed at first. It took Georgie a few precious seconds to realise what was actually going on. Iqbal wasn't running for his own life; he was running for Georgie's. He was drawing the monster-people as far away from her as he could to give her a chance of survival. Georgie knew that to make good on his sacrifice she would need to take action herself. She would need to grant Iqbal his last request.

She would need to get the fuck out of there.

Georgie knew she had to try and block out what was going on outside and focus on getting the plane back onto the runway and into the air; not an easy task with her heart trying to beat its way out of her chest. She told herself that she was taking a practical exam, being tested on what she'd learned from the 'lessons' she'd taken sitting next to Iqbal. She talked out loud, reminding herself of what Iqbal had showed her both on Friday and earlier that day. As she tried things, got them wrong and tried again she did her best to squeeze her ears shut to block out a sound she had never heard before but recognised immediately; the sound of Iqbal howling in agony.

She knew this sound meant two things:

1. Iqbal was being torn apart and/or eaten by the monster-people.
2. The monster-people would soon be finished with that particular distraction and would be coming after her at any moment.

It wasn't like the movies, the creatures weren't almost upon her when she finally managed to get the aircraft moving, and when she'd reached what she hoped was the right speed and pulled herself up into the air, she didn't clear their screeching heads by inches.

But it was plenty close enough.

Any relief that Georgie may have felt from escaping immediate certain death was replaced straight away by the blind panic of being alone at the controls of an aeroplane. Her chest pounded and her forearms burned and she tried desperately to calm herself down. *You don't need to hyperventilate*, she told herself, *and you don't need to hold the yoke quite so hard.* She followed her own instructions; relaxed her grip on the half-steering wheel that she had always thought was called a joystick until Iqbal had put her straight, and she started to breathe more slowly. But within seconds she had slipped back to where she had started; panting and clinging to the yoke like she was trying to murder it. This cycle kept repeating, once, twice, a dozen times, and each time the panic came back it was stronger than before. Georgie could feel herself being sucked into the mental quicksand that was slopping around in her head and in a last gasp effort to break the spell she started shouting her own name. She didn't know why she was doing it; she may not have been conscious that she was doing it at all, but in response an image surfaced in her mind and sat there, waiting for her to notice it.

It was from her desk at work, a sticker that had been in a delegate pack from a conference she'd attended. Georgie wasn't one to adorn her workspace with personal detritus, and she wasn't big on motivational soundbites either, but something about this simple message had connected with her and she had decided that it warranted display. Every working day from then on the sticker had been in her eyeline. It was six inches wide and three inches tall. Three words, black text on a white background:

You've got this.

Whenever Georgie was about to start a new task, a new piece of analysis, she would look at that sticker and say its message under her breath three times. It was her ritual, a way of getting into gear, of pulling focus. She found herself doing it now.

And she found that it was helping.

"Despite what you might think," she said out loud, "you've been incredibly lucky. You got this thing into the air and you haven't crashed it, now all you need to do is get it down again."

Georgie's breathing slowed and she released the tension in

her chest and shoulders. She was still holding on a lot more tightly than a flying instructor would recommend but she decided to give herself a break on that one. For the five or so miles she had been in the air she hadn't felt at all in control of the plane but it now occurred to her that all this time she had been successfully holding it steady, keeping course.

The satisfaction this gave her helped steady her nerves but she knew she couldn't keep juddering along in a straight line forever; the fuel gauge didn't tell a happy story and she needed to find somewhere she'd have half a chance of landing very soon. Steering had seemed so simple when she'd watched Iqbal doing it but she had never been more aware of how delicate the forces that kept an aircraft in the sky were than she was now. She couldn't shake the fear that any attempt to change direction could flip the plane out of control and send her nosediving to her death.

She wished that Iqbal had let her have a go when he'd been flying but he had always been a stickler for the rules and, as he had kept reminding her, he wasn't qualified as an instructor so it would have been highly illegal.

She thought about doing a test; trying a small movement to see how the plane responded and taking it from there, but she knew she was a long way from having the courage even to do that, let alone take the plunge and try and steer properly.

Georgie decided she no longer cared for the phrase, 'take the plunge'.

As she tried to muster the courage to make a move, any kind of move, something on the ground ahead caught her attention: Tarmac, shimmering with rainwater. It was an oasis in a desert. She was over a motorway. And it was pointing in the same direction as she was. She knew she wasn't going to get another chance like this one so she grabbed the opportunity with both sets of white knuckles.

Every one of Georgie's instincts was screaming at her that she was going to die, and Georgie screamed right back at them that they weren't helping. She summoned the image of Iqbal next to her and followed the methodical instructions he had given her before. She eased forward on the yoke and was astonished to find that rather than going into a somersault, the plane began to descend. This was a positive development but it did nothing to relieve her urge to vomit as the ground rose to meet her. Imaginary Iqbal talked her down and at the moment before touchdown she heard him telling her to pull on the yoke and kill the throttle. Georgie did as she was told.

It was by no means a soft landing and Georgie felt bones she didn't know she had jolt painfully with the impact. As soon as the wheels were on the middle lane of the wet carriageway the plane veered to the left and Georgie fought against the drag while forcing herself to go easy on the brakes rather than slamming them on. There was nothing else she could do but try and hold as steady as she could, keep easing on the brakes, and wait to see how hard she hit whatever she ended up hitting.

As she careered along the motorway, numbly waiting to see how things would play out, Georgie realised that it hadn't occurred to her that there might have been traffic using the road. The fact that there wasn't any was good for her immediate safety but it did raise the question: where were all the cars? With her mind released from the single purpose of landing the plane without smashing it into pieces she now noticed that *were* vehicles on the road, but all of them were stationery; crashed or abandoned. They were mostly on the hard shoulder but a few were scattered along the main three lanes. She caught the edge of one of these traffic islands and the collision spun her around so she was facing back up the road from where she had come. Still moving at a fair pace, she watched the vehicle she had hit, a black minivan, clatter onto its side. That's when Georgie noticed she had landed on the wrong side of the carriageway. She was heading north on the southbound lanes; she had created her own contra-flow system. It was the least of her worries. When the final crash eventually came, it was into the barrier that separated the two sets of lanes, a soft landing one might say, and with her speed reduced enough so the impact was a fraction of what it could have been. The plane remained mostly intact. And more importantly, so did Georgie.

Georgie had just performed a stunt from an action-movie; she had crash-landed a light aircraft onto a motorway, and even though a Sunday afternoon in March might not have been the busiest time for this particular road, she knew it should have brought police cars, ambulances and breakdown trucks in a chaos of flashing lights. This had *major incident* written all over it. But as she gazed through the cracked glass of the cockpit at the vehicles that littered the road, she thought about the radio silence on the flight back from Scotland and the horrors that had jumped out at them when they had landed: *Worst surprise party ever.*

And it started to dawn on her that a far more major incident had happened here.

The wheels of her carry-on case rumbled in her wake and she gagged at the sight and smell of the human remains that lay in and around the dead vehicles she passed. If she hadn't just seen Iqbal being slaughtered she would have been confused, as well as disgusted and terrified, by what she saw, but things were starting to look very clear on one point at least; the mob of monster-people at the airfield almost certainly hadn't been a one-off.

As she walked, Georgie turned her phone on for the first time since Friday. She had expected the screen to light up with notifications of messages from friends and family all cheerfully vying for her attention, but there was nothing; no signal at all. She opened every messaging app just in case they had updated in the background but she already knew she wasn't going to find anything. For good measure, she spent five minutes watching her web browser fail to load its home screen.

Eventually she went to the last chat between her and Iqbal and re-read his messages.

Only one more sleep and I get to fly you away!!!!!!
It's today! Just me and you for the whole weekend, I can't wait!
Just leaving, eta is 15 minutes, so stoked that we're doing this.

She clicked on Iqbal's profile picture and gazed at it while her heart broke repeatedly.

Afternoon had become evening by the time she had given up on finding an easy way off the motorway. She stepped through the gap between two sections of barrier at the edge of the hard shoulder and climbed up the steep banking. It wasn't easy, the grass was wet, and she lost her footing more than once. When she finally reached the top she looked at the ghost-motorway disappearing in both directions. She glanced at her watch. It was nearly seven. The roadside lights should have come on by now.

She turned and looked away from the road and could see that she was close to the outskirts of town.

She didn't like what she saw.

Instead of the glimmer of streetlights and the activities of life in a functioning city there was only gloom. Georgie could only tell what she was looking at because of the fires that were scattered across the cityscape. It looked like news footage of a war-torn Middle Eastern city in the aftermath of an attack.

She travelled in quickfire bursts, making a dash for it for as long as she dared, and stopping when she found somewhere relatively unexposed where she could watch and wait for signs of danger. Georgie was in good shape, if she had ever needed a dating profile it would have included 'keen runner' amongst her interests, but all that scurrying, creeping and crouching asked very different questions of her muscles and they burned in response. Her carry-on case was a drag but she couldn't bring herself to dump it; she was literally clinging on to the few possessions that remained from the world she had left on Friday.

Her *run – stop - repeat* approach meant that it took her several hours to cover the few miles into town, and as the natural light faded and then disappeared completely, there was no artificial lighting to keep the darkness at bay.

She constantly saw and heard movement and her stops became more frequent and longer each time as she tried to fathom what was ahead of her and how likely it was to kill her. She used the pockets of fire as reverse beacons, places to avoid.

She didn't see any more of the monster-people but the smashed doors and windows of the buildings that she had been able to see, as well as the human remains she'd wished she hadn't, were evidence enough.

Chapter 3. The morning after

It had felt like it was going to rain all morning but so far it had held off… Georgie couldn't believe that even in this terrifying situation she could still have such boring thoughts. She found herself imagining a TV weather forecaster: "*Today's expected precipitation didn't arrive until later in the afternoon…*" and it occurred to her that she might never hear a weather forecast ever again. This little nugget was just the latest in a series of end-of-the-world realisations she'd had since waking from a sleep so broken that she'd felt more exhausted than before.

She said to herself that she needed to take a time out, to take stock, but since she had arrived in this relatively secure hideout late last night, all she had done was take stock and it hadn't helped, she had just asked herself the same questions on a constant loop:

How many people survived this thing?

How many of those creatures are out there?

What should I do next?

And the most obvious question of all:

What the hell happened?

Early in her journey from the crashed motorway Georgie had ruled out trying to get to her flat across town. Instead she'd focused on finding somewhere to hide that:

1. Didn't have any monsters in it.
2. Wasn't somewhere monsters were likely to pop in for a visit.

The place she had settled on would have seemed unlikely in normal circumstances. But these weren't normal circumstances. Georgie had holed-up in a fire station.

Georgie didn't think she had ever used the phrase *holed-up* before.

Creeping around inside the pitch-black building had been even more terrifying than being out in the open, expecting as she was some shrieking beast to explode from behind every door. At first she had checked rooms at random, just going from one to the next, but as her heart-rate had receded and she had started to think more logically she realised that to have a relatively stress-free night she would have to satisfy herself that she had accounted for every room in the building. She had started again, more methodically this time, noting what rooms she had entered and not been murdered in, and ticking them off her mental checklist.

Georgie had opted against barricading herself in, reasoning that any attempts she could have made to batten down the hatches in this dark, unknown space would have been clumsy and noisy. She had decided that the benefit of any small security improvements she could make would be far outweighed by the risk of drawing attention to herself. The only exterior door had been unlocked when she had arrived, and while she checked the place out she had left it unlocked in case she needed to leave in a hurry. After she had made herself as sure as she could be that she wasn't locking herself inside a building full of monsters, she had crept down the stairs and dropped the latch as quietly as possible. She had returned upstairs, picked the dorm-room that already had the curtains closed and climbed into the bottom bunk of the nearest bed; Goldilocks hoping three monsters weren't coming home for their porridge.

She had wondered about the fate of the last person to sleep in that bed, whether they had suffered and if they were suffering now. She had thought about her family, about what might have happened to them. She had taken out her phone, noticing how little of the charge was left. She had read the last message from her mum:

I can't believe that none of us has been to Scotland before! Can't wait to hear all about it. I love you more than you'll ever know. From mum xxx

And from her younger brother.

Don't come back pregnant!

Georgie had been exhausted and desperate for sleep but the thought that her family might be alive and worrying about her had kept her awake for a long time. When she finally slept she did so like a prey-animal; her senses on high-alert, attuned to anything that might signal danger.

The fire station was a flat-roofed affair with a sizeable car park out front and a tall narrow tower on one side. There was no electricity and the hot taps ran cold, but Georgie was happy to have any water at all. Most of the ground floor of the two-storey structure was taken up by garage space for the fire engines, secured behind sturdy metal rollover doors that Georgie had no idea how to open but was perfectly happy to leave closed. The rest of the ground floor was an entrance lobby with a small office and stairs leading up to what an estate-agent would call a lounge-diner and kitchenette. This is where the firefighters would have killed time between callouts. There were two more offices upstairs as well as two bedrooms with four double bunks in each, and a large bathroom with three sinks and six shower cubicles.

Georgie had been crazy about fire engines as a kid and she had always wanted to slide down a so-called fireman's pole, but as she looked at the one that disappeared into the dark garage below, she realised she had lost the urge somehow.

In the deserted lounge, Georgie took some grim

satisfaction from playing detective. She had watched the police procedural dramas religiously and now she was the investigating officer working the case; sifting through the evidence, painting a picture of what had gone down. The half-empty cups of tea, the unfinished light meals on the coffee table and a pasty, dried out but not yet mouldy, in the microwave, told her that whatever had happened, had happened around lunchtime.

Georgie lay on her back on one of the two sofas, chewing on the crust of the pasty and staring up at the clouds through the big skylight that allowed daylight into the otherwise windowless room.

She pictured the firefighters sitting together on these sofas, the television on while they ate, chatting and gawping at their phones. The sounds of a disturbance outside catching their attention and them all running out to see what was going on, or perhaps to help one of their colleagues. And then... and then, what?

There was no damage in any of the rooms, and the corpses, which were not much more than ragged skeletons were all scattered in the car park. Had they met the same fate as Iqbal, set-upon by monster-people, or had they been the aggressors? Had it been the firefighters who had turned, or *mutated* she realised was a better word, and rushed outside to slaughter whoever had made the mistake of venturing into their territory?

Or had they turned on each other?

Or something else entirely?

The more she thought about it, the more frustrated she became.

But she couldn't stop thinking about it.

In amongst Georgie's revolving procession of thoughts was the question of what had caused people to mutate into monsters. If it had been something in the air then it must have cleared by now or she too would have been affected. If it had been some sort of virus, then it must have spread quickly because there didn't appear to be anybody left who wasn't mutated or dead.

It wasn't curiosity that forced these questions through her head; any information she could work out might help her survive, which was something Georgie very much wanted to do. The other benefit to solving any part of the puzzle was that it would give her an idea of what sort of life she could expect if she did manage to make it through. How many other people might still be alive, for example?

How many of the *mutants* were out there?

What should she do next?

Round and round went the loop.

What Georgie did next, after brushing flakes of pastry from her chest, was sob her heart out. She did this wretchedly, desperately and for a long time. But she did it in silence. Keeping quiet was already becoming second nature to her.

At the bathroom sink, washing the salty tracks from her face, her reflection paid her a surprise visit. This was the first time she had seen herself since the world as she'd known it had ended.

She didn't look her best.

On Friday morning she had been to her hairdresser especially for her romantic weekend. She had been delighted with the result, as had Iqbal, but now, exactly three days later, the tangled mess of long black hair looked like it belonged to someone else. The bags beneath her eyes were like Halloween make-up and her skin was blotchy, crosshatched with hives. The emergency landing had left her bruised and battered and the extreme stress and lack of proper sleep had taken their toll. She looked exactly as she felt; sick and exhausted.

Her breakfast pasty hadn't done much for her hunger and

she went back to the kitchen. Even though the electricity was off, the contents of the fridge were still fairly fresh. As Georgie gulped orange and mango juice straight from the carton she had another end-of-the-world realisation: if the electricity never came back on again then this could well be the last time she would ever be able to eat perishable food.

There was an open packet of bacon in the fridge with four rashers still inside. She opened the cupboard above the worktop. On the higher shelf was half a wholemeal loaf, the best thing she'd seen since sliced bread. On the lower shelf was a bottle of brown sauce. Georgie smiled.

The hob set into the worktop was gas-powered. Georgie tried not to get her hopes up but she saw no reason why the gas would be off as well as the electricity. She had no idea what might have caused the National Grid to shut down, if indeed it had, but gas, to her, seemed like a much simpler proposition. It was just sitting in a pipe, it couldn't be sucked back, recalled by whatever had cut the electricity. That is, unless whatever that thing was had also blocked all the gas pipes, but Georgie thought that humanity couldn't have been *that* unlucky.

Could it?

She turned one of the hob knobs and the hiss of vapour was a symphony to her ears.

With her immediate hunger satisfied, Georgie allowed her mind to look further than the short term. She needed to plan for the coming days, perhaps weeks if she could manage to avoid being ripped into bloody pieces for that long.

Georgie was a methodical person, something that had served her well in her studies. She had landed a first in Physics and had been planning to do a master's after a bit of a time out (although she hadn't meant the time out to last for eight years and counting). She had loved the unambiguity of the scientific method, working within a framework, following a procedure.

She had found satisfaction in making clear, concise yet comprehensive notes so nothing could be missed or incorrectly recorded. She needed to apply that sort of approach here. She needed something to stop her mind from spiralling, something that would allow her to take charge of the situation. She knew exactly what she needed.

She needed a notepad.

Georgie kicked into silent action. She searched the upstairs offices, opening and closing drawers and cupboards slowly and quietly. She started in the smaller of the two offices, grateful that its tiny window had the blind closed so she didn't feel exposed. She came away with a couple of pens and a highlighter. The other office had a big window overlooking the car park, its blinds were open to the post-apocalyptic outside world. Georgie kept low, shuffling into the room on her hands and knees. Her already aching limbs protested against the unnatural position and she was painfully aware of how ridiculous she would have looked had there been anyone to see her. She hit the mother lode quickly: a shrink-wrapped bundle of ten A4 pads in the bottom drawer of a filing cabinet.

With the spoils of her search hooked under her arm Georgie crawled out of the room.

She returned to the smaller office, liking the fact that it had a desk, which would help her feel businesslike and in some kind of control. That was the hope at least.

She shoved aside the monitor and keyboard and ran one of her few unbroken fingernails, like a letter opener, down the length of the polythene wrapping of the stack of pads. She slid one out and opened it to the first, pristine page.

She wrote 'food' at the top, and then underneath, 'make an inventory'.

She realised that she may as well get on with this first task straight away because it would have a big influence on what the next tasks were so, armed with her pad and pen she headed back to the kitchenette…

Food inventory

Fridge/Perishables
Rest of milk: about 1/3 litre
Soya milk: unopened 1 litre
Bacon: 3 rashers (2 days to exp)
Tomatoes: 3 (prob got about 2 days)
Fruit juice: rest of open carton, not much left

Cupboards:
Cereal: ½ opened and 2 unopened 500g boxes
Soup: 3 cans
Baked beans: 2 cans
Chopped tomatoes: 1 can
Spaghetti: 1 unopened pack
Rice: 2 bags
Hoi Sin sauce: 4 packets
Protein shake mix: 1 kg tub (opened but most is left)

Georgie wanted to know how long she could avoid going outside where the mutants were, and to do that she would need to work out how many days' rations her list of supplies equated to. She decided to work in calories. She knew that the guideline daily amount for an average woman was two thousand. She simply had to tot up the calories for everything on the list and see how many guideline amounts it added up to.

Georgie had once been as good as dragged to the cinema by a boyfriend to see a film about a guy who was stranded on Mars. Georgie, not a sci-fi fan, had expected to hate it and had only gone to keep the boyfriend happy. But as it had turned out, she had loved it and it had been the boyfriend who had been bored out of his mind. Georgie had particularly liked the parts where the stranded guy had to do arithmetic to work out how best to use his extremely limited resources in order to survive.

Georgie now felt exactly like that guy on Mars.

She checked the food packaging and was frustrated that the *Nutritional Information* panels didn't show the total number of calories, instead it was the amount per hundred grams, or even more annoyingly, per serving. This meant that she had to note down how many grams were in a serving so she could divide that into the total weight to get the number she needed. Georgie got busy with her notepad and pen.

She did the math.

The results were in: if Georgie was an average woman consuming the guideline number of calories a day, she had enough food for just over seven Earth days. Georgie had no idea what an average woman was, but at five feet five tall and still wearing kids' size shoes she assumed she was below the mean. This, she decided, would buy her at least an extra two days, three if she was disciplined. That made a total of ten days.

Georgie didn't think this was very long, and she also knew that living on those rations would be unbearable. Even if she did manage to stick to the regime for the full ten days, by the end of it she wouldn't exactly be, as her grandma used to say, 'full of vim and vigour'. She certainly wouldn't be in a fit state to go outside amongst the mutants on a life-endangering mission to restock on supplies. There was the chance of course that someone might turn up in that time and tell her that the apocalypse was over, that everything was fixed and life could go back to normal, but Georgie wasn't going to hold her breath on that one.

She decided to park the subject for a while and focus on

provisions of the non-edible kind. As for the food, she needed to make a list of what she already had. This would be a much bigger job than just rooting through a fridge and a few kitchen cupboards, she would have to search the whole building. She could feel herself becoming overwhelmed again. It was a mammoth task and she could feel the mammoth in question bearing down on her, its tusks ready to... Georgie couldn't think of the word that described what a tusk would do when it made contact with a person at full running speed. Jabbed? Not grave enough. Pronged? Maybe.

She tried to fight off the mammoth by telling herself that the task would be therapeutic, something simple to occupy her mind and stop her thoughts for a while. She didn't find herself particularly convincing but got on with it anyway.

The first room she checked was the other bedroom. In a cupboard between two bunks she found a *Scrabble* set. It might not seem a likely source of crushing despair but that is exactly what it turned out to be. It was the text printed in the bottom corner of the front of the box that did the trick.

For 2-4 players.

Georgie had never felt so completely alone.

She sat on the bed, staring at the box, just sitting and waiting for her mind to stop telling her that, even though she was at the lowest point she had ever been, the only way from here was down.

Chapter 4. Special delivery

I don't know what to think. Someone's got to be playing me. It's the zombies, they're messing with my head.

I've had a delivery.

That's right, a package arrived, a little plastic bag wrapped in tape and a letter stuck to it. Or a note, really. One bit of paper folded in half. I read it straight away. Of course I did.

> *Dear hopefully human person (or people)*
>
> *I am a human and I'm living nearby. I won't say where because I don't know who might read this, if anyone.*
> *I've seen that a small group of mutants hang around this building all the time so I think there must be someone inside.*
> *I don't know if you're trapped in there or you control them or you're a mutant (or mutants) too.*
> *If it's the first one (or it's the second and you have a REALLY good explanation for it) then please make contact using the attached. It's set on the right channel, don't touch that dial!*
>
> *You have no idea how hard it was to get this to you.*
>
> *Yours*
> *Hopeful human*

Mute

I pulled off the tape and ripped open the bag. There was a radio inside, one of the two-way ones like security guards use, or coppers. If this is real then all I have to do is turn it on and I'll be able to talk to a real-life other person. I'd really like to talk to a real-life other person.

But...

It's probably not real is it? It's probably the zombies messing with me, either for sport, or to lure me out. Why am I suspicious? Well that's very simple. There's a group of hungry zombies standing guard outside. How could anyone have parcelforced their way past them and dropped this off without getting eaten? I can't really picture it somehow... "Excuse me, scary monsters, I have a special delivery, it's for someone I've never met or even spoken to but who I think lives in this morgue, would you mind stepping aside so I can post it? No, that's okay, Mr. Zombie, I'll politely decline your offer to suck out my spleen if it's all the same to you."

It has to be the zombies, it's a plan to get me to come outside so they can eat me. They must have realised I've run out of bodies. Today's feed is well overdue.

But...

If the zombies are smart enough to set up an elaborate ruse, one involving walkie-talkies and handwritten notes, then surely they'd be clever enough to think of a much easier way to get me out. For starters they could just pour a load of petrol into the drawer and light it up, then keep pouring more and more in and keep it burning. They could keep that up indefinitely, there are plenty of abandoned cars about, and I know for sure that as soon as this place started filling up with smoke I'd try and make a bolt for it. Then they'd have me, and I'd be half-barbecued already. That would be a lot more straightforward than whatever the hell this charade is.

But if it's unlikely that they did this to trick me into

coming out then it means they must have just done it for shits and giggles. If that's it then I refuse to give them the satisfaction of having got one over on me.

Can zombies feel satisfied?

Maybe when they've just eaten a nice brain.

But they don't really seem like the type to do pranks. They seem pretty fixated on that whole eating of human flesh vibe they've got going on.

Oh God I don't know. It's hard to think logically right now. I don't want to be a sucker and I've only got circumstantial evidence to go on, but it does kind of seem unlikely that the zombies posted me the radio.

Okay, let's run with that idea, try it on for size. If it's not the zombies, then who was it? I hope I'll be forgiven for being a bit on the paranoid side these days but I've got to consider that the person who gave me the note doesn't have good intentions when it comes to me. In those movies where the world's gone tits-up there's always a bunch of survivors who go nuts and band together in tribes that go around forcing people to fight to the death in some sort of dome they've inexplicably built from materials they've found lying around. If not that then they take them prisoner and do horrible things to them.

But it's only been a few weeks, maybe a month since the world went tits-up. That's not enough time to organise an army of marauders. And all jokes aside, I can't think what would be in it for someone who's survived this thing to go to all this trouble and danger just to get me to come out so they can do something awful to me.

And the handwriting on the note is *really* nice.

I'm shit scared, I don't mind admitting that, but then I've been shit scared since I left my flat and found that the world had become an arsehole. But there's something else I'm feeling, something that's working my gut in the same way as the fear is.

I've not felt it for a while but I think I know what it is. I think it's excitement.

I don't know what to do. I should just flick the switch and talk. It can't do me any harm. I've got a day, maybe two, until I'm dead anyway so what does it matter?

What if it is an actual person? It's not impossible. There's that excitement again. Oh my dear Lord if it is a proper someone then there's a chance, some kind of chance. And any kind of chance is a million times better than where I am now, with no chance at all.

I'm doing it. I'm turning on the radio.

Jesus, my ears haven't heard much in the way of close-up sounds for ages and the fizz of static is proper harsh. I say hello and leave it for a few seconds, then I say it again and suddenly I hear a voice and it's a girl and I don't know how I know but I'm sure she's not a zombie, even though I know the zombies can talk almost exactly like humans. And as well as knowing she's not a zombie, I know, I can just tell, that she's not someone who wants to do me harm. All she's said is hello and I hope she can't hear me choking up. Even though I know it's completely impossible for her to get me out of here, I'm already thinking of what it's going to be like when she does get me out. Just from that one *hello* I'm pinning all my hopes on her.

I'd forgotten what hope felt like.

"Are you there?" She's whispering but I can hear her fine.

"I'm here." What's wrong with me? I haven't spoken to a human in a month and now the cat's got my stupid tongue. I go for the obvious. "What's your name?"

"Georgie. What's yours?"

"I'm Anthony, but everyone calls me Ant. Well, they used to when there was an everybody."

"I'd love to chat, Anthony, but I don't know how much power these things have got so we need to keep to the important stuff. And I'm going to say 'over' when I finish what I'm saying and it's your turn to speak, and you should do the same, okay?"

I say okay back but realise she hasn't said *over* and I'm talking over her. "Sorry… over."

"That's okay, Anthony. Is it just you in there? Over"

"Yes, just me. And you, are you with people or is it just you? Over."

"I'm alone as well. How long do you have food for? Over."

"I have food for a little while but I've run out of anything for them outside, so I'll be the food soon. Over."

There's a pause and I think she's been cut off but finally she speaks.

"I see. So if we are to get you out it has to be soon, right? Over."

"Yes, it has to be very soon. No pressure, sorry. Over."

"Anthony. I need to be honest with you, I'm not an action hero. I can't work a flamethrower and I can't slide down a power line shooting as I go. If I ever had to shoot someone I'd probably be sick. I need you to know that. Over."

"I understand. Over."

"Okay Anthony, here's what I need you to do…"

Chapter 5. Up on the roof

Georgie, for the second time that day was climbing the ladder to the top of what she now knew was called a drill-tower. She always wore black when she did her rounds and she moved slowly, avoiding alerting any eyes to a sudden movement. The binoculars she had taken from a shelf in the bedroom weren't the highest spec but they were better than nothing. The view, after three weeks, was becoming familiar, and on each watch she had taken notes of everything around her. There was a small parade of shops across to her right, about half a mile away. There was often activity there, mutants going in and out of doorways. She was surprised by their movements, quite orderly mostly, although they had their moments.

A large part of her field of vision was made up of a hospital and the outbuildings that surrounded it. One building in particular caught her interest. It was low and flat, about the same distance away as the row of shops but in the other direction. She wouldn't have noticed it had it not been for the small group of mutants that stood like tattered sentries outside.

Watching for hours on end from her vantage point, Georgie kept a close eye on that building and she made some interesting observations.

She noticed that mutants didn't sleep in the same way as humans, instead they seemed to shut down, slightly slumped like the gold robot in Star Wars when it was turned off. She had seen them stay in that state for hours. This was vital information.

During her scariest moment up on the tower she had found out another useful titbit. Something nearby had exploded, loud enough to make the ground tremble and the tower shake. She had no idea what it was or what had caused it, she had just clung on and kept her eyes fixed on the sleeping-whilst-standing mutants. The sound could easily have been described as being loud enough to wake the dead; the dead, perhaps, but apparently not the mutants, not straight away at least. Of the five inert figures she was watching, one of them came round within thirty seconds of the big bang, while for the others it was over two minutes before they were fully awake. There seemed to be a delay between the sound reaching them and the mutants realising it had reached them.

Georgie didn't enjoy spending time on the tower and it was made even less fun when she was caught in a rainstorm as she lay on her perch, fully exposed to the elements. But she was glad of the deluge when she saw the effect it had on the mutants.

They did not like the rain at all.

As soon as it started coming down they scattered like cockroaches under a switched-on strip light, darting for cover as if it were acid. Their reaction made Georgie panic, thinking that perhaps the rain was tainted and this was going to be how it all ended for her; lying on a platform 50 feet up, frazzled by a toxic cloudburst. When her flesh didn't melt, Georgie relaxed, and would have noted down the extremely valuable information she had learned if her notepad hadn't been soaked by the downpour.

She updated her knowledge store on a new notebook as soon as she got back inside:

1. *Mutants sleep where they are standing.*
2. *Mutants take a while to wake up.*

3. Mutants run and hide when it rains.

After the Scrabble incident Georgie had given herself something of a bollocking. She had told herself that there was no point sitting around crying; things weren't good by any means, sure, but from what she'd seen she had it a lot better than most other people. With renewed purpose she had continued her search of the station. It had gone well. She found she had inherited some clothes that were an okay fit, plenty of bathroom products as well as cleaning paraphernalia and a well-stocked first aid kit. She pulled together enough courage to enter the scary dark garage that housed the fire engines. And that's when things had really started looking up.

When Georgie was little and her local fire brigade had held a *family fun day* she had made sure her family took part in the fun. There had been a barbecue, beer tent, stalls and face painting but all Georgie had cared about was the fire engine that the kids were allowed to climb all over. She'd had an absolute blast and when it had been time to leave, her father had almost had to prise her off the vehicle, much to the amusement of the watching firefighters.

This station must have been about to host a similar event because, stacked against the wall inside the garage, was a treasure trove of supplies. There were burger and hot dog buns; the cheap ones that were low on flavour but packed with preservatives, processed cheese slices, crisps, nachos, salsa, sauces and pickles. This stash alone would have been enough to make Georgie's world look a whole lot rosier but there was more:

Beneath all the brightly coloured packaging was a freezer, and inside the freezer were the burgers and hot dogs that had been destined to fill all those buns, both meat and vegan alternatives. Georgie had no idea how long they would last in the insulation of the unpowered freezer but she knew that her calculation of ten days on meagre rations could be substantially upgraded.

With her mood lifted dramatically, Georgie turned her attention to the four fire engines that were shut in the dark space like dragons entombed in a cave. Here were her childhood toys brought to larger-than-life. Georgie, in her survival-silence, felt overwhelmed by the sheer weight of sound that lay dormant in these machines: the engines, the sirens, the hurried activity in and around them. Given the chance they would, to coin another of her grandma's sayings, *make a frightful din*.

In between her regular trips up the drill-tower, Georgie spent a lot of time in the garage familiarising herself with the controls of the engines, or *appliances*, as she'd heard the professionals call them on that family fun day. At first glance, the dashboard may as well have been the cockpit of the Space Shuttle, but with patience and careful study of the training books and technical manuals she found in the offices it had all started to make sense. Eventually she felt she would be able to drive one of these bright red monsters if she really had to, although she was brutally aware that there would be a world of difference between theory and reality.

There was one hairy moment while she was working through the buttons and levers when she almost set off the siren. She cringed for days afterwards, imagining the horror of what would have happened if she hadn't stopped herself in time. She may as well have leaned out of the window, shouting her head off. *Hey mutants, I'm here, come and get me!*

Her studies of the textbooks also taught her about the communication systems used by the emergency services. She assumed that if some central government still existed and was coordinating an effort to manage the survivors then this is where she would hear from them. There was no power to the desktop radio in the downstairs office and whilst she knew there would almost certainly be a backup generator, she didn't investigate that any further because she was too nervous of the noise that a petrol-powered generator would make. The fire engines had radios though. She turned the volume all the way down and turned the key in the ignition, careful to keep it to one notch, just enough to power the radio, any further could start the engine, which would be as suicidal as sounding the siren. She edged the volume control so it was just about audible and flicked through the emergency channels. She made it part of her routine to repeat the check at various times every day. All she had found so far was static.

From the tower she had noted that the mutants around the shops seemed to have taken their business elsewhere, and now the only ones she could see were those outside the low building at the edge of the hospital grounds. She could see that they spent most of their time gathered around one particular part of the building. Sometimes the mutants huddled even closer and when they came away again it looked a lot like they were eating, but she couldn't be sure from that range.

All she knew was that there had to be something inside that building that was making the mutants hang around. It could very well be people, and if it was, they very probably needed help.

Georgie's first attempt to deliver the radio had been a massive fail. She had been waiting just inside the downstairs door watching the dark sky for the rain and when it was coming down thick and fast enough she had left the building, full of purpose.

But it was all too much. This was the first time she had left her refuge since she'd arrived and she was paralysed by a wave of agoraphobia. She tried to push on through but didn't get past the car park before she turned back.

Georgie refused to chicken out a second time and when it rained again she was ready. She left the package at the foot of the ladder to keep her hands free and climbed the cold wet rungs once more, not all the way, just high enough to see the mutants.

But she couldn't see them. They weren't standing where they normally were, at the front of the low building. This was almost certainly good news; it meant they were round the back, where they always went when it rained. But she hadn't seen them go so she would be risking her life on a guess, an educated one but a guess nonetheless.

She decided to go for it.

She hurried down the ladder and picked up the package. She kept her head as low as possible and ran, the heavy rain stinging her eyes as she took the arcing route she had charted from above. She reached the front of the low building and was grateful that it was still free of mutants but terrified by the thought of them huddled on the other side. She forced herself not to panic; the rain was still coming down heavily and she had never once seen the mutants return until long after it had stopped completely, but it was still hard to keep her fear in check. She could hardly bear being this close to them, and the fact that she couldn't see them only added to her anxiety.

She was tempted to knock on the door and tell whoever was inside that they could get out now if they were quick, but she knew that if it had been her on the other side of that door she wouldn't even have risked answering, let alone opened up.

She looked around for somewhere to push the parcel through. The door had no letterbox and there was nothing around it, no way in. There was a large square hatch that was flush to the middle of the wall, Georgie pushed it but it was rock solid. She could feel her panic returning as she stood there dithering with the parcel in her hand; a quarterback with nobody to throw to. She stepped back from the wall and saw another, smaller hatch to the right. She tried pushing on it, and again it didn't open but unlike the bigger one she felt this one move. Georgie, trying not to think of the mutants on the other side of the building, pushed her fingernails into the tiny gap at the top edge of the panel and tried to prise it open. It hurt like hell and it took several goes but eventually it moved enough for her to get her fingertips inside and pull it open. It was a drawer and it opened about six inches, enough to drop the package in.

She pushed it closed and ran for her life.

Chapter 6. Over and out

Oh man I've been dying to use the radio again, just to hear that voice. There was something about it, not quite posh, but professional, like an off-duty newsreader. Okay, so it's possible that I've only got a thing about her voice because it's the only one I've heard since the world turned zombie. The only human one at least. Either way I want to hear her again. But I have to wait. Those are my orders. I have to wait for rain.

My instructions are that once I know it's definitely a proper downpour and not just spitting I have to wait a few minutes and then turn on the radio, but with the volume proper low. We sorted that out when we spoke last time. She was worried that if the zombies could hear us talking then they'd smell a rat and go nuts. We went through the alphabet letter by letter while I turned the knob down until I could only just hear her:

"A. Over."

"B. Over."

"C. Over."

I stopped her at *G*.

G for Georgie.

I've been doing what I'm told and I've been waiting for rain – more like praying for it. The main zombie's tried talking to me but I've ignored him. I haven't got long until things go south for me here.

I'm shitting myself.

I'm pretty sure it's April now, so that means I'm due plenty of April showers. But I'm not feeling confident, I don't just need it to rain, I need to know that it's raining, and I can't see much out of this box I've shut myself in. If it properly hammers it down then I'll be able to hear it okay but if it's that fine rain that comes down heavy but doesn't make much noise then I might miss my chance.

And it might be my only chance.

I'm trying to keep the sound of my breath down so I can hear any rain but it's not my breathing that's the problem, it's my heart. When did that get so loud? I'm trying to see drops on the glass but it's criss-crossed with wire mesh, it's not meant for seeing out of. I've been like this for ages, watching, listening, trying to shut my heart up.

I think I heard something.

I did, there's a drumming sound on the roof.

It's raining, a proper downpour. Oh Jesus. This is happening.

I do what I've been told. I go and stand at the door and I wait to make sure it really gets going. I start turning bolts so I'm ready to go. I leave the last one. I've got a bag over my shoulder that holds the best knives I found in this place. You never know when you might need a decent blade when there are zombies at every turn.

That's got to be a few minutes. I turn on the radio. "I'm ready," I whisper. "Over."

"Okay, Anthony." There's that voice. She's there, she's bloody there. "They've gone. It's clear. Unlock the door slowly. Keep it quiet. Then, like I told you, as soon as you're out of the door turn right and run straight. You will see a low wall on your right that goes diagonally to the left. Run alongside that and once you're past it, look up and to the right, you'll see the fire station up the hill. I'll be at the door on the right-hand side.

Run as fast as you can. Over."

She told me all that last time and I've memorised all of it, but that's cool, it does no harm to hear it again.

"I get it, coming. Over and out."

I hear her say good luck as I throw the last bolt and open the door. I'm expecting the zombies to jump me but they're not there and I push the door closed behind me and it's properly pissing it down and I'm running like a bastard and it's hard work because I've done basically nothing for weeks but I'm hauling my lardy arse up the hill and I don't look back and I'm in the car park of the fire station and I aim for the door on the right and she's holding it open and oh my dear Lord.

I'm inside and she's locking the door and we're hurrying upstairs but quietly. And we're in the room where all the firemen would have waited to be told when something's on fire and I thought there'd be a pool table and I'm just hugging this girl and I've never been so happy in all my dear life. I swear it.

It's hard to be objective when you're looking at the person who just saved you from certain death, but I'll do my best. She's what the clothes shops call *petite*, a lot shorter than me, but then most people are. Age-wise I'd guess at mid-twenties but a gentleman doesn't ask and I'm a proper gentleman. She's dark, and it'll sound cringe but I'm going to say it anyway, she looks *exotic*. She's got this long black hair that she's pulled back into a ponytail and that means the skin of her neck's on show and I know I've been in solitary confinement for some time and everything, but that bit of her neck looks to me like the softest, smoothest substance on Earth. And obviously I can't help but think about the fact that her whole body must be wrapped up in that same stuff. All over. Jesus.

And I've not even got to her eyes yet. They're green, but a really dark green like I've not seen before, like she's wearing lenses for a video shoot or something, but of course she's not wearing lenses, well she might be but that would be weird in the circumstances and she doesn't look the type. No, that's definitely her natural colour. I reckon, before everyone was dead she must have got a lot of attention just for those eyes alone. And the rest of the package is far from shabby even though I'm sure she's not looking her best. I'm not being judgemental when I say that, anyone who looks their best out here in the Doomsday Quarter has got their priorities totally arse about face and they'd most likely be dead before they could say *because I'm worth it*.

I'm thanking her and I'm probably not making much sense but I'm telling her she's an angel and how she's saved my life and I'm telling her again and I'm all sniffy and snotty and the tears are flowing and she's crying too but not as much as I am, and definitely not as disgustingly.

And she's smiling but she looks a bit worried and she shushes me. She doesn't like noise, this one.

And I say I'm sorry.

And then I just say thank you about a billion times and I tell her I'm sorry that I'm hugging her so much and it's probably invasive and all and I'll definitely stop in a minute and she says it's fine.

And then she kind of eases me away, politely, kindly. And she says, "Would you like to play scrabble?"

And I say why not?

And then for some reason she's the one who's blubbing.

Chapter 7. First night

I'm not sure if Anthony's ever going to get bored of thanking me for saving him from, as he calls it every time: 'absolute nailed-on certain death.' He often throws in an expletive for good measure but I don't need to repeat it. I'm not a fan of swearing. But his choice of words aside, Anthony's gratitude is both overwhelming and humbling. I've never saved anybody's life before and I have to say it's an incredibly satisfying feeling.

During the brief conversations we had when he was in the morgue I hadn't formed much of a mental picture of the man holding the other radio, and even if I had, I'm certain it wouldn't have been anything like the reality. Anthony is a huge man. I would say *giant* but he pointed out to me that at six-eight he falls shy of the official minimum by one inch. If I'd been forced to guess his nationality from looks alone I would have gone with Scandinavian. His orange-blonde hair hangs in a shaggy style that's best described as 'surfer-dude', which I think is from before, not as a result of it being difficult to get an appointment with a barber these days. He has a bushy beard which I don't think is new either. His skin is pale but then it has been starved of daylight for the last few weeks. He's not just tall, he's big too, not overweight exactly - he's probably within the BMI range for his height - he's just big all over, like he's been scaled up. His feet are huge, which I suppose they'd have to be to support his massive legs, and his chest and shoulders are like he's wearing a barrel.

Mute

Put simply, he looks like a Viking.

I'm not suggesting he's wearing a helmet with a nose guard and gripping a horn of mead, I'm just talking about his physical characteristics. In terms of outfit, Anthony is wearing a faded t-shirt, jeans and trainers. I know it's impossible to be anything other than scruffy in an apocalyptic wasteland, but I get the impression that Ant's look has always been this way. I'm not criticising, I'm just noting my first impressions, but I imagine that Anthony could have a suit made for him by the finest Italian tailor and he'd still manage to make it look scruffy. He's so different to Iqbal. Iqbal prided himself on his appearance. He was always perfectly groomed.

I'm not sure why I'm thinking of this now but if someone had asked me before if I had a 'type', I wouldn't have been able to answer. If someone asked me now I'd be able to say exactly what my type is. My type is Iqbal.

But I can't think about Iqbal now. It's too painful.

It's lovely that Anthony is so grateful that I got him out of his predicament but it works the other way around too. In a way, Anthony saved me just as much as I saved him, not from imminent death but from losing my mind. It was only for so long that I could have kept on trying to distract myself from the crushing solitude I felt by occupying my time pottering around inside fire engines and watching mutants from the top of a ladder, all the while making notes I knew I'd almost certainly never read.

Project: 'Save Whoever is in That Funny Little Building', gave me a purpose. It gave my mind something to chew on other than the overwhelming desolation that appears to be a symptom of surviving the end of the world. Now Anthony is out of his prison we have a new purpose; the two of us working together to get through this impossible new reality.

And I'm not lonely anymore.

Last night was amazing. We played Scrabble and I won easily, but it wasn't about the game, it was about laying that two-player ghost to rest. Now Anthony's here I qualify for something other than solitaire. We stayed up well into the night talking about anything and everything. At twenty-six he's younger than I thought, and he acted surprised to find that I was three years older than him, but I think he was just trying to be polite. We both grew up in small villages, Anthony in the Peak District and me just outside Oxford. Anthony has a sister five years younger and she still lives at the same family home with their parents. My mum and dad are also still in the house I grew up in, along with my younger brother Jessie. Anthony thought I was pulling his leg about Jessie's name until I told him about my older brother, Alvin.

There were some awkward moments as we talked about the people in our lives because of the simple fact that we didn't know which tense to use. When I said my parents 'live' in the same house I grew up in, I knew very well that they probably don't, they're not living at all, and the same goes for Anthony's loved ones. But neither of us had wanted to get into any of that stuff.

We talked about what had brought us to London. I'd moved for university and ended up staying on afterwards, while Anthony had a far more romantic story; he'd come chasing stardom. He, along with three friends, had rented a one bedroom flat in Kennington and tried to make a go of their band, *Art I Choke*. They gave themselves a year. In that time, if the music industry failed to respond to their advances they would give up the ghost and take the path of gainful employment. The music industry duly failed to respond and so gainful employment it was. Anthony tried to explain what profession he'd ended up in but I had no idea what he was talking about. It had something to do with marketing, a touch of branding and a dash of influencing. I'm not sure Anthony really knows for sure.

In spite of my very clear explanation of *my* job, Anthony refused to understand what a Data Analyst was. I took a deep breath and was about to talk him through it again, but it suddenly dawned on me that our careers were now about as relevant as our hat-sizes.

Anthony agreed.

I told him about Iqbal, about how we'd left England that fateful Friday as a fledgling couple and fallen hopelessly in love over Armageddon weekend. Anthony was the first person I'd been able to share this with and I was touched by how sympathetic and kind he was.

We speculated over the *what the hell happened?* question, shared our theories, came up with new ones.

We fell asleep as dawn came, Anthony in the bunk opposite mine, his feet poking out of the end. Neither of us had wanted to say goodnight.

Chapter 8. Blindgate

Ant woke up to the joy of being in a bed and not on the floor of a morgue surrounded by monsters. He glanced over at Georgie, sleeping soundly in her bunk, and for the first time in a long time he felt glad to be alive.

He was hungry but decided not just to help himself. This was Georgie's place; he didn't want to take the piss.

Careful not to wake Georgie, Ant slipped his huge frame out of the room and onto the landing. He saw straight away that the larger of the two upstairs offices was an early morning sun trap. Putting on a pair of dead firefighter's Ray-bans, he tilted the venetian blinds open so they angled in his direction. He pulled the lever on the office chair so it reclined as far as it would go, sat back and bathed in the rays.

In his underpants.

He was just starting to doze off when Georgie walked in. She was wearing what she'd slept in, a man-sized t-shirt celebrating the New York Police Department and a pair of football shorts. Ant thought she looked amazing.

"What do you think you're doing? Are you trying to kill us?" Georgie's voice was barely a whisper but her fury was loud and clear.

Ant sat up. He removed the shades. "Calm your farm. It's all good, nobody can see me from outside, I made sure of that."

"Oh well that's just great, there's no problem then."

"Cool beans."

"Except there is. There's a huge problem. What were you thinking?"

Ant was confused. "What do you mean?"

"You opened the blinds."

"Yeah but it's okay, I'm sure nothing saw me. I'm getting a healthy dose of vit-d, you should join me."

"I won't be the only one joining you. You told me all about that first mutant you saw, the one that knocked on your door and said he'd noticed 'activity' in your flat. That means they have at least some level of intelligence, and it also means they have observational skills. Even if nothing saw you open those blinds, the fact that they're open now and they were closed before is a dead giveaway. And I do mean *dead* giveaway, and in case the nuance of that point is lost on you, I mean that we might be dead because you've given us away." Georgie put her head in her hands. "What were you thinking?"

"Oh Jesus." The morning had broken for Ant. The enormity of what he'd done hadn't so much sunk is as landed on his head like an anvil from a clifftop. Panic raised his voice. "Shit, I'm so sorry, what do we do?"

Georgie hastily put her finger to her lips, quietly frantic. "Don't shout, for the love of God, please keep quiet."

"I'm sorry," Ant whispered. And he was. He knew this had been a dick-move. There was no point arguing the case and suggesting that Georgie was overreacting. He knew what he'd done. He was embarrassed and flustered for making such a blunder but most of all he was terrified, as terrified as Georgie was.

When Ant had arrived at the fire station, Georgie had explained that she'd thought about securing the building but had eventually decided that it would have been more trouble than it was worth on account of the noise it would make. Ant had agreed, keen to avoid a siege situation like the one he'd just been rescued from. Their best defence, they'd decided, was not to give any sign to the outside world that they were in there. If the creatures happened to come into the building then that was just bad luck, and they resolved to start planning and rehearsing escape drills in case of that eventuality, but they knew that their best defence was simply not to draw attention to themselves. To Georgie, keeping mute and staying invisible had already become a habit to her. Ant needed to get with the programme, and quickly.

He kept his voice to a whisper. "I'm sorry. I'm so sorry. I wasn't thinking. Shit. What shall we do? Do we close them again?"

"I think we'll have to. It's a huge risk, something might see the movement, but the longer we leave them open the longer we'll be exposed."

Ant went to get up but Georgie pushed him back down again, much harder than Ant would have expected. "Stay where you are. I'll do it."

Ant didn't argue. Instead he watched with dread as Georgie lowered herself onto all fours and shuffled to the window. She rested her fingertips on the sill and gradually lifted her head far enough to see over. Ant could hardly bear to watch as she lifted her head higher still so she could get a good look. Seemingly satisfied, Georgie lowered her head again and shifted across to the right. She reached up with her arm and felt for the bottom of the dangling cord.

Ant didn't know it was possible to close a set of venetian blinds that slowly. It was like they weren't moving at all, and then after several minutes they were somehow shut, exactly as they had been before he'd blundered in and made himself at home.

Georgie collapsed onto the floor, breathing deeply. After a few moments she hoisted herself up and propped her back against the wall beneath the window. She sat listening for any sound outside. Eventually she spoke, or rather, she whispered. "I think we're okay. If something had seen then I'm sure we'd know about it by now. I don't think they're the sort to bide their time, if they see an opportunity they'll just strike."

"I'm so sorry."

Georgie's tone had softened considerably. "It's okay. You didn't mean it, and I know you'll be more careful from now on."

"I will, I promise."

"Okay, I believe you. But please, Anthony."

"Yes?"

"Put some clothes on will you?"

Ant did as he was told while Georgie went to have a shower. He went to the kitchen, planning to make them both a cup of tea, but when he realised that there was obviously no milk he was stuck. He was happy to take his tea black, but he didn't know if Georgie would want hers like that. He didn't want to make one just for himself in case she came in while he was drinking it and it looked like he just hadn't bothered making one for her. He knew he was massively overthinking the situation but he couldn't help himself. He went back and forth a few times on what he should do before realising that there were only a few tea bags left anyway. He decided it was best just to leave the tea.

Ant didn't know where to put himself. He knew he'd messed up and badly wanted to fix things, but he would be the first to admit that he could become a bit of an oaf when he was nervous. He knew there was a very real danger that his clumsy attempts to patch things up would just make everything worse. He felt like the guy who's come home late from the pub and is trying really hard to do everything quietly, but all the creeping and tiptoeing around ends up being more noisy than if he'd just done everything normally, and being extra annoying for his now wide-awake partner.

He decided he needed to change the dynamic. Georgie had been alone for weeks. She wanted some decent company, the last thing she needed was him being all apologetic and nervous and treading on eggshells around her. Basically, she didn't want to hang out with a pussy. The incident was over, she had told him what she thought and she knew he was sorry. She was cool. They could move on. He needed to step up and be the man.

He heard Georgie coming out of the shower and the overthinking kicked right back in. He wanted to go and have a shower himself but he didn't know the etiquette: was there soap for him? Or a towel? Was there a certain cubicle he should use? He decided to wait. He lay on the sofa and stared up through the blue rectangle of skylight. He forced his thoughts away from the image that had nested in his brain: Georgie, still wet from the shower, stepping out of her towel, and instead cast his mind back to the night before. The reason he wanted a shower so much now was because he hadn't got around to having one last night; it had just felt so safe and comfortable sitting and chatting. After all that time in solitary confinement he hadn't wanted to be alone for a second longer than was necessary, and Georgie had made it clear that she felt the same, despite Ant being the opposite of spring fresh.

He wanted to be back there now, back where it was all *oh-my-God-I'm-not-alone-anymore*. Instead of, *oh-my-God-you've-been-such-a-twat*.

Ant corrected himself; one thing he had learned about Georgie in the brief time he had known her was that she wouldn't use the word 'twat'.

After ten minutes he heard her coming out of the bedroom. He jumped up and was standing in the kitchenette when she came in.

"Can I get you anything?"

Georgie was wearing a loose cotton flower-print dress with three-quarter length sleeves. Her feet were bare. She was towelling her hair gently. "No thanks. I'll just get myself some water."

"Cool. Fancy something to eat?"

"Not yet, you go ahead if you want though."

"No, I'm okay. I was thinking I'd have a shower if that's okay?"

Georgie stopped her towelling and touched his hand lightly. "Oh, Anthony, you don't need to ask. Please don't feel like you can't relax now you're here. I'll tell you what. You have a shower and then I'll give you the tour and show you what's what so you can do your own thing. I don't want you thinking you have to ask for everything."

Ant felt the tension melting away. "Fantastic, that sounds like a plan. Oh my God, a hot shower, I can't bloody wait."

Georgie pulled a face. "Sorry, you can only have a cold shower."

Ant slapped his forehead with his palm. "Course, no electricity."

Georgie dabbed her eyes with the corner of the towel. "No, the boiler's gas-powered, but when the hot water's running, steam comes out of the pipe at the side of the building. It doesn't seem to happen when you use the hob, but it's really noticeable with the water."

"I get it, too visible. You're pretty good at this survival lark aren't you?"

Georgie lowered her head and started rubbing with the towel again. "I very much hope so."

Ant got himself a towel from the airing cupboard that Georgie pointed out and went to the bathroom. He took a bottle each of shower gel and shampoo from the shelf above the sink, picked a cubicle and cranked the shower handle. His hair was badly in need of a wash so the first thing he did was to get busy with the shampoo. He regretted this immediately; his hair was long and it was thick and rinsing out the lather in the torrent of ice-cold water was an uncomfortable and lengthy process.

Back in the bedroom, huddled in the towel, Ant was moved almost to tears when he saw that Georgie had put fresh clothes out on his bed for him. Normally he wouldn't expect other people's clothes to be anywhere near his size but there must have been one or two big boys in that particular brigade because the faded denim jeans and black t-shirt that Georgie had salvaged were a decent fit.

He went back into the lounge. Georgie was sitting cross-legged on one of the sofas. She looked up and smiled. "That must have been nice after such a long time, even if it was freezing."

Ant had a rosy glow about him. "It felt amazing. And cheers for sorting out these clothes for me, you're an absolute star."

Georgie hugged her knees. "You're more than welcome, Anthony."

Ant sat down on the opposite sofa. "Thank you, Georgie. For being so nice, especially after me being such a muppet with the blinds."

Georgie waved her hand. "It's forgotten, this is a learning process, we just need to learn very quickly."

"I will, I'm a quick learner."

Georgie leaned forward and picked up a notepad and pen from the coffee table. "I know I said I'd give you the tour, and we'll do that soon, but I was thinking we could take some time to put together all the information we have. I know we talked a lot last night but I think we should go back to the start, go through everything we know between us and try and get organised, start to plan what we might do going forward."

Ant had only heard the term 'going forward' used by his old boss before, and he had always found it, for want of a better description, *a bit wanky*. He opted not to call Georgie on it. There would be plenty of time for that once they'd got to know each other. "Sounds good to me. Where do you want to start?"

"I suppose we start with the mutants, it's as good a place as any."

Ant grinned. "Why do you call them that?"

"Call them what?"

"Mutants."

Georgie looked puzzled. "Well I don't want to state the obvious but it's because that's what they are."

"I disagree."

"What do you call them?"

"Zombies."

"And why would you call them that."

"Because that's what they are, they're zombies."

"What makes you think they're zombies rather than mutants?"

"I've seen loads of zombie films and they look exactly like the zombies in those films."

"Do you know the definition of a zombie?"

Ant hesitated. His smile was starting to feel a bit strained. "Well I don't know the proper scientific criteria that defines a zombie, but I know what zombies are, they're humans but with their minds all gone, dead and just wanting to you eat you, you know, *zombified*."

It had always bothered Georgie when people said, 'you know' to her. It felt to her that it was being implied that if she didn't know what they meant then she was some kind of moron. "Somewhere in the middle there you hit on one thing that is correct. You said *dead*. The definition of a zombie is a revived corpse, a person who has died and come back to life."

"I know what *revived* means." Ant had thought he had just been playing around. Now he was wondering how he had managed to get himself mired in an argument he didn't know how to get out of.

Georgie dropped the notepad back onto the coffee table and leaned back against the cushions. "I'm not trying to be smart, but that's what zombies are, people who've come back from the dead. Those things out there aren't zombies, they didn't die and come back to life. They changed into that state while they were alive, they mutated. So they're…"

"Mutants, yeah, I get it." Ant's smile was long gone now.

"Okay, so you see what I mean."

Ant shrugged. "It doesn't matter anyway. I only meant it as bantz."

Georgie's voice stepped up an octave. "You're only saying that because you lost the debate. If you'd been right you wouldn't be saying it doesn't matter."

Ant folded his arms. "How do you know what I'd say?"

"Okay, so I don't know what you'd actually say, not exactly, but the point stands."

"How can the point stand?" Ant hissed. "You've basically just convicted me for something you've decided I'd do if the outcome had been different, what is this, Minority Report?"

"I've not seen Minority Report."

"Well maybe you should."

"There's no electricity."

Ant shook his head. "Whatever."

Georgie was leaning forward, her hand gestures getting more animated as she continued the whisper-row. "So you're happy are you? You're happy that rather than concede that you've lost the argument, you've just made the argument about something else, something you can manipulate into me being wrong about and you winning?

Ant looked both confused and angry. "I don't know what you mean. And I'm not having this conversation anymore." To Georgie's surprise, he slowly and quietly left the room…

Ant's instinct was to storm out and make a big show of slamming the door behind him, but of course he couldn't do that on account of the noise. But it was too late to pull out, he was committed to the dramatic exit and had to see it through, so he stormed out silently. It wasn't the effect he'd been hoping for, he knew he looked ridiculous; like a sulking mime-artist.

Just like anybody who's ever flounced off during a row, Ant hadn't given any thought as to where he was flouncing off to and as soon as he was out the door he realised how limited his options were. He decided on the bedroom as the best of a bad bunch.

He lay on his bunk and attempted to comprehend what was happening. When he'd been trapped inside the morgue he'd tried not to let himself fantasise about being rescued because the chances of it happening had been so remote, but he'd fantasised all the same. And now, not only had his rescue fantasies come true, he'd been rescued by someone who looked very much like the girl of his dreams.

So how come, not even twenty-four hours later, he was on his own again?

Boredom kicked in very quickly. He had absolutely nothing to do. If this had been pre-end of the world, Ant's phone would have come to his aid. He could have scrolled idly through social media. He could have followed a trail of memes, each more pointless than the last. He could have a done a bit of shopping. He could have watched some porn. The time would have flown. But instead, time was crawling. All he could do was replay the events of the morning in his head. Over and over.

He knew he'd been daft to open the blinds, but that stupid row about what to call the zombies? That had all been Georgie's doing. He'd thought they were having a laugh and suddenly she'd just gone into one. Ridiculous. He wasn't going to be spoken to like that, not by anyone. It didn't matter how hot Georgie was, or how much she'd saved him from an unthinkably awful death.

Or how much he craved human interaction to stave off the crushing loneliness.

Okay, so perhaps, just this once, he could overlook being spoken to like that. Ant wasn't in the business of throwing the baby out with the bathwater, he had to think about the bigger picture. He decided he'd be the bigger man, swallow his pride and go and fix things with Georgie, apologise for winding her up and draw a line under the whole thing.

But his pride wouldn't go down that easily…

Georgie sat under the blank glare of the skylight, legs crossed and a Dan Brown she had inherited from one of the firefighters open on her lap. To anybody watching she was the picture of relaxed focus, but that was all it was, a picture. This was how Georgie wanted Ant to see her if he came in; cool, unbothered, doing her own thing. In reality she hadn't turned a page of the page-turner since she had opened it. She had lost count of the number of times she had read the first three paragraphs, but if someone had tested her on the contents of those three paragraphs she would have scored a big fat zero. She was finding it impossible to concentrate.

All she could do was replay the events of the morning in her head. Over and over.

She was trying to work out why she had got quite so angry with Ant over the zombie thing. He was being annoying, there was no question of that, but not *that* annoying, and Georgie had been horribly alone since Iqbal had been eaten by mutants (not zombies, mutants) so she thought she could have been a bit more accommodating. In her defence, the exchange had come hot on the heels of the fiasco with the blinds, so her hackles were already well and truly up. She'd been cool about that though, at least she had been when she had seen Ant realise how serious it was. After that she had made a real effort to put him at his ease, to make him feel at home. And then it had all gone wrong.

The bottom line as she saw it was that it was ludicrous for what could possibly be the only two survivors of the apocalypse to not be on speaking terms. They had things to discuss, plans to make.

Georgie swallowed her pride like it was a shot of tequila; it was bitter and it made her wince, but she got it down.

Chapter 9. The only girl in the world

Top 20 Things we want to know about all this stuff
By Ant and Georgie

About the big thing
1. What the fuck happened?
2. How much of the world is affected?
3. Why is there no electricity?
4. Why didn't we turn into mutants?
5. What happened to the people we know?
6. Is anyone we know still alive?

About general life
1. How many people survived?
2. Are there top brass in bunkers ready to take charge again?
3. Is there an army?
4. Is there a place that all the survivors should be heading for?
5. Will the electricity come back on?
6. Will the gas stay on?

About the mutants
1. Can they do the things they could do when they were human?
2. If you get scratched or bitten by one do you become one too?
3. Do they all only eat humans?
4. Do they get diseases?
5. How do you kill them?

6. *Do they die of old age?*
7. *Do they go to the toilet?*
8. *What do they do in their downtime?*

Ant tossed the pen onto the coffee table and sat back. He yawned, stretching his arms over his head. "That's pretty comprehensive, well done, team." He held his hand out for a high-five. Georgie didn't leave him hanging.

When the tap on the bedroom door and the apology from Georgie had come, it was a welcome relief to Ant. He apologised right back and started pointing out all the reasons why he had been in the wrong. Georgie had stopped him and pointed out that there was no point in dissecting what had happened, they should just move on. Ant had been more than happy to agree.

They both knew that compiling a list of their top-twenty most pressing questions wasn't going to do much to advance their knowledge of the situation they had found themselves in but it was a good way to focus the mind, to block out some of the background noise.

Now they had their list, grouped into three categories (Georgie's idea), they were working their way through to see if there was any way they could even start to answer any of them.

'What the fuck happened?' had continued to prompt the most discussion. The fact that the electricity had gone down at the exact same time that people had turned into mutants had led them to think that this was a human-made situation rather than a natural disaster, with a nuclear meltdown or extremely complex and well-organised terrorist attack being the two front-runners in their thinking.

Georgie argued that the question of why the electricity was off was already covered by 'What the hell happened?' (as she continued to call it despite Ant's upgrade to the wording). Ant countered that she was absolutely right, but if they followed that argument to its logical conclusion then *all* the questions on their list were covered by that first one and so they may as well just scrap the list completely.

Georgie, wanting to keep the list alive, had backed down.

Georgie liked lists.

Their discussion of the first question had led them seamlessly to the second: 'How much of the world is affected?' They feared and assumed the worst, that this was at least a national event, and possibly the full-on, no messing about, end of the world, although they both very much wanted to be wrong about that.

They were sure there had to be other survivors apart from them. If being on a remote Scottish island had been what had saved Georgie then all the people on all the other remote islands must have been saved too. And if simply staying in while it was all happening had been what had saved Ant, then it would have saved plenty of other people who were inside when it happened, although surviving initially and surviving the aftermath, with its marauding mutants mopping up any human they found, were very different propositions.

Ant had come up with a suggestion to help answer question number two; they should look out for aeroplanes. His logic was that if they saw any, especially larger aircraft or military jets, then they could be sure that the entire world hadn't gone belly-up, unless some mutants had learnt to fly.

"Or," he said, "if they already knew how to fly while they were…" Ant nearly said 'alive' but he checked himself, not wanting to kick off the whole zombies versus mutants argument again, "…while they were *human*, then, as we've put down for number thirteen, they might still be able to do it. But I don't know how it works, I wish I knew."

"If they can fly, or even drive cars, then I think we'll find out soon enough," Georgie said grimly.

"That doesn't bear thinking about." As Ant spoke Georgie's eyes were drawn to his enormous feet that protruded over the arm of the sofa. "Back to the matter in hand," Ant continued, "the experiment has begun." He made a show of fixing his eyes on the skylight above him. "I'm looking for planes."

Georgie sat back on one of the armchairs, rested her toes on the edge of the coffee table and had another crack at her Dan Brown. Ant stole a glance at her, at those green eyes darting along with the words on the page, the long, still damp hair framing her slender face.

Georgie pretended not to notice.

After two hours and no aeroplane sightings Georgie, in a mock official voice, declared the experiment closed. "That's a wide enough data sampling window, we can conclude that no planes are in the air at the moment, in this area at least."

"It's not a window, it's a skylight." This was the first joke Ant had attempted since their recent argument.

Georgie smiled.

Ant was relieved.

"We have to call those results inconclusive as per the experimental design," said Georgie. "If we'd seen any we'd be sure that the world hasn't completely ended."

"Unless there are pilot mutes," Ant chipped in.

Georgie smiled, more convincingly this time. "*Mutes*', is that your creation or is it from a zombie film?"

"Mine, I guess."

"I think I like it."

Ant was delighted by this small note of acceptance. "Me too."

"Our experiment," Georgie continued, "didn't prove that the world hasn't completely ended, but it doesn't prove that it definitely *has* either. The fact that there are no planes could mean that the whole world is affected, or it could just mean that other countries, or other regions of this country for that matter, are choosing not to fly this way because it's not safe, or because they're being cautious. Or there could be any number of other reasons. Our experiment - you on the sofa looking up at the sky – whilst having demonstrated the necessary scientific and statistical rigour, proved to be inconclusive."

"I did conduct it pretty rigorously".

"Strictly clinical conditions, except when I saw you fall asleep for at least ten minutes."

"That was me analysing the data."

Georgie smiled. "Whatever you say, Anthony."

Ant swung his long legs round and sat up. "You do realise that the best experiment we can do to see how far this goes is to pack up, start driving and see for ourselves."

"I disagree" said Georgie. "If we could drive out of the, I don't know what to call it, disaster area? Ground zero? Then someone would have driven in from the unaffected side by now, probably the military."

"If there is still a military, we don't know if there is, it's…" Ant glanced down at the sheet, "…number nine on the list."

"Yes, but if it's only a local event then there's no reason we wouldn't have a military, this goes back to my point about a lot of the questions being linked."

"Fair enough", said Ant nodding. "I'm happy to back your theory, if only for my own cowardly reasons. I don't know about you but I don't feel ready to leave what we have here and go driving off into the forbidden zone just yet."

Georgie leant back and folded her arms. "No, I'm definitely not ready for that yet. But we are going to have to start getting ready for when we do decide to leave."

"Or when we *have* to leave," Ant said.

Georgie pulled a face. "Yes, that could well happen."

"That's why we need to start on those drills we talked about."

Georgie flexed her toes. "True. There's a lot of work to do."

Ant looked pained. "There is, there really is."

"Are you hungry?"

Ant looked like a dog who'd heard someone mention the park. "Yes, I'm hungry, so hungry."

"Cheeseburger?"

"I know you're bored of them, and I'm sure I'll be bored of them soon too, but right now I can't think of anything I'd like more."

Georgie put her open book face down on the coffee table and stood up. "We'd better enjoy them while we can anyway, we'll miss them when they've gone mouldy."

"You sit down, I can do it."

"No, you stay there, you've been working so hard looking out for planes, you must be exhausted." Georgie grinned and turned for the kitchenette, the light fabric of her dress sweeping in her wake.

Ant knew he was in big trouble.

Chapter 10. Shit day

It was a month on from Ant's arrival at the fire station and he and Georgie were still sharing a room, sleeping in the same bunks as that first night together. They hadn't talked about it but they felt safer that way, both knowing that being alone in a post-apocalyptic nightmare is a recipe for heebie-jeebies.

It was early morning and Ant had been awake for the last half hour, but he'd stayed still, not wanting to wake Georgie. He resolved to get up. He pulled the duvet aside, about to swing his legs out of bed.

He could hear a sound from downstairs.

Knock knock knock.

Pause.

Knock knock knock.

It wasn't a branch on the window and it wasn't the wind. It was a knock at the door.

He jumped across to Georgie's bunk and tried to wake her without putting the fear of God in her. He failed miserably on the fear of God part; the first thing Georgie saw as she jerked awake was Ant's panicked face with a finger held to his lips. It wasn't a shock, though, she knew straight away what was going on.

"Someone's knocking on the door." As Ant said the words the rapping came again.

Georgie spoke straight away. "Plan A?"

"Agreed."

They pulled on their clothes and shoes and Ant picked up what had become known as the Shit Day Bags: holdalls that once belonged to the firefighters but were now filled with emergency supplies, for: 'when that shit day comes.' Georgie opened the bedroom door and held it for Ant as he followed. They heard the knocking again as they reached the opening in the floor on the landing. Ant leaned on the top of the pole and dropped each bag into the garage below. He slid down, doing a perfect imitation of the series of pictures in the training manual. Going first was not a lack of chivalry on Ant's part, nothing in this procedure was by chance. Ant was heavier, if he were to follow Georgie down and go too soon it would hurt Georgie more than the other way around. He landed, pulled the bags clear and stepped away. He didn't shout up to Georgie for obvious reasons. After she'd counted to five as per their practice runs, she descended, even more smoothly than Ant had done.

They stood completely still and in complete silence. They were listening.

The knocking came again, louder because they were now closer to the front door. This time it was followed by a man's voice. Loud. Clear.

"Hello hello hello hello hello hello."

The sound of a voice other than their own had a profound effect on them both, but their survival instincts kept them on track. There was nothing that could distinguish the voice between human and mutant, so a neutral observer could be forgiven for thinking they shouldn't be running away, that this might be salvation arriving, or more human company. But it wasn't just the escape procedure they had rehearsed to the nth degree; they had also taken time to agree on the logic they should apply to a whole range of possible scenarios.

The logic that applied in this scenario was that if this was a non-mutant at the door then that person would not be risking drawing attention to himself by shouting so loudly. And even if it wasn't a mutant, somebody who was in the habit of taking that sort of risk wasn't somebody Georgie and Ant wanted to be around.

Georgie was in the driver's seat of their pre-selected fire engine, her door pulled to but not yet fully closed. Ant hoisted the bags onto the row of seats behind. The vehicle was pre-loaded with supplies but their tightly drilled procedure included having a bag each to hand, in case they had to take a different route out when the Shit Day came. Ant stood in the footwell of the passenger side of the cab, a small rubber box in his hand, trailing a cable onto the floor. He held the door open with his free hand and listened.

The knocking and the calling came again, followed by several cracks and the sound of the glass panel in the front door breaking.

Footsteps on the stairs. Lots of them.

Ant pressed the button on the box and the door in front of them opened, a lot more slowly than they would have liked, and a lot more loudly, but the fact that it was opening at all was a huge relief: it was battery-powered, they had been pleased to discover, presumably to allow the firefighters to answer an emergency call in the event of a power cut, and they had tested it, once, in the small hours of the morning, both of them scared out of their minds that the noise would summon the mutants. It had worked but they had feared that they might have used up the last of the stored power doing the test, or that the battery might simply have lost its charge since then.

Ant cast the box aside and pulled his door closed with a slam. Georgie did the same. The sound was no longer a concern. She heard screeching from above. She turned the key in the ignition, the engine bellowed with life.

The garage door was fully open.

Georgie put the pedal to the metal.

They felt a heavy thud on the back of the vehicle as they began to move, and another thud shortly afterwards as the mutant that had jumped from the top of the pole to the roof of the fire engine had failed to clear the gap between the vehicle and the top of the garage door.

Ant looked at Georgie, the steering wheel was huge in her hands, her face rictus concentration. Georgie could feel his eyes on her and for reasons she would never be able to explain she started to laugh uncontrollably. Ant followed suit.

Georgie spoke first. "Why the hell were they knocking?"

"Christ knows, it's like the ones outside the morgue, kind of polite."

"But trying to eat us."

"I know, right? But then that screeching, eurgh."

Georgie took her left hand off the wheel and held it towards Ant. "Kudos to us, all that practice paid off, we executed Plan A."

"Military precision, baby!" As Ant's palm landed on Georgie's she closed her fingers around his hand, holding it for a few seconds before letting go.

Georgie eased off the accelerator. They were clear of the fire station and the mutants that had come-a-knocking, so she didn't see the need to drive at breakneck speed. Handling this behemoth was like nothing she had done before and just keeping them on the road was difficult enough. She and Ant had studied the manual and all the training paperwork they could find but there was nothing to fully prepare her for the real thing. Ant was stealing glances at her in quiet admiration. When they'd made their plans for this eventuality he had taken it for granted that he would be doing the driving.

"Why would you assume that?" Georgie had asked when

she had realised what he was thinking.

"Erm, I really don't know to be honest. It's just the usual thing, you know."

"I don't know. What's the usual thing?"

Ant had sighed. "Okay, I'll say it. In my experience it's always just assumed that it's the guy who drives the tricky vehicle, the hire car on holiday, the van if you're moving to a new flat. It's, like, the default setting." Georgie had gone to speak but Ant had cut her off. "Whatever you're about to say I agree with you, there's no reason it should be the man. I shouldn't have assumed."

"You're right, you shouldn't have."

"I know, I just said that. But I don't think it makes me a bad guy. I get it, we've moved on from that fairer sex bollocks, but some stuff is just hard-wired into us, it takes a bit to get past it. I didn't mean any harm."

Georgie had been silent for a while as she'd considered his words. "That's a fair point. I'll cut you some slack."

"Thank you."

"But I'm doing the driving."

"Fill your boots." Ant had been sorely tempted to say *heels* but thought it too much of a high-risk strategy.

Ant hadn't admitted it but he'd still had doubts about Georgie being the designated driver, it wasn't so much the fact that she was female, more that she was so petite and the fire engine so huge, but now it was happening and she was getting them out of danger he was eating his unspoken words.

They drove through the eerily empty town. There were cars either abandoned or crashed on both sides of the road but no long procession that would have indicated an attempt at a mass exodus. Whatever had happened must have happened quickly and without warning.

They were moving fast but not going flat-out, something

which seemed to undermine the cinematic nature of their scenario of fleeing in a fire engine through a desolated city. In the movie version they would have been flying around corners and ploughing through legions of mutants, but until Georgie saw a convincing reason to do otherwise, she was happy to carry on at their current pace.

Although 'happy' wasn't quite the word for her emotional state.

The mutants they did see paid them close attention, but unlike the ones that had entered their former home, most didn't attempt to board the vehicle. Instead they watched in silence, like displaced refugees in news broadcasts as the aid convoy rolled past.

She felt almost sorry for them. "These ones don't look dangerous, do they?"

Ant turned sharply. "Don't even go there. Trust me, I lived for ages with them outside my door. They *are* dangerous, they're all dangerous. They're clever. These ones we're driving past know there's no point in acting crazy, so they don't bother. If they thought they had a chance of getting to us then things would be different. Don't even think about slowing down."

"I wasn't thinking about slowing down, I was just making an observation."

"That's good to hear. And if you fancied going a bit faster then I wouldn't object at all."

"We're fine like this. I'll speed up if I need to."

"Okay, any time you think you need to then you have my blessing."

"I'll speed if I need to."

"I know! I was just saying."

"Anyone who says *just saying*, isn't ever *just saying*. They always have an agenda."

"Okay, you got me. I've got an agenda. Can we go a bit

faster please?"

Georgie sighed and put her foot down, but only slightly, nowhere near as much as Ant was hoping. He decided not to pursue it.

They passed through the suburbs of town and into semi-countryside. Georgie pointed at a hand-painted sign declaring that the Coach House pub was next left. "What do you think, worth a look?"

Ant checked the mirrors and the road ahead. "I guess so."

"You don't sound very convinced."

"I know, I'm shitting myself."

"I wouldn't put it quite like that but I'm the same. But then there'd be something wrong with us if we weren't scared."

They were nearing the turn, Georgie glanced at Ant. "Shall we?"

Ant swallowed hard. "Go on, let's do it."

Georgie eased them off the main road and into the narrower track that looped left for few hundred yards and then straightened up. The ground was flat. They could see the pub half a mile ahead and it was open fields either side of them. Georgie looked into her mirror and across at the one on Ant's side.

When they had talked about eventually having to find another hideout, they'd agreed that their highest priority was that no mutants saw them arrive, because that would make them sitting ducks. The irony of stealth being their most valuable tool whilst they were driving a fire engine wasn't lost on them.

They pulled into the long car park that ran alongside the road with the pub at the far end. "This feels a bit open," Ant said.

"Yes, we can't park here. If the mutes are even half as smart as you say they are then it won't be hard for them to notice a big red truck that wasn't here before."

"How about down there?" Ant was pointing to the left of the pub: A sign saying 'private' marked a narrow turn that sloped downwards.

"Good spot," Georgie turned towards it. The road was steep and she slowed down to walking pace as she followed it down. As the ground levelled again she pulled the vehicle to a stop past a big oak-tree on Ant's side. Georgie peered out of her window. "I don't think anyone would be able to see us from the road or the car park."

"Agreed."

"And you didn't see any mutes on the road before we turned off?"

Ant frowned theatrically. "Don't you think I would have mentioned it if I had?"

Georgie shrugged. "Alright, I'm just making sure. I didn't see anything either."

"I know you didn't, or you would have said something too."

Georgie's eyes narrowed. "Not now, Anthony."

"Sorry."

Georgie scanned the area around them. "If there's anyone in the pub, or any*thing* I should say, then they've already seen us."

Ant swallowed hard again. "Agreed."

"Actually," Georgie said, "this is a terrible place to park. If there is something in there then we'll need to get out quickly, and we're tucked in at the bottom of a hill. My bad." She reached for the ignition key.

"But if we park nearer the road we're exposed."

Georgie sat back. "Fuck."

That was the first time Ant had ever heard Georgie swear. "Listen," he said, "We're never going to find somewhere that's got everything exactly as we want it. Yeah it's a risk, of course it is, but it could be more dangerous to keep driving, this thing makes a right old racket. Let's leave it here and check the place out."

"You think so?"

"Yes, I think so."

"It's not just because it's a pub and you really want a drink?"

Ant's smile wasn't very well hidden. "I have no idea what you're talking about."

It could have just been the fact that someone else had made the call, but Georgie was relieved they had decided on a course of action. She took the key out of the ignition. "Let's do it."

The Coach House was a traditional olde-worlde country pub, white walls with black trim, the structure slightly crooked from having stood for at least two hundred years. The difference in colour and regularity of the brickwork on one side showed that an extension had been tacked on at some point.

As they approached the back door they stopped. This was the first time either of them had been in the open air for weeks and they both felt extremely exposed. Ant reached out for Georgie's hand and she took it without a word. Ant looked up and around. "I haven't been out in the sticks for a while but shouldn't there be, like, some birds in the sky or something?"

Georgie stared up at the empty sky and nodded. "There should have been cows in the fields we just drove past, surely."

"Did you not see the bones?"

Georgie looked pained. "What happened?"

"I'm not sure I really want to know." Ant took a deep breath and squeezed Georgie's hand. "Ready?"

Georgie squeezed back. "Ready."

Neither of them was ready.

Chapter 11. Gastropub

The wooden door creaked like in the cheesiest of horror movies and Ant was grateful it was daylight. They stepped inside into the pub kitchen and Ant had a flashback to his morgue-residency: long, deep stainless-steel worktops, industrial sized refrigeration. A lot of knives.

The pans on the hob of the range cooker contained whatever had been simmering inside on that last day and was now just dried-up goo. A row of meals, encrusted with mould, waited to be served to hungry customers. Soiled plates, glasses, bowls and cutlery, filled a plastic rack ready to be loaded into a dishwasher.

The contents of the fridges spilled out from open doors. Watermarks soiled the floor.

The smell was disgusting but there was no sign of life.

"Clear," Ant whispered.

"Clear?" Georgie snorted, her nose gripped between her finger and thumb. "Okay, Mr. Navy Seal."

"Yeah alright, I have no idea what I'm doing, it seemed like the right thing to say."

Georgie touched his arm. "It's okay, I was only playing with you, it's better to laugh than…"

"Than wonder about that?" Ant was pointing at one particular set of human remains on the floor. In amongst the bloodstains on the shredded cotton around the sticky bones they could clearly make out a harlequin pattern; chef's trousers.

He gestured to the double swing doors on their left. "That must be the bar through there. And that one…" there was a single door on their right, "… don't know, into the rest of the house, whatever."

They approached the swing doors. There were no handles, designed as they were for fully loaded waiting staff to open with their backsides. Georgie pushed her cheek (the facial kind) against the left-hand door and eased it open, enough for her to peer through the tiny gap with her left eye. She was silent for a few seconds then pushed the door inwards another two inches. Ant was kicking himself for not bringing any weapons to use against whatever might be through those doors. He wanted to pick up a cleaver from a rack that was within reach, but he elected against it. He didn't want to startle Georgie with the sound of metal against metal.

Georgie pushed the door open and stepped through.

Ant was hot on her heels.

There were no mutants in the room.

"Clear," Georgie whispered.

They were in the restaurant section, half of the dozen tables of varying sizes were turned over. Plates, cutlery and glasses were on the floor as well as on the still-standing tables. There were piles of bones and bloodied clothing everywhere.

The bar itself was around thirty feet long, with dirty glasses crowding the end nearest Georgie and Ant. The bar was lined with high stools, several on their side on the floor.

"The police would call it signs of a scuffle," said Ant.

They crept through the building just as Georgie had when she had searched the fire station, their confidence stepping up a notch every time they entered a room devoid of deranged ex-humans.

The living area for whoever had run the pub was upstairs. It comprised a kitchen, bathroom, lounge and three bedrooms;

two doubles and a single. There were the remains of what looked like two people in the smaller of the double bedrooms but nothing in the other rooms. They checked everywhere several times over, upstairs, downstairs, and then further downstairs: the unspeakably creepy descent into the darkness of the cellar where the beer kegs cast ominous shadows in the torchlight.

They finally accepted that the building was free of mutants.

They made a cautious trip to the fire engine to retrieve the Shit Day Bags, with the day feeling a lot less shit than it had earlier. They put the holdalls at the bottom of the stairs.

"Fancy a pint?" said Ant. He wasn't sure whether to trust what was in the pumps so he poured himself a glass from a bottle of ale he'd taken from the unlit fridge behind the bar. "So what do you think, should we stay or should we go? The place stinks to high-hell."

Georgie smiled. "Yes, it smells truly awful, and there are corpses. But I think that's how the world is now. I think we have to stay. It has everything we need. We'll do a clear-out tomorrow, get rid of the skeletons and the rancid food. But we'll do it quietly."

Ant was relieved, he could not have faced going back on the road again just yet. Although he wasn't sure how well he'd be able to face cleaning up all the gore.

He took a long swig of his drink and sighed. "God that's good. That's so fucking good."

Georgie looked appalled. "Really? Sort yourself out why don't you? Get me one of those fruit ciders. No, on the left, no, one down, left again. Yes, that one."

"So," Ant said, "about all these corpses. Do you think only some people turned into mutes and the rest got eaten?"

"I've been thinking about that," said Georgie.

They were both still whispering and the sound of Ant popping the cap on Georgie's bottle sounded louder than it should. They glanced around, nervous. Ant listened for a while, heard nothing and carefully filled Georgie's glass.

"When the thing happened," Georgie took a sip, "oh yes, that *is* nice, it's been a while." She took another sip and put the glass down. "When the thing happened, I think it took some people longer to change into mutes than others, and they got eaten by the ones that had already turned."

"Or not everyone turned into mutes, and the ones that did ate everyone who didn't."

"Yes that's possible too. But I don't think that's what happened."

"Why?"

Georgie shrugged. "I have no idea to be honest."

Ant laughed. "It's basically the biggest murder mystery ever."

Georgie raised her glass, "Did we not do this?"

"Jesus," said Ant, "I don't think we did. Cheers!"

"To solving the biggest murder mystery ever," said Georgie.

"To surviving," said Ant.

They chinked glasses.

Georgie leaned back on her barstool. "Do you think the mutes eat each other?"

"They don't seem to, not the ones I've seen anyway, but maybe they do, maybe they just don't within their little packs. Maybe if the ones we drove past on the way here met the ones that were outside my morgue they'd kick off against each other."

"Like tribes?"

"Yes, I suppose. I don't know." Ant returned to his beer.

"I think I know why there are no mutes here by the way."

"Do tell."

"There's nothing else around here, just this place. Once the mutes had eaten the humans there was no point in them sticking around so they headed elsewhere, probably into town."

"I bloody hope so."

"And if that happened then it answers one of the questions in the top twenty."

Ant was all ears.

"I think it's number fifteen," Georgie continued, "the one about whether they eat anything other than humans. You said that the ones at the morgue weren't interested in anything else but the corpses… and you."

"Yeah," said Ant, "but to be fair, the other stuff I had to offer wasn't great."

"But surely if they were hungry they would have eaten what was available. And from what you said they were definitely hungry."

"Christ yes, the way they went on you'd think they were starving."

"Exactly," said Georgie, "and there's plenty of food in the kitchen here, fresh meals that have just been left to rot. If they could have eaten them, then surely they would have done."

"Maybe they didn't like the food here. I looked at the menu and it does look a bit poncey. I mean, it's a bloody pub, why do they have to go all *gastro*, what's wrong with fish and chips?"

"They did do fish and chips."

"I didn't see that."

Georgie reached out and took a menu from a stack near the till. She opened it, scanned it and read aloud. "Cracked pepper-battered hake served with triple fried potato croquettes."

Ant snorted into his drink.

"Before we go into what's starting to sound like a very predictable stand-up comedy routine about trendy pub food," said Georgie, "let's get back to the point I was making. I think the mutes got hungry when they ran out of longpig and that's why they left."

Ant opened a packet of dry-roasted peanuts. "What's longpig?"

"It's said to be the word cannibals used for human meat."

"Did they really have cannibals in Africa then?"

"Pacific Islands I think."

"If they only eat humans," said Ant, "then they're going to run out of food soon, if they haven't already."

"Unless they're adaptable and can change their diet."

"Wait a minute," said Ant. "They ate all the cows – unless something else did that. And I bloody well hope it was them because if there's something else roaming about out there that can do that then we're double fucked."

"So you're saying they only eat live animals? I'm including humans in the animals category by the way."

Ant frowned. "I need to pop out to the kitchen. Are you okay on your own for a second? I'm not being patronising but, you know, it's a new place so you might not want to split up until you feel a bit more settled here."

"I appreciate the sentiment, Anthony, but I'm fine, I'm okay to be on my own."

Ant stood up. "Okay, see you in a second." He didn't move.

"You okay, Anthony?"

"Yeah, I'm fine, I was just thinking."

"You're not ready to be on your own are you?"

"No I'm bloody not! Just come with me, will you?"

Georgie smiled. "It's okay, I don't think I am either, if you'd have gone I think I would have just followed you out."

She stood up and they started for the kitchen. "What do you need to do in the kitchen anyway?"

"Testing a theory. You saw that the fridges and the freezers had been properly ransacked, right?" Ant held the swing door open for Georgie as he walked through.

"Yes, everything's all over the floor, all soggy. There it is, *bon appétit*."

"I didn't see any meat, though." He leaned on the opened door of the fridge and stood as closely as he could without treading in anything terrible. He scanned the mess. "No meat." He checked the other one, "nothing." He lifted the lid of the freezer. "Hold on, here's something." He lifted out a click-lock container and pulled off the lid. "Chicken, but it's cooked, and there's cooked meat on these plates that have been left…"

Georgie finished his point for him. "They only eat raw meat, whether it's alive or dead."

"Exactly," said Ant but I get the feeling that, given the choice, they'd go for something alive.

They returned to the bar and Ant lifted his empty glass. "Fancy another?"

"I've only just started this one. Please don't get drunk, Anthony, we need to keep our heads clear."

Ant thought he noticed a tenderness in the way Georgie had said his name. "Get us," he said, "we sound like an old married couple."

"No we don't," said Georgie.

Ant got himself another bottle. "Sure you don't want one?"

"No, it's okay thanks." Georgie paused. She looked at her drink, back up, and back to her drink again.

"What?"

"I may as well say it, I know you must have thought about it."

"You're not talking about meat now are you, human or otherwise?"

"No, I'm talking about beds."

"Oh, I see," said Ant, putting his drink down.

Georgie smiled awkwardly. "Yes. I'm sure you see. One of the double rooms is out, even when we've got the corpses out, the smell's going to linger. That leaves the single, with a single bed in it, and the other double, with a double bed in it."

"So if we stay in the same room then we've got to share a bed."

"Yes."

"Right," said Ant, "I'm going to be perfectly honest with you. If I was staying in a room on my own I'd be too scared to go to sleep. So yes, I'd much rather we shared a room. And I know it probably sounds like I'm just trying to get you into bed, and I'll level with you, in normal circumstances I'd be doing everything I could to get you into bed, but this right here, is about keeping sane. I don't know why it makes a difference having someone else in the room but I know that out here in the sticks in the dark, with whatever the fuck is out there, if I'm alone I'll go off my fucking nut."

"That's a very eloquent argument, Anthony."

"I thought so. What do you think?"

Georgie sighed. "I agree with you, I couldn't be on my own either. It's not just about being scared, it's about being safe. If we're in the same room we've got more chance of one of us waking up if something comes."

"I could bring the single mattress in from the other room."

"Don't bother. We have to get used to the fact that we're in a different world now. The rules of polite society don't apply anymore, maybe they will again but right now survival is most important."

"Suits me," said Ant.

"But don't get any ideas. I'm grieving the love of my life."

Georgie didn't see the flicker of a smile that played on Ant's face. She hadn't said she wasn't interested in him; she'd said she was grieving. Ant knew there was a world of difference.

They sat quietly for a while, enjoying the peace, finally achieving something close to relaxation after the stress and upheaval of escaping the fire station.

Georgie suddenly looked puzzled. "Who turned the hobs off?"

"What do you mean?"

"The chef was killed. The other kitchen staff were either killed or turned into mutes. There were pans on the hob, but the hobs weren't on. Somebody turned them off, and the ovens too."

"Maybe the chef did it."

"While he was being attacked? I think that's a stretch."

"Maybe it was the mutants." Even as he said this, Ant knew it wasn't at all likely. He shook his head. "You're right," he said. "It's a bit weird, that."

Chapter 12. A quiet night in

Their first full day in the Coach House was hard going, not least because they slept terribly the night before. The smell of decay wasn't conducive to restful slumber, and whilst the silence of their new surroundings should have put them more at ease compared with the random noises that had been the soundtrack of their stay in town, it had the opposite effect entirely. The June night was lit by a full moon and they imagined that if they looked out of the window they would see an army of mutants marching over the open countryside towards them.

Sharing a bed had also made them both feel uncomfortable. Ant worried for most of the night that he might do one of those sleep-twitches and unwittingly nudge Georgie, making her think he was copping a feel while she slept. As a result, he was frightened to drop off, and as he lay there, eyes open, the urge to wrap his arms around her became almost irresistible, if only just to feel some human comfort, to hold her close and pretend that everything was fine with the world.

For Georgie, sharing a bed with a man had taken her back to her last weekend with Iqbal. The sense of loss that had been rumbling along in her gut since she'd lost him spiked to the point of desolation. She had wept silently, and at one point almost reached out to Ant. Just to feel some human comfort.

But she hadn't wanted to give him the wrong idea.

In the morning they started the big clean-up, and their first task was to clear the building of corpses. Before they did so they collected wallets, purses, jewellery and keys that lay close to the remains or in the pockets of the torn and bloody clothing. They put the items in clear plastic food storage bags from the kitchen, doing their best to keep the possessions of each person separate. They placed the bags neatly on the bed in the single room. They knew they wouldn't be able to dig a hole big enough to store all those bodies so this was the best they could offer as some kind of memorial. It would also mean that the victims could be identified at some future date in case a miracle happened and the world restarted.

They did shuttle-runs in and out of the building, collecting human remains and putting them in a wheelbarrow that they had taken from a utility shed outside. When the barrow was full they wheeled it to an area far enough away from the pub for the smell not to reach them but not so far that the heap of awfulness could be seen by prying mutant eyes. There they deposited the barrow's grisly contents.

It was long, heavy and disturbing work.

Next was the rotting food. This took even longer than the unceremonious bringing out of the dead. It seemed to be everywhere on the ground floor, and the actions of pouring, scooping and scraping the putrid food seemed to dislodge trapped odours strong enough to permeate the scarves they tied around their faces to protect them from the stink.

The food waste was added to the pile of human waste and the whole thing covered with a tarp weighed down with empty beer barrels that had been stacked outside, awaiting a collection that would never come.

After all of that, the task of cleaning and scrubbing every room seemed almost relaxing by comparison. Georgie hadn't had the best experience of men doing domestic chores, mostly because of her two brothers who had always seemed to be overcome by crushing laziness and stupidity when there was work to be done around the family home. Ant, by contrast, showed an impressive level of industry. He didn't wait for her to tell him what to do and he didn't ask daft questions. He just got on with whatever needed to be done.

When it was over they rewarded themselves by taking full advantage of the gas-fired boiler and taking their first hot showers in longer than either of them could remember. Just like it had at the fire station, steam billowed out of the flue when the water ran; a smoke signal to any passing mutants, but they agreed, in an impromptu policy-setting discussion, that they would allow themselves hot showers as long as they kept them short and only had them after-dark.

Ant had suggested that they could halve the time they were running the water by showering together. Georgie had told him not to push his luck.

They checked everywhere for provisions, mostly food to supplement what they had brought with them. They hit the jackpot in the cellar where they found catering sized tins of beans, fruit and soup as well as pasta and other dried food that would see them through a good few weeks at least. Georgie opened a cupboard full of tea-lights and holders meant for the tables in the restaurant and bar. The discovery prompted another policy discussion; with no lighting it would have been convenient - and rather nice - to have the candles around the bar where they were sitting. They considered it but the front of the pub looked out over the garden, dotted with picnic tables, the dormant road and farmland beyond. The windows were frosted, shielding the view from outside but not enough to block the flicker of candlelight at night. They agreed not to take the risk.

They were enjoying the moment. They felt clean, satisfied with a good day's work and much more comfortable in their new surroundings. Ant had tested the draft beers and found that two of the lagers and a cider were still very drinkable. He had moved a stool to the other side of the bar and was enjoying playing landlord, with Georgie already his favourite regular.

"So how about you, Anthony? We've talked about Iqbal a lot but what was your situation? I know you were single when… when it all ended, but was there someone, you know… someone you liked?"

Ant blushed. "What, like a crush you mean?"

"You know what I mean."

"Yeah, okay, I do know what you mean and yes there was someone. Suzie. We worked at the same place. We'd go for coffee at lunchtime and drinks after work sometimes, she'd only just split up from her fella, so it wasn't like I'd made a move or anything, I was giving her time, you know? Didn't want to be that douche stepping in fancying myself as a knight in shiny armour."

"Isn't it *shining* armour?"

"What did I say?"

"Shiny armour."

"Same thing isn't it?"

Georgie nodded, smiling. "Maybe. I think I quite like your version though. It's a shame you never got to see if your strategy worked."

"Yeah, we literally ran out of time. But I suppose I should be grateful I wasn't gaga over anyone because it means I haven't got the heartbreak like you're going through. Except my mates I suppose…" He thought back to that last session with Pete and Rachel and wondered how it ended for them, "…but I've tried not to think about them really. Then there's my family. I miss them like mad."

Georgie sighed. "That's the hardest part. How often did you see them?"

"A few times a year at least. I'd go up there for the weekend. Sam, my sister, and me were really close and we'd all have a right laugh. My mum was the bollocks, she loved having people round. She was proper funny. We'd stay up playing cards and my mum would be on the sherry and she'd tell these stories about the people she used to work with, she worked for the NHS, used to be a nurse, but she'd got more into the management side of things. She seemed to work with some right crazy bastards and she'd make us all wet ourselves with the stuff she'd tell us about them. We'd forget all about the cards. My dad was potty about her. I'd watch him watching her while she was talking, it was the same look I saw him have when we went to watch Sam singing a solo at her school end of year thing, like he was going to split open with pride. I'm… I'm sorry." Ant's lip was quivering and in moments tears were streaming down his face. "I'm sorry." He put his hands to his face and sobbed.

"Please don't be sorry." Georgie stepped off her stool, raised the hinged counter flap and went through to Ant. She pulled him close, resting his cheek on her shoulder as she too started to cry. Ant returned the hug and they stayed like that for a long time, weeping for themselves, for everyone they had lost and for each other. It felt perfectly natural, comfortable, comforting. They eventually ended the embrace, wiping their eyes and becoming present again, like volunteers at a stage-hypnotist show being brought back into the room.

And suddenly they both felt incredibly awkward.

Neither of them knew how to make the transition from the intensity of that shared moment to just going back to chatting. Georgie was over on Ant's side and now needed to go back through the bar to her stool and her drink. She patted Ant on the shoulder clumsily and Ant raised a hand but didn't know what to do with it. Georgie took it and shook it, like she was closing a business deal. "Good work," she found herself saying. "I mean," she shrugged. "I don't know what I mean. I'm just going to sit down. Let's have another drink." She went back to her stool.

"Yes, more drinks," said Ant. "What can I get you?"

"Same again please."

"Coming right up." Ant topped up both their glasses.

They drank in silence for a while, both of them thinking about the people in their old lives.

It was Georgie who spoke first. "Do you think any of them are still alive?"

Ant let out a breath slowly. "That's the question isn't it?"

"How come we've never asked it before?"

"Simple," said Ant, "because we knew we wouldn't have been able to handle any of the likely answers. Either they're alive and living God-knows what sort of existence, scared out of their minds and in constant danger, or they're dead. Or worse, they're mutants. At least I think that's worse. Is it worse?"

Despite the awful subject matter Georgie couldn't help but smile at Ant's question. "Yes, Anthony, I think it's worse."

Ant had lifted his drink but held off as he thought about Georgie's answer. "Yeah, I think you're right. It's worse." He took a swig. "So anyway, we knew there was nothing we could do for them, we had no clue what we were doing, so we just kept quiet about it."

"We can't keep doing that though, can we?"

Ant locked eyes with Georgie. "So what do you think?"

Georgie looked nervous. "You mean, do we go looking for them?"

Ant nodded slowly. "We're going to have to, aren't we?"

"We are, yes."

"Your folks are closer. Oxford's just the other side of

town."

"Well not really," said Georgie, "not just the other side, it's a fair few hours away, but yes, it's not an impossible journey. My mum, dad and youngest brother live there. The same house I grew up in."

"We start there then."

"That doesn't seem fair on you."

Ant took another pull of his pint. "It's not about fairness anymore, it's about logic. Your family are close. Mine are three hundred miles away. We'll try your 'rents pad first and if we get through that then I'd like to check in on some friends, see how they got on."

"Let's do it. But we can't rush it, we need to take a few days to get ready, make plans."

Ant put his drink down. "Oh God yes, I wasn't suggesting we leave now."

"We need to prepare ourselves for the worst though, Anthony. We have to be realistic. It's a fair bet that everybody we know is gone."

"I know, this is probably what they used to call a fool's errand. But if we don't try then we'll never forgive ourselves."

"That's about the size of it."

"It's a big old size." Ant finished his drink.

Chapter 13. Sunday worst

The next day, according to Georgie's records, was a Sunday and she sat behind the bar with a newspaper open in front of her. The paper's date was several months of Sundays in the past; the day the world had ended. Above the title on the front-page Ant had scrawled *Apocalypse Edition* in black felt-tipped pen.

Detective Georgie had already deduced that the catastrophe had been on the Sunday of her weekend away rather than the Saturday. She had established this from a combination of evidence, namely that the last message on Ant's phone had been sent to him that Sunday morning and included no mention of the disaster, along with the fact that the Sunday menus had been put out on the tables in the pub restaurant. If final confirmation had been needed then the existence of a newspaper from the Sunday in question proved, beyond doubt, that the world could not have ended the day before.

Ant was upstairs reading the Dan Brown he had inherited from Georgie. They'd settled quickly into their new home and found that they'd become brave enough to spend some time on their own, in daylight at least.

As Georgie scanned the newspaper she was overcome with thoughts of that last morning, when everybody had gone about their business as if nothing was about to happen, because as far as everybody was concerned, nothing was about to happen. And then the something had happened and now here she was, sitting with this historical document that captured a moment in time, before time as she understood it had ended.

She thought about the journalists who had submitted their stories, probably stressing to a deadline but managing to get the job done and moving on to the next thing. She thought about the staff running the printing presses, the delivery drivers, the shopkeepers that sold them, the paperboys and papergirls. The paperpeople.

She thought about her family, she thought about Iqbal.

The main news stories, as she had expected, gave no indication of what might have brought about the End of Days. She turned the page to a piece about the leaders of Iceland and Greenland meeting to discuss shipping routes through the Arctic Circle. More of Ant's handiwork was visible: Speech bubbles drawn on the picture of the two leaders shaking hands.

"I'm a Green man from Greenland."

"I'm an icy man from Iceland."

And he'd drawn penises coming out of their heads.

Georgie, despite having been feeling what can only be described as a deep melancholy, found herself smiling.

She turned the page to the crossword. She looked around for a pen.

She heard a key turning in the lock of the front door.

She dropped off the stool and ducked low under the countertop.

The door opened and she heard footsteps followed by a voice. "Hello, hello. Late opening, had to use my key. Anyone about? Oh there you are, hello Cynth. What are you looking for down there?"

Georgie glanced over her hunched shoulder at the mirror behind the bar and locked eyes with a mutant.

In the last few months of Georgie's life, she had been scared for almost every minute of every day, feeling a constant background fear that was as difficult to ignore as toothache. On top of this ever-present bedrock of dread were the moments of bone shaking terror she had endured, the first of which being seeing her boyfriend chased away and killed by mutants.

This was one of those bone shaking moments.

She raised herself up from under the bar. "Morning." She was surprised she was able to form that one word coherently.

The mutant, a man, quite elderly as she could make out in spite of the purple stretched skin, the drool, the lumps and the bulging eyes, wore baggy brown trousers tucked into knee-length boots and a wax jacket. He was gripping the curved handle of a wooden cane. He removed his cap, revealing sparse white hair sprouting between pockets of yellow discharge. "It's two past twelve," he said, glancing at his watch. You should be saying good afternoon." He lifted the cane and tapped the head of one of the pumps. Pint of the usual please."

Georgie's hand shook as she took a pint jug from the shelf above the bar. The nozzle frothed and spat as she pulled on the pump, a result of both the length of time it had been unused and Georgie's lack of technique; she had worked several jobs to help her through university but never behind a bar. She shook the foam that had quarter-filled the glass onto the floor and took another run at it, tilting the glass as she'd seen bar staff do, and easing the pump more smoothly this time. It was an improvement but not by much. She stole a few glances at Farmer Mutant as she carried out the botched job. He was staring straight ahead, his eyes seemingly unfocused on anything specific.

She held the glass in both hands in an attempt to keep it steady and lifted the half-liquid, half-foam apology for a pint onto the bar. It smelled all wrong, but then so did he. She slid the mug across and twisted it so the handle pointed in the mutant's direction. The base of the glass left moist residue in its wake.

"Thank you my dear." His eyes looked straight through her, glazed, lifeless, Ant's word: *zombiefied*.

In spite of her all-consuming fear, Georgie's scientific mind was fascinated by what she was seeing. She was particularly curious to see a mutant drink.

His fingers closed round the handle of the pint-pot and he lifted it towards his face, touched the rim with his mouth. He held it there for a few moments but was just going through the motions; no beer passed his discoloured lips. Georgie watched, baffled, as Farmer Mutant lowered the glass back onto the bar and, to complete the charade, wiped some of the drool from his mouth as if it was foam from the beer. "First of the day, can't beat it." His eyes continued to look vaguely in Georgie's direction. "Jack not about?"

Georgie managed to speak again. "He's out at the shops." From a stack of mail Georgie had found in a drawer upstairs she knew that Cynthia and Jack had run the pub, and from the photos on the mantlepiece she knew that she, Georgie, looked nothing at all like Cynthia. Either this mutant had poor eyesight or he was not connected to reality, either due to some pre-existing dementia or something related to his mutant-state.

The mutant touched the handle of its glass again but didn't go through the drinking motion this time. "All work and no play makes Jack a dull boy."

"He does his best."

"Plenty in today."

Georgie glanced at the empty pub and back at the mutant. "Yes, we're rushed off our feet."

"Preferred it when it wasn't just about food. A pub's for drinking in, not for eating. It's when they started letting kids in that it all changed. You used to be able to say what you wanted in a pub but now you have to watch your mouth because someone's brat might hear. You could smoke too but they put a stop to that along with everything else. You can't do anything anymore. It's a nanny state is what it is." Georgie's mind rolled back to the two bodies in the bedroom and felt sympathy for Cynthia, not because she had been killed by mutants and had her body picked clean as they devoured every last morsel of her flesh, but for all the times she must have had to endure the same old repeated patter from not only this regular, but from all the others who would have had her as a captive audience for their relentless opinions.

Farmer Mutant did the mock-drinking thing again then turned his head from side to side as if taking in his surroundings. He mentioned Jack again and muttered something about the work ethic of Eastern Europeans, his pupils starting to dart around under eyelids that had started to flap open and shut. His head moved left and right again, and Georgie was reminded of a movie she had seen where humanoid robots went out of control, their behaviour becoming increasingly erratic before they went berserk or their heads exploded. Or both. Georgie had not altogether relaxed since the start of the exchange but her fear of being eaten had subsided a great deal since Farmer Mutant had shown more signs of boring her to death than pulling out her heart and chewing on it. But now she was back on full alert. The mutant was either going to seize up and drop to the floor or it was going to attack her.

It did the latter.

It jumped at the counter, its arms flailing in Georgie's direction and suddenly there was a flurry of movement from the far end of the bar. It was Ant, his eyes as crazy as the mutant's and his hands flashing, a psychotic Edward Scissorhands. But it wasn't scissors in his hands, it was a combo of a scalpel, his most cherished cutting tool from the morgue, and a cleaver, the one that had caught his eye in the kitchen the day they had arrived. He swung the cleaver into the side of the mutant's neck, using his momentum to maximise the power of the blow. It nearly took the thing's head off, but Ant wasn't stopping to take stock of the result, he was busy bringing the scalpel upwards with his other hand, hard into the monster's chest. It went up and under the ribcage, buried to the hilt. Ant, now disarmed of his two weapons went back to basics and started punching the thing on either side of the head, a whirling dervish; the bullied kid at school finally losing it at his tormentors. Ant was, as he would have put it himself, going proper apeshit. Farmer Mutant fell to the floor and Ant followed him down, kneeling astride the lifeless body and pounding with his fists and elbows.

The rain of Ant's blows eased from a deluge to a downpour and finally to a light drizzle as his knuckles began to land on the mulch of exposed soft tissue rather than shattered bones. The mutant's head was a bloody pulp and Ant started to come down from the adrenaline-fuelled state he had entered as soon as he saw Georgie in danger.

He rolled off the corpse, completely drained and choking down the urge to vomit. Georgie was kneeling over him, holding him, pulling him away from the dead mutant. She whispered reassuring platitudes but most of all she just repeated one phrase: "Thank you."

They lay on the floor for a while, stunned into silence by what had just happened.

"Fuck," said Ant.

"Fuck indeed," said Georgie, and started to laugh, feeling that same hysteria as when they had left the fire station.

This, of course, set Ant off too and they lay there, literally rolling on the floor laughing. "What just happened?" Georgie managed to say between breaths. "What on earth just happened?"

"I don't know," said Ant, rolling onto his back and starting to pull himself together. "I heard voices and knew there had to be someone here, so I tooled up and crawled into the room and watched. I thought it was going okay, he was just talking."

"He was for a while."

"But then he turned."

"Yes, he definitely turned."

"And you know the rest."

"You went ballistic."

"I'm no good at fighting, I've been in plenty of scraps but lost almost all of them. The only way I was going to take that thing out was to lose my shit. But I don't think it was, like, a conscious decision, I think I just lost my shit. Seeing someone you care about being attacked by a monster will do that I guess."

Georgie kissed his cheek. "Thank you," she said again.

"You don't need to keep thanking me." Ant's eyes went from Georgie's face to her upper arm and his face darkened.

"What?" said Georgie, following his gaze. "Oh," she said.

She had three deep scratches in her skin, all of them oozing blood.

Chapter 14. Guilty pleasure

"What happens now?" Georgie asked. "Do you lock me in the cellar in case I turn into one and turn on you?"

"Are you serious?"

Georgie looked nervous. "I'm not really sure, but I'm calling it because it must have crossed your mind. You've seen the films."

Georgie was wrong, the thought hadn't remotely crossed Ant's mind, but now she had injected it into the forefront of his thoughts he was forced to face it: the image of Georgie locked in the cold cellar, alone in the dark. Ant could no more shut his grandmother in that cellar than do it to Georgie. He tried to picture himself walking up the stairs after having locked her in, sleeping upstairs in a bed while she was down there in the blackness.

Just the thought of it made him want to throw up.

"Come on." Ant stood up and reached out for Georgie's hand to help her up. He led her to the kitchen and stood her next to the sink. He went to a cupboard and took out a first aid kit, opening it up and pulling out a large clump of cotton wool. He rolled up the arm of her t-shirt and gently bathed her wounds, using water as hot as she could stand. He dabbed it dry with a clean tea-towel from a drawer and then soaked some more cotton wool in an antiseptic solution and carefully applied it along the length of each gash. It stung but Georgie didn't complain. She was surprised by how gentle this huge housemate she'd been landed with was being, and she couldn't help but notice the not at all unpleasurable tingling that his touch set off in her skin. He wrapped the finished article in a bandage and stuck it down with adhesive tape. "How's that?" he said.

Georgie nodded, genuinely impressed by the neatness of the dressing but more aware of the mild ache in her stomach and the flush rising from her throat. "It feels clean and sterile, what more could a girl wish for?"

"To not have been scratched by a mutant?"

"Fair point, but we can't have everything we want in life, can we?"

"I'll make up a bed for you in the cellar."

Georgie studied Ant's impassive face. "I really can't tell if you're joking or not."

"Of course I was joking dummy! We've just been over that, we're not locking you up, that would be ridiculous. The thing where people turn into a zombie, mutant, whatever, after a scratch or a bite, that's only in films, there's no evidence that it happens for real."

"Yes, but bloodthirsty mutants only happened in films before, and they're very real now."

Ant chewed on his bottom lip. "Yeah, that's true, but it's very simple, I'm not locking you in the cellar and that's that."

"You're sure?"

Ant laughed, "Yes, I'm sure! I've told you before, I'd shit myself sleeping on my own."

"But what if I turn?"

"You've seen what I'll do if that happens, I'll murder you with kitchen utensils."

"Okay, that sounds fair," Georgie said, smiling. "But seriously," her tone changed, "thank you, Anthony."

"You don't need to keep thanking me, you would have

done the same thing, and anyway, you *did* do the same thing, you got me out of that morgue when I was a goner for sure."

"We're quite a team it would appear."

Ant smiled again. "It's certainly looking that way."

They did go down to the cellar, not to imprison Georgie but to retrieve some plastic sheeting to wrap up Farmer Mutant. They dragged his body through the kitchen and out the back to take its place amongst the rest of the artefacts in their open-air Museum of Carnage.

They scrubbed the carpet in front of the bar and when they were satisfied that they had got rid of as much mutant blood and other unknown bodily fluids as they could, they voted unanimously to make an exception to their recent showering policy on the grounds that not washing thoroughly after handling mutant remains was just asking for trouble.

"Where do you think he came from?" Georgie asked. They were on the sofa in Cynthia and Jack's upstairs lounge, clean and dry.

"From across the fields I suppose," Ant said. "Seemed like a regular who always came for his Sunday pint, and it seemed like he was re-enacting his visits."

"He had a key."

"Yes, maybe he kept an eye on the place if the owners weren't around, helped out sometimes, brought firewood, whatever."

"Do you think it was him who turned the hobs off?"

"I hadn't thought of that, but yeah, it could well have been him."

"I wonder how close his farm is. It's creepy to think that he's been nearby all the time we've been here. Makes me shudder. Oh God, do you think he has a family, a mutant family and they're somewhere over the fields? Do you think they'll come looking for him when he doesn't come home?"

"I think we're okay. He was pretty old so if he had kids they probably would have left home by now."

"Farmer's kids don't leave home. They take over the farm."

"We don't know he's actually a farmer! If everyone who wore wellies and a wax jacket was a farmer there wouldn't be enough countryside to go around. It might be worth us taking a recce out across those fields though. It's farmland, probably not his, but if we can find a farmhouse then we should be able to find a shotgun."

Georgie's eyes widened. "Have you ever fired a shotgun?"

"I did paintball once at a mate's stag."

"Were you any good?"

"Didn't find out, I got hit really early on, right on the knuckle of my little finger, it really hurt. It swelled right up. I had to go to A&E."

Georgie was shaking with laughter.

"What?"

"Did you fire any shots at all?"

"Got one or two rounds off, yes."

"And you think you can handle a shotgun?"

"Who said I'd be the one handling the shotgun? Why would you assume it would be the man who'd take on the gun responsibilities?"

"Okay, you got me, well done. I'm a bad feminist."

"The worst. How about you, ever fired one?"

"A shotgun? Actually I have. Last year, on Lucy's hen weekend, we did clay pigeon shooting."

"Well there you go then, you're definitely in charge of shotgun duties. How did you get on?"

Georgie smiled bashfully. "Well I don't want to brag but I was really good at it. I got the top score by miles. The instructor couldn't believe I'd never held a gun before."

"I'm glad to hear it, that could be a very useful skill."

"Do you think we really need a gun then?"

"It can't do us any harm. We just had a really close call. I don't want to make a habit of getting into hand to hand combat with mutes."

"You did a pretty good job of the last one."

"Thank you, Georgina, that's very kind of you to say, but I think we got lucky there. He wasn't particularly strong, he was ancient."

"His mental state," said Georgie, "do you think that was from before?"

"The blank stare, the vagueness? I reckon it's a bit of both, the mutes outside my morgue had a similar look but seemed a bit more with-it. Come to think of it, only one of them really talked to me, the leader one. So maybe it varies. I don't think Farmer Mute could have been too far gone while he was human otherwise Jack and Cynthia wouldn't have given him the keys. All due respect to people with dementia but you probably wouldn't trust them with a key to your house, would you?"

"No, you probably wouldn't."

"But what about the thing he did where he, like, mimed drinking?"

Georgie pulled her feet up onto the sofa in front of her and hugged her knees. "Yes, that's really interesting. I think it's what you said, *re-enacting*, like he was going over old behaviours. Did any of yours outside the morgue do anything like that?"

"Well the first one I saw, the one that knocked on the door of my flat. He was done out like he was a rep for the council or something, he had a clipboard and he was all, like, businesslike. That could have been the same sort of thing."

"It's useful data."

"Not sure how useful it is."

Georgie rested the side of her head on her raised knees.

"Any information is useful."

Ant had to look away from the sight of those green eyes peering out from her cocked head because it was making his heart hurt. He was worried he was going to say something soon. There was never any doubt that he 'fancied' Georgie, and he knew that was a childish word but he could never think of anything that did the job any better. He definitely fancied her, found her attractive, was aware of her charms, all of the above, but what was new was this affection that was taking hold like one of those weeds that grows around trees and strangles them to death. Ant forced himself to speak. "Talking of information, we'll soon have the answer to one of our top twenty, I forget which number, the one about whether a scratch turns you into one."

"Sure you don't want me to go and live in the cellar?"

"Well if you really want to, be my guest. How are you feeling anyway? I don't mean, like, are you starting to feel like you want to eat human flesh, I mean how are you after being through what you went through? It was quite a trauma in anyone's book."

"I feel a bit woozy, that's all, and I think that's just shock, the arm is fine, you did a good job there. You weren't a paramedic in a previous life, were you?"

"No, I'd be no good, I hate the sight of blood, and I'm incredibly lazy."

"Neither of those things is true," said Georgie. "You beat that mutant to mush and you didn't even retch afterwards, and you're definitely not lazy, you work like a pack horse, I've seen you."

Ant was very tempted to say that he was hung like a pack horse too, but he resisted the urge. "I'll take that as a compliment, thank you."

"You should. Talking of previous lives, do you miss your

job?"

"Not really, not the work anyway, I miss some of the guys I worked with though, I made some good mates there. And when I say *guys* I don't just mean blokes."

"I got what you meant. Did you do a lot of socialising as a team then?"

"It was Relationship Marketing, it was almost all socialising. That's why I said I didn't miss the work, there wasn't much work to miss. How about you?"

"Do I miss my job, or was my job sociable?"

"Both I guess."

"It wasn't sociable, no. People just did their hours and went home. A lot of people did compressed hours so they could finish early and go to the gym or to see their families. We didn't go out after work, except at Christmas, but that was never a biggie, just a dinner and then most people went home."

Ant's face was pained. "That sounds fucking awful."

"It wasn't so bad, I liked it." Georgie frowned. "Actually, come to think of it, I don't think I did like it. I think I would have liked to have worked somewhere were people did stuff together."

"I always used to say to people who said they didn't want a beer because they had work to finish off, when you're on your deathbed, you're not going to say to yourself, *shit, I wish I'd worked more.*"

"I'm not on my deathbed, Anthony."

"I know, but it's the end of the world, it's sort of the same thing."

"Not if you're saying that I am at the end of my life and now can only regret things that I didn't do."

"Erm... no, didn't mean that, sorry. Plenty to look forward to." Ant winced as the last sentence left his mouth.

Georgie clearly wanted to change the subject. "I'll tell you what I do miss, and I never thought I would. I miss what my older brother always called dicking about on the internet. That was my guilty pleasure when I was studying or working."

"I really hope you had guiltier guilty pleasures than that."

She put on her best innocent look. "That would be telling now wouldn't it?"

"What sort of stuff did you look at when you were dicking around?"

"Any kind of pointless clickbait that you could think of. Quizzes, pictures of actors from old films and TV shows where they look older than they used to, riddles, pictures of random things that half the population thought were a certain colour and the other half thought were a different colour, and lists. You know the lists, best things, worst things, most unbelievable things. Lists of facts about a thing or things."

"That's quite a list."

"Ha ha, Anthony."

They'd both relaxed since the shock of the attack but Georgie was carrying heavy anxiety over being scratched. She knew she only had popular culture to go on but she couldn't help but fear the worst. She tried not to let on to Ant but she kept glancing at the skin of her arm to make sure it wasn't turning purple or growing lumps. Ant wasn't being completely honest either. Despite casually writing off the whole thing as nonsense he was very afraid. He'd seen a lot more zombie movies than Georgie, a lot more than most people for that matter, and it was difficult to shake one of the most common tropes of the genre. If a zombie, mutant, whatever, bit or scratched you, you turned into one. That was the rule. He knew it was fiction but he had seen it happen on the screen so many times that it was hard not to believe it now he seemed to be living inside one of those movies. He was on edge for the rest of the day, watching out for Georgie to suddenly go all woozy, fall into a fever and then come out the other side a crazed monster. He watched her for half the night, too, after she had fallen asleep he lay there for hours. But she didn't turn into a monster, she remained, in Ant's eyes, an angel.

Chapter 15. Hey Georgie, it's your birthday, we're gonna party like it's your birthday…

10 things we don't miss since the apocalypse
Brought to you by Georgieslists.com

Everybody misses something about the world before the human race was as good as wiped out, but what about things we don't miss? What have we happily said good riddance to as we take our chances in the dystopian chaos that's now our home? Our panel of experts have sifted through the possible options. They've distilled, they've filtered and they've filtrated (which is pretty much the same as filtering but we needed a third thing because there's always a third thing) and without any further ado, we can reveal, in no particular order, the top 10 things we DON'T miss since the end of the world.

1. *People who sniff every 5 seconds.*
2. *Your friends trying to educate you with their self-righteous social media postings.*
3. *Being on a train while someone's playing a game on their phone that makes really loud babyish noises whenever they get, like, 10 unicorns lined up or whatever.*
4. *The News.*
5. *Talking to those people who hijack the conversation and make it all about them.*
6. *Going to work.*
7. *Having to hear about other people's fantasy football teams and how*

they would have got, like, a hundred points if they'd included so and so in their team that week but they thought he was injured so left him out but he wasn't injured and he played really well.
8. *Having to sponsor your friends so they can do something they've always wanted to do without having to pay for it themselves.*
9. *People who talk without noticing they've got loads of phlegm in their throat.*
10. *People telling you how many thousands of steps they've done that week.*

Related articles

Best places to forage for supplies.
This app shows you what you'll look like as a mutant!
Where are they now? Your friends and family.

Ant had had limited means at his disposal: a notepad, a pen and his brain, but he had done his best. He had wondered if he'd gone a bit too far with the name of the last spoof article, but he hoped the gallows humour would be appreciated.

He had folded it in half, written 'happy birthday Georgie' on the back and left it on the coffee table in the upstairs lounge. This had become Georgie's favourite hangout spot since Farmer Mutant had come through the front door and tried to kill her in her previous favourite hangout spot.

Ant was down in the kitchen making them his breakfast special: soup and crisps. He heard Georgie hurrying down the stairs and within a moment she had burst into the room, waving the list and grinning. "Thank you, thank you, I love it." She put her hand to her mouth as she noticed the sheets of paper taped to the kitchen walls and cupboards, a letter on each and one for the exclamation mark:

H A P P Y B I R T H D A Y !

"Thank you, Anthony, I love it!" She threw her arms

around him. She had to stand on tiptoes and he had to stoop so she could kiss him, on the cheek, disappointingly for Ant. It was less disappointing when she pulled him close and held him very tightly and for a long time.

Ant heard a sniff from the face buried in his chest and realised she was crying. "You okay?"

Georgie pulled her head back so she could look at Ant but kept her arms loosely around him. Her eyes were red but she was smiling. "I am, yes, thank you. This is really nice, I love it, I love…." She hesitated, "*it*." She sniffed again and her smile grew bigger. "Thank you, Anthony."

"You are most welcome, Georgina. I'm glad it made you smile."

"How did you know?"

"That you liked stupid internet lists? You told me last night."

"You know very well that I don't mean that. I can't believe you remembered my birthday! We only talked about it once and that was weeks ago."

"Weird as it might sound, I do actually listen to the things you say. Happy birthday!" Ant took the opportunity to pull Georgie in for another hug. He eventually released her and gave the soup a last stir and turned off the gas. "Won't be a minute, don't go away."

While Ant was out of the room Georgie poured the soup into bowls and put the crisps on a plate. "You're not supposed to do that," Ant was back in the room, "it's your birthday."

"It wasn't too much effort." Georgie put the saucepan in the sink.

"No, I guess not." Ant said, producing a bottle of champagne from behind his back. "Okay, so it won't be properly chilled, but I left it in that really spooky corner of the cellar where it's the coldest so it's the best we can hope for."

Georgie noticed for the first time the two champagne flutes that were already out on the counter. She clapped her hands and grinned. "Oh Anthony, thank you."

"You don't need to keep thanking me, it's a pleasure. You okay to go into the restaurant for your birthday breakfast?" Ant started loading their drinks and food onto a tray.

"Yes, let's. You sure I can't carry anything?"

"No, you're not to lift a finger, it's your birthday."

"Can I at least get the doors?"

"Go on then."

Georgie gestured at the tables in the restaurant. "Any preference?"

"Actually, yes." Ant smiled, a little embarrassed. He nodded his head in the direction of the window. "That one."

Georgie didn't notice straight away why Ant had picked that table but when she saw the flowers, six stems wrapped in a single sheet of tissue, she clapped her hands together again and beamed.

"Happy birthday Georgina. Sorry they're not roses, unless roses come in purple."

"I'm pretty sure they're geraniums," said Georgie, sitting down. "And they're beautiful. Where did you find them?"

"I had them delivered, obviously."

Georgie placed her hand flat on her chest, "I believe you, Anthony."

Ant raised his glass. "Cheers Georgie."

Georgie raised her own. "Cheers Anthony." She took a sip and put the glass down. "You do realise you've made a huge problem for yourself." She held up the list he'd written for her. "You're going to have to come up with more of this stuff, you need to give the readers of Georgieslists.com the content they need, or they'll take their clicks elsewhere."

"Don't say that! I can't lose you, you're my most

important subscriber."

Georgie reached across the table and put her hand over Ant's. "I couldn't bear to lose you either." She leaned back but didn't take her hand away straight away.

They were quiet for a while, eating and sipping their bubbly. Ant eventually spoke. "So, Georgina, what would you like to do for your birthday."

"I'd really like to have a bath actually, but I know I can't, it's daylight."

"I think we can take the risk, it's your birthday. Go up after you're done with breakfast. I'll keep watch while it's running."

"You sure?"

"Yes I'm sure."

Georgie's eyes were moist with tears. "Thanks, Anthony, for everything."

"It's my pleasure. Here," he topped up Georgie's glass.

After breakfast, Ant gave Georgie another refill to take up with her and got another peck on the cheek for his efforts.

As soon as he heard the water running upstairs, Ant went from window to window, binoculars in hand, checking no mutants had been drawn by the plume of boiler vapour and were coming to eat them. He kept checking long after the water had stopped running.

He took the plate and soup bowls into the kitchen and rinsed them under the tap, then returned to the restaurant and poured himself another half-glass of champagne. He nursed the drink whilst he thought about Georgie in the bath. She was taking her time. Ant was insanely jealous of the water.

Ant was bowled over by Georgie's response to his birthday fussing over her. Ant prided himself on getting good gifts for people he cared about and it bothered him when others didn't put in as much effort as he did. The phrase 'it's the thought that counts' was a real bugbear to Ant, because, as he would insist whenever the subject came up, *the thought* in that phrase didn't mean remembering the birthday, it meant putting some thought in to getting the person something they'd genuinely like. He'd put a lot of thought into Georgie's birthday and had expected her to be pleased, but not literally moved to tears.

Ant was feeling very satisfied with himself.

"Anthony."

Ant was startled by the sound of Georgie's voice and the sight of her in the doorway.

"Sorry," Georgie spoke softly, "I didn't mean to make you jump."

Her hair was wet and combed back from her face. She was wearing nothing but a silk bathrobe, but had put on some make-up, not heavy, but enough to be noticeable. The effect, to Ant, was intense. She looked incredible.

She walked towards him and untied the cord around her waist, she let the robe fall open and put her hands to his face.

Ant, his hands already inside the robe, pulled Georgie close and they kissed softly and slowly. Eventually they broke apart.

"Take me upstairs," said Georgie.

Ant didn't need telling twice.

An undisclosed amount of time later and Georgie and Ant were in the traditional bathing-in-the-afterglow position: Ant on his back with his arm looped around Georgie's head as she lay on her side and rested it on his chest.

"Wow," said Ant.

"Wow indeed," said Georgie.

Ant was no fool, he'd seen the signs that Georgie had started seeing him as more than just some guy she was surviving the apocalypse with, but this turn of events was still a huge surprise.

He was dying to get answers to those questions that everyone has when they've finally got it on with somebody they've held a candle to for a while:

When had Georgie started seeing him in 'that way'?

Had she been wanting to do this for a while?

Was it always on the cards?

But Ant knew better than to ask. He knew from bitter experience that neediness was not an attractive quality.

Since realising he'd fallen head over heels in love with Georgie he'd started to wonder how it would turn out if she never came around to his way of thinking. He had pictured the frustrating future, seeing out the rest of his days in the sole company of the object of his unrequited affection. Sharing a bed with Georgie had already been becoming unbearable. She was always just there, right next to him, and he couldn't touch.

It was an ordeal to rival Tantalus.

He knew this one event didn't mean they were about to ride off into the sunset together, Georgie may have just been swept up in the moment of Ant remembering her birthday or she may simply have missed sex as much as he had and needed that itch scratched. Or the champagne may have just gone to her head.

One swallow, Ant knew, didn't make a summer.

But lying there with her in his arms, feeling that warm body he had craved for so long, feeling her skin against his and re-living the recent memories of their lovemaking, Ant decided that this was the best birthday he could remember.

And it wasn't even his.

Georgie shifted her position and propped her chin on Ant's chest so she could face him.

"I've got to ask," she said. "How come you've got condoms?"

Ant laughed, blushing. "There was a stash back at the fire station, in some guy's washbag."

"And you thought they might come in handy?"

"Well yes, I guess." Ant paused. "I thought I may as well take them. It's not like you can pop out to the chemist anymore."

Georgie smiled, "There's no need to be embarrassed, you did the right thing, it's best to be prepared." She kissed his chest.

That was the moment, right there. More than her grand gesture of opening the bathrobe, more than the intimacy of the foreplay or the intensity of the sex, it was that casual kiss, done without even thinking, done just because it seemed like the natural thing to do, that's when Ant knew he was onto something.

Georgie rested her head sideways again and he held her a little tighter.

Ant eventually broke the longest, most comfortable silence they had experienced together. "So, Georgina, what else would you like to do for your birthday? I propose we have a day off the Shit Day Drills."

"Best. Gift. Ever." Said Georgie. She looked up and around as if trying to narrow down a long list of options. "Actually, there is something I'd like to do."

"Name it," said Ant.

"I want to go for a walk."

"I see." Ant breathed in. "Okay."

"You sure?"

"Course I'm not sure, I doubt you are either, but it did look pretty nice out there when I... erm... went outside to meet the delivery guy from the florist."

"Bless you Anthony." Georgie kissed him again. "It should be nice out there, it's the summer solstice."

"How do you know that?"

"Because it's the twentieth of June, my birthday, remember?"

"Is that the same as the longest day?"

"Yes, but it can be the twenty-first or twenty-second depending on the year."

"Every day's a school day."

"So, shall we?"

Ant eased onto his side and kissed her. "Christ, yes, let's do it."

"I meant shall we go for a walk."

Ant kissed her again. "I know, but, well, while we're here and all…"

"Oh go on then…"

Chapter 16. The birds

Georgie and Ant had brought a few clothes with them in their Shit Day bags but after they had arrived at the Coach House they had sifted through Jack and Cynthia's drawers to see if there was anything worth having. As Ant had expected, Jack had been a lot smaller than him, but there had been rich pickings for Georgie. Cynthia must have been close to her in size, and as well as the silk bathrobe, she had found plenty in the dead publican's wardrobe that suited her tastes.

Now, after Ant had finally agreed to let them get out of bed, they put on their summer collection; Georgie in a denim skirt and peach-coloured vest top and Ant in a pair of grey joggers that were like drainpipes on him but would have been baggy on Jack, and a Liverpool football shirt, size XXL that they could only assume had been a badly judged gift for the landlord. They topped off the look with his-and-hers sunglasses that they had found on the console table in the hallway, Georgie's hooked over her ears while Ant's were tightly wedged on either side of his enormous head.

Ant filled a plastic bottle with water and put it into the drawstring bag he'd found upstairs. "We should look for some sun cream. Have you seen any about?"

"No, Anthony, I haven't seen any sun cream and I don't think we need any. What I think we need is to stop procrastinating and just get outside."

"Fair enough." Ant glanced at the dressing on Georgie's

exposed upper arm, "That reminds me, I'm taking this." He picked up the meat-cleaver that he'd had to wipe clean of Farmer Mutant's insides and dropped it into the bag.

"Good idea," said Georgie.

They stepped into glorious sunshine and Georgie locked the front door behind them. They walked along the crooked paving slabs and down the few steps between the gap in the overgrown hedge that would once have been the main way into the pub before the road had been widened and the car park built. They crossed over and Ant leant down and pulled the two strands of the wire fence apart for Georgie to step through. Once she was on the other side she returned the favour.

They walked across the middle of the field.

"Okay," Ant whispered. "I won't lie, I'm feeling proper exposed."

"I'm trying to focus on enjoying having the sun on my face." Georgie took Ant's hand and it seemed to absorb some of his fear. "As you said before, any mutes should be long gone now. There's no food for them out here, unless they're foraging for whatever wild animals are still around."

"Poacher mutes."

Georgie suddenly stood to attention and saluted. "Hello, Mister Magpie! Where's your wife?"

"What the fuck?"

"Look." Georgie pointed to the far edge of the next field in front of them.

Ant did as he was told and could just make out a black and white bird. "Well that's a turn up, first living thing we've seen in for ages. That's got to be a good thing. But what was all that saluting about?"

"It's what my dad always did if he saw a magpie."

"All due respect to your old man but isn't that a bit weird?"

Georgie laughed. "Okay I can imagine if you've not come across it before then it would seem a little strange, but I don't think it was only my dad, lots of people did it, but only when the magpie's on its own."

"I'm sure this is an obvious question," said Ant, "but I'm going to ask it anyway. Why did your dad only salute magpies and ask after their wives when they were on their own?"

"I would have thought that was obvious, Anthony, if Mister Magpie was in the company of another magpie then we would have to assume that she's his wife."

"But we don't even know if the magpie is a mister, we can't see its bits or anything. And even if we do know Mister Magpie is a mister, how do we know he's with his bird, I mean missus?" Ant stopped and thought. "Actually, I do mean bird. How do we know he's with his bird?"

Georgie facepalmed. "You're a very literal man, Anthony."

"I'm just really confused by this magpie thing."

"You don't know the rhyme, the magpie rhyme?"

"There's a rhyme?"

"Yes, there's a rhyme. One for sorrow, two for joy, three for a girl and four for a boy... I forget the rest. If you see one and you're superstitious then it means sorrow is coming, so you salute it and ask about its wife, to, I don't know, ward off the oncoming sorrow."

"Was your dad superstitious then?"

"No, I think he just thought it was funny, or he knew we thought it was funny. It was one of those dad things that dads do."

"I'm not liking the sorrow thing at all. I'm a lot more superstitious than I used to be."

"It's okay," Georgie said, shielding her eyes from the sun with her hand. "There's another one, look, two magpies. We're onto joy. Looks like my saluting did the trick."

"What are they doing? They're moving about in that one spot."

"I think they're eating something," said Georgie as they moved closer. "Dead rabbit maybe. Actually, that's too big for a rabbit."

"Jesus," said Ant. "It's a mutant, still quite a bit of it left, too."

Georgie's hand was over her open mouth. "It's two mutants."

"Is there a rhyme about dead mutants?" said Ant.

Ant's glib tone was replaced by the sound of his retching as they reached the mutant corpses that lay on their backs, side by side. The birds, which hopped away as Georgie and Ant approached, had evidently pecked their way through the stomachs, worked their way under the rib cages and had been busy feasting on the organs inside when they had been rudely interrupted. The bodies were otherwise undamaged and the faces, despite being the now-familiar shade of mutant-purple and having eyes that were seemingly too big for their sockets, would have been recognisable to anyone who had known them before they had turned.

Georgie squatted down; her hands clasped against her face. "It's a mother and daughter."

"Give me a minute," said Ant, who was doubled over and taking deep, controlled breaths. He glanced at the bodies, shook his head and faced the ground again. He held up a finger. "Another minute."

When Ant was able to look without risking losing his breakfast, he could see that Georgie was right. Even if they ignored the matching long blonde hair that looked fake, like dolls' hair, the resemblance between the two faces was unmistakeable.

"She can't have been more than five," said Georgie.

"That's so sad."

Ant, now upright and with his dry heaves under control, took her hand.

"What do you think killed them?" Georgie asked.

"Magpie attack?"

Georgie narrowed her eyes.

"Too soon?"

"Yes, Anthony. Far too soon."

"Sorry, couldn't resist, but I think your theory's right, they ran out of food. They probably came out looking for something to eat and didn't make it."

"I don't see it." Georgie screwed her face up. "They wouldn't have starved to death at the exact same time."

"That's not what I meant. Probably the mum died first and the kid didn't know what to do, she didn't want to leave her mother and there was nothing to eat, so…"

"So she stayed and died."

"Pretty much, yeah."

"It's as good an explanation as any I suppose. I wonder how far they came from to get here?"

"Not far I'd say, we'll probably find houses soon. They might even be something to do with the mutant who came for his lunchtime pint. Maybe the mum is his daughter. Maybe they lived with him and when he didn't come back from the Coach House they came looking."

"Why would he come wandering across the fields for a beer that he can't even drink when his daughter and granddaughter were half-dead from hunger?"

Ant snorted. "You saw the guy, you, like, *interacted* with him, did he seem to you like he was making strong choices?"

"Okay, I guess." Georgie looked back at the bodies. "Maybe it was him who killed them."

"Why would he do that? It's not like he wanted to eat

them. The jury's still out on whether they eat each other but even if they do, he hasn't fed on these. This," Ant gagged again as he looked at the half-eaten entrails on the ground, "is all down to Mister Magpie and his wife."

Georgie leaned over the body of the mutant child. "There's bruising on the neck. She's been strangled."

"Who called the coroner?"

"I'm serious, Anthony, take a look."

"I'm good thanks."

Georgie turned around; her face deadly serious. "Anthony, I need you to look at this."

Ant sighed. "Go on then." He stood next to Georgie and looked at the dead girl's throat. Even to his untrained eye he could not fail to see the marks that could only have been left by fingers gripping tightly. "Oh God I think you're right. Who would strangle a kid, even a mutant kid?"

Georgie stood up slowly. "It was the mother. She knew she was going to die and couldn't bear to think of her daughter trying to survive without her."

"A mercy killing? Wow, that's deep."

"It means they have feelings."

"Or some of them do at least. Come on, let's keep moving."

"Gladly," said Ant.

They resumed their walk and the magpies hopped back to their awful smorgasbords.

The house was like something a child would draw, completely square with a blue front door, four equally spaced windows and a tiled roof. The only thing missing from the image that had been stuck on the side of so many fridges was the curl of smoke from the chimney.

They had crossed two more fields and climbed through another wire fence and down a bank onto a narrow winding road which they'd followed for half a mile or so. They had rounded a bend and had just about managed to read the sign saying 'The Cottage' despite the bush that all but engulfed it. The low wooden gate was open, wedged against the raised corner of a paving slab with weeds sprouting from the cracks that ran across it. The narrow path was long and straight, flanked by more overgrowth.

They stopped after every few steps they took towards the house, watching and listening for movement inside. They reached the front door and found it locked so they followed the path round to the side where there was another door. This one opened into a small kitchen. Ant took out the cleaver as they stepped cautiously inside.

They went through the now familiar check-out-a-new-building rigmarole; nerves on full alert, creeping between rooms, expecting death through every doorway.

The house was empty.

They went back to the kitchen and Georgie sat at the table that filled more than half the room. "I like this," she said, patting the solid wood surface. "Rustic." She looked around, taking in the room. "This is the sort of kitchen I always thought I'd have if I ever had enough money to buy my own place. Not fancy, just homely, homely and functional."

"Nothing to stop you having this one," Ant said, opening and shutting cupboards.

"That wouldn't be the same. This isn't house-hunting, this is looting."

"That's a bit harsh. At worst it would be squatting." Ant opened the final cupboard. "You beauty!" He lifted out a bottle of red. "Now *this* is looting." He rattled around in a drawer.

"Could you be less noisy?"

"Yes, sorry."

"It's a screw top anyway."

"I'm such a dick!"

Georgie smiled. "Well I didn't want to say, but…"

Ant returned to a cupboard he'd checked previously and took out two wine glasses. "I love these big ones, like goldfish bowls. These are the sort of wine glasses I always thought I'd have if I ever had enough money to buy my own wine glasses." He poured and sat down opposite Georgie, putting the glasses between them. Cheers, happy birthday!"

"I think that's enough birthday cheersing now, but cheers anyway."

"Shall we see if there are outside chairs? Or we could take these ones out."

"I'm happy here thanks. Nice to cool down a bit."

"Are you having a good birthday?"

"It's been very unexpected." She leaned forward and gave Ant's hand a squeeze. "Thanks again for making such a fuss."

"You're welcome."

Georgie rotated her glass, staring into it from above.

"What's up?"

Georgie kept her eyes in the glass. "It's nothing."

"It's not nothing is it?"

Georgie looked up at Ant, her face earnest. "You're right, it's not nothing. Thanks for calling me on it. Can we make that a thing that we do in this new world, actually say what's on our minds, not just say that nothing's wrong when something obviously is?"

"Might take a bit of getting used to but I'll give it a go. So, what's up?"

"It's the obvious really. All the death, all the loss, I know I should be getting used to it but it's really starting to get me down. Those two out there in the field, just awful. And here in this house, there are no bodies but the chances are they're all dead too. Did you see the pictures on the dresser in the lounge?

It looks like there were three children, two girls and a boy. Did you see the kids' bedrooms?"

"Yes, I saw them."

"Their toys, clothes on the floor. Their *stuff*, the stuff of being alive. And the parents, they would have rushed around in the mornings, getting breakfast ready, probably preparing school lunches or maybe the Ancient Rome themed artefact that one of the kids was meant to take in that morning but had forgotten to tell the mum about. The dad would have done dad jokes and everyone would have groaned and pretended they thought they were awful, but they wouldn't have been able to imagine a world without him and those jokes." She shook her head. "And now we're in that world. It's all gone. And none of them had a chance to have their turn at living." Georgie stopped talking. She drank some more wine.

Ant covered Georgie's hand with his own and thought long and hard for something to say that would be in any way reassuring. Nothing came. "I know, it's fucking horrible, there's no way of making it not horrible. It's just awful and sad and horrible." He stopped talking.

After almost a minute of silence Georgie spoke. "Thank you, Anthony."

"You've really got to stop thanking me, and I'm not sure what you're even thanking me for this time."

"For not telling me that everything's alright, for just listening. For not trying to fix it with some bullshit."

"Sweary!"

"Perhaps you're rubbing off on me."

"Do you want a top up?"

"Yes, Anthony, I do very much, but I need you to kiss me first."

Ant was both shocked and delighted by Georgie's relaxed affection. His heart pirouetted as he leant across to carry out her orders.

As Georgie sat back down she licked her lips. "You taste nice, that's good wine."

"You taste bloody delicious, and I don't mean the wine."

"Do you think they'll die out?" Georgie said.

"Wow, that was quite a change of tone. You mean the mutes?"

"Yes. There's not much left for them to eat. It looks like all the cows and sheep out in the open have been had, and it'll be the same for any pigs or chickens. Battery farmed animals will either have died inside their sheds or the mutes will have got in and eaten them. All that'll be left will be wild animals, rabbits, deer, foxes, badgers. I wouldn't imagine the mutes would be smart enough, or quick enough, to catch them. There's the smaller stuff too. Mice, rats, oh," a look of realisation crossed Georgie's face, "and birds of course."

"Voles," said Ant, "and squirrels."

"Yes, Anthony. There are other animals. We could list a lot more I'm sure. What I mean is, there won't be many left that will keep a large population of mutants fed."

"Hedgehogs?"

"Yes, thank you Anthony."

"There's wild boar up in Scotland, I read a thing a while back about them being reintroduced."

"Can we stop listing animals now please? The point is that I think the mutes will become an endangered species if they haven't done so already. They've hunted their most common prey almost to extinction…"

"You mean longpig?"

"Yes. There's probably only a few of us left now so now they'll be feeding on scraps. I think we're going to start seeing more mute corpses like we did earlier."

"I think you're right, their numbers will drop, but I don't

think they'll die out completely, not straight away anyway, not while there are still animals around that they can live off. The population will fall, then it'll, like, stabilise at a lower number."

"But presumably," Georgie said, "and hopefully," she added, "they'll die out in the end because they can't reproduce."

"Good point. So really we've just got to stick it out long enough for them all to keel over, or maybe the longpigs will rise up and stamp them all out before that. It might be that we've not been hunted almost to extinction. There could be loads of survivors and we just haven't seen them. Me and you have been concentrating on keeping ourselves safe, staying in the shadows as much as we can. It could be that there's a colony of survivors, all in one place and we just don't know about it."

"You mean like you've seen in zombie films?"

"Exactly like that. In a football stadium or something."

"Not sure why anyone would pick a football stadium, it's not very comfortable. Surely a housing development would make more sense."

Ant thought for a moment. "Yeah," he said, nodding. "That would make more sense. I'm sure it's usually a stadium though."

"Are you saying that we should go looking for this refugee camp that you think might exist just because it's been done in films?"

"No. I'm just saying we wouldn't know about it if there was one."

"There's been nothing on the radio."

"You're right, but there could be a million reasons for that."

Georgie looked back down into her drink. She spoke finally, "We need to get on the move soon don't we?"

"You mean back to the pub?"

"No, I mean what we talked about, seeing if anything's left

of our loved ones."

Ant drank some wine. "Yes, we need to do that."

"And while we're at it we can look for evidence of these groups of survivors you've talked about. I'm not sure what we'd be looking for exactly though."

"We'll check every lamppost for notices."

Georgie frowned. "I'm not sure anyone would risk that, it's not clear whether the mutes can read or not."

Ant grinned. "I was joking. You take things very literally don't you?"

Georgie put her head in her hands, smiling and blushing. "It would certainly appear so."

Chapter 17. My girlfriend the murderer

On the way back to the pub they took a less direct route to avoid an update on how the magpies were getting on with the mutant corpses. They followed a rough path that skirted the edge of the fields. There was woodland to their right. "Fancy a walk in the woods?" said Georgie.

"Can do, yes." Ant didn't, not really, he was more interested in getting Georgie back to the pub and picking up where they had left off with that cottage-kiss.

"That's not very convincing but I'm playing the birthday card, let's do it." Georgie took Ant's hand and they navigated through a gap in the fence where a tree had split almost down the middle and broken the wire.

They walked through the wide gaps between oaks that probably stood before the Coach House had been built.

With no warning at all, Ant let out a whimper of terror. Georgie turned, her pulse ratcheting up to breakneck speed. Ant's face was a grimace of alarm and Georgie, her panic rising further with each moment, flung her eyes around to see what had prompted his distress. "What is it?" Her voice was a hissed whisper.

Ant flung his hand to his face, "There, look."

Georgie followed his terrified eyes, reminded of that moment back at the airfield when Iqbal had seen the horde of mutants coming for him. "I can't see anything."

"You need to lean in, you can see it where the sun comes

through the trees. Jesus, "Ant shuddered, "it's hideous."

Georgie moved closer to Ant and could finally see the source of his abject horror.

The web stretched between two trees, revealed by clinging droplets of moisture that caught the sunlight that dappled the woods. Its maker sat in the centre, reddish in colour, its eight legs uniformly splayed around its plump body, seemingly unperturbed by the drama it had caused.

"Don't ever do that again! I thought it was something really bad."

"What do you mean? It *is* bad, it's terrifying. I could have walked into it, it would have been on my face, can you imagine? No, me neither." He shuddered again. "Makes my skin crawl."

Georgie breathed deeply, letting her body come down from the fight-or-flight state Ant's panic had set off in her. "Please," she said, "I'm scared out of my mind almost all the time. If you react like that then I'm going to assume it's something dangerous, something that could kill us."

"Okay," Ant nodded, "I get it, sorry."

"There's something dangerous behind you right now, something that can kill you."

They jolted at the sound of the voice behind them. As they turned to face the figure standing a few yards away they assumed at first that it was a mutant, one that lived in the woods, surviving on wildlife as they had talked about. But there was no tell-tale purple skin, and no bulging eyes.

But there was a shotgun.

The man looked to be in his forties and had the weather-beaten complexion of someone who spends a lot of time outdoors. He wore hiking boots and thick multipocketed cargo trousers, khaki, a long way past their first flush of youth. The one nod his outfit made towards the heat of the day was the rolled-up sleeves on his black woollen jumper.

The gun at his hip was loosely pointed at Ant. The man nodded at Georgie. "She'll be coming with me. Best you don't make a scene."

Ant turned to Georgie. "Are you going with him?"

"Not that I was aware of," said Georgie.

"What makes you think she's coming with you?"

The man held the gun a little higher. "Because I said so."

"Have you asked her?"

"I don't need to ask her."

"I think that would be your best approach, ask her, see if she wants to go with you. She might want to. That would make everything a lot easier. Although you've not really sold it very well, you've not really made it clear what 'going with you' means exactly."

The man looked directly at Ant. "Funny boy are you?"

"I have my moments."

"I told you not to make a scene."

"Okay, let's settle this." Ant turned to Georgie. "Do you want to go with this guy?"

Georgie's eyes darted from the man, to Ant, then back again. "No, I don't, thank you."

"That's that then," said Ant. "We're done here. We'll be on our way."

"I don't think you understand."

Ant stepped forward. He towered over the man. "No, it's *you* who doesn't understand. This isn't a film and we're not doing that scene. It's too much of a cliché, the redneck throwing his weight around in the lawless, post-apocalyptic world. What are you trying to gain exactly?"

"The girl."

"Mate! Stop it. The *girl* has a name, it's Georgie and she doesn't want to go back to your weird lair with you. What do you think is going to happen here?"

"I'm expecting to blow your brains out and take her for myself."

"Take her? And how's that going to work? Okay, let's say you do blow my brains out, what's going to happen then? You'll have just killed Georgie's very good friend, someone she's got very attached to, and you think she'll just go with you and that'll be that? She won't try and fuck you up the first chance she gets?"

"I'll tie her up."

Ant snorted with laughter. "Oh for fuck's sake. How would that work, and for how long? The logistics just don't add up, she'd be fighting you at every stage, it would be a nightmare. I'll tell you what's going to happen. You're going to lower your big gun and you're going to go back to your nest and once you're there I'd suggest you have a great big wank, get all this out of your system. Then go back to eating spiders or whatever it is you do for fun."

The man raised the gun and pointed it at Ant's face.

Ant stepped forward, as he did so he let the drawstring bag slip off his shoulder onto the ground behind him. He took another step so he was within inches of the man but at least a head taller. The man tilted the shotgun so it was under Ant's chin, but Ant held his ground, listening for the sound of Georgie picking up the bag and pulling it open. "If you pull that trigger," he said down the barrel of the gun," then my friend, *the girl*, is going to throw a meat cleaver at you. It's extremely sharp, extremely easy to throw, and already has one notch on its blade, so to speak. If you try and stop that happening by pointing the gun at her instead of me then I'm going to punch you to the ground and proceed to beat the shit out of you and finally kill you, either with the meat cleaver, my fists or with your gun." Ant stopped to let all this sink in. The man tilted his head to see past Ant and saw that Georgie was indeed, brandishing the cleaver. Georgie took a step forward to make sure he got the point. "Your one remaining option," Ant continued, "is to very carefully and slowly put the gun flat on the ground and walk away."

The man did not take any of the options offered to him, instead his face twisted, his lip wobbled and he began to cry. The gun fell to the ground as he fell forward onto Ant's chest and wrapped his arms around him, sobbing bitterly.

Ant reciprocated the hug, not out of affection but to keep the would-be-assailant where he was.

"I'm sorry," the man said through his sobs. "I've been on my own too long. It's been hard, just surviving. I was wrong to do what I done. I'm off the meds. I ran out. I've not been able to get me prescription since it all happened. I've been too scared to go into town. I shouldn't have done what I done. I'm sorry."

As Ant looked down over the shuddering shoulders of the weeping man he was pleased to see Georgie retrieve the gun from harm's way. He released his grip a little. "It's okay," he said, "don't worry." He found himself patting the man on the back, like he was a kid who'd lost his puppy. He stopped short of saying 'there there'.

The man pulled his face from Ant's chest and looked up at him. "Will you help me?"

Ant saw the pain, the regret, the tragedy in the man's eyes and no longer felt angry. His only emotion was pity. He couldn't imagine what this desperate figure had endured. Ant knew that what this guy had done was inexcusable and he wouldn't ever be able to forgive him, but he knew he could at least try to understand him.

"Let go of him." At the sound of Georgie's voice, Ant and the man ended their clumsy embrace and turned towards her, neither of them knowing which of them she was talking to. The answer was either of them, or both. But it no longer mattered. Georgie had lifted the gun to her shoulder and had the barrel pointed directly at the man's head. "Ant, step away."

Ant did as Georgie said, taking a few paces back so he was behind Georgie, understanding her caution but keen to disarm her in both senses of the word. "Okay babe, good not to take any chances. But I think we're cool. I think he's over it."

The gunshot sounded even louder to Ant because it was so unexpected.

The sight of the man's head exploding looked even more horrific to Ant because it was so unexpected.

The sight of Georgie lowering the gun, vapour streaming from both barrels was, to Ant, incomprehensible.

He stared at her, his mouth gaping.

Georgie stared back at him. "It had to be done."

Ant was surprised he was able to talk. "You sure about that? He was unarmed, he'd broken down, he was a mess."

"He was a threat, Anthony."

Ant held his hands up placatingly. "Look, I get it, the things he was saying, the thing he was planning. I'm not going to pretend I know how you feel..."

"No," Georgie said, as firmly as if she was telling a child to step back from a fire. "Don't do that. This isn't about me being a woman, this isn't about me trying to settle the score with a man who was trying to rape me. I'll tell you what this was about. It was about survival. We are here in this new, awful world. Everything is binary now, it's safe or it's unsafe, it's no longer about consideration of why people act like they do, it's not about whether people should be forgiven or not. It's about what will keep us alive and what might stop us from being alive."

Ant went to say something, but Georgie carried on.

"While he was crying his heart out on your chest I thought

about the options we had. We could have helped him, taken him under our wing, drove him into town to find his meds, if they were even a real thing, but we both know that at some point he would have turned on us. The only reason he broke down like he did was because he knew he'd lost and had no game left. If we took him with us, as soon as he had the chance he would have gone all lord of the wasteland again. The other option we had was to send him back into the woods, but again, he would have either followed us home or come looking for us later."

"He didn't know where we're staying."

"There aren't many houses around here, he would have found us. We have enough to contend with without having to worry about him creeping in on us some dark night."

"If everything you've assumed is right then you did the right thing."

"I know I did the right thing."

"But what if everything you've assumed isn't right, what if he wasn't going to turn on us?"

"We both know that's not true."

"But what if it was?"

"Okay, Anthony, let's say it was. Let's say that during that brief exchange he'd become a reformed character and would never again have threatened strangers at gunpoint. If that's the case then it's a shame I killed him, it's a waste of human life. It's a tragedy and my heart bleeds. But you're not getting it. This isn't the world we used to live in, this isn't a world where our liberal views on morality, on giving people the benefit of the doubt are relevant anymore. We're not debating the rehabilitation of offenders here, we're trying to survive, and the odds are already stacked against us."

"So you think we should throw out everything that makes us civilised?"

"Of course not! We can still be civilised. I'm not saying we become survivalist freaks, shooting everybody we come across. I took one decision and explained why I took it. Making that decision hasn't changed who I am. I'm still the person you made breakfast for this morning, the one you cuddled up to after making love. We can still be civilised, we can still be *us*, we just need to be ready to make the decisions that need to be made. Do you think I don't feel completely shaken up after having done what I did?" She dropped the gun. "I feel horrible, Anthony, I feel sick." As she said those few last words, tears sprang to Georgie's eyes, as if the adrenaline that had flooded her system had served its purpose and now receded, allowing her normal human emotions to function again.

Ant saw her face crumple and felt his own do the same. He had no more arguments to raise, he just knew he needed to hold Georgie, not to comfort her but to comfort himself. He reached out to pull her close, his own face flooding with tears. "I love you, I bloody love you."

But the Hallmark moment wasn't to be. Georgie batted Ant's hands away. "We need to get away from here, anything could have heard that gunshot."

Chapter 18. Aftermath

Bollocks.

The day had started so well. She couldn't have been more chuffed with the fuss I made over her birthday. And then, Jesus, when she opened that dressing-gown I thought I was going to lose my shit. Talk about birthday wishes coming true. I've never really known why people call sex 'making love' but I found out the difference today. It didn't feel like it's ever felt with anyone before. It felt like we were, and I know this is going to sound as soppy as shite but it's true, it felt like we were *connected*.

But then we went outside, and apart from some nice moments, it all went to shit in the end.

And now it's worse than shit.

I admit I was shocked – appalled is a better word - when she shot that poor fucker. When someone you… I'm just going to say it, when someone you *love* commits what can only be described as cold-blooded murder right in front of your face it's a bit tricky to take in at first. But I've thought about it a lot since it happened, I've thought about what she said about why she did it and how things are different now. And I get her point. You might say I've come around to her way of thinking.

And I've tried to tell her that, but she doesn't seem to want to know. It seems like, because I reacted negatively (or completely understandably) at the start, then she's locked in that response and won't let me budge from it. She won't accept that I've taken her explanation on board, seen her point of view and want to move on. I'm just tagged as the bad guy because I didn't see things her way from the get-go.

I don't pretend to know anything about relationships, not full-on ones anyway, but I'm pretty sure that when you're with someone then you're meant to be able to listen to each other, take in each other's point of view and move the conversation forward. Georgie's not letting the conversation go anywhere. It's stuck. And I'm stuck because I can't fix it if she gets pissed off every time I try and talk about it.

So I've stopped talking about it, and now it's just awkward.

I'm trying not to but I can't help pussyfooting around her, which is the worst thing to do because I'm nervous and tense and that means I'm clumsy, banging into things, knocking stuff over. I know I'm annoying the crap out of her.

I'd go and sit in another room, leave her be, but that would just look like I'm sulking. So I'm hanging around her, like the proverbial bad smell.

This is all wrong. We shouldn't be sitting in silence. Apart from anything else we've just got so much to talk about. Like meeting the first non-mutant survivor since this all began. If Woody Woodsman survived and we survived, then who knows how many more did too? That's what we should be talking about. But we can't talk about it because we can't talk about anything.

Bollocks.

It couldn't have come at a worse time. It's hard enough as it is to know how to act when you've just got it on with someone you're into. You've got to be keen but not too keen, make them know you're interested but not scare them away. And you've got to carry on being you, not try and act like you think they think they want you to act. They can see straight through that stuff. They can smell it. Like dogs can smell fear.

And because of what's happened I'm doing all the things I know I shouldn't be doing. I'm coming over as the most uncool person ever.

There was this kid at my school, Josh Hartley, his name was. Josh was what you might call, unfortunate-looking, and his personality didn't do much by way of compensation. Josh didn't have much luck with the girls, or with anyone come to think of it, but there was this one time when Lisa Yaxley gave him a Christmas card. Lisa Yaxley was hot, definitely one of the cool kids, so her and Josh didn't really move in the same social circles (Josh didn't even have a social circle), but because their Chemistry teacher, Mr. Sutton, at the start of each term would put everyone's names into a hat and draw them out to pick lab partners, Lisa and Josh got paired up. Lisa was a nice person, so in the last lesson before we broke up for Christmas she'd got Josh a card. It had seemed perfectly natural to Lisa, no biggie. But to Josh it was a very biggie indeed. The next morning he turned up with this massive bunch of flowers with all ribbons and bows and stood next to Lisa's locker and waited for her. It was bad enough because there were loads of people about when Lisa turned up and even though she tried to be nice about it, she looked properly embarrassed and everyone took the piss. But it didn't end there. Suddenly Josh had whipped out this roll of paper and unfurled it like he was the Town bloody Crier or something and then he proceeded to read out this poem he'd written, a poem all about his feelings for Lisa. Josh hadn't been popular before but he'd always been anonymous. Now he was unpopular and everyone knew who he was. The worst possible combination.

And that's how I'm coming across right now, less cool than Josh Hartley.

Me and Georgie's relationship shouldn't matter. Compared with everything else we've got on our plates the whole boy-meets-girl thing shouldn't mean shit. We should be focusing on keeping ourselves safe, fed and sheltered in the short-term and planning what we should do in the long-term to find out what's left of the human race. Me and Georgie falling out shouldn't matter, it shouldn't even be a thing.

Except it really does bloody matter. It's a huge thing.

It seems that even when we humans are facing the most extreme circumstances, our most basic desires still matter to us. I guess that's evolution doing its bit. Our programming doesn't get overridden because there are tons of more important things to deal with, if anything it gets even stronger. I know for a fact that I'll get through this situation a whole lot better if me and Georgie get together properly. It would give me something to fight for. It would give me something to feel nice about. But instead it just feels shit, and feeling shit is not a helpful state of mind to have when you're facing the end of the world.

I should check myself really, here's me talking about evolution and human urges as if I'm in the heads of all the survivors. The sample I'm working with is precisely one so I shouldn't talk as if I know what anyone other than the one – me - is experiencing. Maybe it's just me who thinks this stuff matters, maybe any other survivors are only fixated on staying alive, not on copping off with their co-survivors. Maybe it's the same for Georgie too. Maybe she'd get on just fine without any romantic entanglements. Maybe she'd even prefer it.

I hope not.

I hope I haven't fucked it up.

It's bedtime now and we've reached this weird polite stage. Georgie asked me if it was okay if she used the bathroom first. She always uses the bathroom first, it's never in question, but for some reason she asked this time. I said it was okay and she went and did her thing. She came out wearing the t-shirt she likes to sleep in, the man's one, it comes halfway down to her thighs. Jesus, those dark, delicious thighs. It's worse now because I know what it's like to touch them, to taste them. She's in the moonlight that's coming through the curtains and it's not an exaggeration to say she looks like an angel.

Girls wearing guy's t-shirts is my favourite look. It normally means they've stopped over at yours without planning it. I've had a lot of good nights where girls have stopped over at mine without planning it so I've become a big fan of that look. It's made better because of what it represents, that early-stage excitement, where nobody knows where it's going to lead but it might lead somewhere really fun. That's the feeling I should have now, that excitement. I know the circumstances are different, it's not like we came home from a club or anything, and its not even my shirt, it's some dead guy's, but it's still that first time feeling, and now we should be enjoying the next stage, where the pressure's off, and we get to just go at it like rabbits. But instead of being exciting and sexy it's awkward and stilted and uncomfortably polite.

It's awful.

"You've got a bit of toothpaste." I point towards the corner of her mouth.

But she's miles away. "Pardon?"

"On your mouth, there's some toothpaste."

"Oh, thanks." She licks her finger and wipes at it. She's not got it all but she doesn't ask me, and I don't tell her because I know it'll just piss her off.

By the time I come out of the bathroom she's in bed, the duvet's pulled right up, covering most of her head. It may as well have *Stay Away* written on it. She's lying on her side and crucially she's facing outwards, away from my side.

I thought I was done with wearing undies and a t-shirt in bed after this morning but that's where I am again now that I've slid down that fucking snake.

Mute

I get into bed next to her back. I turn onto my side and face away in the opposite direction too.

I'm lonely and I'm horny and it's horrible.

"Goodnight," I say.

"Night."

I can't sleep of course and as I lie here I'm starting to get pretty pissed off myself. How can she just switch off and go so cold after what happened this morning? Okay I get it, she did something she never thought she'd have to do, and I'm sure it was really traumatic, but she could turn to me on that, we could be a team on it. I've had my fair share of trauma too. If she knows the effect this is having on me then surely she'd be acting differently, and if she doesn't know the effect it's having on me then she bloody well should know. It's not like we're strangers anymore. We've been through a lot, more than most people go through in a lifetime.

But it's not really her I'm pissed off with, it's me. I'm pissed off that I've broken all the rules, become that guy, lost any game I might have had and given all the power to her. There's nothing in the world less appealing than someone who's needy and desperate, and that's how I've come across all evening. Christ, I even told her I loved her right after she killed that guy. What was I thinking? I need to get my shit together. I don't want to play games because apart from anything else, she'd see straight through it if I did, but I need to get some pride back, she won't respect me if I don't get my game back.

I've got to put it out of my mind, the fact that this should have been an amazing night, it should have been the kickstarter for something bloody wonderful to take us through the rest of the shit we're living through. And now she's turned her back on me.

Okay, I *am* pissed at her, I'll admit it. We could have had a good thing and now she's robbed it off us because she can't listen, she can't see how much I'm trying. Fuck her. That's it, I'm done. Even if she became all sweetness and light right now, I'd tell her we should leave all the romantic stuff aside, focus on the business of survival. I wouldn't give her the satisfaction. Not anymore. She's had her chance.

It feels good to have set my mind straight on it, to put things in perspective. I didn't fuck it up. She did. It's her loss.

I can feel myself dropping off now. At last.

There's movement next to me and I'm awake again. Georgie's turned round.

"Anthony, I'm sorry."

I don't answer.

"Are you awake?"

"Just about, yes."

"I'm sorry for being silent all evening, I've been thinking things through."

"Okay."

"I think I love you too, Anthony."

Ignore everything I just said, all of it. I was talking out of my arse.

I don't remember ever feeling this happy.

Chapter 19. Homecoming

Georgie and Ant had exchanged the 'L' word. They were a thing. Their relationship was a fast-tracked emergency passport application; approved, rubber stamped and issued overnight.

Things became easier for them straight away. For starters, now they had seen each other's game-faces and everything that went with it, they didn't have to worry about protecting each other's modesty anymore. Obviously there were limits, Ant didn't wander around the place with his meat and two veg hanging out or burst in unannounced when Georgie was in the bathroom, but he no longer found himself waiting around downstairs in case he bumped into her while she was going to or from the shower. Apart from the nudity thing, their general awkwardness all but disappeared. Georgie and Ant had never discussed it but the dynamic that had loomed over their situation since they'd met was very simple: Ant was keen to make something happen with Georgie and Georgie wasn't keen. This dynamic had been a big influence on how they had both carried themselves. It's difficult to act normally around a person when you have a huge crush on them and Ant was no exception to this. He had known he probably wasn't Georgie's type, and that she was mourning her lost love to boot, so he had tried not to make a thing out of his feelings for her; he didn't want to make her feel uncomfortable on top of everything else she was going through. But the fact that he was trying so hard meant he was never properly relaxed. He was never really being himself.

If it's hard for the holder of a crush to act normally around the object of their affection then it's even harder for the person on the receiving end, the *crushee*. Georgie wasn't arrogant but she had got used to the fact that she was desirable. She wasn't an idiot, she had seen 'that' look on guys' faces and noticed how they acted around her. Her own experience and the repeated advice from her two older brothers had taught her to be cautious, to assume that men weren't just nice for no reason, that they usually wanted something from her. As a result, Georgie had got into the habit of being guarded about how she came across, about what she said and how she said it. And because, despite Ant's best efforts, it was obvious that he was completely gaga over her, Georgie had been doubly cautious; she hadn't wanted to give him false hope. As a result, she had never been properly relaxed either.

What had happened between them surprised them both, but at a stroke it had levelled the playing field. Ant was no longer the puppy dog trying to please its master; they were on an equal footing now. All the tension that had been bubbling away in the background had been cleared, like bleeding a radiator, or maybe more like lancing a boil.

The next few weeks were as close to a honeymoon as is possible while living under the constant threat of mutant attack. They did their daily chores and their Shit Day drills but they just took everything a bit easier. Ant had been fretting about the pile of human remains they had made when they had cleaned up the carnage from inside the pub. It had become a thriving tourist attraction for all kinds of wildlife. At first Ant had been pleased to see so many birds and other animals out and about again, but he had started to get nervous that they might catch the attention of any rural mutants that might be passing. He had suggested burying them, but Georgie pointed out that it would take a week, if not longer, to dig a hole big enough, which was far too much effort, especially when they were leaving soon anyway.

Because they were indeed leaving.

They had continued to talk about checking out Georgie's parents' place and it was obvious to them both that they needed to turn the talk into action soon or it would never happen. They knew it wouldn't be easy to leave the Coach House with all its comforts (and, as Ant kept repeating, its well-stocked bar), but they knew they had to at least try, so they began preparing for the trip.

They had decided on a change of wheels, something a bit more discreet than a fire engine, and set about finding a replacement in the twenty or so assorted cars parked at the pub.

It felt disrespectful rummaging through the bags of personal effects they had collected from the dead pub patrons, but they hoped the departed would understand their position as they collected car keys and took them outside. They stood in the middle of the car park and pressed fobs. The beeps and flashes told them which cars were up for grabs; twelve in all.

Neither of them knew anything about cars but the BMW estate was the obvious choice. It was the newest car on offer, it was big enough to store all their stuff but, unlike the fire engine, wouldn't feel like they were driving a monster truck. It was black, so wouldn't stand out, and it had Sat-Nav, a big plus in a world without phones. It hadn't occurred to them that the Sat-Nav might work and it was a nice surprise when it did. "I suppose," Ant said, "that the satellites are just up there doing their thing, beaming up, beaming down, whatever. They don't know the world's ended."

"You have no idea how it works do you?"

"Not a bastard clue."

"Me neither."

As an extra precaution they took a map from one of the older cars. Georgie marked their route with a highlighter pen. Georgie liked highlighter pens.

The beamer only had a quarter of a tank of fuel so Ant got busy siphoning the rest out of other cars using a tube and bucket he had found in the scary cellar. He could taste petrol for days afterwards.

Ant made sure that the scalpel and the meat cleaver were packed close to hand, like putting the crisps and chocolate at the top of the shopping bag for easy access on the way home from the supermarket. It occurred to them that the shotgun was now only good for one shot, what with Georgie having emptied the other cartridge into someone's face. Angry with themselves for not thinking of it at the time, they took a walk out to the body, which they found under a murder of hungry crows. It wasn't looking so good and was smelling even worse. Georgie insisted that she searched what was left of the corpse seeing as she was the reason it was a corpse. She found another five cartridges in a pouch on the belt and held them up victoriously while Ant stood a few yards away, bent double and puking.

When departure day came they were up before the sun. Ant won the toss and opted to drive. The roads were deserted save for the vehicles strewn on either side.

At the Coach House it had been part of their daily routine to listen to the emergency radio frequencies in the fire engine. Now they had switched to the car they would have to make do with just the civilian channels. They had decided that if an official body did somehow materialise and started to organise survivors to safety then it would most likely broadcast on standard radio anyway. They stepped through the stations early in the journey. Not a peep.

They had chosen to drive through town, rather than

around it, both out of curiosity and so they could look out for human survivors. They didn't see anybody, human or mutant, on their way, but saw plenty of birds, as well as cats, dogs and foxes brazenly stalking the streets, chasing, fighting and fucking.

Georgie was fascinated. "This is what a world without humans looks like."

"We don't know if it's a world without humans just yet."

Georgie pushed her seat back and rested her feet above the glove compartment. "I wish I shared your optimism."

"I'm not sure you could call it optimism, more like blind hope but I'm going to hang onto it as long as I can."

They passed shops, bars, cinemas, libraries, leisure centres, some that either or both of them had known well, and they struggled to comprehend how permanent these places had once seemed and were now just museums for their old lives.

Ant was visibly more relaxed as they got closer to the western outskirts of town. "I'm not complaining, but where are all the mutes?"

"All moved on I suppose, looking for something to eat."

"What about all the animals? I'm sure a fox would make a decent snack for a mute."

"They're better at running away than humans."

Once they were out of town the roads were less littered with vehicles and within another two hours they passed the sign that welcomed them to Georgie's home village. Ant drove more slowly and Georgie directed him left at a fork, up a hill past a church. They turned left again into a residential avenue with grass verges and a footpath between the road and the four- and five-bedroom mock Tudor houses that lined it.

Ant read the sign aloud. "Loxwood Road."

Georgie put her feet back on the floor and sat up. "Do you mind pulling over?"

Ant, out of habit despite there being no chance of any traffic behind them, checked his rear-view mirror before stopping the car.

"Sorry, I just need to get my head together."

Ant took Georgie's hand. "There's no need to say sorry. I get it."

Georgie pointed out of the window at the house nearest them. "The Lawrensons lived there, number forty-seven. I used to feed their cat when they went on holiday. Their youngest son had such a crush on me, he made me a Valentine's Day card, it was so sweet."

"Did you take him up on his offer?"

Georgie's sombre expression broke into a smile. "I was sixteen. He was eight."

"I see," said Ant. "By the way, you said *lived* there - past tense - you never know, they might still live there."

"I don't think we're going to kid ourselves on that one, Anthony. If they do still live here then Mrs. Lawrenson is a lot less particular about her front garden than she used to be."

Ant followed her gaze to the overgrown lawn and the weed-ridden flowerbeds. "Good point, well made."

"And their front door is wide open."

The door wasn't just open, it was hanging off its hinges. "Yeah," said Ant, "I'd noticed that with most of the places along here."

"It doesn't bode well, does it?"

"No, I won't pretend it does, but you never know." Ant leaned over the steering wheel and peered through the windscreen; an undercover cop on a stake-out. "How far along is your house?"

"It's number fifty-three, three along from the Lawrensons'. You can just see mum's car on the driveway, the dark blue one."

Ant nodded slowly. "Okay."

"What do you think we'll find in there?"

Ant knew exactly what he thought they would find, the remains of human bodies, stripped to their skeletons. "I have no idea," he said quickly.

"I don't believe you."

"Okay."

"You're not going to answer, are you?"

"Would you answer if it was the other way around?"

Georgie squeezed Ant's hand a little tighter. "No, I don't think I would."

They sat in nervous silence, listening out for any sound that might suggest they had been seen or heard by mutants. Ant was darting his head about, checking all the windows and mirrors in turn for any movement around them. The street was dead.

He heard Georgie sniff and saw that she was on the verge of crying.

"I'm scared, Anthony. I have no idea what I'm doing."

"You and me both, babe. This is unchartered territory."

"Don't you mean uncharted?"

"No, it's unchartered, I reckon the term would have come from a place that nobody had chartered a boat or a plane to before."

"I don't think that's right," said Georgie. "It will have come from a time before the world had been fully explored. A map of the sea is called a chart, so an area that nobody had sailed before would have been called uncharted."

"I think they both work."

Georgie wiped her eyes and smiled. "Let's go with both then." She leaned across and kissed Ant's cheek. "Thanks for this pep-talk, you'd be surprised how much it's worked. I think I'm ready now."

"I didn't know I was trying to give you a pep-talk, but whatevs, if it helped then I'm not going to argue. What is the plan exactly?"

"We drive up, we park, we get out. You take the cleaver. I take the shotgun. We go and see if my family are home."

"How about I go in first?"

"In case I'm faced with the remains of my slaughtered family?"

Ant decided not to sugar-coat his response. "Yes, because of that."

"I think I'm already resigned to that."

"Fair enough. Okay then, let me know when you're ready and we'll do it."

"I'm ready."

"Let's do it."

Georgie's mum's blue car turned out to be a Mercedes and Ant stopped himself from commenting on how Georgie's family must have been minted. He parked on the road outside rather than the driveway in case they needed to leave quickly.

"Dad's car's not here," Georgie observed.

They walked up the still-pristine paving to the front door, their weapons at the ready.

The door was ajar.

"No sign of forced entry," said Ant, trying to sound hopeful but knowing he didn't. He eased the door fully open and they stepped into a wide hallway with a staircase on the left. Immediately inside the door was a console table with a few assorted knick-knacks: an ornamental candle, a dish of loose change and a family photograph featuring a teenage Georgie. Ant saw Georgie's eyes fall onto the picture and quickly move away. Ant followed her lead and didn't mention it.

The open door to their right took them into a lounge-diner, its plush carpet and furnishings spotless save for the build-up of dust on every surface.

Where Ant would have expected the TV to be there was a polished wooden cabinet instead. "The telly's inside," Georgie said. "My dad didn't want to have one at all, he said they were tacky. This was the compromise."

Ant saw Georgie's eyes reddening again at the mention of her father. "Fair play," was all he could think of to say.

They walked through to the dining half of the lounge-diner. There were more family photos on a wall unit on the far side of the table. One was of a very young Georgie sitting at the wheel of a fire engine, which Ant thought was hugely ironic but opted to keep his thoughts to himself. Another was of Georgie's graduation. Her face beamed in delight out of both pictures and Ant felt a knot of pain. He would only ever know Georgie in this end-of-the-world world. He'd never get to see her looking that content in person.

They looped through the kitchen and back into the hallway where they'd first come in.

"There's nothing here," said Georgie.

"Let's check upstairs."

It was more of the same upstairs: tidy, ordered and devoid of life. Georgie was painfully quiet. Ant had expected her to stop and reminisce in every room, and he would have happily listened to her stories, but it was like she was deliberately closing herself off from the memories that must have surrounded her.

They went back downstairs and through the kitchen into the garden, a big lawn flanked by flowerbeds as overgrown as the grass. There was a narrow passage at the side of the house and a door into the garage. They had a nervy moment peering into the gloom and imagining what might be in there but the garage was empty, save for a chest freezer and a storage unit that lined the wall.

They went back to the kitchen and sat at the breakfast bar.

"They can't have been here when it happened," Georgie said. "Or they left as soon as it started. Dad's car has gone and there are no keys in the bowl by the door, that's where he'd always keep them." Georgie's elbows were on the counter and she put her head in her hands. "I suppose that's that. I'm never going to see them again. Even if they did get away, they could be anywhere."

"Any idea what 'cabin' might mean?"

Georgie lifted her head and followed Ant's eyes to a small whiteboard hanging on the wall with 'to remember' printed on the top and a marker pen hanging on a cord. Someone had written the single word on the board. 'CABIN'.

"My parents have a place in the West Country, we always call it the cabin. It's not really a cabin, it's technically a small house, but it's in the middle of nowhere and it's close to the sea. We used to go there every summer."

"Why would someone have written it on the whiteboard?"

"It was probably there before the big thing happened, something that mum and dad needed to remember about the cabin, book a cleaner, get the boiler fixed, or…"

Ant interrupted. "Or it's a message. A message written for you in case you came back here. A message telling you that's where they've gone. They didn't add any detail because they didn't know who might end up reading it, but they knew there was a chance that you'd get what it meant."

Georgie thought about this for a long time, so long that Ant wondered if she had fallen into a trance.

"You okay?"

Georgie blinked a few times. "Yes, sorry. It's a lot to consider."

"It sure is."

"Let's think this through," said Georgie. "First, is it

possible that they weren't caught by whatever it is that turned everyone else into mutes?"

"We don't know that everyone else turned into mutants, and the amount of bodies we found suggests that a lot didn't."

"Unless the mutes *do* kill and eat each other, and some of the remains we've found are mutant remains."

Ant shrugged. "We're back to that again. We have no way of knowing." It had occurred to him more than once that if Georgie hadn't blown Woody Woodsman's head off quite so hastily then they might have got some useful information out of him: where he had been when the big thing happened, how he had survived, what he had seen, all that stuff. He might even have been able to answer some of the questions on their list, or some they hadn't even thought about yet.

But Ant knew better than to point that out to Georgie right now. Or ever.

"All the broken front doors," said Georgie, "that suggests that mutants went rampaging along the road, attacking every house."

"But your parents' door was left open and the house is immaculate."

"Yes, they weren't attacked, not here anyway. Maybe they turned into mutants and it was them who slaughtered the neighbours."

Ant couldn't tell if Georgie was joking. He played it safe. "But why would your dad's car have gone?"

"Maybe he'd popped out and it was just my mum and brother who mutated and went on a frenzy."

"If any of your folks had gone on a killing spree, wouldn't they have come back afterwards? The mutant who came to the pub stuck to the same routine he did when he was alive, wouldn't your family have done the same and gone home?"

"They might have left since, gone to find more living

meat."

"Babe, I really don't think your family murdered your neighbours. If they'd come back here the place would be a tip. I've never been in a house with a mutant but I reckon they're a proper messy bunch."

Georgie put her head in her hands.

"One more variable to chuck in here," said Ant. "If your folks *had* scrawled that word on the board as a message to you and then done a runner, then leaving the door open would have been the smart move. It would have meant nobody would have needed to have broken in. It could be another message to you. If you'd got here to find it all smashed in, you'd have assumed they'd been killed, you might not even have come inside."

"Or they might have just been in such a rush to leave that they didn't think about shutting the door behind them."

"Yeah," said Ant. "That's possible too." He put his hand on Georgie's leg. "So what you… what *we* need to decide, is this. Do we think there's enough to go on? Do we think there's a possibility that your folks are still about, are still human, and they've bolted for the seaside?"

Georgie shook her head. "I don't know. I honestly don't know."

"Okay," Ant said, "I'll tell you what I think. I think that the chances are remote."

Georgie looked disappointed and hesitated before she answered. "I agree," she eventually conceded.

"I wasn't finished."

Georgie looked confused.

"What I think," said Ant, "is that if we don't follow up on this then it's going to creep around in your brain forever. It'll eat away at you and you'll go fucking nuts wondering what might have been. You'll end up resenting yourself for it, you won't be able to live with yourself. If my vote's worth anything then I say we head west, we go and find your holiday retreat."

Georgie looked overwhelmed. "You'd do that for me? You'd come all that way on a half-chance, probably even less, a one-hundredth of a chance?"

"Well yes, that's exactly what I'm saying, I don't see any other option. And before you go making me a saint, I do have a selfish reason. When I said you'd resent yourself, I think you'd end up resenting me too, for not pushing you to do this. You might not ever say it out loud but it would be in there somewhere, festering. Really all I'm doing is covering my arse. I suppose it's also worth mentioning that I love the shit out of you and I'd walk into the fires of fucking hell for you. But please don't make it a thing."

Chapter 20. Go west

"A supermarket is a definite no-no, have you not seen the films?"

"No, Anthony, as you well know, I haven't seen as many zombie films as you."

"It's always supermarkets, or malls really because they're normally in America, but the principle's the same. There's always a big set-piece scene where the survivors are trying to get supplies and it all goes to shit and the zombies pour in and get them."

"Those weren't documentaries, you do know that don't you?"

"Yeah, but it makes sense. If I was a zombie, sorry, *mutant*, I'd set myself up near a supermarket and catch any humans coming in."

"If they're clever enough to think in advance like that."

"We've got to assume they are, just in case."

They agreed to rule out the supermarket for now. Instead they decided on a more low-key, methodical approach: to go house to house in leafy, affluent Loxwood Road and raid the kitchen cupboards of the neighbours. They prioritised tinned food: tuna, meat, soup, vegetables, beans and fruit, but took anything that was still okay to eat: nuts, crisps, cereal, dried fruit.

The scenes inside the houses confirmed what the broken front doors, and more than a few windows, had suggested: that there had been carnage in this picturesque piece of England. Only Georgie's parents' house, and one other in the dozen they visited showed no signs of fatal violence.

They didn't meet any mutants or people, but they had a few run-ins with the road's surviving dogs and cats. Now feral and in regiments within their species they'd carved up the territory like post-war Berlin. The other family pets had fared less well. Rabbits and guinea pigs, cruelly confined in hutches outside hadn't stood a chance, and the same went for the caged birds inside. Ornamental fish had been scooped from ornamental ponds and the upended aquariums showed that their indoor brethren hadn't been overlooked.

There had been plenty of choices for a car-upgrade but they were happy with their current set of wheels. Ant got busy with the tube and bucket combo and topped up the tank from Georgie's mum's Merc. He hadn't got any better at it. "I love the taste of petrol in the afternoon," he said grimly.

By three in the afternoon they were ready to go. Ant had suggested staying the night at Georgie's parents' place and making an early start in the morning, but Georgie said she wouldn't be able to relax there. "Too many ghosts," she had explained.

"We're banking on them not being dead," Ant had replied, "and like you said about the definition of a zombie, you've got to have died to be a ghost."

"You're really hanging onto that optimism, aren't you?"

"Sorry," said Ant, "I just think it's worth staying positive."

Georgie's eyes sparkled, "I didn't say stop."

It was Georgie's turn to drive. The day had warmed right up, which prompted a policy discussion over whether to turn on the aircon. Turning it on meant they would get through more fuel but, as Georgie pointed out, leaving it off would result in "Death by body odour".

Georgie won the debate and turned on the aircon.

They tried the radio again and found nothing again.

"If this was all a terrorist thing, what do you think the aims of it were?" Ant said, breaking a ten-mile silence.

Georgie shrugged. "The usual I suppose, bring down the western capitalist structure."

"But that seems pointless if you've destroyed almost all of humanity in the process."

Georgie adjusted her sunglasses. "Maybe the aim was to establish a mutant caliphate. Or perhaps it wasn't the sort of terrorists we'd got used to, perhaps it was more like an evil mastermind."

"Yes!" Said Ant. "Maybe it *is* like the films after all. Maybe this was all the work of a Bond villain. Bending the world to his will."

"To his nefarious ends."

"What do you think his ends would have been then?"

Georgie laughed, "You really want to run with this don't you?" Ant was nodding enthusiastically. "Oh, you really do," she shook her head, still smiling. "Okay, maybe he just hated people, perhaps he had his heart broken and it made him into a psychopath, or maybe his parents were eaten by a bear in front of him. Or most likely he just had a small penis."

"Or all of the above," said Ant. "Or maybe he doesn't have a beef with humanity, he just really enjoys the company of mutants."

"Maybe he's a mutant himself."

They had climbed a hill and the road plateaued, revealing a countryside panorama that caught Ant's attention. "Wow look at that view."

Georgie was keen to keep her eyes on the road ahead but allowed herself a few stolen glances across the rolling scenery. "That is beautiful."

"Fancy a break? We've been driving for ages."

"Do you think it's safe?"

"We can see the road ahead and behind us, it's just fields either side for miles. I don't think there's anything up here. And we'll stay close to the car and be ready to go at the first sign of any trouble. And I'm sorry but I really need a piss."

"Okay," said Georgie, "Let's take a break."

They took turns to answer the call of nature behind a big elm tree and sat on a stone wall. The view, in the early evening sunshine, was nothing short of spectacular; the hills opposite and the fields in the valley beneath them, chequered by the different colours of the crops growing in each.

Ant put an arm around Georgie's waist and she returned the gesture, leaning in close and resting her head on his shoulder. "You and I have the perfect height differential for snuggling," she said, and Ant thought his heart was just about ready to explode.

"It feels good being alive doesn't it?" he said. "Despite everything."

"I agree," said Georgie," this is why we've gone to so much trouble to keep on living."

Ant turned and kissed the top of Georgie's head, feeling the sun's warmth on her hair. Georgie tilted her face upwards and they kissed gently and for a long time.

They sat in silence, allowing themselves to enjoy the simple happiness of that moment.

"I love you, Georgina," said Ant.

"I love you, Anthony, said Georgie.

They sat in quiet contentment. Pooh and Piglet.

Neither of them wanted to drag themselves away from that slice of heaven but they knew they had to get moving. Georgie's family's cabin-that-wasn't-a-cabin was nearly as far west as the West Country went before becoming the Atlantic

Ocean so they still had a long drive ahead of them.

They hit the road again, Ant taking his turn at the wheel.

They dipped low into a valley and climbed steadily to another flat, high road on the other side. "This scenery is really something." Georgie was enjoying being able to look around without risking running them off the road. Look at that lake down there, it's incredible, it's like an artist painted it."

Ant could only glance but immediately saw what Georgie meant. The water was impossibly blue and the yellowing sunlight captured in its surface looked like the work of a Renaissance master.

Georgie's face was a puzzled frown as she peered intently out of her side window. "There are animals by the water, cows, maybe sheep."

Ant's head turned quickly, excitedly. "Where?"

Georgie pressed a finger on the glass. "Down on the left side."

Ant looked again. "Those aren't sheep."

"They're people," Georgie said.

Ant pulled the car over. Georgie took the binoculars out of the glove compartment.

They got out and leaned on a gate into the empty field next to them, staring at the scene below. The figures they saw moving by the water's edge were tiny from that distance, even with the binoculars, but they definitely weren't animals.

"Are those tents?" Georgie asked, handing the binoculars to Ant.

Ant screwed his face up, trying to see more clearly. "I think so, yes, it looks like a campsite."

"Or more like a shanty town."

"Yes," said Ant. "That."

"We should get down. They probably can't see us from down there but let's not take any chances."

"There was a time," Ant said as they squatted behind the gate, "when I would have said we should just go down there and say 'hello', but after meeting Woody Woodsman I think we should be careful."

"Took the words right out of my mouth," said Georgie.

"So what do we do?"

"Well we've got to check it out."

"Of course," said Ant. "This could be huge, we can see at least twenty people just from up here, there's no telling how many others there might be."

"A proper community," said Georgie. "This could be the colony you were talking about."

"As long as they're not redneck rapists."

They didn't have an address to punch into the Sat-Nav so they went for the old-fashioned option. They took the map from the car and spread it on the ground. It took a while but they finally found where they were and where the lake was, which allowed them to plan a route down. They targeted a road on the hillside on the eastern side of the water. From there they would be able to look down, from much closer range, at the figures they had spotted.

"How will we know from looking at them if they're friendly or not?" Georgie had asked.

Ant shrugged. "No idea, but I don't think either of us has got any better suggestions."

Georgie nominated herself as navigator and sat with the map open on her lap while Ant drove slowly and carefully.

It was just after six when they parked at what they decided was far enough away for the car not to be seen or heard and they set out on foot, weapons in hand. After walking for half a mile, they could hear the sound of voices rising through the trees on the slope beneath them. They left the road and, squatting almost on their backsides, they eased themselves downwards. They passed through a small copse of trees and huddled behind thick gorse bushes. They couldn't hear individual conversations or even words, just a hubbub of speech, like trying to eavesdrop at a football match. They sat for a while, trying to pluck up the courage to raise their heads above the thorny parapet.

Ant took Georgie's hand. "Ready?"

She squeezed back. "Ready."

They peered over the bushes.

It wasn't a lake they were looking at; it was a reservoir. The paved banking gave that away, along with the big sign displaying various water-based activities that said at the top: 'Welcome to Westwater Reservoir'. At various points along the water's edge were some of the advertised activities: paddle boards, pedalos, a rack of kayaks, another of windsurf boards. A water-ski ramp rose out of the still, clear water on the far side.

A low building, all art-deco curves, was surrounded on the two sides that they could see by rows of wooden picnic tables. Each table had an umbrella sticking up through a hole in the middle. These were what Georgie and Ant had thought were tents. Their shanty town was, in reality, the outside seating area for the *Waterside Café and Bar*.

Every seat on the picnic tables was occupied, and most of the space nearby was taken. Georgie and Ant couldn't count the number of people they could see.

But, just as they'd found out from this closer range that the tents weren't tents, they could also now see they had been wrong about the people they had seen. They weren't people. The skin was too purple, too lumpy. The eyes bulged far too much.

They were looking at a colony of mutants.

Georgie and Ant didn't speak, they just ran, scrabbling up

the hill back to the road and then non-stop to the car. They ran so hard they thought they were going to be sick, but there was no time for that so they kept going. They got into the car and drove with the sole intention of putting enough tarmac between themselves and the mutants to feel able to breathe freely again.

An hour felt like enough.

Ant turned off the main road and drove for a few minutes more before seeing a row of three houses in the moonlight. He pulled over.

Their luck was in, all of the houses were clear. They chose the one at the far end because it didn't have any human remains inside and also had the luxury of gas, supplied not from the mains but from a big tank outside. Ant made them a dinner of tinned ham and tomatoes with some cheesy footballs on the side.

After dinner they went upstairs to the only double room in the small house and proved the theory that fear can be a strong aphrodisiac.

"I was always going to get some after serving up such fine cuisine," were Ant's first words afterwards.

"Anthony, if you ever call what we do in bed 'getting some' again then you'll never get any again."

"Fair enough."

"You're forgiven."

Since they had run away from the reservoir they hadn't talked about what they had seen and now Georgie decided it was time they discussed the biggest collection of mutants since (their) records began. She propped herself up on one elbow and looked down at Ant, lying on his back. "So much for them dying out."

Ant put his hand over his eyes. "Really? We have to talk about it now? Aren't we meant to be bathing in the afterglow of our romantic union?"

Georgie kissed him. "We've finished doing that."

"One more kiss."

Georgie obliged.

"Thank you. And yeah, that wasn't a species in danger of extinction we saw there. It's like they've been breeding."

"I very much hope not."

Ant's expression was a pained one. "Please God, no."

"We forgot about fish didn't we?"

"When we were talking about what the mutes might eat when the longpig ran out? Yeah, we did."

"It seems so obvious now."

Ant nodded. "It really does. They've eaten every living thing they've come across. Why wouldn't they set up camp next to a lake full of living things?"

"It reminds me of a documentary I saw at school, in Geography. It was about how shifts in population are driven by resource availability."

Ant grinned. "That sounds like a hoot, I hope I get to watch it sometime."

Georgie slapped his chest lightly. "Shut up and listen. Fish are probably the biggest source of meat now, so we're seeing population shifts as a result, mutes forming colonies around lakes and rivers."

"How do you think they're catching the fish?"

"You mean are they using a rod and line?"

"Yeah, or nets maybe. It would be a worry if they were smart enough to use either. I'm assuming they just get in the water and scoop them out."

"I'm not sure how many you'd be able to catch that way, and it would take a lot of fish to feed that lot."

Ant bit his lower lip. "Jesus."

"It would be really useful if we could find out how they're doing it, it would give us an idea of what else they might be able to do."

Ant turned onto his side and faced Georgie. "It wouldn't be useful enough to risk going back there."

"I wasn't saying we should go back there."

Ant screwed up his eyes and made a point of intently searching Georgie's face. Eventually he looked satisfied. "Good."

"Can we get back to my point?"

"Remind me what your point was?"

Georgie rolled her eyes. "Population shifts, mutes setting up near water. My parents' cabin is by the sea."

"I'm not so sure about the sea. Whatever way you're catching fish, it's got to be harder to do it in the sea, unless you've got a boat."

"I hope to God they can't use boats."

"I didn't see any boats out on that water."

"We weren't looking for long, but yes, that tells us something."

Ant lay on his back again. "It's tricky. We're trying to find colonies of humans and avoid colonies of mutants, but they're likely to be in the same sort of places, because they both need food."

"Except that mutes only eat uncooked meat."

"Yeah, that's the difference. Human survivors could be foraging for nuts and berries like in the stone age or whenever it was. Or they could be near the big fields of crops that we've passed, but it's a lot of effort, to, like, *harvest* that stuff, and they're not going to get far chomping away on corn all day."

"I think humans are more likely to be in towns because the easiest food is there, the tinned and dried stuff that we've been eating." Georgie moved onto her back. "My arm's gone numb."

Ant gave Georgie's arm a rub, noticing that the healing

wounds from Farmer Mutant's attack were going to leave a scar. "Or they could be doing what we're doing, which is just moving about and blagging it, finding food wherever they end up."

"And wherever humans are, mutes will be there too, hunting them." Georgie moved her arm away and curled her forearm slowly up and down. "Thanks, I can feel it again now."

"You're welcome. So basically we've got to watch our backs wherever we go."

Georgie propped herself back up onto her side. "I think that's where we started wasn't it?"

"Yep."

"Next time we hit a town, shall we stop and take a look, see what's about, or do you think it's too risky?"

"Well according to what we've just been talking about, it'll be no riskier there than anywhere else."

"I thought not," said Georgie. "Fancy it then?"

"I'm not sure that *fancy* is the word but go on then. Let's do it."

The next day was another glorious one and they allowed themselves a lie-in, enjoying the sunshine streaming through the bedroom window. Georgie took the wheel when they eventually hit the road, and Ant stepped through the radio channels, finding nothing again.

After thirty miles they hit a junction. Left was signposted to the town centre, while right meant they would stay on the A-road.

Georgie glanced at Ant. "Still up for it?"

"We've already agreed, haven't we?"

"Yes, we have, but I wanted to give you another chance to say if you didn't want to."

"You mean you wanted to give *you* another chance?"

Georgie smiled, "yes, maybe. But you're right, we've

agreed, nothing's changed." She checked herself, "Oh, I just thought of something, it's a seaside town, I can't remember if we decided if that meant it was safer or not."

Ant puffed his cheeks. "I don't even remember anymore. Fuck it, nowhere's safe. Let's just go for it, check it out."

"Fuck it," agreed Georgie, taking the left turn.

Ant grinned. "I really am rubbing off on you aren't I?"

"Try not to sound so pleased with yourself Anthony."

As they got closer to the centre of town they could see that the place had seen some serious action. They hardly saw a pane of unbroken glass, a car that hadn't been burnt out or even a bin that was still standing.

Georgie was leaning over the steering wheel, scrutinizing the scene in front of her for any signs of danger. They saw the now-familiar cohorts of dogs, cats and foxes roaming the dystopian landscape but no mutants. "What do you want to do, just drive on through or do you want to get out and take a closer look?"

"I'm not sure why I'm saying this but I think we should take a stroll."

"Good answer. I want to see the sea." Georgie parked the car.

They spent at least ten minutes checking the area immediately around the car for mutants before following the smell of salty air towards the sea. Georgie gripped the shotgun in both hands and Ant held the cleaver tightly to his chest. They kept to the shadows as much as they could.

They turned a corner and saw the sea for the first time, sparkling in the sunlight at the bottom end of a terrace of whitewashed Edwardian houses.

As they followed the road down they started to regret leaving the car but felt too committed to suggest turning back. Their fear built as they passed the broken fronts of the houses, expecting mutants to come pouring out of each one. They reached the end of the street and tasted sea air, heat and panic. They hurried across the wide seafront road and down some steps onto the waterfront walkway that was raised above the edge of the beach. They stopped for the first time since leaving the car, shrinking back against the foot of the steps.

Georgie was breathing hard. "What possessed us to do this?"

"It seemed like a good idea at the time. But we need to calm down, we're getting ourselves into a state. We haven't seen any mutes, just a lot of damage. Let's take a breather, sort ourselves out. When we've got our shit together, we'll just play it safe, head back to the car and get the fuck out of Dodge."

Ant felt his arm lurch as Georgie pulled on it, dragging him behind a row of recycling bins. Ant nearly soiled his pants but he didn't protest, just let himself be led, knowing that Georgie must have had good reason, and knowing too well what that reason almost certainly was.

They squatted down in the filth behind the bins. "Mutes?" Ant whispered.

Georgie nodded; her face was expressionless but her eyes told a story.

"How many?"

Georgie looked at the ground.

"It's loads isn't it?"

Georgie's head moved, almost imperceptibly. Up. Down.

"Hold on." Ant stood up. He kept his body hunched low and edged sideways to the end of the row of plastic containers they were hiding behind. He peered out, saw that nothing was immediately around him and stepped out, shuffling towards the bottom of the steps they had come down. He kept his eyes fixed in the direction Georgie had been looking when the blood had drained from her face.

That's when he saw them. Mutants, too many to count. They were fifty yards away. They were surrounding a building that the brightly coloured signs outside announced was an aquarium. The building was flat, landscaped into the concrete of the promenade. Ant's view was towards the east-facing main entrance which had wide, curved concrete steps on either side that led to the walkway above.

On every space on every step sat a mutant, like pigeons in Trafalgar Square. Those not able to sit were standing. They were all completely motionless, their heads lowered.

Ant crept back to Georgie. "It's like a mutant music festival, except without any music. Or dancing. They're doing that thing you said you saw them do. I know what you were talking about now, sleeping while they're standing, like they're powered down."

Georgie let out a sigh, not of relief, but as an effort to unfreeze herself, to allow her body to function again.

Ant took her hand. "Come and look."

It took a few goes for Georgie to agree but eventually she went with Ant and stole furtive glances at the scene. "Why are they all hanging out here?"

"Because of all the fish inside?" Ant didn't' sound convinced by his own answer.

"I don't think they're so stupid that they think it's worth waiting outside an aquarium until the fish come out."

"We should leave," whispered Ant. He started to move but Georgie pulled on his arm again, less violently this time but no less firm.

Her voice was almost inaudible. "We can't."

Georgie gestured with her eyes towards a point above where the mutants were congregated: a flag bearing the face of a cartoon dolphin that fluttered above the entrance to the building. Across it was handwritten, in large readable letters:

HELP US INSIDE.

Chapter 21. Georgie's choice

"We can't help them. It would be suicide to try."

"I haven't known you for long, Anthony, but I know you wouldn't be able to leave here knowing there are people trapped inside that building."

"It's not that I don't care, it's a horrible thought, but what can the two of us do?"

"We can try and get them out."

"But we'll die."

"Maybe. But I wouldn't be able to live with myself if I didn't try, and nor would you, so if we die trying then the problem of living with ourselves goes away."

"Interesting logic."

"It's very strong logic when you think about it. Can you imagine us driving away and then just going about our business knowing what we've left behind? We'd always be wondering if they were still alive, if the mutes had got them yet, or if they'd starved to death. Good luck getting any sleep from now on."

When Georgie had said "at least hear me out," Ant had reluctantly agreed. What he hadn't realised was that hearing Georgie out included locating themselves in the top floor flat of a four-storey block that, as the estate agent's listing would never say, afforded good views over the pack of mutants laying siege to the town aquarium.

Entering an unknown building in an unknown town was stressful, but they were less worried about there being any mutants inside than they might have been because they couldn't imagine there being any mutants in town that hadn't already joined the crowd outside the aquarium.

Georgie and Ant had moved some chairs from the dining end of what the estate-agent *would* have described as a light and airy double-aspect lounge-diner with original feature sash windows. They sat at one of those windows, grateful for the cover of the venetian blinds that were open enough to allow them to watch the sunlit scene below.

From their vantage point they could see the walkway that doubled as the aquarium's roof and could tell immediately that there were even more mutants in the still, silent swarm than they had originally thought. To the right as they looked was the beach. The sea sparkled in the sunlight, looking ridiculously inviting.

Ant had long since met his side of the hearing-Georgie-out bargain but the argument about whether they should try to help the besieged survivors rumbled on. Georgie did most of the talking while Ant tried to come up with different ways of saying "but we'll die" so he wouldn't just be repeating himself.

"There are kids in there, can you imagine what it's like for them?"

"I'm not saying it isn't horrible for everyone inside, I'm saying it's impossible to get them out. And anyway, how do you know there are kids inside?"

"It's an aquarium, it was the weekend, there has to be kids in there." Georgie pointed at the jolly dolphin banner hanging above the entrance next to the *kids go free* sign.

"That's only if they've been stuck in there since the thing happened. They might have gone in there more recently."

"You can tell yourself that if you like. I don't think you believe it though."

"What if there's a nutjob in there like Woody

Woodsman?"

"We can't leave them to die just because that's a possibility."

"Okay, but what if they're all dicks? What if we got them out, and I'm not saying we could, because we definitely can't, but what if we did, and found ourselves stuck with a bunch of dicks."

Georgie's face wore a weary smile. "Oh, Anthony, really?"

Georgie didn't know but Ant was well on the way to coming around to her point of view. She was right, he wouldn't have been able to live with himself knowing they had left the survivors at the mercy of the mutants. He knew what they were going through. He had been in the exact same situation. And in that situation Georgie hadn't said to herself "But I'll die" and left him to it. She had saved his life.

All they knew about the aquarium building was what they could see. They assumed that it went at least one more level down because otherwise it would have been too narrow to fit all the exhibits that were advertised with cartoon pictures outside. They studied the flagpole and saw that the loop of rope attached to the flag disappeared into the building through a gap around the metal pole. They assumed this meant it could be lowered from inside the building, all the way down into the entrance lobby. This explained how the survivors had been able to write their SOS on the flag without being set upon by the mutants; they had done it from inside.

Going through the front door wasn't an option, unless they could find a way to distract the mutants and lead them, Pied Piper style, to an alternative location. The only other possible entry points they could see were a row of three boxy metal ventilation shafts that stuck out of the rooftop pavement.

If they could manage to get to one of the shafts on the roof without being noticed then they would need to remove the stainless-steel domed cap, along with whatever filtering system might be underneath, again, without the mutants noticing. Even if they were able to do all of that, they had no idea if the shaft would be wide enough inside for a person to climb into. Or out of.

Ant was sure the situation was hopeless but he couldn't bring himself to say that to Georgie again. He searched his brain for something constructive to say instead, and while he was rummaging about in there he stumbled across the semblance of an idea. "If only we knew someone who could work a fire engine," he said eventually.

Georgie was smiling for the first time in a while. "There he is. That's my Anthony."

Chapter 22. Redelivery

'Ensure your own oxygen mask is fitted before helping others with theirs.' Georgie and Ant applied an extension of that logic to Operation Sea Life, making sure their own immediate needs were met before they started their rescue mission.

Their own needs included:

Having sex, Ant insisted and Georgie didn't argue.

Having dinner.

Having sex again.

They had time anyway, because the first step of their not yet fully complete plan was simply to watch the mutants. They did this for two days and nights, taking it in turns to sleep for an hour or so while the other sat at the window, pinching themselves to avoid dropping off when the sound of the waves rhythmically lapping at the beach became unhelpfully soothing. There were of course no streetlights, but the moon, which seemed much larger than normal, bathed the scene outside in the proverbial milky glow, which was a little eerie but extremely helpful.

They learned during this time that these mutants seemed only to be active at dawn and dusk. Georgie edified Ant with the official name for this behaviour: *crepuscular*. As the sun rose (at five in the morning) and set (at ten past nine at night), the creatures woke up from their stasis and wandered about for a while, then they would bang on the shuttered doors of the aquarium before shutting down again. The total period from the first one waking up to the last one going back to sleep was about an hour.

The scientist in Georgie wanted more data, but her practical side, which tended to get the upper hand these days, knew their limited sample would have to be enough. The people in the aquarium were on borrowed time.

They argued over who would carry out the next stage of the plan and despite Georgie's protestations, Ant won. "Listen," he had said, "it's not because I think I can do it any better than you, especially not because you're a girl and I'm a man, I just wouldn't be able to watch you do it because I couldn't bear losing you, simple as."

"But what about me having to watch you?" Georgie's question wasn't unreasonable.

"Tough, you're the one who talked me out of leaving town, I'm having this one."

So it was Georgie who watched nervously from the window at five past one that afternoon, exactly halfway between sunrise and sunset.

From where she was standing she knew she wouldn't be able to see Ant coming out of the front door of the apartment block, so she kept her eyes fixed on the road that ran across the inland side of the aquarium. This is where she knew Ant would appear. They had made a scary trip back to the car to pick up a couple of things and Georgie now kicked herself for not getting the binoculars while they were there. On the other hand, she thought, perhaps it would be better not to be able to see too well.

Since she had kissed Ant goodbye Georgie had tried to gauge how long it would take him to make it down the stairs to the ground floor, go outside and walk due north before turning right and joining the road she was looking at, but her estimation fell way short of reality. While she waited for Ant to show, she felt frustration that she had never known; the frustration of a partner waiting for their other half outside a clothes store changing room raised to the power of one million.

Ant eventually appeared and Georgie was seized by the urge to shout at him to come back inside, to call the whole thing off. But of course she didn't. She couldn't. Instead she was forced to watch in silent horror as Ant edged his way along the upper road, hiding whenever he could behind parked and abandoned cars while the mutants stood in their silent droves.

Ant had made progress. He had reached the pavement that cut down from the road that would lead him down to the walkway-roof of the aquarium.

Georgie didn't know whether to look at Ant or the mutants, who seemed to have multiplied since she last looked. Where they had looked like pigeons before, covering every square foot of concrete, they now looked like bats, bats in an upturned cave.

There was no way she could see the detail in Ant's face from where she was watching, but she was sure she could, she could see the fear in his eyes as he walked down the path with nothing at all to shield him from view. It would take just one of the mutants to stir and he would be toast. Or more accurately he would be pulled pork.

He crossed the boardwalk within ten feet of the nearest mutant and reached the middle ventilator duct. He lowered himself onto one knee, his head scanning back and forth around the crowd of mutants and offered up the package in his hand to the underside of the dome that covered the shaft. Georgie was whispering to herself, to Ant, "That's it, drop it in and go, just drop it and go," but he still had the package. He shuffled around and tried again at the far side of the capped shaft but his hand was still full when he pulled it away.

Apparently the package didn't fit.

Georgie could hardly breathe as she watched Ant drop to both knees and lay the package carefully beside him. He put his hands out in front, palms up, like he was taking communion, and slid his fingers beneath the rim of the metal duct cover. The sea-breeze caught his hair as he leaned back, silently straining, all the while keeping his eyes fixed on the monsters that slept all around him. Georgie realised what he was doing, he was trying to bend the metal to make more room. She thought she heard the steel creak but told herself she must have imagined it, because if she had heard it then all the mutants that stood between her and Ant would have heard it too, and as far as she could see they hadn't stirred.

Georgie knew she wouldn't be able to take much more of this.

Ant had stopped pulling and his head darted around, a giant meerkat, checking on the status of the deadly predators around him. With his eyes flitting from mutant to mutant to mutant, Ant picked up the package and put it under the bent rim of the shaft. He pushed gently, once, twice, a little harder the third time, and it dropped.

The clatter of the walkie-talkie landing on something hard inside the shaft shattered the silence.

Ant was up and running, sprinting up the pavement. He reached the top and disappeared behind a car.

Georgie watched in impotent terror as the mutants came to life. Two, now three were fully conscious and others were quickly following. She studied the road for signs of Ant running or crawling back but she saw nothing.

The mutants that had woken up first focussed their attention on the main entrance, running to the doors and banging on the metal shutters. The ones that woke up after them followed suit and soon they were all at it, flocking and banging.

Georgie felt a wave of relief. She hadn't seen any mutants go after Ant. He had completed his task and would be back at any moment. But as the minutes dragged by the relief evaporated and Georgie learnt what the phrase 'worried sick' really meant.

After fifteen minutes the mutants' stopped their banging, but they didn't go back into shutdown mode, instead they began to walk around, as if searching for something or someone. They were calling out, like parents looking for a lost child in a shopping mall, but all of them calling different names.

The sight was both strange and terrifying and Georgie thought she might just lose her mind as she watched, now kneeling, with her hands clamped over her mouth to stifle the screams that she couldn't trust herself to keep in.

Ant definitely should have been back by now.

Georgie breathed, long and slow, if something had happened to Ant then it meant that he needed help, and that meant she needed to get herself downstairs and do whatever she could to help him. She jumped to her feet.

She was startled by the sound of feet on the stairs and the apartment door opening.

"Honey, I'm home!"

Georgie ran to her man in the cheesiest tradition of the Hollywood melodrama, flinging her arms round him and kissing him over and over. "It didn't fit, did it?"

"No it bloody didn't," Ant was laughing as Georgie buried her face into his chest and neck. "I had to bend the metal thing, did you hear it? I thought they were bound to wake up."

"So it *did* make a noise. I thought it had, but none of them moved. I thought I must have been hearing things."

Ant pulled her closer. "And when the radio landed, Jesus, I've never moved so fast in all my life."

"Yes, you did, for about five seconds, and then what

happened?" Georgie pulled her face away and slapped Ant's chest gently but insistently. "What happened? You were ages, I thought they'd got you. What happened Anthony? I was so scared. I was just on my way out to come and find you."

Ant pulled Georgie back again. "I'm sorry babe. When they all woke up and started banging I didn't know what the fuck was going on, I just crawled along that road and then I slid under a lorry and waited it out. Then they all started shouting that stuff so I just stayed where I was. I couldn't risk leading them back to here, to you. I'm sorry."

"But that wasn't the plan." Georgie pulled away and looked up at Ant, tears streaming down her face. "It wasn't the plan."

"I know, I'm sorry babe. I'm really sorry."

"Don't do that again, Anthony, always stick to the plan, please. I was going out of my mind."

"I promise."

Georgie sniffed back her tears. "Okay."

Ant took hold of her shoulders and looked into those green eyes. "When you said you thought they'd got me and you were going to come looking, that's true isn't it? You were going to come outside to find me, with all those mutes wandering about?"

Georgie looked up into Ant's face, she looked puzzled, like she didn't understand the question. "Of course I was."

It was Ant's turn to cry. He hadn't thought he could love Georgie any more than he already did, but she had just proved him wrong.

They had to cut their swooning reunion short and get to business.

Georgie turned on the two-way radio.

"Hello, over."

The answer was so immediate and so panicked it caught

them off guard.

"Who is this? Who are you? What's happening?" A man's voice. There were a few seconds of silence and then a click and the 'talk' light on Georgie's receiver glowed green.

"Please say 'over' when you've finished speaking and release the button so we can speak properly. Do you understand? Over."

"Who are you?" More silence, another ten seconds before the person at the other end released their talk button and Georgie could answer.

"I will explain but first we need to be able to talk. When you speak, say 'over' at the end and then release the button so I can respond. Please confirm that you understand. Over."

Some indecipherable noise followed by a woman's voice. She spoke calmly and clearly. "We understand. Over."

Georgie relaxed visibly. "Thank you. I'll explain our position now. Please listen carefully and then respond with as much information as you can. Does that sound okay? Over."

"Yes, okay. Over."

"I am Georgie and I am with my friend Anthony. We can see that you are inside the aquarium surrounded by at least a hundred mutants. We want to help you if we can but it will be extremely difficult. I need to stress that we are not an official rescue operation, we are just two civilian survivors, we haven't met any other survivors." Georgie ignored Ant's raised eyebrow, now wasn't the time to talk about Woody Woodsman. "We need to know as much as possible about you. How many of you are in there, how secure you are inside, how much food you have, what your physical condition is. Anything that can help us work out if we can help you. Please answer now. Over."

"Hello Georgie and Anthony. I am Naomi. I will give you the information but please answer me a question first. Please tell us how we can know that you are not zombies..." Ant grinned, "...I am sure you will understand why I am asking. Over."

"Hello Naomi, yes I understand. You obviously know that mutants can talk and are able to carry out simple tasks. They appear not to be intelligent enough to know that without too much effort they could get through the ventilation ducts to get inside. If we were mutants we would not be telling you this because we would already be inside. Over."

There was a pause before Naomi's voice kicked in again. "One more question. How did you get past them to get the radio inside? Over."

"We saw that the mutants are active in the morning and evenings and sleep in between. While they were asleep Anthony put the radio down the shaft. This sounds infinitely more simple than the reality." Impatience had crept into Georgie's voice, raising it an octave. "Anthony risked his life for you. That's how you got the radio." There were a few seconds of static before Georgie remembered the radio etiquette she'd insisted on. "Over."

"Please don't misunderstand, we are more grateful than you can imagine, just to hear another human voice is wonderful and I hope we are able to thank you properly. I will tell you all the information that I hope can be useful to you now. Are you ready for that? Over."

"We're ready," said Georgie, more levelly than before. "Over."

"There are seven of us in here. I will not list their names now. Five adults and two children." Ant started scribbling notes. "There were more, a lot more, but many turned and many are dead. The main door is secure as well as the fire escapes on the south and south-east side of the building. As you say, the air ducts are the weakness. We do not know why the zombies have not come through them. We keep a lookout but we are careful not to be seen because then they may realise and we will be dead. I am stopping to confirm you have heard all of this and to allow you to ask any questions before I continue. Over."

"We can hear you and understand. We are sorry for your losses. Thank you for giving us the chance to comment, please continue to do that in case it is needed. Over."

Whilst Ant wrote his notes he watched and listened in awe of the mad skills Georgie and Naomi were showing. This was their first contact, the circumstances were at best, unlikely, and yet they were communicating with military precision. Their words were clear, concise and without ambiguity. It was really something to behold. He could see why Naomi had shoved that first guy off the mic, and he knew that if he, Ant, had been doing the talking he'd have been stumbling over his words, mumbling, rambling and generally messing the whole thing up.

"I'm sure you have lost plenty too," continued Naomi. "Regarding our physical condition. It would be inaccurate to say that any of us is ill but just as inaccurate to say we're fit and healthy. We are confined in semi-darkness and the constant fear of death takes its toll. In terms of technicalities, when the mains power shut down, a backup generator kicked in, providing emergency lighting, keeping the electrical appliances running as well as the filtration in the fish-tanks. We have mains water and we have gas to cook with but limited food. The cafeteria store ran out some weeks ago. We have enough to eat for perhaps another week. I will stop talking again. Please tell me if you need anything repeating or need to ask anything. Over."

"We heard it all clearly. One question. What are you eating? Over."

"We are eating the exhibits. Over."

Georgie looked at Ant, who mouthed the word 'wow'. The penny took a while to drop for her. She pressed the button but not the issue. "I understand. Please continue. Over."

"I think that covers all the information that you may find useful at this point. Over."

"Understood. I have one question. I will ask it now. Understood? Over."

"Understood. Please go ahead. Over."

"What is the most accessible exit for you?"

"We have barricaded all the doors very heavily. The fire door on the south-east side of the building, the opposite end to the main entrance, is the easiest to get to and open. Over."

"That's very helpful, Naomi. Thank you. Do you have any questions? Over."

"More than we currently have time for, but I will ask the most obvious. Do you think you can get us out? Over."

Georgie and Ant looked at each other, both shrugging with the age-old *who the hell knows?* gesture. Georgie pressed the talk button. "There is definitely a chance, Naomi. It'll be hard, we can't pretend otherwise, but Anthony and I have overcome every obstacle we've come across so far..." she and Ant allowed themselves a satisfied smile, "...and this is just another obstacle for us to overcome. What I *can* tell you for certain is that we will do everything we can to get you out, you have my word on that. Over."

"Thank you, thank you. I understand and appreciate your honesty. I wish you the best of luck. I have another question if that is okay. What happens now? Over."

"Anthony and I need to prepare some things. If we can do what we need to do, then we will be attempting to get you out at around the same time tomorrow. Would you be able to leave at that time? Over."

"We will be ready anytime you say. Over."

"And do you have at least one working watch between you? Over."

"We do, yes. Over."

"Okay, Naomi. Thank you, you have been brilliant. Please turn off your radio after we have finished talking. We need to conserve the batteries. We will need to talk again before we try to get you out, to go through the details. Please turn the radio on at eleven o'clock tonight for five minutes. If you don't hear from us in that window then turn it on again at twelve and on each hour until you do. Do you understand? Over."

"We understand. Over."

"Do you have any more questions? Over."

"One, but it is not a question, it's a statement." Emotion slipped into Naomi's clipped professional voice for the first time. "Thank you, we are more grateful than you could ever know. Over."

"You are welcome Naomi. Thank you for all the information. I hope we meet in person tomorrow. I am going to turn the radio off now, okay? Over."

"Likewise, Georgie. Thank you again. Over and out."

Georgie turned off the handset.

"I think we're doing this aren't we?" said Ant.

"Yes, I think we are," said Georgie.

Their plan, as Ant had mentioned, involved a fire engine. They had considered driving back to the Coach House to get their trusty vehicle but had written off the idea as too risky and time-consuming. They decided instead to find a local replacement.

A few years ago, Ant's mate Pete had spent his gap year travelling in South America. Ant had forgotten which city Pete had been talking about, perhaps it had been Rio, perhaps Buenos Aires, maybe Montevideo, or possibly all three, but Pete had found the security situation stressful. Pete had said how tourists, or *travellers* as Pete insisted was the word that applied in his case, were advised not to wander too far away from where they were staying and always to take a taxi when going to a different part of the city.

Pete's views on the security situation in South American cities had been part of a package of *I went travelling and I did...* stories, that Ant had endured in the pub a few days after Pete had got back from his travels. Ant hadn't been particularly interested, or even listening particularly closely at the time. He was surprised that he even remembered it. But as he considered heading out into this English seaside town to find a fire station, he couldn't help but see the similarities between his current situation and Pete's Latin American megacity experience.

But instead of muggers, who apparently would go away without hurting you if you simply gave them everything you had, there were killer mutants.

And the advice of keeping close to where they were staying definitely didn't apply here.

And he knew a taxi might take a while.

They had no idea where the nearest fire station was and Ant was thinking they'd just drive around until they saw one, or a sign to one until Georgie reminded him of the Sat-Nav. He felt his stress-level ease down a notch. It was still a hundred notches too high, but every little helped.

The local fire station had a different layout from the one they had stayed at before. The garage was in a separate building and they checked that first. The second of the four up-and-over doors had already been forced up and over. Georgie checked between and around the vehicles while Ant, torch in hand, checked underneath, slithering around on his belly like a snake wearing a miner's helmet.

A helmet of any kind would have been useful for what happened next.

"Can I help you?" said a female voice that wasn't Georgie's.

Mute

Ant jumped out of his skin and cracked his head on the underside of an exhaust pipe.

Chapter 23. The meek shall inherit the earth

Jesus. That really hurt. I can see little sparks in front of me. Now I know what people mean when they say 'seeing stars'. I've not had that before, it's weird. I touch the back of my head and check my fingers but there's no bleeding.

But my head's not really the issue right now.

The issue is, who the fuck said that?

I slide out from under the fire engine and stand up.

It's a mute.

Jesus.

She's small, about the same size as Georgie. She's wearing glasses. I've not seen that on a mute before. Her hair's all pulled back, it's a mousey colour. She looks a bit like a mouse actually. She's wearing a jumper but it's one of those summer ones, thin, ribbed, with short sleeves. I've not seen mutant arms before. The lumpy purple skin clashes with the peachy colour of the jumper. And there's that thing with the eyes.

I shouldn't be thinking of it as a *she*.

It's standing outside the garage, the sun reflecting off its glasses. It's got something in its left hand, like an old-fashioned paying-in book. Its right hand is fiddling with a St. Christopher on a thin gold chain around its neck. It looks nervous, which looks weird on a mute but it has every right to be nervous because Georgie's only a few feet away and she's got the shotgun pointed at its head.

"Can I help you?" it says again. "Are you looking to take

Alpha Two out?"

"Yes." I touch the wing of the fire engine that I've just crawled out from under. "We need to take out Alpha Two. It needs a repair."

"Is it not an in-house repair?"

"No, it's an…. it's an out-house repair. It needs to be taken out."

Georgie's looking at me like I'm nuts, but she hasn't pulled the trigger yet and I'm happy with that. I don't want Georgie to shoot, Christ knows how many mutes would come running if that thing went off. I'm hoping Georgie's worked that out but I'm not going to tell her. First, because I know she won't appreciate being told, but more importantly because I don't want to take any game away from us. When the person you're pointing a gun at knows you don't want to pull the trigger it limits your options.

But to be honest, it doesn't look like the gun is worrying the mute, I'm not sure it's even noticed it. It does look nervous, sure, but more like a kid at school who's been made to stand up and speak to the whole class. I think it might just be nervous by nature. A shy mute. But I'm not taking any chances. Farmer Mute was a boring mute but it still tried to kill Georgie.

Shy Mute's staring a little bit past me and it's not talked for a bit and I'm wondering if it's shutting down, going to sleep, whatever. But then it does speak. "You'll need a checkout docket."

I just go with it. "Yes, yes I think we will. Have you got one?"

"I have one here. I can complete it for you but you'll need to sign it or I won't be able to give you the keys."

"Can we sign it before you fill it in?"

It stares again. I wait for it to speak. It doesn't this time.

"Can we sign the checkout docket before you complete

the checkout docket?"

"Please sign the checkout docket so I can give you the keys." It holds out the pad to me. As I take it I see an engagement ring on its purple finger and wonder if it misses its fiancé.

There's a biro clipped to the cardboard base of the pad by its lid. I remove it and tear off the first form in the stack. It's actually two pages, a yellow top sheet and a pink copy underneath. I turn over the pad and rest the form on the cardboard. I sign my name on the bottom, write a date that I hope is close to whatever today's date is and hand it back to the mute along with the pad and pen.

It's still staring straight ahead. "I can complete the checkout docket."

"Can you get the keys?"

"Follow me to the office and I'll get the keys."

Georgie and I exchange *what the fuck* looks, but I can't think of anything better to do and it doesn't look like Georgie does either, so I walk with the mute across to the main building and Georgie walks next to us with the gun pointed at the mute's head the whole time.

I'm scared already but I get proper scared when the mute walks through the door into the building and I have to follow. I'm scared because I'll be between Georgie and the mute while I go through the door and if she needs to shoot it then she won't be able to until I'm out of the way again. I could step aside and let Georgie through first, but I'm getting the feeling that if we stray from the scene that's going on in the mute's head then things could go tits up. I think Georgie's thinking the same as me because she hangs back and gives me a hopeful nod with this sort of wince on her face.

I follow the mute into the office. There's a desk, a couple of filing cabinets and a big framed group photo of the station crew outside in the car park. I don't want to look too closely but I think she's in the picture, standing at one end. I'm sure it's her, she's wearing the same peach top and looking nervous. Next to the picture there's a key cupboard.

The mute goes and stands at the other side of the desk. Georgie's got a good clean shot again and I feel a bit better. On the desk there's a telephone and a computer. Both of them look like they were made before telephones or computers were invented. Next to the phone there's a mug. There's mould growing on the black liquid inside and on the front it says *100% vegan*. I really hope Georgie's seen it.

It opens a drawer, takes out a key and opens the key cupboard. It takes one, two, three sets of keys off their hooks and turns back to the desk and puts them down. They're marked A1, A2 and A3. I take the middle one. "Thank you, we'll check it back in tomorrow." The mute just stares into space and I give Georgie a look that says 'result!' but Georgie doesn't move and she's got this different look on her face and I'm scared again.

"We need the section of the manual," she says to the mute, "that covers locating and connecting to public hydrants."

I frantically shake my head at Georgie, whispering "We need to go" under my breath.

Georgie touches a finger to her lips.

The mute carries on staring into space.

"Where are the manuals stored?" Georgie says.

The mute stares into space.

I can't believe Georgie's doing this. We've got no idea if this thing is on its own, there could be a whole nest of them in here and if that's true I don't want to be around when they wake up. I want to tell Georgie this, I want to scream it in her beautiful fucking face, but I can't do that. I can only stand and watch.

The mute finally moves. "Manuals," it says. "It goes to the key-box and takes another bunch down. It comes out from behind the desk and I have to step back to let it through the narrow space and it's right up close to me as it goes past. If I breathed in I'd be able to smell it, but I don't think I've breathed in - or out - for a while.

It goes through into a corridor. Georgie turns to me and whispers "Stay here, watch out for anything outside." She follows the mute along the corridor and into a room halfway down on the right.

I do what Georgie tells me, for about a second, then I stare down the corridor she's just walked down, waiting for her to come out.

She's been gone for ages. It's horrible. What's she doing?

At last, at bloody last, she comes out. She's got this huge ring-binder wedged under her arm and she's hurrying up the corridor towards me. There's no sign of the mute. I follow Georgie's lead and we run to the garage. When we get close I swap the keys with her for the binder and the shotgun. I realise I've left the cleaver underneath but decide to leave it. Georgie presses the fob and the doors unlock and we're up and we're in.

Georgie's got the key in the ignition and it's not like in the films because it starts first time and we're off.

"What happened to the mute?" I'm almost shouting with relief.

Georgie's pissing herself as she steers us out of the compound and onto the road. "I asked for the section in the manual about helmet etiquette. I guess she must still be looking for it."

Chapter 24. Operation Sea Life

The flock of mutants that surrounded, or engulfed would be a better word, the front of the aquarium was as silent as the grave.

Georgie, squatting on the hot concrete, hidden from the mutants by an upturned rowing boat, shielded her eyes from the sun and watched the fire door.

Ant leaned against a closed and shuttered ice-cream kiosk fifty feet closer to the mutants. He ignored the sweat that stung his eyes.

The door crept open and a tall woman, made taller still by the afro that had obviously grown wild during her confinement, stepped out. Sunglasses covered her eyes as she peered into the full glare of a summer's day for the first time in a long time. This was Naomi. She was, to put it mildly, a striking figure. She saw Georgie and gave her a cautious thumbs-up. Georgie pointed east along the seafront, confirming what Naomi already knew from their run-throughs over the radio: the way to the van that waited for them.

Naomi, holding the fire door open, fanned her hand towards her as if guiding a cautious driver into a tight parking space. A woman emerged holding the hand of a young girl who Naomi kissed on the forehead before pointing in the direction Georgie had indicated. The shared features of mother and daughter were unmistakeable: The black hair, the pale blue eyes and sharply angled cheekbones, the broad, upright shoulders.

They looked like two pieces in a set of Russian dolls. Neither of them looked at the mutants, they just ran where they'd been told to run. They were barefoot and made almost no sound.

Next out was a man, tall and skinny. His eyes darted everywhere. He saw the mutants holding their silent vigil and quickly covered the eyes of the boy he was carrying. Two more men followed, one in his early twenties and the other maybe twice that age. They walked hand-in-hand and quickly caught up with the young man carrying the toddler, who was noticeably struggling. The kid was obviously too big to be carried, but he was also too small to make the run to safety on his own. As the two men passed, the older one turned, offering to help the skinny man with the wriggling child, but his partner pulled him away. As the skinny man adjusted his hold on the toddler his hand slid away from the kid's eyes and the boy did what any four-year-old would do when faced with a crowd of monster-people.

He screamed.

Loud enough to wake the dead.

Loud enough to wake the mutants.

Georgie didn't blink, she cranked the lever on the brass valve that sat above the fire hydrant, turning it as far as it would go. Ant braced, holding the hose the way the training manuals had told him, knees bent, one hand cupping from below and the other on top, gripping it firmly in place. As the floppy length of hose was made solid by the water, the mutants started to stir.

Naomi, bringing up the rear of the aquarium exodus, ran to the skinny man with the wriggling, screaming cargo. She took one of the toddler's hands, the man took the other, and together they ran with the kid hanging between them.

At least three of the mutants were fully awake and were starting to react to the live flesh that moved in front of them.

The hose bucked, jerked and exploded in Ant's hands, but he held on fast and trained the jet on the approaching mutants. He wasn't picky with his aim, he just blasted from left to right and back across again.

And the mutants went down like targets at a funfair.

Those closest were felled by the power of the jet, and the rest simply ran in the opposite direction, traumatised by being soaked to the purple skin. This had been a huge risk on Georgie and Ant's part; the mutants outside Ant's morgue had run for cover when it rained, but they had no idea if this lot would suffer from the same phobia. Georgie and Ant had effectively bet their lives on this, along with those of everybody inside the aquarium.

But their bet had come in, and half of Naomi's group were now in the van. Georgie called to Ant that it was their turn now. She found herself paraphrasing Iqbal's last words; that they needed to go go go, they needed to get the fuck out of there. Ant dropped the hose and ran after Georgie. With the still-spurting hose breakdancing in front of the manic mutants, Georgie and Ant covered the ground quickly. They reached the van as Naomi and the young man had hoisted the stricken boy into the back and jumped in behind. Georgie ran around to the driver's door and Ant, after checking that all seven passengers were safely inside, slammed the back doors closed. The van lurched away. Ant ran to their trusty estate and followed, leaving the pandemonium of mutants behind.

Georgie drove in a loop, cutting north-east and then almost back on herself to head west, across the full width of the town with Ant clinging to her tail throughout.

They had thought about what they would do once they had got everyone out, not least because they hadn't dared to dream that they would actually manage to get everyone out, not without being killed in the process. The closest they had to a plan was that Ant would follow Georgie to the first safe place she found outside of town.

They left the suburbs, still heading west and crossed an enormous toll bridge. Ant, already jacked up on adrenaline, suffered a bout of vertigo that nearly took him into the safety barrier. Once they were safely off the bridge Ant willed Georgie to find a place to stop soon; he wasn't sure his chest could keep his thumping heart in place for much longer.

They passed several places that Ant thought were perfectly good places to stop, but Georgie clearly didn't agree and kept to the meandering A-road. Ant, losing patience, took the walkie-talkie from the passenger seat to ask Georgie what was going on. Turning it on wasn't easy with one hand on the wheel and one eye on the road, but he was spared the effort when Georgie indicated left and slowed down. Ant dropped the radio and followed her onto a smaller road. After a few minutes Ant could see where they were headed, a huge stately home in a walled estate set on a hillside in acres of grounds of grass and woodland.

Georgie flashed her hazards and then slowed, indicating right. She stopped outside a pair of gatehouses either side of an archway that formed the main entrance into the grounds of the estate, marked with a sign that read, 'Welcome to Historic Hoxley House'.

Georgie and Ant had just accomplished an almost impossible mission, a mission where the preparations had been at least as dangerous as the final execution. Making contact with the trapped survivors had been difficult enough, as had been getting hold of the fire engine and driving it as close to the rescue site as they dared, then killing the engine and rolling the last hundred yards without waking the sleeping mutants. But that wasn't even the half of it. They'd had to locate the right tool on the fire engine and, in complete silence, prise the cast-iron cover off the underground hydrant. They'd had to unload fifty feet of fire hose and connect it to the mains outlet using heavy, clunky, copper fittings that seemed designed to make the most noise possible if they happened to clang against each other. They'd had to find a van that worked and had fuel. They'd had to rummage through human remains to find the keys. They'd had to start the engine in the deadly silence of a town full of monsters. They'd had to drive the van to within easy access of the aquarium, again, without waking its sleeping sentries.

Georgie and Ant could, and probably should, have died several times over in the last two days but they had come through, they had done it, and because they had been in something of a hurry when they had completed the final stage of their mission, this was the first chance they'd had to celebrate. Georgie jumped out of the car almost before she had parked it and in a few strides her and Ant were buried in each other, kissing, crying, laughing.

Their reunion was interrupted almost immediately.

"Mulțumesc!" Neither of them knew Romanian but they were in no doubt that the word being repeated by the woman who had led her mini-me daughter out of the aquarium, as she assaulted them with hugs and kisses, meant 'thank you'.

Her seven-year-old daughter was less boisterous than her mother but no less grateful. Georgie had to squat down to hear the shy little girl's voice.

She held up a battered teddy bear. "Cici wants to say thank you for saving her."

"Your teddy bear is a girl!"

"She's a Cici bear."

"And what's your name?"

"I'm Sophia."

Georgie took one of the toy's threadbare paws and shook

it carefully. "Cici is very welcome, and it's lovely to meet you, Sophia."

"Her friends want to say thank you too."

"Where are her friends?"

Sophia's dark hair, uncut and unwashed for four months, swung as she turned her head from side to side to indicate the others who had escaped the aquarium siege. "All of us are her friends."

Maria and Sophia were the Russian dolls who had been the first pair out of the aquarium, although Russia was a few thousand miles east of their homeland. Maria's fiancé, Luca, had been called out to work that Sunday morning and had been meant to meet them at the aquarium afterwards. He had promised to take them for pizza and ice-cream and had said how much he had been looking forward to hearing his best girl tell him all about the fishes she'd seen.

Neither of them had any idea where Luca might be now.

Lewis, twenty-seven, had been on a weekend getaway with his husband Frank to celebrate Frank's fiftieth birthday. "I'd wanted a party," Frank said, "but Lewis didn't want to advertise the fact that I'm half a century old." Just like the others in their group, both men bore the signs of months of incarceration. Frank's hair, which, he told them, he had shaved every two weeks in his previous life to "blend in with the bald patch" had grown bushy all the way round.

"You look like a monk," Lewis said unpleasantly. "Thank heaven for small mercies though, at least being on food rations has got rid of that gut you had before." It was obvious from the expression on Frank's face that this was not the first time his trophy husband had made this point.

The four-year-old whose screams had nearly brought Operation Sea Life to a miserable and messy end was Ronnie, whose blonde hair was cut, albeit not recently, in what could only be described as a mullet. Ronnie, apparently over the shock of starring in his very own monster-movie was the picture of childish glee as he went from person to person in his grubby dungarees, clapping his hands and demanding, what he called "Sunny cuddles". Georgie watched him going about his excited business, amazed at the fortitude of a boy who had spent over ten percent of his life so far trapped inside a windowless building. The skinny man that Georgie and Ant had assumed was Ronnie's dad turned out to be Blaze, his seventeen-year-old half-brother.

Blaze, in his jogging pants and hoodie tied around his waist, had the look of the TV stereotype of a 'wayward youth'. His features were gaunt and the pale skin on his face had the scars of serious acne from his earlier teens. His eyes, as he had been told by various figures in authority, looked 'shifty'. Although he was thin, his chest and upper arms showed that he was no stranger to the gym, a regime he had managed to maintain, with a bit of improvisation, while he was cooped up inside the aquarium.

Blaze and Ronnie had been with their mother that fateful day. "One minute she was paying for the tickets and saying she'd catch us up, and the next thing we know she's this monster and she wants to eat us." Blaze seemed unconcerned that his little brother could hear every word. "Luckily I had my blade. He touched his belly. I've always got my blade, and I always know how to use it." Georgie and Ant both wanted Blaze to confirm if his last statement meant what they thought it did, and for him to explain why, in a pre-apocalyptic world, he felt the need to carry a deadly weapon with him at all times. But right at that moment neither of them felt able to deal with what Blaze might say.

Ant was used to being the tallest person in any group and this remained true here, but Naomi gave him a run for his money. It wasn't just her height that caught the eye; she had removed her sunglasses and Georgie and Ant were seeing her face properly for the first time. Like everyone they had rescued, she needed a shower and a change of clothes, but even in those reduced circumstances she was something to behold.

"It's like her features were made in a lab," Georgie whispered, "like someone had been asked to design and build the most beautiful face possible."

Ant, sensing a trap, was thinking carefully about how to word his response and was massively relieved when Naomi saw them looking and came over before he had to come up with an answer.

Ant went to shake Naomi's hand but the angel with the afro went straight in with a hug. "I've had a chance to say it to Georgie but not to you, thank you for everything."

"You don't have to keep thanking us, I'm glad we could help. And anyway, you helped loads. As soon as you took the radio. It made everything so much easier."

"Yes, I could see straight away," Naomi glanced over at Frank who seemed to be on the receiving end of crossed words with his young husband, "that Frank was struggling, so I stepped in."

"Do you answer emergency calls for a living or something?"

"No, but I have experience working a radio, and keeping calm in a crisis was a big part of my job description. I'm a Marine Biologist, I've been going on expeditions for more than twenty years, leading most of them for the last ten. I've sailed on every ocean on earth and let's just say it doesn't always go to plan."

"I have two questions," said Ant.

"Please say them now, over."

Ant laughed at the in-joke. "Why would a Marine Biologist

be visiting an aquarium? Do you miss fish when you're off-duty or something?"

"That's a very good question, Anthony. I was contractually obliged to be there. They kept Green Sea Turtles there and the authority I worked for was responsible for the welfare reviews for that species. It's the only part of my job that I hated. I see no reason to keep any kind of animal in confinement. What was the other question?"

"You said you've been on expeditions for over twenty years, that means you must have started at, like, ten years old?"

"I appreciate the compliment, but no, I was twenty when I had my first paid project, measuring reef propensity in the Indian Ocean, which was a lot more exciting than it sounds. I was out on boats from a young age though. At home in Kenya my father was a fisherman. I think he took me out before I could walk. Everyone in the village called me 'Mtoto wa maji', it means *water baby*."

Georgie looked astonished. "You're from Kenya? English isn't your first language?"

Naomi shook her head. "It's my third."

"Wow."

Finding their way to Hoxley House hadn't been an accident; on the drive out of town Georgie hadn't minced her words, she had brought her passengers bang up to date on how things were in the outside world. She asked if anyone with local knowledge had any suggestions of somewhere they could go that might be safe and secure. Maria had suggested the estate and directed them to it.

The sign across the locked gate said it was closed for the season, and the information board behind the glass of the small entry kiosk showed that it had been due to reopen at the start of April. This felt like good news to Georgie. "Less people in the grounds on the day the world ended," she said, "means less mutants."

"Apart from any who came afterwards," Lewis pointed out.

"Of course," said Georgie, "but the starting point is lower, and I'll take that as a positive."

"Does anyone live here?" Ant said, looking at Maria.

Maria stood behind Sophia with her hands resting lightly on her daughter's shoulders. "A baron. Rich family, old money. Might say on the board."

The information board as good as confirmed Maria's answer, although it was an earl rather than a baron. He was the head of the Ashcroft family, but how many were in the family was not specified.

"Let's say there were twenty of them," Ant said, "and another twenty staff, a butler, maids, a cook or two and a few groundskeepers. Does that sound reasonable? I'm happy to be corrected here because I haven't got a bastard clue how many people live in a stately home."

"There's a church inside too," said Maria.

Ant managed to smile and frowned at the same time. "Well that's all we need, a mutant vicar."

"I think the church only opened for the big events like Christmas and Easter. Sophia went with school once. To the festival of the harvest."

Ant smiled, he liked Maria's accent. "Okay, no mutant vicar. Good, but I'm going to give up trying to work out how many could be inside."

Blaze sniffed loudly and, to Georgie's dismay, swallowed whatever he'd dislodged even more loudly. "Have we got weapons?"

Georgie's revulsion showed on her face. "Nothing to write home about. I have a shotgun with a few cartridges, Anthony has a big scalpel. We have two axes from the fire engine."

"And my blade," said Blaze.

Maria stroked Sophia's hair absently. "How to get inside?"

Ant pointed at the intercom next to the gate. "I think we should ring the doorbell."

"I doubt it'll work, no power," said Lewis.

Ant approached the metal panel. "I reckon there is, all these little lights are on." He looked carefully at the choice of locations on the panel: General Manager, Accommodation, Trade, Corporate, Private Residence.

He pressed all of them.

They waited for over a minute and pressed them again.

Nothing.

"Nobody's home," he said after the third try. "Nobody who can operate an intercom at least."

"Or maybe nobody who feels safe enough to operate the intercom," said Georgie.

"Fair point. I wouldn't answer it either." Ant put his hands behind his head, stretching, and looked through the gates. "Anyone got any ideas on how to get in?"

"We climb over the wall easy," said Maria.

Naomi spoke. "We need to get the gate open so we can take the vehicles in with us. We might need to get out fast."

Blaze held up his little brother. "Can someone take Ronnie?"

Maria obliged and they all watched as Blaze disappeared into the bushes next to the gatehouse.

After several minutes of nothing happening Georgie spoke. "Has he just…. gone?"

Nobody seemed sure.

A loud scraping made them all jump. It was the wooden sash window in the kiosk being lifted open. Blaze's grinning face peered out. "I'm afraid we're closed for the season." He pointed at the information board. "It's all on the sign here.

Please come back in April."

"You open the gate from in there?" Maria adjusted her hold on Ronnie, who was giggling excitedly at his brother-in-the-box.

"Okay, I'm feeling generous, I'll give you the group rate." Blaze pressed down on a button under the ledge in front of him and the gates swung slowly open.

Chapter 25. Stodge

Despite everybody fearing the worst about what might be waiting for them, they were all impressed by the opulence that surrounded them as they drove through the grounds and saw the house at close range for the first time. It wasn't quite a castle but the brickwork on the flat roof looked very similar to battlements. It all looked like the backdrop to a period drama. It had probably been used in a few. Ant kept expecting to see a Henry VIII lookalike come striding onto the lawn.

Naomi parked the van against the ivy-covered wall at the south-west corner of the house and Georgie and Ant parked the beamer behind. They all got out of the vehicles a lot more quietly than they had outside the main gate.

After a quick huddle it was decided that Georgie, Ant and Naomi would check the place out and the others would stay by the vehicles. They had a brief discussion on a code word to shout if either group got into problems. They agreed on 'help'.

The three of them crept along the edge of the once-manicured lawn behind the building. The first few of the tall windows they passed were shuttered, but the next, a large bay window formed from the bottom half of a turret that emerged from the centre of the house, allowed them a clear view inside. They were looking into a banqueting hall, its rows of tables overlooked by a vast centrepiece chandelier.

Georgie let out a quiet whistle. "This is exactly the sort of place my dad would have wanted me to get married in."

Ant's face was pressed against the glass. "Whenever I've been to a wedding I've hated it when the tables are set out in rows like that. You're all sitting in big lines. If you've got someone boring next to you or opposite then you're fucked. I prefer round tables, then you've got more options for decent chat."

"Fair point," said Georgie, "but would you have the bride and groom on a round table too?"

Ant thought for a moment. "You mean instead of the long table across the front? No, I think I'd keep that, the parents like that don't they? Being on the top table, looking at everyone who's come to their kids' special day."

"The room looks very tidy," said Georgie.

"No sign of a scuffle," said Ant.

"Guys," said Naomi.

Georgie and Ant pulled their faces from the window.

"Oh," said Georgie.

"Shit," said Ant.

"Drop the gun please." The owner of the voice was a squat woman, late middle-aged, wearing a red and black checked shirt, light jeans and leather sandals. Her grey hair was pulled into a tight bun. Next to her stood a man of similar age and not much taller. He wore a flat cap and what hair they could see was white. As with Maria and Sophia, the family resemblance was obvious, particularly the hooked nose, which might in some circles have been called aristocratic.

The barrel of their shotguns glinted in the afternoon sunshine.

Georgie did as she was told.

The woman pointed her gun at Ant. "You can put whatever that sharp thing is down too please."

"This old thing? Oh, go on then." Ant slowly put the scalpel onto the ground. "Help," he shouted, half-heartedly.

The woman laughed, not unkindly. "Your friends are inside, in the same boat as you."

"Worth a try," said Ant. "Pleased to meet you. I'm Ant, this is Georgie, and this is our friend Naomi. You must be the lady of the house."

"I don't think titles matter anymore, if they ever did before." The woman lowered the gun and held out her hand to Georgie, Naomi and then Ant for cursory but unexpected handshakes. "I am Alice. This is my cousin, Douglas." Douglas tipped his cap, but kept his gun trained on the trespassers.

Georgie forced a smile. "It's a lovely place you have here. We wondered if you might have room for a few guests."

The older woman smiled and cocked her head. "Let's all go inside."

They were led further around the building onto an expansive patio and through a door into a reception area. The room was smaller than the dining hall but no less impressive in its grandeur. The others from the aquarium were sitting on a row of upholstered wooden chairs under the watchful gaze of a bald-headed man with a white beard. He was also armed. Shotguns seemed to be *de rigueur* for the household.

The lady of the house addressed them all. "I have introduced myself to our three friends here, but for the rest of you, my name is Alice." She nodded to the guy in the cap who shared her nose, "and this is my cousin Douglas. We may well be the last surviving members of the Ashcroft family, the family that has had the good fortune to own the Hoxley House estate for generations. More recently our fortunes have been less than favourable." She gestured towards the bald man with the beard who responded with the barest trace of a nod. "This is Arthur. As well as being as good as family, he was the head, and only surviving member, of our groundskeeping staff. When the cataclysm occurred that Sunday afternoon, everybody who was caught outside became one of those *creatures* and in order to defend ourselves we were forced to destroy them." She tapped the stock of her shotgun and looked around the room, her face solemn. "This meant killing people we knew and loved. That day I lost eleven members of my family, including my father, Grandma Beatrix and my brother Sebastian. Douglas and Arthur both lost their wives." She paused to let her words sink in before continuing. "We also lost eight other employees and an extremely pleasant young couple who were visiting our facilities with a view to holding their wedding here." Lady Alice searched her memory, gave up and shook her head. "Sadly, their names escape me." She paused for gravitas once again. "That is our story, I am sure you all have stories of your own. You will all have lost loved ones, and some of you will have had to do the unthinkable, just as we have. I hope you will forgive me the lecture but I wanted to give you the background to what we have been through and acknowledge that you have endured something similar."

Lady Alice stopped talking and scanned faces, making sure she had everybody's full attention.

She did.

"I am not used to holding people at gunpoint and I am hoping there is no need for guns, except to defend ourselves against any further attacks from those creatures. Myself, Douglas and Arthur have been getting by, we have been surviving, but there are only three of us and I am sure you will have noticed that we are not spring chickens. Douglas and I are the wrong side of fifty, and Arthur, well it's not my place to tell you his age but let's just say he grew up with my father. The most logical path for all of us here would be to join forces. Strength in numbers, pooled knowledge and experience, a wider variety of skills and improved social interaction are just a fraction of the obvious benefits. But I am no fool. Human nature being what it is means that obvious benefits are often forsaken in place of petty, selfish short-term gains. This is particularly true in a world where order has been replaced with chaos. I am therefore cautious, hence the rifles that are currently trained on you. I cannot know your minds, you may not know each other's yet, but I can make a start by asking you this very simple question."

Lady Alice scanned her captive audience once again before speaking.

"Do any of you intend to cause us harm?"

Lady Alice's Gettysburg Address proved to be effective. None of the new arrivals wanted anything more than a safe place to stay. For everybody in that room, hostilities would only be tiresome, and just surviving up to that point had been tiresome enough.

After some more relaxed introductions and trading of stories, the newcomers were led up the wide mahogany staircase that swept grandly from the centre of the lounge. Georgie and Ant were given the first room on the right. This was currently Douglas's bedroom and he was more than a little affronted at having to relocate, but Lady Alice insisted that the old and new residents be in alternating rooms. This would, as she put it, "Hasten integration."

Lady Alice kept the room next door to Georgie and Ant, and she put Blaze and Ronnie in the next one across. This meant that Arthur also had to uproot. The groundskeeper was considerably more pragmatic than Douglas had been. "It's just somewhere to sleep," he said, "I don't care where I sleeps."

Blaze carried Ronnie across the threshold of their room, finding the youngster a lot easier to handle than when they had been running for their lives. He sat Ronnie on the bed and the boy, with two fingers in his mouth, looked around at his new surroundings. "Mummy coming?"

Blaze had been investigating the room, his never-still eyes darting into every corner and cupboard and out of the tall arched windows at the view of the grounds outside. At the sound of his little brother's voice he stopped his pacing and focused his attention on Ronnie. He took the knife from the waistband of his joggers and put it on the nightstand. He lay on the bed, taking the boy in his arms. "I wish she was, little man. She'd have loved the shit out of this place."

"Where's mummy?"

"She's gone. It's just us now. But I know you're going to make her proud."

Naomi, in the room the other side of Blaze and Ronnie, found herself standing and staring at the full-length mirror, not recognising the woman who stared back, the woman with the face calloused by unrelenting fear, both for herself and for those she had been fighting to protect. The face in the mirror wasn't the face that had wowed Georgie and Ant; Naomi saw a different face entirely. Her eyes used to sparkle, they lit up any room, everybody had told her so, but now she could barely see them. They were sunk into their sockets like glass beads on a broken doll. She tried a smile, but it looked false; a grimace.

Naomi couldn't picture a situation where she would ever light up a room again.

When she had been inside the aquarium Naomi had taken charge. She was the go-to girl for everything, organising, planning, fighting to keep spirits up, and when they had been thrown a lifeline it was her who had seized it with both hands. Now it was over, all there was to do was face this new world. And she didn't see where she would fit into it, or how.

It is said that if a shark stops swimming it dies. Naomi, an expert in her field, knew this wasn't completely accurate, but it served as a perfect analogy for how she now felt. Her work, taking responsibility for the lives of everybody trapped inside that building, was over. She had stopped swimming.

And now she could feel the black depths pulling her down. She had felt it before, in between expeditions, but it felt stronger, more final this time. She couldn't see any options in her life anymore.

Back down the hall, in the room across the deep-pile carpet outside Georgie and Ant's door were Maria and little Sophia. Sophia, having had to sleep on the floor of a tourist attraction for four months, burst into tears when she saw the huge bed that now belonged to her and her mummy. She instantly started bouncing up and down on it in celebration. After a handful of bounces she almost as instantly curled up and fell into a deep sleep. She was out for the count and couldn't see her mummy fall to her knees and weep at the sight of her daughter enjoying a moment of pure contentment after everything they had endured. Maria kissed her daughter softly and, remaining on her knees, tried to offer up a prayer of thanks for their deliverance and hope for their continued safety.

But the words wouldn't come.

Arthur was in the next room along, with Lewis and Frank on the other side, which just left Douglas, who was given the room at the end. Douglas was still angry about being kicked out of his room in the first place and this new arrangement made him angrier still. When Lewis and Frank were out of earshot, Lady Alice asked him why he was so bothered about his new neighbours.

"It's just not normal is it? Men aren't meant to go with men. And don't give me that look. I bet Arthur's just as narked about having two of *them* next to him. And if you don't believe me then I'd advise you to go and ask him."

Lady Alice went to Arthur's room and did exactly what Douglas had suggested.

The old groundskeeper's answer was brief and familiar. "I

don't care where I sleeps."

Frank closed the bedroom door. He leant back against it and let out a long sigh. "At last! It's just us, hun. We're safe and we've got privacy. Can you believe it?" He walked over to where Lewis was flopped on the bed.

Lewis recoiled from his husband's touch. "What I can't believe is how you could be so polite to that posh old bastard, the one who so obviously hates queers."

Frank's shoulders sagged. He perched on the edge of the bed, his hands in his lap. "Oh baby, we have to pick our battles."

"You don't pick your battles, you run away from them."

"Don't talk to me like that, hun, please. Douglas is just a lonely, scared man. Everything he knows has been taken away from him, his wife was killed, probably in front of him, possibly even *by* him, and suddenly a group of strangers has moved into his family home. He's a mess, he doesn't know up from down. Is he homophobic? Probably. Is it acceptable? Absolutely not. But is it understandable? Maybe."

Lewis, his back still turned to his husband, snorted in disgust.

"Listen babe, there'll be time to talk to him, to challenge his prejudice, but right now we should focus on the fact that we've been saved from a gruesome death. We need to work with these people, with this community. This could be the start of something." He patted the thick mattress. "And it's pretty luxurious here too." He reached out his hand.

Lewis ignored his husband's touch. He spoke quietly, but very clearly and very deliberately. "You can dress it up however you want but I know what you are. You're a weak old man who ducks every fight. You're a sell-out."

Lewis yelped in shock and surprise as his husband took his shoulder and yanked him round to face him. Frank's face was no longer the picture of calm passivity, it was unbridled rage. "You listen to me you spoiled little brat, I've fought, I've been fighting since before you were born. You have no idea what it was like back then. It was hard, harder than it is now, harder than you can dream. You can call me what you like, you can call me old, fat, bald and boring, all the shitty things you enjoy saying to me so much, but don't you ever call me a sell-out."

Lewis didn't answer, he just stared in shock, his mouth hanging open.

"Do you understand me?"

Lewis closed his mouth and nodded.

Neither Georgie, Ant, Lady Alice, Arthur or even Douglas had mentioned the fact that the ex-residents of the aquarium, having not seen the inside of a bathroom for more than a quarter of a year, stank beyond belief, and it was a big win all round that all the rooms had functioning en suite showers. It was a bonus that there were enough clean clothes in enough sizes in the many wardrobes and storage cupboards to give everybody something fresh to wear.

Two hours later, the smell of cooking brought everybody downstairs and they were told to take a seat in the dining hall. To Georgie and Ant's surprise this was not the room they had peered into while discussing wedding-day seating arrangements. That, they learned, had been the banqueting hall. "I get that," Ant had said. "You definitely need a banqueting hall as well as a dining hall. Imagine, right, trying to have a banquet in a *dining* hall, you'd feel like a proper prick wouldn't you?"

They sat at an oval table, large enough for them only to fill half the chairs around it. Arthur rattled into the room with a trolley-load of plates, cutlery, condiments, jugs of water and glasses. "Give me a hand with this lot would you?" Blaze and Naomi jumped up and started unloading it all onto the table. "I won't lie," said the old Cornishman," it's best for everyone that you do it, I'm cack-handed, see? I'd probably break something."

When the trolley was empty Arthur took it back into the next room, which the sleuths amongst the group had correctly guessed to be the kitchen, or one of the kitchens at least. He was back in a few minutes, wheeling in a platter of sausages and one of chips. The guest's *oohed* and *aahed* like they were watching a firework display. Arthur, shuttled in and out of the kitchen again, minus the trolley this time, carrying a huge tray of bread and butter. "I'm sure I'm breaking some rules here, this ain't silver service, but I reckon it all goes down the same hole."

Lady Alice followed with the trolley, laden this time with wine glasses and three bottles of red. "You're doing just fine Arthur. Maggie would have been proud of you."

Arthur's expression was blank but his eyes darkened. "God rest her soul."

"She was one of a kind." Lady Alice touched his arm gently. She saw the empty plates in front of her guests and frowned. "Oh no, please do not stand on ceremony, it will get cold. Help yourselves. You must be terribly hungry."

Nobody needed telling twice.

Lady Alice sat down at one end of the table. "I hope this hits the spot. It's not *haute cuisine*, of course, but it's what we have most of and it was the easiest to prepare in a hurry."

Blaze was cutting up Ronnie's portion for him, grinning through a mouthful of sausage and bread. "It's bloody amazing." The rest of the room murmured their agreement.

"Where's Douglas?" asked Frank.

"He's up on the roof, taking watch," said Arthur.

"That's very kind of him." Frank felt Lewis' eyes on him as he spoke.

This was definitely not the kind of formal affair that the salubrious surroundings had hosted in the past, but as Lady

Alice watched her guests demolishing their platefuls and gratefully accepting seconds, she felt more satisfied than she had in a very long time.

Arthur poured the wine and the glasses were passed around the table. Both the children tried their luck and both were told to stick to water.

Lady Alice stood up. "It seems right to make a toast and you will be glad to hear that I will keep it brief." She raised her glass. "To our new friends, may we make a future together."

Everybody got to their feet and echoed the sentiment, loudly. Frank raised his voice to be heard above the noise. "I would like to say a few words if I may," he paused. "Nobody has said I can't, so I'll proceed. I would also like to propose a toast, to our host for this wonderful hospitality and for welcoming us into your home."

There was a loud consensus of approval.

"I would also like to thank Naomi who kept us all going while we were inside that wretched building."

Naomi showed a keen interest in the tabletop as the cheers rang in her ears.

"And, of course, the heroes of the hour. To Anthony and Georgie for risking their lives to save us. What you did for us was unimaginable. Thank you thank you thank you." He raised his glass high into the air. "Thanks all round!"

Everybody drank.

They cleared the table and returned to their seats. Ant sat to Lady Alice's right with Georgie the other side of him, followed by Blaze, Ronnie and Naomi. On Lady Alice's left were Arthur, Maria and Sophia, and finally Frank and Lewis.

The inaugural meeting of the new Hoxley House community had begun.

Ant patted his belly. "Lady Alice, that food was bloody marvellous. Thanks again."

"Just Alice is fine, and you are extremely welcome."

"You said that the food was what you had most of, I've got to ask, how much of it do you have?"

"Fortunately, at the time it all happened our personal freezers were full, mostly with the various meats one would expect on a country estate with old relics like my family as residents. We have not dipped too far into those stocks yet."

"But how come all the chips and sausages?"

"The estate hosts music festivals and other events throughout the summer. To cater for these, the freezers tend to be kept full of simple foodstuffs, not so much to serve to the attendees, but to feed the workmen who set up whatever equipment is needed and erect the fencing, marquees and the like."

Ant looked pleased. "So you have plenty of meat, and plenty of good old stodge."

Lady Alice smiled. "Indeed. If the cataclysm had been considerate enough to have taken place a few months later, then we would have had some more sophisticated fare in stock as there would have been supplies brought in for the weddings that were booked throughout the summer."

"Where does the power come from for the freezers?"

The lady of the house patted her groundskeeper's forearm. "Would you be so kind as to answer that, Arthur, it's much more in your area of expertise."

"Certainly, m'am." Arthur looked at Ant. "We've got more than half a dozen generators on the property for the music festivals and all the other business. I hooked our electric up to those. We keep the generators in the wine cellar so the noise don't travel. We don't go overboard on the power though."

Lady Alice nodded earnestly. "Absolutely. That is something for all of you to note. We impose strict rules on ourselves governing the use of the electricity. This is to preserve the petrol that feeds the generators, and for common sense reasons of security. The most obvious being that we never have lights on at night if they can be seen from outside."

Georgie was reminded of their showering rule back in the Coach House. It already felt like a very long time ago. "What else do you eat apart from the frozen food?"

"Arthur and Douglas have a knack for fishing and we have access to both a river and a well-stocked lake. As you saw on your arrival, we all know our way around a shotgun so it would be possible to hunt game too. We are refraining from doing that for now though, gunshots would attract unnecessary attention and we think the ammunition is best saved for the purposes of defence."

Georgie took a sip of her wine. "Very wise."

Lady Alice's face brightened, "Oh, I have just remembered. We have chickens too." She turned to Arthur. "How are they getting on?"

"I checked on them this morning and they're going very well indeed. I'd say the hens are two weeks into the brood, we have five nests. Mabel and Maisie are sharing one, bless 'em."

"So, a fortnight you think?"

Arthur nodded. "I would say, yes. We should be looking at a dozen or so chicks, and at least a few of them'll be cocks, so old Roger'll be dethroned when they're full grown. He's had a good stint though."

Lady Alice spoke to the group. "We have been treating our cockerel, Roger, as something of a golden goose. He is our one and only male and if we lose him then that would mean no more chickens after this current crop. All being well we will be in a much less tenuous position when these clutches hatch. When you come to take your turn on lookout you will see that we keep an eye out for foxes as much as we do for the monsters."

"That's right," said Arthur. "Me and Doug worked hard on securing the enclosure, nothing should get in, but Mister Fox is a wily devil and you can't be too careful."

Lady Alice looked at Arthur proudly. "If there was a guidebook advising on how to start a new life in the wake of an apocalypse, then the very first entry would say 'you need an Arthur or you may as well give up immediately'. What I would have done without him I do not know."

Nobody could be sure but there seemed to be a touch of a blush behind the grey beard. "Don't be daft, m'am. We've all done our bit. You and Doug have done as much as I have."

"We will have to agree to differ on that, Arthur."

Arthur finished his wine and looked around for a bottle. "Agreed."

"One more thing on the subject of food," said Lady Alice, "we also have a small plot of vegetables which are coming along nicely. In summary, we have started preparations for self-sufficiency, which I think is key to our survival, we must build on these preparations. More people living here means more mouths to feed, but it also means more hands to carry the load. It is the third week of July, there is plenty of summer left. We can plant more crops which will serve us both in the short term and to prepare for next spring. With the right planning and utilisation of resources, this community could not just survive, it could flourish."

"I'll drink to that," said Blaze. "If someone'll give me a refill."

Chapter 26. Purple Rain

The next item on the free-flowing agenda was the burning question at the very top of Georgie and Ant's top twenty: *What the hell happened?*

Georgie, a fresh notebook in front of her, clicked the button at the top of her pen and opened the discussion. "Anthony and I have wondered for a long time what caused people to turn, and why some people became mutes, sorry, *mutant*s, and others didn't." She looked at Lady Alice. "I think you answered at least half of that when you talked about that day. You said that everybody who was outside turned, and those who were inside didn't."

"That was our experience, yes. Anyone who was outside in that freakish downpour."

Georgie sat up. "Freakish?"

"Yes, it came up out of nothing, it was a clear day and suddenly the heavens opened, and the rain, well the only way I can describe it is that it seemed to be boiling. It only lasted for a few minutes then it was all clear again. And yes, we do think there is a link." Arthur nodded in agreement.

"Where I was," said Georgie, "there'd been heavy storms but they'd cleared by the Sunday morning." She thought for a moment, "But yes, I remember there was a sudden downpour during the day. It stopped nearly as soon as it had started. We were indoors and didn't pay much attention to it," she supressed a smile. "We were a bit… distracted." Ant tried not to turn green at the thought of her and Iqbal as Georgie continued, "I couldn't tell you what temperature the rain was. I didn't see any mutes afterwards but then I was on a tiny island with only a handful of people living there. Maybe nobody else was outside when it happened."

Blaze cut in. "A weird storm kicked off where we was too. Mum was outside the museum paying for the tickets…"

Georgie looked up from her note-taking. "Museum?"

Blaze looked confused by the question. "Fish museum. Anyway, while we was outside it was one of them nothing days, not sunny but not raining or nothing, not even cloudy really, just this boring white sky. Ronnie really needed a piss so they let me and him go in while mum stayed in the queue. When we came out of the lavs I could see it was proper hammering it down outside, it came out of nowhere just like the baroness said, and it was all, like *fizzing* when it landed. Shit started happening after that."

"I am not a baroness, please just call me Alice, but thank you, Blaze. That backs up our theory. What about you, Anthony? Can you make it four sudden toxic downpours out of four?"

Ant looked sheepish. "I was…"

Georgie cut him off, "He was out of it."

Lady Alice's brow furrowed. "Out of it? I'm not sure what you mean exactly."

"Let's just say he'd been over-indulging."

A smile formed on the older woman's face. "I see!"

"I had a fever," Ant muttered.

Lady Alice touched his wrist gently. "If you insist, my dear."

Ant didn't bother arguing.

Lady Alice turned her attention to Blaze. "What time did it happen?"

"About half past one."

"Exactly the same as here. Georgina?"

"Please just call me Georgie. And I couldn't say what time exactly, but that would sound about right."

"And you, young man, you cannot vouch for where you were because you had your fever."

Ant shook his head.

"It is limited evidence," Lady Alice continued, "but it is consistent. I think we can assume that whatever was in that rain caused anybody beneath it to turn into one of those creatures."

Frank squeezed Lewis's hand. "We didn't see anybody turn did we hun?"

Lewis pulled his hand away. "I'm surprised you saw anything. You ran away screaming."

Frank looked long and hard at his husband.

"No one else saw anybody turn," said Naomi. "We've discussed it over and over. The rest of us were already well inside the building when it happened. The zombies all came from outside."

"How did you get rid of them?" Ant asked.

"Most of the first wave left after the initial massacre," said Frank, "I don't know if it was because they thought there were easier pickings outside. We overcame the few that remained, although it was by no means easy. This young man..." he pointed at Blaze, "and Naomi too, they displayed incredible bravery, we owe our lives to them."

"We all pitched in," said Naomi.

Lewis made a show of turning his back on Frank. "This one didn't."

Naomi fixed her eyes on Lewis and repeated her statement. "We all pitched in."

Lady Alice spoke up. "If we can please focus on our main line of enquiry, we have evidence enough to conclude our simple theory that the storm caused people to change. Can we agree on that?"

"It's the best we've got for now," said Georgie.

"Forgive me," said Maria, "but I not see how knowing this way or that way helps us, unless we think the poison rain it is to happen again. Then we must stay inside."

Arthur spoke. "We tried that for a bit, but you can't stay indoors forever."

Lady Alice took up the point. "I talked earlier about the crops, the power, the fishing, all these tasks entailed going outside. We have to be careful, of course we do, but as Arthur says, we cannot keep ourselves cooped up, not just for practical reasons but for our physical and mental well-being. The human spirit does not take kindly to confinement, as I am sure those of you who were trapped inside that building can attest."

There were a few murmurs of agreement.

"And besides," the lady of the house continued, "I don't think it is going to happen again."

Maria wiped some ketchup from the corner of Sophia's mouth. "Hope you're right."

Lady Alice smiled at the little girl and looked up at her mother. "Arthur, Douglas and I have all been caught in the rain since it happened, and we have been unaffected."

"Same for me and Anthony," said Georgie.

"It is only when the hot poison rain comes," said Maria.

"The wrong kind of rain," said Frank.

Georgie spoke again. "The mutes are scared of rain. There has to be a connection."

That caught everyone's attention.

Georgie carried on. "They hate the rain. They run and hide from it. I've watched them do it many times."

Lady Alice's eyes sparkled. "That is a fascinating observation. That can only back up our working theory that the freak storms were responsible. What else have you observed? It feels as if you have a lot to share."

Georgie drew a line under the last thing she had written in her notebook. She thought for a while before speaking. "That's right, I have a lot to share, Ant does too, but you were right earlier, we need to stick to one line of enquiry at a time, otherwise we'll keep going off in different directions. That's what my brain was doing for the first few days of this and it did me no favours at all. For now, I think it's best that we stick to what we're discussing, the event itself. When we've finished that, then Ant and I will tell you everything we've learned about the mutes. Does that sound sensible?"

Lady Alice looked impressed. "It sounds very sensible indeed."

Georgie turned to a new page. "Good, now let's talk about the power going off."

"The electricity," said Arthur, "went off at half one, same time as the storm."

Frank nodded emphatically. "It was the same for us. The emergency lighting came on just before those things came pouring in."

Lady Alice saw that Georgie was chewing her pen and frowning. "Penny for your thoughts my dear."

"I was just going to say that there was no power cut where I was, but now I think about it, the house didn't have mains electricity. It was a zero-carbon place, which is why the shower wasn't great. It was all powered by wind I think, which makes sense because it was a really windy place. I remember Iqbal being very excited that it used alternative energy. What I'm trying to say is that the electricity probably went down on the island too, I just didn't notice."

Ant pushed his hair back, tucking it behind his ears. "It's sounding like it was some kind of natural disaster then, not a terrorist attack."

"Or a Bond villain," said Georgie.

"It still could have been man-made," said Lady Alice. "A storm that turns humans into monsters whilst simultaneously causing the National Grid to fail does not sound like a natural phenomenon."

Lewis let out a sigh. "All sounds a bit far-fetched to me."

"I'll say it does, lad," said Arthur, "but if you've got any other ideas then feel free to share."

Lewis folded his arms and said nothing.

Blaze leaned back in his chair. "While we're getting everything straight in our heads, we should agree on what to call them, the monsters I mean. The baroness says creatures, or things. Us lot have all been going with zombies and Ant and Georgie call them mutes."

Georgie glanced at Ant and smiled. "They're definitely not zombies."

Lady Alice cut in, not quite angrily but definitely impatient. "Feel free to decide between yourselves what to call them in your own time, I do not think we should trouble ourselves with that now. And again, I am not a baroness."

Ant turned to Lady Alice. "Have you had any attacks? Since that first day I mean."

"We have indeed. On three occasions."

Ant was impressed. He looked from Lady Alice to Arthur. "And you lived through them, you must have done something right."

"We were lucky," said Arthur. "They came in pairs. The most was a three. We picked them off easy, like we were shooting clay pigeons. We were most worried about the sound of the guns to be fair, didn't want to attract any more of the buggers."

"Sounds cool," said Blaze.

Arthur looked daggers at the skinny youth. "It most certainly weren't cool, son. Those things were people once."

It was obvious from Blaze's face that he still thought it was cool.

"Anyways," the old groundskeeper continued, "all the attacks came from the woods. That might be because it's the easiest way to get into the estate because there's no wall that way. Or it might be that they're living in those trees."

"You mean like monkeys?"

Arthur's eyes blazed at Blaze. "Are you trying to piss me off, lad? Because if you are I can tell you that you're doing very well."

Blaze held up his hands, his pockmarked cheeks red. "No mate, honest. I thought that's what you meant by them living in the trees."

Arthur wearily gave him the benefit of the doubt. "I meant living in the woods. On the ground."

"I get you."

"Glad to hear it." Arthur didn't look at all glad. "The point is that those woods are out of bounds. We've got more hands now so we'll look to put up some protection, but for now, stay away, it's not worth the risk."

Lady Alice patted Arthur's hand. "Thank you Arthur." She turned to Georgie and Ant. "I think it's time for you two to share with us what you have seen of these creatures if you'd be so kind."

Georgie and Ant hit play on their montage of mutant encounters.

They started at the end; Operation Sea Life. They described the army of mutants laying siege to the aquarium. Georgie explained how the creatures had shut down for most of the day, suggesting that they conserved energy that way, allowing them to go longer between feeds.

She described Ant's heroics delivering the walkie-talkie to the aquarium and the bizarre scene after the mutants had woken up and made like parents searching for their lost offspring.

She had no theories on that.

Georgie and Ant talked about the curious incident of Shy Mutant, the fire station employee. How she hadn't shown any signs of hostility towards them and how she seemed to be acting out her working routine; producing dockets for them to sign, looking up the training manuals. They wondered aloud if she had stuck to her vegan diet after she had turned.

They took their time over the reservoir story, ratcheting up the tension, trying to convey to their rapt audience the same level of shock they had felt when they were close enough to see that they hadn't discovered human survivors, but a community of mutants.

They described Farmer Mutant's visit and how he too seemed to be re-enacting his life before his transformation, but, unlike Shy Mutant who had given them the keys to Alpha Two, this one had gone ballistic and tried to kill Georgie.

Ant blushed a deep red as Georgie went into great detail about how he had saved her life and he moved the conversation on, describing the gashes on Georgie's arm and how it wasn't like in the films; you couldn't catch it from a scratch.

They described the mutant bodies they had found in the field, and their theory that the mother had killed her daughter in a mercy killing. This, Georgie explained, made them think that at least some mutants experienced emotion.

They didn't mention Woody Woodsman.

They described what they had encountered in every building they had visited on their travels: the human remains, what had been damaged, what hadn't. They explained why and how they had worked out that mutants only ate fresh meat, live or otherwise.

It already seemed like a dream to both of them, but they relived their close encounter at the lakeside commune and their thoughts on how it had made sense that fish would be their most obvious food source.

They recounted their escape from the first fire station, the experience of driving the engine out of town; how the mutants they had passed had been awake but had not bothered to chase them.

They talked about the mutants outside the morgue, their respective testimonies coming from very different perspectives; Ant from inside the tiny building and Georgie studying them from up on the drill-tower. Ant explained how talkative some of them had been, much more so than any they'd seen since, and how the first one who came to his flat had tried to catch him out.

Georgie blushed a deep red as Ant went into great detail about how she had saved his life.

Georgie revisited her point about the mutants' fear of the rain, listed her observations. She went into detail about the mutants going into shutdown mode, how it took them a while to wake up and how some individuals took longer than others. She warned that this was something to be wary of, that they had to be careful not to expect all of them to behave in the same way and make too many assumptions based on what they had seen. By way of example she pointed out the differences they had observed in different groups, how the ones outside the morgue had shut down in the same way to those outside the aquarium, but for much shorter periods, while the ones camped at the reservoir seemed much more active and may not have shut down at all, possibly because they had a regular food source.

Georgie did most of the talking but Ant helped wherever he could. The download of their experiences took a while, and there were almost no interruptions as they talked. When they had finished they felt drained, shattered, like they had endured an intense therapy session. It took them a few moments to get their heads back into the room and once they had, they realised that at some point they had taken hold of each other's hands and were still gripping tightly.

The room fell silent. Everybody around the table was staring at Georgie and Ant, most with their mouths cartoonishly open.

Frank was the first to start applauding and the others, even Lewis, were quick to follow. It became a standing ovation.

Georgie and Ant blushed a deep red.

Chapter 27. Gone fishin'

"This is where we buried them." Lady Alice pointed with the butt of her shotgun at a row of shallow graves.

Georgie, Ant, Naomi and Arthur had taken up Alice's offer of a walk around the grounds, leaving the rest of the occupants of the house, aside from Blaze and Ronnie, who had taken the morning watch, sleeping soundly. They were at the southern edge of the graveyard that sloped down from the imposing flint-grey twin towers at the front of the church.

Lady Alice stopped at the first grave of the neatly ordered row and knelt down. She reached into the front pocket of her blouse and carefully took out a daisy chain. She placed it on the mound of soil and made it into a circle with her fingertips. She stayed hunched over the grave for a while before standing up and crossing herself.

Georgie allowed what she thought was a respectful amount of time before speaking. "Your father?"

Lady Alice nodded, blinking away tears.

"I'm so sorry. Losing him would be bad enough, but what you went through, what you all went through. I can't imagine."

"Thank you my dear. And thank you for not uttering that monstrous platitude that people say."

Ant had to ask. "What do people say?"

"They say, 'sorry for your loss'. I cannot bear it when I hear that phrase. It is so impersonal. If someone wishes to express sympathy at the loss of a loved-one they should say something that expresses that sympathy properly, they should not use an off-the-shelf term."

Ant exhaled slowly with relief. He had been about to say that exact phrase.

Lady Alice gazed down at her handiwork. "One of my earliest memories is of daddy taking me for a walk in these grounds. It was a warm day just like this one. He had me on his shoulders and we stopped in a meadow further up the hill. He sat on the ground with me on his lap and he picked daisies and made them into a chain. I can distinctly remember being amazed at how his big fingers were able to make the tiny holes, and thread the stems through. I watched him make this beautiful thing for me and then he put it on my head, and…" she choked on the words, "…he told me it was a crown for his princess."

"That's beautiful," said Georgie.

"I still have it. I pressed it. It became our little tradition, every spring when the daisies started sprouting I'd make him a chain." She put her hand over her nose and mouth and closed her eyes tightly, holding in a sob. "He didn't make it to spring this year."

Arthur pitched in. "We wouldn't be standing here if it weren't for him. He stood up to them, he bought us valuable time."

"Yes, yes he did."

Arthur bent down and dropped a pine cone onto the next grave. If anybody was expecting an explanation they were disappointed. "That lot in there," he said, pointing at the house, "are gonna want a decent dinner tonight and I reckon us lot will too. I'm off to the river. I've got one spare rod, who's coming?" He was looking straight at Ant.

"I've never fished before."

"Well that's all the more reason you should come with me,

lad. You need to learn."

"I suppose so."

Arthur was already on his way out of the churchyard.

Ant called after him. "You mean right now?"

Arthur kept walking.

"Looks like I'm off." He turned to Georgie. "You okay with that?" Ant suddenly felt self-conscious. His relationship with Georgie hadn't followed what anyone would call a normal path. Since they had met they had never been apart. It felt weird to be leaving her now, which is why he had instinctively asked her if she minded. Now he just felt like a teenage kid who has been badgered by his mates into ditching his girlfriend to go to the park with them. "I mean," he stuttered, "I know you'd be okay with that, why wouldn't you be okay with that? I'm not saying you can't survive without me for a few hours, just, well, y'know…"

Lady Alice was loving it. "Try closing your mouth, young man, it'll help stop the words from tumbling out."

Georgie's smile told Ant that she understood. "I'll be fine." She took his hands. "You go and do your boy's stuff with your new bestie." She went onto tiptoes and kissed him. "See you in a while. I love you." She kissed him again.

"Love you too." Ant hurried after his new fishing buddy.

Arthur, his shotgun over his shoulder, led Ant along a well-trodden path to a bend in the river that ran along the eastern edge of the estate.

In Ant's head they were going to be sitting on the riverbank with their feet dangling over the water. He realised it was going to be a bit more civilised than that when he saw the wooden platform that extended from the bank.

Arthur went to a hut that was almost completely hidden by the bushes that grew wild around it. He unlocked the padlock of the slatted wooden door, covered entirely in green moss.

"Hold this open will you?"

Ant held the door while Arthur got the equipment together; folding chairs, a net, tackle box, holdall with various containers inside. He took out two rods, their reel and line already attached. "This one's yours," he said. "Let's go."

Arthur taught Ant how to attach the float and weights to the line, and how to tie the hook, making sure his student carried out each task himself. He showed Ant how to cast and after a few tangles Ant picked it up.

"You're ready," Arthur said after Ant's float had landed in the exact position he had been told to aim for. Ant felt a rush of pride. He was taken back to a time when he had scored a goal in a school football match and his dad had made a huge fuss of him afterwards. Arthur broke his reverie. "Let's get your hook baited, lad."

Ant had known when Arthur had pulled the lid off the plastic tub that whatever was inside wasn't going to be pretty, but the seething mass of maggots was still a disgusting surprise.

Arthur scooped up a handful of the writhing grubs. "This'll tell the fish it's time for breakfast." He threw them into the water.

The hook-baiting lesson was even more unpleasant.

"It's got a little beard, lad, just catch that with the point and it'll hang nicely."

Ant wasn't sure he could see the 'beard' that Arthur was talking about, but he aimed where he thought he meant. The hook skewed straight through the wriggling larva, bursting it open.

"Chuck that one in, try another."

"How do you, like, unthread it from the hook?"

That was the first time Ant saw Arthur smile. "You don't *unthread* it, lad, you pull it off. Like you're pulling a grape off its stalk. I don't think that little fella's coming back from this so let's not mess about. Just rip the thing off."

Ant took a deep breath and did as he was told.

He disembowelled seven more of the wretched creatures before he finally got the hang of it and watched the latest dangle in front of him as Arthur baited his own hook.

"You go first, lad."

Ant's cast was a good one, and Arthur expertly landed his own float ten feet away. Arthur sat down, laying his shotgun within reach, and Ant lowered himself carefully into the faded canvas of the decades-old garden chair.

Ant's hands felt slimy. "Don't suppose you've got any wet-wipes have you?"

That was the second time Ant saw Arthur smile.

The sun rose higher and the colours and sounds of their surroundings changed. Ant told Arthur about how there'd been no wildlife in the fields around the Coach House but then they'd seen the magpies and it had all started to come alive again. Arthur said the same had happened there, and now it was back in all its glory. Ant could hear in the Cornishman's voice how much he loved and respected nature, and as he sat by the gently flowing river in the shade of a tree, he was starting to see what all the fuss was about.

It dawned on Ant that he was feeling a sensation that had become very unfamiliar since the world had become a bad dream. He felt completely relaxed. He was happy just watching his float floating. "I could get used to this."

"There's worse ways to spend the day."

"How did you end up here, as groundskeeper I mean?"

"I grew up here, my old man had been the groundskeeper since God was a boy. When he snuffed it, the job fell to me. I don't remember it ever being talked about. It just happened. Mind you I've not been here the whole time. I've come and gone, for the army, see?"

Ant started doing mental arithmetic and realised that Arthur was looking sideways at him, his eyes narrowed against the sun.

"You're trying to work out which war I fought in aren't you?"

Ant laughed, blushing. "You got me, that's exactly what I was doing. I'm not sure what the etiquette is, is it rude to ask?"

"I don't know nothing about etiquette lad, and yeah, it's prob'ly rude to ask but it does no harm me telling you. The only proper action I saw, the type of action you'll be thinking about, was down in the South Atlantic."

"Falklands?" Ant remembered from his History classes.

Arthur scratched his beard. "That it be."

"What was it like?"

The old man let out a few feet of his line. "Now that, lad, is a very good question. It were horrible. It were cold, wet and it were frightening. We were a long way from home and the Argies'd got there a long time before us. Got themselves well settled they had."

Ant watched a dragonfly hover near the tip of his rod and fly away. "I can't imagine."

"No, you probably can't. But that's not all of it. Nasty as it were, and it were bloody nasty, it were also one of the best times I can remember. We all felt part of something. We were there to do a job for everyone back home and we did that job. I made friends for life in those short weeks." He hesitated. "Lost friends too."

"I'm sorry."

"Not your fault lad." Arthur stood up, reeled his line in and re-casted. "Something's gonna bite soon."

Ant scratched his ankle. "I think something's already bitten."

"Oh yeah, nasty them mozzies, think they've got fed up

with the taste of me over the years, they don't bother on me no more."

"Can I break etiquette again?"

"I told you, I don't know nothing about etiquette."

"Fair enough."

"You want to know if I've killed a man."

"Yeah," Ant conceded. "Yeah I do, sorry."

"Nothing wrong with being honest, lad. Yeah. I killed men. Not in the Falklands, at least I don't think so. But a long time after, in Bosnia."

"You fought in Bosnia too?"

"We weren't officially fighting there, they called it *peacekeeping*. I were more senior then, meant to be training some boys. But we got caught in the wrong place at the wrong time and, well, I suppose you'd call it an ambush."

Ant pulled a face. "Oh my God."

"I've never seen no god in a warzone, lad. I'll spare you the details but I had to take those boys out or they were gonna take me and my boys out."

"How many?"

"Two that I took care of. My mate, Coop, he took another one, and the others bolted. I often wonder what would have happened if they'd stuck around. I reckon it's best for everyone that they didn't."

"I can't possibly imagine what that would have been like."

The old man turned to face Ant. "Oh yes you can, son. You've done it. That lass you're with told us all about it."

Ant shook his head. "That was different. That wasn't a person."

"Oh yes it was, son. That was no different." He turned to look out at the river again. "No different at all."

They were silent for a long time.

"I've got to ask."

"You got a habit of introducing your questions, son. Just ask what you're going to ask."

"Okay, I'll just ask. What was that thing with the pinecone?"

Arthur smiled. "Well that's another good question. That was Maggie under there. Now, I never saw Maggie happier than when we were out with Lulu, our little border collie. She loved that dog, we both did, she were something special that one. Maggie were never happier than when she were out with Lulu, and Lulu were never happier than when there were pine cones on the ground. And that's because pine cones on the ground meant it was Lulu's favourite playtime. I'd scoop them up and I'd throw one, and Lulu would go running for it, then as quick as lightning she'd spin round and she'd be looking up at me for the next one, so I'd throw that and she'd be ready for the next and I'd throw that and, well, you get the picture lad. I'd be there tossing pine cones about, and in return my dog and my wife would show me what happiness looked like."

Ant wasn't a dog person and the story would have meant nothing to him if he hadn't been able to see the eyes of the man telling it. "What happened to the dog?"

"She had a name, lad. Lulu."

"I'm sorry."

"That's okay. But a word of advice, it does no harm to remember the name of a person's dog. It might mean nothing to you but it sure as hell means something to them." The chair creaked as Arthur shifted his position. "Anyways, we lost Lulu a year or so back. She was old and she was ready. I gave her the injection myself, it was the kindest way, it meant she had no idea, no stress, just kisses from her old dad and a little bit of a scratch." Arthur shuffled in his seat again. "It's the hardest thing I ever done in my life." His voice cracked a little. "Until the day Maggie turned."

It took a while for Ant to realise what the old man meant. "I'm so sorry."

Arthur caught eight fish that morning, six sea bass and two flounder.

Ant didn't have so much as a nibble.

"It'll come," the old man said as they walked back to the house, their gear packed away in the hut that was being swallowed by the bushes. He hoisted his shotgun. "We'll show you how to use one of these too. You ever had a go?"

Ant shook his head. "Georgie's your one for that, she's deadly."

"Good to know. That'll come in useful. As Madam Alice said, we don't use them unless we have to, they make such a bloody racket. But we need folk who can shoot." He gazed into the trees. "I don't think we've seen the last of them purple buggers."

Chapter 28. Ancient history

When Ant jilted them at the church, Lady Alice took Georgie and Naomi on a stroll around the graveyard, pointing out the headstones of her ancestors as they went. She was a good tour guide, colouring the walk with gossip and factoids about her forebears that had been passed down to her through the generations.

When they had covered all the resting places, Lady Alice gestured towards the church. "Shall we take a pew inside?"

They were about to go through the big oak doors when a copper plate on the wall outside caught Georgie's eye:

In memory of Sir Donald Ashcroft.

His body is across the sea but his soul will be here for eternity.

Georgie read the dates stamped at the bottom. "Is this for your husband?"

"It is indeed. We were unable to give Don a burial on account of his body being halfway up Kangchenjunga. Have you heard of it?"

"I'm guessing it's a mountain."

"Correct. Not the highest but tremendously difficult to climb as I understand."

"I'm so sorry."

"Don't be. I miss him of course, but I loved him and he loved risking his life on wild exploits. If he had stopped pursuing those exploits then he would have stopped being the man I loved, so I did not try to stop him. There was always a risk that it would end the way it did. Or it would be more accurate to say that it was more than a risk, it was a statistical probability. Don had the last laugh, though. When you and I and everybody else here are rotting in the ground, Don will be perfectly preserved on his mountainside, enjoying the view."

Georgie wasn't quite sure what expression to have on her face and she settled on a pained smile. "That is quite a thought."

Lady Alice looked up, shielding her eyes from the sun. "Until global warming makes the snow melt."

Naomi, who hadn't seemed interested in the conversation until then, surprised them both with her contribution. "Without the human race, climate change will no longer be a problem."

"That is a very astute observation," said Lady Alice, "and probably very accurate." She smiled.

Naomi didn't smile back. "The sooner the earth is rid of us, the better."

Lady Alice reached out to take Naomi's hand. "Are you okay my dear?"

Naomi pulled her hand away. "I'm sorry, I can't do this." She hurried down the narrow path and out of the churchyard.

Lady Alice turned to Georgie, baffled by what had just happened. "Do you think we should go after her?"

Georgie's response was emphatic. "Absolutely not. She needs to be on her own, we have to respect that. Chasing after her won't fix anything, it'll just make drama. I'm done with drama."

"I'm not so sure, she seemed quite upset."

"She'll talk to us when she's ready."

Lady Alice thought for a moment and then shrugged. "Okay my dear. I'll defer to your youthful wisdom on this one."

Inside the church Georgie's head immediately tilted

upwards to take in the impressive structure. The sweeping arches, the colour and detail of the stained glass, the intricate statues carved into the walls. "It's more like a cathedral."

"Well technically it is a priory but the monks left long ago, and nowadays it functions as a church. Well not so much *nowadays* but you see what I mean."

They walked slowly towards the alter and Georgie took a chair in the front row. "It's a shame we can't actually take a pew," she said.

Lady Alice sat beside her. "Indeed. They were removed some years back, rot had set in and replacing them would have been prohibitively expensive. It was also felt that chairs were easier to rearrange for different types and sizes of service." She shook her head, smiling and blushing. "I am so sorry. I am sure I already bored you with the potted history of my ancestors and now I am boring you with the background to the removal of the pews."

Georgie was smirking. "Not at all, it's all very fascinating."

Lady Alice clasped her hands together. "Thank you, my dear, I am not in the least bit convinced, but I appreciate the gesture."

Georgie gazed up at the figure of Christ crucified, almost life size, above the alter. "Are you religious?"

"No. Don and I were married here, and I would attend the services at Christmas and Easter, but only out of family duty. The scriptures leave too many unanswered questions for me to have any kind of faith. There are a good deal more unanswered questions now, most notably, was this part of His grand plan? And if it was, then the most obvious question that follows is *why?*"

Georgie's eyes stayed fixed on Jesus.

"My apologies dear, are you a believer?"

Georgie broke out of her semi-trance. "It's funny. I

actually see more reason to believe now than I ever did before, but no, I can't say that I think there's a deity watching over us. Please don't tell my parents, though." Her voice tailed off. "If that's even possible."

"Where are they?"

"It's most likely they aren't anywhere but there's a slim chance they could be on the coast, further west. That's where we were heading when we saw signs of life at the aquarium."

"I see, so this is something of a detour for you."

"I suppose so, but I'm very glad we took it. Finding the others, finding you, finding this place, it's changed everything."

"You are still going to try and find them though, your parents?"

Georgie nodded quickly. "Yes. I need to know either way."

"Tell me about them."

"What would you like to know?"

"Anything you think is worth telling."

"My father was a vet. I'm using the past tense not because I don't think he's alive but because I don't think that occupations count anymore. He was a local councillor as well. He was what you might call a pillar of the community, extremely well-respected. It meant that he didn't have much time for us, but it's like you said about your husband, mum knew how important it was to him so she didn't get on his case about it too much. I wished she did though. I wanted to see him more. Everybody called me *daddy's girl* when I was younger, which suggests we were close. We were in a way, I knew how much he loved me, but really I was just happy with any attention he could spare on me. It was unfair on mum, really. She paid the price for being the ever-present, she took all the flak from me. All my moods, all my dissatisfaction, it all went on her. Dad just had to throw a look my way and I'd turn into an angel."

"I'm sure she understood."

"I think she did, yes. And things changed as we all grew up anyway, for mum in particular. She'd always been the archetypal homemaker. Everything in her life was about her husband, her children, making life run smoothly and neatly for everyone. But after Jessie, my little brother, started uni, it was like she reinvented herself." Georgie searched for the right word. "Or perhaps she *found* herself. She signed up with a group and went trekking in the Andes for a month, and if you knew her that was the last thing you'd ever expect her to do. She suddenly became really active. She enrolled herself on a part-time degree course. Social Sciences, very broad. It covered politics, economics, a bit of criminology. She said she wanted to learn what made people tick, and what made society tick. It probably sounds like the old cliché, what they'd call a mid-life crisis in a man but they patronisingly put down to empty nest syndrome in women. Whatever it may sound like, I was proud of her, of the changes she'd made. It was like she was seizing life, taking her share. But it made me feel quite sad too. It made me realise that we'd never really seen her as a person before, a person with her own intellect, her own ambitions. She'd just been our mum. As we'd become teenagers, and like all teenagers thought we had the answers to the world's problems, it was dad we'd go to for the discussions, for the debates, never mum. We never considered that she might have an opinion."

Lady Alice touched Georgie's arm. "Do not worry yourself about it my dear, it is often the way. And a mother knows."

"Are you a mother?"

"I certainly hope I still am. Two girls, both of them with families of their own. One in Canada and the other in Argentina. You could say they are both in medicine, one became a surgeon and the other married one."

"They fell a long way from the tree then."

"They certainly did, there does seem to have been something of a wanderlust in their genes."

"Anthony and I have talked a lot about whether this thing has affected the whole world. It must be something you think about too, with your daughters so far away."

"Oh yes my dear. I have thought of little else. Unfortunately, the same practicality that makes me spurn the notion of a god leads me to believe that this cannot merely be a local problem. If other countries were unaffected then we would have been made aware of it by now."

"I think you're right."

"Will you be moving on soon then, to find your parents?"

"Not sure if *moving on* is the right term. We'll go to the cabin to see if they're there, but we'll come back. If we find them, we'll bring them back here." Georgie hesitated, "if that's okay with you of course."

"Oh yes, my dear. The more like-minded souls that live here, the better."

Georgie frowned. "What do you mean by *like-minded* exactly?"

"Nothing sinister my dear! I do not mean that we have to share the same political views, favourite colour and whatnot. I mean that we need people who are able to cooperate with each other. If we maintain a community then we have a much better chance, both of survival and of a certain quality of life."

Georgie considered this for a while. "What if people turn up and want to live here who aren't like-minded, who don't want to cooperate?"

Alice suddenly looked all of her fifty-two years. "Now that, my dear, is an extremely good question. I wish I had an answer to it."

Chapter 29. Blaze on the roof

From his lookout post Blaze watched Naomi leave the churchyard. She looked like she was in a rush even though there was nowhere for her to go. She walked down the slope to the wall at the bottom edge of the estate and put her hands flat against the stone in front of her. Blaze thought she was going to try and climb it, which would be impossible, it was far too high, but she just lowered her head and stood there, like she was praying. He watched her turn to her right and walk slowly along the edge of the grounds and back up towards the other side of the house. Blaze crossed the roof to keep watching but he lost sight of her as she passed underneath.

Blaze liked Naomi. Where he came from, the word 'respect' was used a lot. It was used so much that it didn't really mean much anymore. But Blaze had plenty of respect for Naomi. He knew he could look after himself, but Naomi, she could not only look after herself but everybody else too. When they'd been stuck in that hole it had been Naomi who'd kept them going. She'd been like a saint, like that Mother Teresa. That is, Blaze thought, if Mother Teresa had been hot, and proper hard.

But she'd seemed different since they'd got out.

One of Blaze's earliest memories was from before his dad had popped out for a swift half and never come back. Blaze was a few years older than Ronnie was now. The London Marathon was on the telly and Blaze remembered that with about five miles to go, the guy who'd been in the lead the whole time suddenly stepped off the course and stopped while the other leaders kept on going. Blaze had been confused. His dad had told him that the guy was called a 'pacemaker', that it was his job to put in the effort to get his team-mates up to the right speed and then, when he was knackered, he stopped. Blaze had wondered what was in it for the pacemaker. He was obviously a good runner and if he'd gone a bit slower to start with then he could have been in with a shout of winning, but he'd agreed not to go for the glory. He'd burnt himself out so his mates could benefit.

That memory had stuck with Blaze over the years. He'd realised that his dad probably hadn't known about pacemakers any more than Blaze had, he'd just repeated what he'd heard the commentator saying so his son would think he knew his shit. Blaze's dad always wanted people to think he knew his shit, like it was a weakness if he didn't.

Blaze thought now that Naomi was like that pacemaker. She'd kept them moving, kept them up to the speed they needed to be going. Now she'd done what was needed she'd burnt herself out. She'd stepped off the track. Blaze didn't have too much to go on, but he was worried about Naomi. He decided he'd try and talk to her, even though talking to women wasn't what he was best at.

Blaze liked it on the roof. He liked the views and he liked the silence. He liked being up as high as the trees. Blaze had never really paid much attention to trees, never really looked. But he was looking now and he liked what he saw.

He liked the feeling of doing his bit too. If anyone or anything showed up on the grounds then it would be down to him to raise the alarm. He was responsible.

When he'd taken over the shift from Douglas, Blaze had asked if he could have a shotgun. The answer had been no.

He'd been told that until he'd been shown his way around a gun he should leave any shooting to what Blaze called *the aristos*; Lady Alice, Douglas and Arthur.

Blaze already knew his way around a gun, he knew it wasn't hard, you just pointed it and you pulled the trigger. The trick was to brace yourself, to be ready for what's coming so you can hold steady when the thing goes bang. Blaze also knew that the reason he hadn't been given a gun was nothing to do with him needing to learn how to use one, it was because the aristos weren't ready to arm their guests just yet. There'd been plenty of good vibes around that dinner table, a ton of talk about the new community, about everyone pulling together for a bright shining tomorrow, but nice though all that big, warm talk was, Blaze knew that they were still just two groups of strangers who had no idea what the others had in their locker.

Blaze didn't blame the aristos for holding back; if he'd been in their shoes he wouldn't have handed out the hardware straight away either. It made sense that they'd have to earn each other's trust, he got that.

The drill to follow, if he saw something, was to get on the radio straight away. If nobody answered, which he'd been told would never happen because the aristos had a radio each and knew to have them switched on, Blaze would use the megaphone. He'd been told which way was north and they'd tested him on where that meant south, east and west was so he'd be able to say where the danger was coming from without any messing about.

While he'd slowly done laps of the roof, watching and waiting, there'd been plenty of time for Blaze to imagine a whole range of possible attack scenarios. He'd come to the conclusion that if they were serious about defence, then shotguns weren't going to cut it. For starters, if the mutants came mob-handed then having to reload after every two shots would get old very quickly. And that wasn't the only problem; Blaze knew a bit about guns and he knew that a shotgun was only good up to about fifty yards. That would be about as useful as a paper crash helmet if mutants came pouring over the wall.

He decided he'd take it up with the old guys; Douglas and Arthur, suggest they change up. It would mean a mission outside to get what they needed, not that Blaze had any idea where they'd be able to get the sort of firepower he had in mind, this wasn't downtown LA. The only thing he could come up with was a military base, but getting inside a military base, even one where everyone's been eaten, would be easier said than done.

He'd take it up with the old guys anyway, see what they thought.

Blaze had been surprised by Ronnie's reaction to being on the roof, he thought he'd have been a pig in shit up there but he hadn't seemed fussed at all. He'd tried to get him into it. He'd pointed out landmarks and tried to get Ronnie to say what he thought they were, but Ronnie hadn't wanted to play so he soon gave that up. It made Blaze miss their mum. She'd have got Ronnie interested; she was good at all that stuff. She would have come up with a game, a proper game, a better game than 'Do you know what a water tower is?' She'd have had Ronnie clapping and laughing away. She hadn't always been good at that stuff though. There'd not been any games when Blaze was a kid. There hadn't been much of anything when Blaze was a kid. Blaze missed out on his mum being a good mum because it took her a long time to get there.

Blaze hadn't known the word 'enabler' when his dad lived at home and he hadn't heard of 'controlling behaviours' either. When Blaze's mum drank, she'd get crazy. If her shouting didn't wake up the entire block, then the noise of her smashing anything she could get hold of would. And Blaze's dad always made sure there was plenty of booze in the house. There was no money for new stuff for Blaze, if he asked he'd be told they didn't have a pot to piss in. But there was always plenty of piss for the pot.

Whenever Blaze's mum went nuts, his old man would come into his own. He'd shout, he'd give her a slap, he'd tell her it was all over, that he was out, and Blaze's mum would collapse. She'd go all desperate and weepy and beg for forgiveness. She'd swear that she'd be good for him, that she'd behave herself if he'd give her another chance. And Blaze's old man would say he didn't believe her. He'd make her persuade him.

Blaze didn't say at the time but he was glad when his dad had done a runner.

His mum took it badly, really badly.

It was Blaze who found her. He was ten years old. He didn't know why he'd woken up in the small hours of that Sunday morning and he didn't know how he'd known something was up, but he'd known. He found her on the bathroom floor, curled round the toilet. She'd been there a while, lying in her own sick. Whenever he looked back on that night he wondered how he'd not woken up earlier on, while she'd been puking all that up, it wasn't a big flat and she must have made plenty of noise. At first he'd been sure she was dead but then she'd moved when he shouted her name, not much but enough to show that she'd heard him. The house phone had been cut off months before and Blaze's mum was too far out of it to unlock her mobile, so Blaze had gone out into the hallway and knocked on doors until someone had answered his cries for help.

He spent time in care while his mum got her act together, and fair play to her, she really did get her act together. She didn't cut out the drinking completely, instead, and Blaze thought this was probably harder than stopping altogether, she started drinking like normal people drank. She'd have a few glasses of wine on a Friday night or maybe a gin, but she'd stop before it got too much, before it got nasty. She wouldn't smash it back and get psycho-drunk like before.

Soon after Blaze moved back in with his mum she'd got serious with another guy and he'd moved in too. Blaze could see his sort straight away. He was just like his dad, had to be right, had to be the one talking all the time, couldn't say anything nice to anyone, especially not Blaze or his mum. It looked to Blaze like it was going to go just like it had before, different guy, same story, repeat to fade. But Blaze was wrong. His mum took the guy's shit for a while, and Blaze had to take it too, but then Ronnie came on the scene and something in his mum seemed to change overnight. It was like she was a washing machine, recalled by the manufacturer because of a faulty part. His mum had been taken back to the factory to get fixed so she wouldn't catch fire.

Just like Blaze's mum had decided she wasn't going to be a car crash on booze anymore, she'd made up her mind that she wasn't going to be pushed around by dickhead guys anymore either. And that was it. She didn't give the guy a *this is how it's going to be now* speech, she just told him that she and her boys didn't want him in their lives and that he needed to do one.

Blaze could have been jealous of Ronnie for getting so much better from their mum than he had, but he wasn't, he was grateful. He was grateful to his dad, too, and to Ronnie's old man, they'd taught him a lot about people. They'd taught him that the guy who talks the loudest usually ends up with nobody listening to him.

Yeah, Blaze thought as he looked out at the trees, his mum definitely would have made Ronnie see how cool it was to be on the roof.

That Romanian Lady, Maria, had come up a little while after Blaze and Ronnie had got up there. She'd said her little girl, Sophia had wanted to see Ronnie, but Blaze got the feeling that she had another reason for coming up. Maria was old, maybe thirty, but Blaze thought she was in good shape. He thought Naomi was hotter, but Naomi was older, and Blaze knew she would just see him as a kid, even though the old rules were out of the window now there were less people to go around.

He was a big fan of that one from the new couple, too. That Georgie. He liked that look, Indian or Arabian or whatever - Blaze wasn't too fussed about the geography. She was off limits though. She was well into the Viking guy. And fair play to them both, Blaze knew he'd be dead without them.

The Romanian lady was more in Blaze's range, he had more of a chance with her. When she'd come up with her kid she'd been friendly but she'd been shy as well, like she was nervous. Blaze had taken that as a sign that she was into him. They'd got on okay when they'd been in the Fish Museum but everything was different in there, it wasn't a place for copping off. When Maria had come up they'd chatted for a while and it had looked to Blaze that she wanted to stay longer, but her kid had kept on tugging at her arm and whining for them to go back downstairs. The little girl had asked if they could take Ronnie with them and it had looked like Ronnie was up for it, so Blaze had said it was okay.

Blaze had a good feeling about Maria.

He looked out to the woods, which the aristos had told him were at the north side of the building. Something caught his eye, something moving, and he was ready for it to kick off. But it was just Lewis, that bratty one who gave his husband grief all the time. He was walking into the woods.

Mute

"Everyone's out and about today," Blaze said out loud.

Chapter 30. Rock bottom

Naomi didn't know what to do with herself. She didn't want to talk to anybody and she didn't want to be anywhere. She felt trapped, not by the confines of the estate walls, which technically she *was* trapped inside, but by the confines of her own head.

Walking hadn't helped. Walking had made it worse. Walking had underlined the fact that she could go anywhere and it wouldn't make the slightest bit of difference; wherever she went she would be carrying her sack of despair with her.

She had tried to rationalise what she was feeling. She knew that if she could convert the general cloud of dread into real things, actual specific problems, then she could take each one on, prioritise and action them like tasks on a project plan. But severe though her problems were (including the fact that everybody she knew and loved was dead or had become a monster), she didn't think those problems warranted the level of hopelessness that she felt.

Panic bubbled up inside her again and again. She choked it down each time but it just fizzed up again like some emotional acid-reflux. She had never felt anything like this before and she didn't know what to do. She knew she should probably talk to somebody, but just the thought of interacting with another person made her feel ready to throw up. And even if she could talk to somebody without being sick, there was no way she would be able to convert the mess that was inside her head into

anything approaching a conversation.
   Naomi kept walking.

Chapter 31. Drama

Blaze was surprised it was Lady Alice who came up to take over his shift. He thought that keeping watch would have been too menial for her, or more accurately, he thought that *she* thought that keeping watch would have been too menial for her.

Lady Alice didn't bother with any pleasantries. "Have you seen Lewis or Naomi?"

"Yeah. I saw Naomi, at about one. And Lewis just after that."

Lady Alice looked at her watch, her face pinching into a scowl. "That's three hours ago?"

"Yeah."

"Where did they go?"

"Naomi didn't go nowhere. She came from the church and she went down there." He pointed at the perimeter wall. "Then she came back up again. I think she went into the house."

"You *think*?"

"Well she got pretty close and then I couldn't see her no more cos of the angle. Like when you're on the top floor of the bus and it stops at the lights and a bike comes up the inside and you can't see it cos you can't see straight down through the window."

Lady Alice didn't let on that she'd never been on a bus. "That's the last you saw of her?"

"Yeah."

"She's not in her room."

"Yeah I guessed that, else you wouldn't be asking me where she'd gone."

"And what about Lewis?"

Blaze gestured with his thumb over his shoulder. "He went up there, into the woods. Where the grass is all worn down."

"Three hours ago."

"Nearly, yeah."

"And you didn't think to tell anyone?"

Blaze's eyes narrowed. "Listen, *lady*, I was looking out for things coming from outside, like them monsters, I didn't know I was meant to be keeping track of our lot."

Lady Alice rolled her eyes and held up a hand to stop him talking. She pulled a radio from her belt and spoke slowly and clearly. "Lewis took the dog-walk path into the woods soon after one pm. Naomi was seen outside just before that but it is not known where she went. Over." The response was too buried in static for Blaze to make it out, but Lady Alice's ears were obviously better tuned in. "Yes, I will let you know if I see anything. Over and Out."

"How come this is such a big deal?" said Blaze. "They've just gone for a walk."

"You said it yourself, young man. There are monsters out there. Real, live monsters. So yes, it is a *big deal* as you put it."

Arthur, Ant, Georgie and Frank were downstairs with Douglas. They had all heard what Lady Alice had said on the radio. Frank had been crying and looked like he was about to start again. Georgie had a hand on each of his shoulders, trying to keep his attention while she talked to him. "What exactly did he say?"

"He said 'what's the point of a sugar-daddy when money doesn't matter anymore?'"

"Yes," said Georgie, "you already told us that, but what did he say about where he was going?"

"You see what that means? He's saying I don't serve a purpose anymore."

"Yes, I get it, it's a rotten thing to say. But where did he say he was going?"

Frank looked at the floor. "Just that he was going away from me."

"And when was this exactly?"

"One o'clock."

"Did he mention Naomi?"

"No."

"Has he mentioned her before?"

Frank looked up again. "What do you mean?"

Georgie was struggling to keep her voice controlled. "I mean that she's been gone for the same amount of time as he has so I'm trying to work out if they might be together."

"What do you mean, *together*?"

Georgie felt like shaking him. "I mean exactly what it sounds like, are they in each other's company, are they in close proximity to each other, are they together?" Georgie realised her tone had gone up more than a notch and she forced herself to lower it. "Please, Frank, we just need to work out where they are. It's not safe out there."

"Don't you think I know that?"

Georgie relaxed her grip on Frank's shoulders. "Of course, I'm sorry."

"I'm the one who's sorry." Frank swallowed hard. "He's a drama queen, always storming off, and I always go after him. It's exactly what he wants. This time though, after what he said I decided I wouldn't follow him. I'd show a bit of pride for once." His face twisted as he fought back more tears. "I just thought he'd be somewhere else in the house. If only I'd gone after him, if only I'd stopped him."

"It's okay, Frank, it's going to be okay. We're going to find him."

Douglas's voice cut across Georgie's reassuring words. "I'm not so sure about that, young lady. They might come back, and I hope they do, but we're not going to find them, because we're not going to go looking. It's far too risky."

Georgie turned to Douglas, ready to disagree, but Arthur stepped in. "Doug's right, if they've chosen not to come back then we're not going to find them. And if it weren't their choice not to come back then what we'll find of them won't be worth finding."

Georgie looked to Ant for backup. Ant looked very awkward. "I'm sorry babe but I don't think we can risk it. We can't keep putting our necks on the line. They chose to go."

At first, Georgie couldn't believe what she was hearing. She felt betrayed, humiliated. But as she looked at Ant's face, heavy with its solemn apology, she knew he was right. She pulled Frank close. "I'm sorry," she whispered. "I'm so sorry." She let go.

Frank looked at her in shock before turning on Douglas, his eyes narrowing into angry red slits. "I hope you're happy. This is exactly what you wanted, one less freak of nature in your family home." Frank turned to Arthur, then Ant, and back to Georgie before shaking his head in disgust and making for the door.

"Where are you going?" Georgie called after him.

"Where do you think?" Frank slammed the door behind him.

Douglas was happy to see him leave. "Just let him go if he wants to. It's his funeral."

But Georgie and Ant were already at the door.

They were both surprised at how quickly Frank covered

the ground and they were well into the woods by the time they had caught up. Frank did his best to keep ahead of them, zigzagging between and around trees, but Ant had a quarter of a century on him and brought him down with a diving rugby tackle. Ant, sitting on Frank's legs to make sure he didn't go anywhere, tried to explain why it was crazy to go searching these woods. Frank kicked and thrashed, and Ant was finding it hard not to use excessive force, when Frank's body went limp and he fell silent. He was looking at something between the trees. Ant craned his neck to see what it was but he didn't have the same angle as the older man. "What is it?" he asked.

Georgie answered for him, her hand over her mouth. "Jesus."

Ant released Frank, stood up and peered between the trees.

In his haste to stop Frank from going after Lewis, Ant had forgotten all about Naomi.

He wouldn't forget her again in a hurry.

She was hanging from a tree, her arms slack at her sides, her bare toes a yard above the ground. It wasn't until they got closer that Ant could make out what it was that stretched between her neck and the branch above. Naomi obviously had the same curtains in her room as he and Georgie did in theirs. He recognised the black and gold rope of the tie-back cord cutting into Naomi's throat.

Nobody knew what to say. They just stood and looked at Naomi's slowly rotating body like visitors to a macabre art gallery.

Frank pulled himself out of his daze. "I've got to find Lewis," he muttered. He stole a glance at Georgie and Ant, saw that they no longer had the will to give chase, and hurried further into the woods.

Georgie and Ant didn't move.

Ant had never thought about the mechanics of suicide, but now as he looked at Naomi's lifeless body he couldn't think of anything else.

A short but thick stub of branch stuck out from a point low on the tree. Ant made an educated guess that this would have been Naomi's first foothold as she'd started the climb. He looked at the next branch up, where her left foot would have gone, and the branch up on the right, which she'd have used to steady herself as she shifted her body weight to the higher position. He continued to recreate Naomi's last moments and wondered whether, once she was sitting on the final branch, which he presumed she had chosen for its thickness and height off the ground, she had tied the cord around the branch first, or around her neck. He tried to imagine what had been in her mind in those last moments; if she had been scared as she pushed herself off into nothingness, or if she had just felt relief.

Ant's reconstruction was interrupted by the sound of footsteps moving quickly and in their direction from deeper in the woods in front of them.

And the same sound from behind.

They edged together, standing hand in hand in the moving shadow of Naomi's corpse, regretting not picking up weapons when they hurried after Frank. They saw the mutant coming from in front of them. It was fifty yards away, making its way over and around the thick roots of the ancient trees that warped the already uneven ground. It was a woman, or had been once, tall and thin with long red hair. It was shouting but they couldn't make out the words, like a street-drinker ranting in the small hours.

They could hear that whatever was coming from behind was closing in on them too. They didn't want to look because they didn't want to know, but they turned and they looked.

And they saw Douglas running at them, the blood vessels

on his face nearly bursting from the effort. He shouted for them to get down and they did as they were told. The country squire ran between them, on a collision course with the screaming mutant, a collision that was only averted by Douglas raising his shotgun and giving the creature both barrels, the first in the chest and the second full in the face.

The creature fell to the ground, its head only vaguely connected to its body.

Douglas, standing over the dying mutant, snapped open his gun and plugged in fresh cartridges. "We need to go, now."

Leaving Naomi hanging, Georgie and Ant started following Douglas back through the trees towards Hoxley House but the sound of another shotgun blast somewhere in the woods stopped them in their tracks. "That was Arthur," said Douglas. Georgie and Ant had no idea which direction it had come from but Douglas was a human gundog. "This way," he barked. As they followed him back into the woods they heard another shot. It was dead ahead, confirming the accuracy of Douglas's senses, and was followed by a mutant-screech that set the inside of their heads down the same path of logic:

At least one mutant was still alive.

Arthur had fired twice, he needed to reload.

The path they were following, if it could even be called a path, narrowed between dense walls of hawthorn and they were forced into single file. Douglas, still leading, held his gun upright in front of him like a guard on parade as the brambles whipped his elbows. The path widened into open woodland and they could see figures moving ahead of them, indistinct at first, just flashes of colour between the trees, but as they got closer the scene became clearer:

Five figures. Two on the ground, not moving. Two others, both male, one of them a mutant, the other, a human, naked from the waist up, fighting to the death. The fifth and last figure was Arthur, standing at the edge of the clearing that played host to the gruesome scene. Arthur prodded his rifle ahead of him as he ducked and bobbed, trying to find the angle to take a shot at the mutant without killing its opponent.

As it dawned on the three onlookers who the shirtless man was, he plunged his knife into the mutants throat and kicked it to the ground, bringing his foot down hard on the creature's chest to keep it in place while it died, howling in pain and anguish.

By the time they reached the scene the thing was dead.

Blaze, the knife shaking in his trembling hand, stepped back from the body. He was covered with blood, some of it from the mutant but plenty of his own; oozing from the scratches, gashes and bite marks on his face, arms and torso.

Arthur lowered his gun. "Strong work, lad."

Georgie, Ant and Douglas could now see that the two figures on the ground were Lewis and Frank. It was obvious that one of them wouldn't be getting up again.

Chapter 32. Progress

I used to wonder if I'd ever fall in love, and then I go and do it twice in the space of a few months. And to two men who couldn't be more different.

I'll never know how things would have turned out with Iqbal in the long-term. That future was stolen from us. But now there's Anthony and who knows if we'll even manage to stay alive for the long-term, let alone stay together.

I don't know why it works with Anthony; it just does. That's not true. I know exactly why it works with Anthony. It works because he's funny and he's kind. And this isn't a quality I would have particularly looked out for in a man before, but it certainly is now: he's the bravest person I've ever met.

And I love him.

That's why it works.

I've heard the line 'they make me a better version of myself' in the bride or groom's speech at more weddings than I can count, and I always thought it was overblown sentimentality. But now I can see what they were all talking about. I know it's the same the other way around too, I make Anthony a better version of himself. And that's not me being big-headed, it's the simple truth. I've seen him grow in the short time I've known him, seen him rise to every challenge. I don't know how either of us would have survived in this mess had we not found each other. We've both needed to be the best versions of ourselves to get past everything that's been put in front of us. But we've done it, we've overcome every single obstacle. And I think we've only been able to do that because we've been together.

And to think I wasn't sure about him at first. To think I thought he wasn't my type.

It's been six weeks since we started this… what should I call it? *Community*, that's it. It's tempting to say that the Ashcrofts were generous for letting us stay in their home, but I don't think that's really true. The arrangement benefited them at least as much as it did us, possibly even more. I'm not sure it's right to call Hoxley House their home anymore either. The idea of ownership, not just of property but of anything, is very different now.

There should have been twelve of us, but we're down to ten since what we call 'that day in the woods.' When I say that's what we call it, that's only if we ever mention it, and we hardly ever do, especially not in front of Lewis.

Lewis knows that Frank would still be alive if he hadn't gone flouncing off that day, he doesn't need us reminding him. Although Douglas does take it upon himself to remind him from time to time.

While we're on the subject of blame:

"Chasing after her will only make drama."

Those words I said to Alice when Naomi left us in the churchyard that morning will haunt me for the rest of my life. I've tried talking to Alice about it but whenever I do she just gives me her stock answer: she says that what happened was Naomi's choice, that nothing we could have done would have made a difference. I couldn't disagree more, we could have talked to her for a start, asked her what was wrong, but Alice won't let me have that debate, she just shuts me down.

Maybe it isn't a debate I want. Maybe it's a Confession. Maybe there's a part of me that thinks if I get to say out loud that I could have stopped Naomi from killing herself, and have someone agree with me, then it will somehow allow me to move on. But everyone's trying so hard to protect my feelings they won't give me that, not even Anthony.

And especially not Blaze. Blaze has his own claim to blame. He says he'd noticed that something was wrong with Naomi but hadn't got around to doing anything about it. I found myself answering him with the same nobody-could-have-done-anything platitude that Alice had spooned out to me. There is no way of knowing if anything we could have done could have stopped Naomi from doing what she did. All that we can do is learn from this and just do everything we can in future to make our achievements outweigh our regrets. That's what I said to Blaze. I don't know where all that from, it sounds like it came from a self-help book.

It sounds, as Anthony would say, like utter bullshit.

Even if Blaze was responsible in some small way for Naomi's death, he's already gone a long way to making up for it. He saved Lewis's life that day, and Arthur said he would have been next if Blaze hadn't arrived on the scene, stripped to the waist and leaping at the mute with his knife flashing, like Tarzan doing battle with a rogue leopard.

The drama hadn't ended with the dead mute at Blaze's feet. We had no way of knowing if more were coming and we had to get Lewis back to the house before he died from his assorted wounds, most worryingly a gaping hole in his right thigh that pulsed horribly with overflowing blood. Arthur had stepped in, and with a calm authority that he'd apparently picked up on the battlefield, he tore a tourniquet from his shirt and used it to stem the flow, before he and Douglas picked up Lewis's barely conscious body and carried him back to the house where they proceeded to save his life. They actually sewed him up with a needle and thread. It was disgusting, and awful. And amazing.

I thought that Arthur had shot Frank, not deliberately of course but by mistake while he was trying to take out the mute but I found out later that I'd got that wrong. Arthur had missed with both shots, probably because he was trying so hard *not* to hit Frank. It was the mute that did it, Frank hadn't stood a chance.

Blaze was able to walk, unaided as they say, back to the house, and we were all astonished and hugely grateful that his injuries, once the blood and the muck had been cleaned off, weren't at all serious. It did take a while, though, for Anthony and me to convince him that it wasn't like in the films; the bites and scratches weren't going to turn him into a crazed mutant. After Maria had been told what had happened she set about Blaze like a wife to a returning war-hero, insisting she was going to give him round the clock care. I saw the look in her eyes, and in Blaze's too, and offered to have Ronnie and Sophia sleep in our room that night.

Anthony forgave me. Eventually.

I still can't stop thinking about Naomi, about what she must have been going through to do what she did. Ant and I went back into the woods to get her. Alice and Arthur tried to stop us, telling us how risky it was, but we knew we couldn't leave her out there. It wouldn't have been right. I'll never forget her eyes; they were still open. So full of sadness.

We buried her in the churchyard, the last place anyone had spoken to her. The place where I let her walk away.

We put Frank next to her. After Lewis' battle surgery all he would talk about was how he was going to go and get Frank as soon as he could stand up. Alice and Arthur argued even harder with Lewis than they had with Ant and me; Frank was further into the woods than Naomi had been, it was crazy to think about bringing him back. Nobody saw Douglas leave but he was gone for two hours. I can't believe he moved that dead weight on his own.

Since that day, security has been our top-priority and we've been busy doing whatever we can to help us sleep a little more soundly each night. We know the grounds of the estate are far too large to secure completely, so we've allocated our limited resources to the areas where we think they'll have the most effect.

We've strung rows of barbed wire, recycled from neighbouring farmland, tightly between the trees at the edge of the woods. We know it's not impenetrable, and anyone who has their mind set on getting through could climb over if they were careful, or just take a longer route and go around. But we're hoping that whatever minds would be set on getting to us aren't particularly sound, and their owners not particularly careful.

Where the ground floor windows have shutters, we've bolted them, and where they haven't, we've boarded them over. It's the end of August and it's still hot, so we'd all rather have the windows open, but it's either that or risk mutes getting in.

We've stepped up the lookout duties too. There are two people on the roof at any time and a pair of us walk round the grounds three times a day to check for anything we should be worried about.

The estate already had security cameras but the screens were out in the gatehouse. We've moved everything inside, set up a control room in one of the spare bedrooms and hooked it all up to a generator. There's somebody at the desk at all times, linked by walkie-talkie to whoever is on the roof. If anything comes for us we'll know about it.

On the hour, every hour, whoever is on shift in the control room has to work their way through all the radio channels to check for any activity, then record it in a log like the ones you used to get in pub toilets saying when they'd last been cleaned. When I'm on duty I check the radio the whole time. I find the white noise quite therapeutic while I'm staring at the monitors. I roll the dial from one end to the other and slowly back again, then flick to the next frequency and go again.

Nobody has ever heard anything on the radio.

I've been worried for the children. I can't imagine what any of this could have been like for them but they've been amazing. They've just got on with it. I think it's helped that Blaze and Maria have coupled up. The two of them have been almost inseparable since that day in the woods. I use the word 'almost' because we've insisted on splitting them up for lookout and patrol duties; we'd never forgive ourselves if we all had our faces eaten off because our security guards were busy eating each other's faces off.

Ronnie seems to share his half-brother's adoration of Maria, and Sophia sees Ronnie as the little brother she always wanted. I won't pretend to be a child-psychologist but I'm sure this convenient arrangement won't fix the trauma of what those little ones have been forced to live through. But it seems to work for now, and that's all anybody can hope for.

As for the rest of us; the grown-ups, it's been surprisingly harmonious.

There has been plenty of work to go around and everyone has done their fair share, including Lewis, who's been something of a revelation. He's completely unrecognisable from the brat I met that first day, polite, friendly and always first to volunteer for any job that's going, however dirty or dangerous it might be. He was disappointed when Anthony, Douglas and Arthur wouldn't let him go with them on an expedition into the outside world to pick up supplies. Luckily when they got to the retail park they didn't see a soul, human or mute, and they all came back safe and sound, but Lewis wasn't to know that when he put himself forward, anything could have been waiting for them out there.

Perhaps this is his way of working off his guilt. Just as I wanted my Confession and subsequent absolution, perhaps this is Lewis's penance for his role in Frank's death. Whatever the reason, his eagerness to please has been welcomed by all of us. Even Douglas has cut him some slack. In fact, if I didn't know any better, I'd say the two of them were forming something approaching a friendship.

It's a strange world we're living in.

Maria's taken on the role of house hairdresser. She's not been trained or anything, she said she learned from her mum. She's not half-bad either, especially after the boys brought back some proper scissors and clippers from their shopping mission. We're all a lot less worried about our appearance these days for obvious reasons but I have to admit that I do feel really nice after having a trim. Ant says that Maria's a bit much when she's doing his hair, he says she deliberately pushes herself up against him. I told him that she does that to me too. I'm not sure if he was appalled or excited by that.

It's good that there are nice little things like getting a haircut to lift our spirits, because otherwise life here is something of a grind. With only eight adults and so much work to be done to protect and feed the community it's a struggle for everybody.

It's going to be even more of a struggle when that number goes down to six.

It would have been sensible for Ant and me not to have got so involved with these people, to have taken a back seat in the workings of the community. That would have made it a lot easier to leave. Or maybe just a little less difficult. But that was never going to happen. As it is, we've become major players in this fledgling human society, particularly Anthony. Everybody loves him. And without wanting to sound conceited, they seem pretty keen on me too. We've definitely made our mark here.

It would be so much easier if we hadn't.

We've not told anybody yet but we're leaving in a week. I'm trying not to feel guilty, there's no reason I should. We can put our hands on our hearts and say we've done more than our fair share in getting this place up and running. Now it's time to get back to our original plan, to find out what happened to my family.

I had to check with Anthony that he was still into the idea of going to the cabin. I'd noticed that he hadn't mentioned it since we took this detour, and it had occurred to me that maybe he'd changed his mind. There would have been no shame in it if he had. It was an unbelievably selfless offer even by his standards, to risk everything to help me chase what we both know is probably a lost cause.

I was careful when I brought it up. I said if he'd changed his mind about making the trip then I'd completely understand. Hoxley House is comfortable, we have supplies, provisions and company. I could see why he might want to make this home. The only downside is the fear of being attacked again, but that would be the same anywhere. I told him that obviously I'd be disappointed if he'd had a change of heart, but I would let him decide, and respect whatever decision he made.

Anthony didn't hesitate. He even made a joke out of it. I don't know why I was ever worried. It's settled. We're leaving.

It's no secret that we were always going to move on, so it shouldn't be a surprise to anybody. Even so, it does feel like we're going to be walking out on our new comrades, leaving everybody in the lurch. But it's not like that, we'll be back soon.

Hopefully.

Chapter 33. Fight or funny

I was thinking about that night at the start of all this when me, Pete and Rachel went out and got blasted. When I look back now it doesn't seem like it really happened. It feels like a dream, and not even my dream, it feels like someone else's.

And what I can't get my head round is that it was only six months ago. That's right. It's only been six months since the world went to shit.

Jesus.

It's nuts how quickly this has all become the new normal. I already can't picture what it would be like to live in the world like it was before. So many things have become second nature already, keeping quiet, keeping watch, being careful with food, fuel, power.

It's become second nature to *not* do things too. Not using the internet. Not watching TV. Not going to pubs. Not watching bands. Not going to museums, galleries, the theatre. Yes, alright I didn't go to museums before, or galleries, or the theatre, but it was nice to have the option. Not going to festivals. Not going to parties. Not meeting mates. Not going to the park. Not having barbecues. Not going shopping. Not seeing films. Not going on holiday.

Not enjoying ourselves.

All we're doing is surviving. Fun has had to take a back seat to function.

Stripping barbed wire off a fence is not an easy task. That

stuff's not loosely attached to those posts, the staples are hammered in really hard. And once you've managed to get it off you've got to move it all to where you need it to be, and that's basically impossible. You'd think you could just roll it all up and chuck it on the back of a truck wouldn't you? No, no you can't. Barbed wire's not wool. It's really hard to roll up. And it's really spiky. There's a reason they call it *barbed* wire.

We work very hard here, and it's been lucky that everyone's done their bit. They're a good bunch. Okay, so I prefer some more than others, Blaze is a bit intense, a little too keen on his knife for my liking, and I'm going to be careful what I wish for here but Lewis has been a right dullard since Frank copped it. He may have been a proper knobhead before but at least he wasn't boring. But on the whole they're a decent bunch. Nobody's impossible to live with and some of them can be proper funny. I wasn't sure about Douglas at first but it turns out he can be a top bloke once you get to know him. I think he's what you'd call an *acquired taste*. He's definitely got a taste for the sauce, too. That's one of the positives of being holed up in a wedding venue, there's plenty of booze.

But it's Georgie who makes all the difference. I know how lucky I am to have her. Without Georgie I'd think of Hoxley House as nothing more than a convenient place to scrape out an existence. With her here it feels like home. It's as simple as that. If only she was up for staying. We'd have it made.

But she's not up for staying. We have to go. Apparently.

It would be wrong to say I regret suggesting we try and find Georgie's family. At the time I genuinely thought it was the right thing to do. I'm as worried about my family as Georgie is about hers but I think visiting their house made all the difference. That word on the blackboard, it was like a clue in a TV drama. I knew that if Georgie hadn't followed up on that one lead then she'd have ended up tearing herself up over it.

Even back then I didn't think we had an ice-lolly's chance in hell of finding her family alive and I don't think Georgie did either, but it gave us a purpose and we both needed that.

Shit, I wonder if I'll ever have an ice-lolly again.

But back to the point. Back to me suggesting we go searching for Mr. and Mrs. Georgie.

I'm sure some wise person once said something about regret, that if you do something that feels right at the time then it's the right thing to do, and that shouldn't change when you look back on it afterwards. I get that completely, but if you've made a decision and then new information comes up that gives you a good reason to change your decision, then you'd be a twat not to take that new information into account.

If we hadn't decided to go check out the cabin by the sea, then we wouldn't have come in the direction we did. That would have meant that we wouldn't have seen the flag outside the aquarium and decided to help the gang escape. And we wouldn't have ended up here. But now we *are* here, and everything we went through to get here, all the danger, everything we saw, it's all new data. The chances of Georgie's family still being alive haven't got any bigger, but our knowledge of what's out there has.

The sensible thing to do now would be to stay right where we are.

So how come I couldn't bring myself to tell Georgie that? Because I'm a pussy that's why.

In my defence, she did lead the witness a bit. Actually, I think the word is *corralled*. Let's take a look at her tactics:

Tactic 1. She threw in some fluffy bollocks about how she'd 'understand' if I'd changed my mind, but at the same time she made it very clear how disappointed she'd be if I had.

Tactic 2: She couldn't help but remind me about the danger of the monsters in the woods if we stayed here, even though those woods might be perfectly safe now.

Tactic 3: (and this was the killer). She put all the responsibility for the decision onto me. She said it was my choice and that she'd go along with whatever I chose to do. That was a low move. There's no way I could have then turned around and said, "Okay, I've made a decision. Let's abandon your family and stay here. We cool?"

We would not have been cool.

Oh, and…

Tactic 4: We were in bed when she brought the whole thing up, and she knew how horny I was.

I don't want to use the word 'manipulated' because it sounds too devious, so let's just say that Georgie *massaged* me into going along with what she wanted. It did piss me off a bit at the time, still does a little, but I didn't call her on it for the simple reason that I can't risk losing her.

To say Georgie is out of my league is like saying a horse is better at running than a slug. Okay, so I realise she has less choice than she had before, what with the human race having been decimated and all, but she isn't the sort of person who needs a partner to feel like she's complete or whatever. I think she'd rather go without than settle for someone who didn't tick all her boxes. And I'm not sure how I've managed to tick her boxes but I'm not going to spoil the whole exam paper just because she used everything in her locker to make sure I'm at her side when she goes looking for her family.

I put up a bit of a fight. I tried a Jedi mind trick of my own, but I'm nowhere near as skilled in the ways of the force as Georgie is. What I did was to use the old joking-but-not-joking technique. I had this half smile on my face and I lay back on the bed, stretched, and said, "Well I am getting pretty comfy here."

She was meant to come back with something about how, even though she knew I was joking, I'd still stumbled onto a valid point, that this wasn't a bad place to live, especially compared with taking our chances on the outside. This would have opened up some chat about the pros and cons of the original plan (with particular emphasis on the cons) and we'd have ended up coming to the same conclusion that I'd already come to, that the safest and most convenient way forward was staying put. All without me looking like I'd gone back on my offer.

But my joking-but-not-joking technique fell on its arse.

She just thought I was joking.

And then she started doing things to me with her mouth. Incredible things.

So it's settled. We're leaving.

Everyone says a relationship is about give and take, and I get that now. I'm happy to give Georgie whatever she wants. And she can take whatever she likes. It works for me.

If I needed reminding why I'd literally follow Georgie to the ends of the earth to keep her happy then all I'd have to do is listen to the sound I'm listening to right now. The sound of her breathing as she sleeps next to me. Yes, I know I'm being as soppy as shite but I don't think I could sleep without that sound anymore. Actually, fuck it, I don't think I could *live* without that sound anymore.

Jesus, if I wasn't me I'd find myself unbearable.

I'm wide awake now. I've got no idea how late it is, or it could be early. Those curtains block all the light right out so I'm getting no clues from that direction. I don't like to look in that direction anyway, when I look at those curtains I think of that gold and black rope, and then all I can think of is what happened to Naomi. Fuck, now I'm thinking about it. Poor Naomi. What a fucking waste.

I know I'm not going to get back to sleep for ages now. I know how this goes. I'm going to start fidgeting like a little kid soon. I'll decide that I can only get comfortable if I turn over, and then as soon as I've turned over I'll realise I was better off before. Then I'll get an itch somewhere and I'll try and ignore it for a while but then it'll get loads worse so I'll scratch it. Then I'll get an itch somewhere else. And I'll turn over again…

We all know the drill.

I'm going to get up. I could do with some water anyway.

I rummage about on the floor for a while trying to find my pants. I don't expect to see anybody on my way to the kitchen but you never know. I wouldn't want to bump into Lady Alice with my knob out. I finally find my undies and I'm surprised Georgie sleeps through the palaver of me trying to put them on in the dark. It's like a hippo trying to put on a onesie. I get there in the end.

I creep out onto the landing and follow the bannister down the stairs. At the bottom I take the wrong door and find myself in the banqueting hall, or the dining hall, I still don't know which is which. Either way, it's the wrong room, so I turn around and head for the kitchen. The door's closed, that's what must have confused me.

I open it and nearly shit my pants when I see that there are two people in the room. It's just Arthur and Douglas but I hadn't banked on seeing anyone at all so it had caught me on the hop. They're sitting at the breakfast bar. The only light in the room is coming from the fridge. Its door's been propped half open with a stool.

"Can't put the lights on," says Arthur. "Don't want to be seen from outside."

"Yeah, I get it. What are you up to?" The whisky bottle on the counter answers my question.

Douglas sees where I'm looking. "Fancy one?"

"Go on then." I pull up a stool on the other side of the counter across from them. Douglas reaches into a cupboard down to his left, gets a glass out and pours. He's not tight with his measures.

I'll be honest, I'm not a big whisky drinker. I've been on God knows how many stag weekends and I always dread that moment that always comes, the one when the brother or the father of the bride makes a big show of being all generous and ordering a round of single malts, and everyone sits around cooing like aunties at a baby shower over how smooth yet oaky this particular ten year-old is. And they all sit and they sip and they tell their stories of other times when they've drank expensive whisky, normally in spectacularly large measures in far-flung parts of the world, and nobody's listening to anyone else because they're all just waiting to tell their own story.

And they sit. And they sip. And they coo. And they tell their stories.

And I just hold my nose and knock it back.

And they all look at me like I'm nuts.

And I say I'm sorry, but it tastes fucking disgusting.

And they make their comments about how I'm a philistine or whatever and I go get a beer and by the time I've come back they're telling their stories again.

I think I've made my point. I'm not a whisky man. I'll drink the stuff but only to get drunk. I won't savour it, because if I do I'll start to gag. But this stuff that Douglas has served up. Jesus. Whatever it is, well. I don't know what to say.

Wow.

I hold up the glass and study the dark liquid, as if I'll find some clue as to why it tastes so bloody nice. I put the glass down, none the wiser.

Douglas tops me up, smiling. "Thought you'd like it."

Arthur pushes his glass forward for a top up of his own. "What brings you down here lad?"

"Couldn't sleep."

Mute

Before Arthur replies, Douglas laughs, and I wouldn't have thought anything of it but Arthur gives him a look and I know straight away that they've been talking about me. And I'm not having that. "Come on then, out with it."

Arthur goes to speak but Douglas talks over him. "Fair play to you, son. You're right to call us out. Full disclosure. I said it to Art before and I'll say to you now. Your better half. I'm impressed, she's... impressive."

I'm just about ready to knock him off his stool, and if I'd had as many drinks as he has then I'd have done it by now, but I can see in his eyes that he's not trying to mug me off. I think he's actually trying to give me a compliment, he's just not very good at it.

He shakes his head and carries on. "I don't know why it's such a, such a *thing* to notice when another chap's got a hot bird. I mean, isn't that what every man wants? To have a hot bird and have everyone else notice?"

Even though I'm doing my best to cut Douglas some slack, the way he says 'hot bird' makes my toes curl. It reeks of posh bloke trying to talk like a lad. He pretty much pronounces the quote marks around the words. It's cringe.

"I don't think we're allowed to call them birds anymore". Maybe Arthur noticed the look on my face, or maybe the hot bird thing grated on him too. Or he could just be trying to get Douglas off the topic of my girlfriend.

"Fair enough." Douglas takes a huge gulp of his whisky. "I can embrace modern thinking. I will drop that term from my vernacular. And very soon I'm going to forget the point I've commenced so I will curtail it." He puts his drink down and claps a couple of times. "Suffice to say, good work old boy. Georgina is unspeakably beautiful and you are a very lucky man. But I think you have earned your luck." Before I can answer he's divvying up what's left of the bottle between the three of us and raising his glass. "Congratulations."

I'm still mulling over whether I should give him a slap but realise there's no point being a dick about it. He doesn't mean any harm. He's just being clumsy. And I've been guilty of that more times than I can count. I drink with him and I'm wondering if this whisky is even whisky at all because it's just so bloody delicious.

Jesus, what if I become a whisky guy?

We move on from the fact that Douglas thinks Georgie's hot and we chat about other things. We talk about mutants and death and the wars they've fought in, because it turns out that Douglas is a war hero too. And I feel all insignificant but they're both really good about it. And we have a moment about Naomi and we all go quiet for a bit because we feel so shit about it and still can't believe it even happened. And then we get to gossiping and we talk about how much Blaze loves his knife.

And then Douglas brings us back round again. "I'm not going to bang on about it because I fear I have done so more than enough already, but do you realise how lucky you are to have a lady on your arm? Look at Me and Arthur here. We are both widowers now. It would have been hard enough for chaps of our age to get back into the swing of things as it was, and now, with the population of available females having reduced to almost zero, it's as good as impossible.

Arthur's stool creaks as he shifts his weight. He raises a finger. "I'd like to take... what's the word?"

I suggest one. "Offence?

"No, not that strong."

"What are you trying to say?"

"That I disagree with some of his points."

It's funny seeing Arthur like this. Douglas has been doing most of the talking and I hadn't noticed how hammered Arthur was. I take another punt at the word he's looking for. "Objection?"

"No."

Douglas's face lights up. "Exception!"

Arthur grins, touches his nose with his finger and points at Douglas with the other hand. "Five points to you sir!" Now Arthur's got all the words he needs he goes back to what he was saying. "I'd like to take… *exception*, to two of your points."

"I'm surprised you can remember any of my points," says Douglas. "I don't think I can."

Arthur's mouth smiles but his eyes are completely gone. "I'm surprised as the next man." He cocks his head towards Douglas. "Which is you, you're the next man. Anyway. The first point I except to is you saying 'of our age' when you're talking about us. I except to that. I'm not *of our age*."

Douglas pulls a face, which turns out to be his only answer.

Arthur carries on. "And the other point I except to is that you're suggesting I want to get back into the swing of things. I don't want to be in the swing of things. I'm staying faithful to Maggie." He looks down at the counter and I think that he's going to get all maudlin on us, but he suddenly jolts into life and lifts his glass. "To Maggie!"

We all drink to Maggie but it's no surprise that Douglas, has something to say on the matter. "I'm sure you absolutely mean what you say old boy, but I think you will change your mind soon enough. Once you are hungry enough."

Arthur screws up his eyes and shakes his head, like a little kid refusing to eat his broccoli. "I'll never be unfaithful to Maggie."

Douglas is at that stage of arseholed where his thoughts appear on his face. I'm not saying I can read his mind but from his changing expressions I can definitely see that he's arguing with himself about whether or not to say the thing he's about to say. His drunken gobshite side wins through, obviously. "You weren't so faithful in Banja Luka, in that pub that turned out to be a knocking shop."

It's one of those moments, the ones where you've got two guys who are totally out of their minds and one's just pushed it a bit too far and you don't know if it's going to be a fight or if it's going to be funny.

Arthur locks his red, hooded eyes on Douglas and there's this long silence. It's like at the end of those TV talent shows where the last judge on the panel takes ages before they tell the wannabe singer, ventriloquist, or whatever, if they've made it to the live final.

Eventually Arthur makes his move.

He puts his finger to his lips. "Ssssssh." Loads of spit sprays out and a drop lands on the back of my hand. I go to wipe it on my trousers, which reminds me that I'm only wearing pants.

"That was a good night," says Douglas. "Oh, those Eastern European girls. They know how to play."

Arthur's eyes are completely glazed over now and he's grinning like a bastard. His mind's obviously back in Banja Luka.

I don't know where Banja Luka is.

"Sounds like you should have taken a run at Maria," I say to Douglas.

I was only joking but I think he's taken me seriously. "I was planning to, young man, but then that spotty adolescent went and did his superhero act and she went all potty over him."

"Quite an age gap," I say.

Douglas nods enthusiastically. "My sentiments entirely. She has to be in her thirties, and how old is he, fifteen?"

"He's seventeen I think, but I meant more the gap between you and her."

Douglas wags his finger. "It's different in their culture. The girls like an older man."

Arthur's back from wherever he's been. "You'll get your chance. That lad will mess it up."

"There is one person who's available," I say.

I can see the workings of Douglas's head again as he runs through the residents of the estate. "Who?"

"Lewis. He seems to like the older men."

"Fuck off!"

Out of nowhere the conversation takes a turn. This time it's Arthur, asking me a question that isn't really a question:

"When are you leaving us?"

And it's that last word that does it. That 'us' that changes it from being late-night drunken chat to it being an accusation.

And there's this long silence and I realise that it was still technically a question and they're both looking at me, waiting for an answer and I'm sitting on the stool, looming over them both, wearing only my underpants, and I realise I've been drinking whisky like it was lemonade and I find myself answering. "Yeah, we're going. It's the last thing I want to do and I think it's the wrong thing to do, but Georgie wants to do it, and she pretty much railroaded me into going along with her. And like you said, she's fucking hot, so I'm not going to argue."

The two old guys are both looking straight past me and I think it's down to their eyes being all out of focus because of all that whisky. But I realise they're not struggling to see straight, they're just looking at something behind me. So I turn around, in my pants, holding my whisky.

And there's Georgie.

And she must be telepathic, because before I ask her how long she's been standing there, she says, "Long enough to hear what you just said."

Chapter 34. Trouble in paradise

It was convenient timing that it was Georgie and Ant's turn to take patrol duty. Ant had spent what was left of the night before lying next to the impenetrable fortress of Georgie's back, holding auditions in his mind for sentences that he might use to break the deadlock. But none of the candidates had got the gig. The result had been the frostiest of silences, during which he and Georgie had both been painfully awake but thought the other was sleeping soundly.

Even if Ant had been able to get a discussion going it would have been restricted to an exchange of whispers in case their drama was overheard by the occupants of the rooms on either side. Now they were in the open, in the mid-morning sunshine, they were able to talk freely.

But there hadn't been much in the way of talking since they had started their first lap of the grounds.

Georgie adjusted the strap of her shotgun and served up the opening salvo. "I never thought we'd be that kind of couple."

"What kind?"

"The kind that keeps secrets from each other. The kind that talks to outsiders before talking to each other."

"They're not exactly outsiders."

"They're outside of our relationship. That makes them outsiders."

"Okay, whatever, but I wasn't talking to them."

"What were you doing then, flying a kite?"

"Well obviously I was talking. What I mean is I wasn't, y'know, confiding in them. I wasn't going behind your back. I just blurted that stupid shit out."

"Yes, you blurted out that I'm forcing you to do something against your will, something that you think is completely the wrong thing to do. What was the term you used?"

"I don't remember."

"So now you're lying to me too."

"Hold on, don't start lashing out. I'm not a liar, I just don't remember. I was pretty hammered."

"You have to agree it's pretty convenient."

"None of this is convenient. Let's keep this in perspective. I had too much whisky and gobbed off when I shouldn't. I'm really sorry for that, it was stupid, but it's not the end of the world."

"Is that meant to be a joke?"

Ant couldn't help but smile. "Actually, it wasn't, but now you mention it…"

Georgie started walking faster.

Ant hurried after her. "I'm sorry, that was daft. Please slow down."

Georgie didn't slow down.

"We're meant to be on patrol."

Georgie stopped.

"Thank you. Listen, I know it's a lame excuse but I was hammered. That's the only reason I said anything to them two."

"And if you hadn't been drunk, you wouldn't have said anything at all."

"Exactly. And we wouldn't have this problem."

Georgie shook her head and breathed out very slowly.

"The problem isn't that you said it to them, although that didn't help, the problem is that you couldn't talk to me about it. You were just going along with what you thought I wanted because I'm, as you so poetically phrased it, *fucking hot*."

"I guess I was trying to be one of the boys."

"One of the boy*s*? Their combined age must be a hundred and fifty. And you're missing the point again. The problem, well one of them anyway, is that you don't trust me enough to tell me what's on your mind, in case I don't like it." Georgie started walking, at a more reasonable pace this time.

"Can I say something?"

"Oh, *now* you want to talk about things."

Ant pressed on with his argument. "If you think about it…"

"All I've done is think about it."

"Yes, okay, fair point. What I mean is, when push comes to shove, having a boyfriend who'll go along with whatever you want to do because he's so crazy about you - which, by the way, is what I should have said to those two instead of saying you're hot - isn't the worst thing in the world. Is it?"

"I don't want a Stepford boyfriend."

"I don't know what that means."

"Google it."

"I can't seem to get a signal."

"Stop trying to make a joke out of everything. This matters to me, and it should matter to you too. I thought we were a team. I genuinely believed that together we could take on anything. Yes, I know that sounds cheesy but it's true."

"There's nothing cheesy about it. We *are* a team and we *can* take on anything. We've proved that more times than we can count."

"Yes, all the practical stuff. The rest hasn't really been tested."

"What do you mean, *the rest?*"

"All the normal things about being in a couple. Trusting each other, respecting each other. Being honest with each other."

"All I can say is I'm sorry. You're right. I should have told you. I know now. I won't keep anything from you again."

"Well of course you'd say that now."

"I'm saying it now because I mean it now. Look, I get it. I really do. I didn't want to be the guy who took away what might have been your last chance of finding your family. But that was stupid of me. You're right, we're a team and we should be able to talk about anything."

Georgie stopped walking and looked Ant in the eye for the first time that day. "Perhaps we've just mixed up our ability to get through all those crazy situations together with being in love."

"Please don't say that."

Georgie started walking again.

Ant followed. "I fucked up. It was once. It doesn't mean everything we've got has gone."

Georgie stopped again. "I don't think it's gone. I think that maybe it was just never there in the first place. Maybe we were mistaken."

Ant looked crushed. "No, you're wrong. You're mistaken now."

"If we were the couple I thought we were then I wouldn't have to worry about you telling everybody that I'm the sort of woman who forces her partner into going along with whatever she wants." A look of realisation came over her face. "*Railroaded*, that's what you said. I railroaded you into going along with me. Now you tell me, Anthony, is that how my loving partner, my *teammate*, would talk about me?"

During the long sleepless night before, Ant had sworn to

himself that he would not, at any cost, say what he was about to say, but his policy of almost complete contrition was not only proving to be unsuccessful, it was starting to feel downright unfair.

"Well you *did* railroad me."

Georgie's face was a cocktail of shock, disbelief and anger. "I don't…. I can't." She gave up trying to form a response and marched off.

"For fuck's sake." Ant hurried after Georgie again. "Are you going to pretend you don't know what I'm talking about?"

They reached the north-west corner of the grounds and turned left, following the high wall that ran south. "No, Anthony, I'm not going to pretend anything. I have no idea what you're talking about, except that you are accusing me of something that I know I'm not guilty of."

"Oh come on! You knew what you were doing. All that stuff about how you'd understand if I'd changed my mind, but how disappointed you'd be if I had? How you'd leave it up to me to make the call? You knew I couldn't do anything but agree with you when you put me on the spot like that."

Georgie's voice wasn't much more than a whisper. "You really think that. You actually think that." Although technically the words were aimed at Ant, she seemed to be speaking more to herself.

Ant could only see Georgie's face in profile as he walked beside her but he could see that she was fighting back tears. It started to dawn on him that perhaps he had been wrong about the whole thing, a realisation that became more certain with every step, until he was at the point where he wished he had something to yank back the last few minutes of time like that button that retracts the power cord on a vacuum cleaner. "Oh God I'm so sorry. I've been such a knob."

Georgie didn't look at him. "Let's just get this patrol done.

Please don't speak anymore."

As they walked, the knot of shame and regret in Ant's gut grew. He kept going to speak but thinking better of it, knowing that anything he said wasn't going to improve things, and would most likely make them worse.

They reached a ladder that lay on its side against the wall and Ant was glad of the brief respite of a procedure to follow. "Think it's my turn to go up," he said.

In silence, they lifted the ladder and propped it against the wall. Georgie held the base while Ant ascended, keeping his huge frame hunched down as he neared the top. He stopped climbing, wiped away the dollops of sweat on his forehead just before they fell into his eyes, and slowly and carefully raised his head. This part always made him nervous. He knew that any mutant activity this close to the wall would have been seen by Lady Alice and Blaze, currently on lookout duty on the roof. And besides, Ant was fifteen feet up so unless the mutants had mastered using ladders themselves, or trampolines, then he knew he wasn't going to come face to face with one. But a steady diet of horror movies told him that the slow creep upwards, the unseen unknown on the other side of the wall, the big reveal; it had all the ingredients of a jump-out-of-the-skin moment.

His head was above the last row of bricks.

The field beyond was empty.

Satisfied there was no imminent danger, Ant hooked his left arm over the wall to steady himself as he pushed his gun further over his back and lifted the binoculars that hung from his neck. He did a sweep from left to right of the area in front of him and repeated it in reverse. He lowered the binoculars and scanned the view once more, checking for anything that he might need to zoom in on, any movement, anything.

He turned and looked back down the ladder. "Nothing.

I'm coming down."

Georgie nodded.

He was halfway down when the jump-out-of-the-skin moment arrived. A crunch of static and Maria's voice over the radio. "I see them on the screens. They are coming. They are coming. Over."

Lady Alice's voice quickly followed. "I see them. Southeast, at the gatehouse, they have it open. They are coming through. Thirty at least. No. Fifty. Over."

Georgie and Ant instinctively looked to the roof but realised that Alice and Blaze were out of sight, they were on the far side of the building; the side that faced the danger. Georgie and Ant were almost as far from the mutants as they could be while still being inside the grounds of the estate.

Ant jumped off the ladder, straightened up and gripped his shotgun, ready to run back towards the house. He looked at Georgie and stopped. Her face carried an expression he hadn't seen on her before, but one that he recognised straight away. It was nothing to do with their argument, that was insignificant now, ridiculous even, it was something else. It was the look he'd had on his own face that awful day when Frank had wanted to go and find Lewis in the woods; when Douglas and Arthur had said no and Georgie had looked to Ant for backup. It was the look that said: "We can't keep doing this. We can't keep putting our necks on the line."

Ant understood Georgie's unspoken point.

They heard shotgun blasts and saw movement on the roof. Alice had come across to Georgie and Ant's side. She was waving frantically. The radio crackled with her voice again.

She spoke like she was dictating a telegram. "You two must run. There is nothing you can do from out there. You will die if you try. We are barricaded inside. We have planned for this. We will try to pick them off."

The sound of two shotgun blasts underlined her point.

Georgie held the radio limply between them. She looked at Ant and then back at the roof.

Alice was flapping her arm forwards, shoeing them away. Her voice came through the radio again. "Go, please go. Over."

The shrieks of the mutants were loud and clear now. Georgie looked at Ant once more. He nodded.

She nodded back and turned away, lifting the receiver to the mouth, struggling to speak through the tears. "We understand. We are so sorry. We will never forget you, any of you." She had to force out the final word: "Over."

"Stop talking and go. Over and out." They saw Alice's silhouette disappear from view.

After all the dangers they had overcome in the last six months, after everything they had faced, bailing on their friends while they were under attack was the hardest task of all.

But they did as Alice said. They knew the drill, both figuratively and literally.

Ant held the foot of the ladder while Georgie ascended. At the top she shifted her body off the ladder and onto the wall, straddling it. She held the ladder as steadily as she could while Ant climbed. The uproar of gunfire and screams in the near distance made it hard to focus as he reached the top and hauled himself onto the wall on the other side of the ladder from Georgie. He overbalanced and nearly went down head first but managed to hang on. They pulled the ladder up between them, and when it was high enough they tipped it over the wall, then carefully but quickly slid it down the other side until it braced on the ground.

Taking the pole down to the garage in the fire station seemed a lifetime ago but the same logic applied here. Ant went first, almost abseiling onto the grass below. He stepped aside to hold the ladder steady while Georgie followed. They lowered the ladder and laid it in front of them. Ant went in front and they picked up the ladder in their right hands, like they were carrying a long, comedy briefcase between them. They knew which way to go, due west, across the fields, taking the far edge where it was less exposed. They knew that the mutants that had breached the estate were unlikely to be following but they were well aware that the noise of the attack could bring more to the party so they moved as quickly as they could. The ladder hampered their progress but they knew better than to stray from the script; it was the least they could do not to leave an easy way over the wall for anything coming from this side.

As they moved in their encumbered two-step, Ant stopped himself, several times, from checking if Georgie needed to stop and rest. He knew the plan and knew she did too. If Georgie had a problem she would say so, otherwise there would be no talking unless absolutely necessary. Those were the rules.

Their ladder-carrying arms were almost numb within ten minutes, and they stopped and switched hands. After another quarter of an hour the burning pain in their other arms was eased by the sight of a church spire. This told them they were close to the pick-up point which was also the drop-off point for the dead wood they'd been dutifully carrying.

They carried on for another hundred yards, to where a straggly row of bushes separated the field from the back of the church grounds. They dumped the ladder and stretched their aching limbs in silence. An exchange of nods signalled they were both ready to move again and they eased through the straggly bushes.

They gave the church as wide a berth as they could; none of the reconnaissance trips had reported any activity in there but they didn't want to take a chance. Their target was on the other side of God's house, next to the front gate. They made their way slowly and purposefully around.

In the September sunshine it was hard to picture the grit bin's contents being used to stop the church path from freezing over, but it was its more recent contents that Georgie and Ant were after. The shiny padlock stood out against the faded yellow of the bowed lid and Georgie put a hand under her chin and retrieved the silver chain from beneath her sweat-soaked t-shirt. The key twirled in the sunlight.

The bin was only a quarter full of the grit it was designed to hold, which left just enough room for two Shit Day Bags. The bags weren't tailored for Georgie and Ant, their contents were generic; for anyone from Hoxley House who happened to find themselves in that position. There were basic survival rations: nuts, biscuits, crackers, bottles of water. The water, despite not being chilled, hit the spot after their long trek with the ladder. Besides the food and water, the Shit Day bags contained a trinity of toiletries: toothbrushes, toothpaste and tampons, as well as some soap and a limited first aid kit. One of the bags contained a map and both contained a torch, a sawn-off shotgun and a box of cartridges.

These were their worldly goods now, aside from the clothes on their backs, the guns already on their shoulders and Ant's binoculars.

They carefully closed the lid of the grit bin and reattached the padlock. The chances of a mutant even seeing it, let alone noticing it had been unlocked, were slim, but neither of them was in the business of taking risks anymore.

The stash point for these Shit Day Bags was chosen because it was in the first village due west of the estate. More had been hidden to the south and east, but not the north, nobody was going to enter those woods after what had happened to Frank.

The church was on the intersection of two wide A-roads, and on the opposite corner was a car showroom. There may have been more to the village but Georgie and Ant weren't about to hang around. They gave each other the nod and hurried across the road.

The glass-fronted car dealership had obviously been busy on the day of the apocalypse and the air was ripe with the smell of rotting corpses. Even Georgie and Ant, veterans of the stench of death, struggled with their gag reflexes as they entered. They walked beneath a 'staff only' sign into a large office. They didn't need to search the place; a key cupboard was on the far wall, its door open. They took all the car keys and returned to the showroom where they hunkered down low and checked the registration numbers stuck to the fobs against the plates on the cars outside. They agreed on a white saloon, less interested in the car itself than how easy it would be to get it off the forecourt. It was next to the exit and facing the right way, an easy sell for the dead dealers.

They were on the road in less than a minute.

Chapter 35. Peaky blinders

Since their enforced departure from Hoxley House, Georgie and Ant had communicated in grunts, nods and the odd monosyllable. They were on the road for half an hour before they had a proper conversation, and even that only barely qualified:

"I propose a new policy," said Ant in the passenger seat. "We don't stop for anything other than the necessaries now. No turn-offs, no distractions, we just keep going until we reach your folks' place."

Georgie kept her eyes on the road ahead. "I agree."

"Okay."

Ant, realising he wasn't going to get anything else out of Georgie for now, occupied himself by checking out the glove compartment. Inside he found a flat, resealable polythene bag that held all the official bumph about their brand-new Toyota. He fished out the owner's manual and went to work with the small, thick textbook, trying to get it to tell him how to operate the Sat-Nav. It didn't go well. As far as Ant could tell, the instructions in the manual bore no relation to what was on the display in front of him. He knew he must have been driving Georgie up the wall; stabbing at the screen with his huge fingers, and muttering in frustration when the result was the exact opposite of what he'd been trying to do, but Georgie didn't seem to be paying attention. She was busy somewhere inside her own head.

Ant gave up and sat back in his seat, his arms folded.

The initial shock of the attack on Hoxley House was starting to fade, and Ant had finally managed to force himself to stop picturing the range of gruesome fates that could have befallen the friends they had left behind. Instead his mind returned to the argument he had been having with Georgie. It had been rendered trivial by the attack but now it stepped out of the shadows and took centre stage in Ant's production of *Things to Feel Uneasy About*. He felt bad that he was worrying about a lovers' tiff when there was probably a massacre going on back at the estate, but he couldn't pretend it wasn't a big deal to him. And anyway, it was a lot more than a lovers' tiff. Where they had left it, it was clear that Georgie had been leaning very heavily towards them splitting up. Ant had no idea what the practicalities of splitting up would entail, what with them being joined at the hip for the sake of survival, but he knew it would mean at least three things:

1. No more sex.
2. A return to life in Awkwardville.
3. Ant's heart being smashed into a billion squillion pieces.

He knew he couldn't go back to how things had been before they had got together, it would be unbearable. He didn't want to overdramatise it, but in his eyes it was a matter of life and death. If he didn't fix things with Georgie his life simply wouldn't be worth living.

He knew he had to talk to Georgie but also knew that, right at that moment, talking was the absolute last thing that was needed. Ant was no expert on relationships but he had messed things up enough times with enough women to know that if he tried to rake it all up now he'd just be the guy making the whiny apologies, and that would push Georgie further into her bunker. He also knew that their argument was probably the last thing on Georgie's mind; she would be focused entirely on what was happening back at the estate, and would think Ant was unbelievably selfish, obscenely inconsiderate, or some kind of sociopath if he had the gall to think that their relationship was even worthy of a mention right now.

Ant turned his mind to more practical matters. When they had taken the car they had just started driving; they hadn't talked about which way to go. Ant had failed to get the Sat-Nav to work and he didn't know if Georgie was waiting for him to give her directions. He opened up the map that had been in his Shit Day bag. The rough location of the cabin was fairly easy to find; he remembered the name of the nearest town from when Georgie had marked it on their map from before, and there weren't too many towns near that stretch of west coast to search through. The destination wasn't a problem. The problem was finding where they were now. Ant, to use his own words, didn't have a bastard clue.

Ant was fully aware that, at a time when the last thing he needed was anything more to mark him down in Georgie's eyes, being the guy who couldn't find their location on a map was not a good look. He stole a glance at Georgie, she seemed to know what she was doing, so he decided to stay quiet, he would leave it up to Georgie. She would say if she needed any input from him. In the meantime, he would keep an eye out for any road signs that could help him find out where they were. He would *triangulate their position*.

In the silence that followed, Ant shut his eyes and started to doze. He had just reached that point where his thoughts began morphing into dreams when he was pulled out of his sleepy netherworld by Georgie's voice. "You were right," she said.

Ant took a few moments to get himself back into the here and now. "Right about what?"

"I knew you were having doubts about leaving the estate and I..." Georgie thought carefully before she spoke again, "... well I didn't *coerce* you exactly, but I didn't give you much chance to say no. I don't think I was even conscious that I was doing it, but looking back... well, like I said. I think you were right."

Ant was astonished at this turn of events but he worked hard to keep his cool and not mess it up. "I think all that happened was that you were dead keen on finding out what had happened to your folks and you wanted me to be there with you, that's not a crime. I shouldn't have been such a dick about it."

Georgie glanced across at Ant; the first time they'd made eye contact since they'd left the estate. "You were a bit of a dick about it."

"Alright, I just said that."

Georgie smiled.

Ant felt awful. His friends at Hoxley House were at best under siege from a legion of mutants and at worst all dead, and here he was struggling not to punch the air with delight.

But Georgie wasn't done quite yet. "I need you to promise me something."

"Go on..."

"I need you to promise that if there's something on your mind, you'll just come out and say it."

"Of course."

Georgie shook her head. "No, Anthony, not *of course*, I need to know you mean it. We shouldn't even have to be talking about this, it should just be accepted as part of us being together, but after what I heard in the kitchen I need to know that you'll always talk to me, even if you think I might not like what you've got to say."

Ant put his hand on Georgie's arm. "I promise. I'll always

talk to you. Whatever it is, even if I think it's going to piss you off."

"It'll piss me off a lot more if you don't."

"Yeah, I'm getting that."

"It's really important to me that we're a team. That's what brought us together, everything we've been through, everything we've overcome, I knew we could rely on each other. It made me feel invincible, and to feel like that in a world like this, well it's magical. Then when I heard you going behind my back, it didn't just feel like a betrayal, it felt like I'd been wrong about everything."

"You weren't wrong about anything. I was just being a dick, and you always knew I was capable of being a dick."

"Yes, you do have enormous dick capabilities."

"I'll try and keep the dickness in check."

Georgie pulled the car over and put the handbrake on. "Come here you."

Ant gratefully took her in his arms. "I missed you so fucking much."

Georgie kissed him softly before resting her forehead against his. Ant could have stared into those eyes all day…

That is, if the handbrake hadn't been poking painfully into his leg and he wasn't worried about mutants creeping up on them.

Georgie was obviously thinking something similar. "We'd better get moving."

Ant needn't have worried about directions. Georgie knew exactly where she was going. "We basically just follow this dual carriageway almost to the end, right the way across Cornwall, then we take a few smaller roads up to the cabin."

"Why didn't you tell me that when I was trying to get the Sat-Nav to work?"

"I didn't want to interrupt, you looked like you were

enjoying yourself."

Georgie had been driving carefully, taking no chances with the abandoned and wrecked cars that cluttered the tarmac until they reached a point where the road was completely blocked by a pile-up of cars and lorries. There was no way through so Georgie improvised. She did a quick U-turn and drove back up the road to a roundabout they'd recently crossed. She took it anti-clockwise, looping all the way around before taking the exit that took them the wrong way down the carriageway that ran parallel to the one they had been on. "This is fun," she said as she accelerated past the pile-up.

It was early evening when Georgie turned off the dual carriageway and joined a country road that took them through open moorland. They passed stone-built houses, some of them centuries old while others were more modern; new-monied variations on the theme.

Georgie took another turn off into a much narrower road that rose higher before levelling out over a wide, windswept plain. Ant could taste salt in the air. "Are we close?"

Georgie turned and nodded, and Ant could see the anxiety on her face. Ant had been drifting along with the journey and his mind had drifted too. He hadn't forgotten the purpose of their trip; it had just become buried under a hypnotic repetition of scenery, of towns and villages looming in their windscreen and disappearing in their wake. Georgie, he realised, had had no such time out. Her mind had been completely occupied on what they might find when they reached their destination.

Ant sat up straighter in his seat. "Do you want to pull over? I think we should have a chat, make a bit of a plan."

There was a lay-by a few hundred yards ahead and Georgie pulled in behind a petrol tanker, its cab door hanging open; its driver long gone.

"How far exactly?"

"Ten minutes, max."

"Don't call me Max." Ant regretted the crappy joke almost before it was out of his mouth. "That was twatty. Sorry, I'm nervous."

"It's okay. It makes two of us."

"Is the cabin close to other buildings or is it out on its own?"

"It's on its own, in ten acres of open land. No neighbours for miles."

"Is there a fence around it?"

"No."

"Is it far from the road?"

Ant was starting to think that his questions might be getting annoying but if they were, Georgie didn't show it. If anything, it seemed to be helping her focus her mind on the job in hand. "It's a few hundred yards from the road. There's a turning on the right and then there's a bumpy track that goes across the field to the cabin. There's no cover. If anything's in there then they'll see us coming."

"So you think we should park up before we get there and walk it?"

"Definitely."

"Do you think we should wait until it gets dark?"

"Yes, we definitely should." Georgie rubbed her eyes. "But I really don't want to." She turned to Ant. "How did it come to this? Creeping across a Cornish moor in the dead of night to see if mutants have eaten my parents."

"I know, babe. All I can say is that I'm right here with you."

"I'm glad you're here."

"What a soppy pair we are. I'd hate us if I wasn't one of us."

Georgie's face broke into a smile. "We'd be unbearable."

Ant looked at his watch. "It's nearly six. We should give it three hours, a couple until sunset, then give it an hour after that. What do you think?"

"Sounds about right."

Ant patted his knees. "What do we do in the meantime? I'd like to get out of this lay-by."

"Me too, I keep thinking something's going to come bursting through that hedge." Georgie thought for a while. "Do you want to go to the beach?"

Ant hadn't been expecting that question but answered without hesitation. "Yes, I do."

Georgie took off the handbrake and pulled away. "The sunset will be amazing."

Ant had grown up in the Peak District so he knew a thing or two about striking views, but he was suitably wowed by what he saw as he stood hand in hand with Georgie on that Cornish clifftop looking out over the violent drama that is the Atlantic Ocean. They were overlooking a bay, the beach beneath them bookended by steep banks of jagged granite. The tide was coming in and the wind was whipping up the waves that broke onto the rocks and sand.

In that moment, Georgie and Ant weren't apocalypse survivors seeking out relatives who were most likely dead already, they were a young couple on holiday, taking the clifftop walk that the guidebook heartily recommended.

Georgie pointed at a path that twisted down to the beach. "Do you want to go onto the sand?"

Ant was standing full-on to the wind, his hair blowing horizontally behind him and his face feeling the light sting of the drops of water that had got caught up in the gusts. "I'm happy up here actually, if you are?"

"More than happy."

Something Ant had missed out on in the Peak District for

obvious reasons was sunsets, and this one was exactly as Georgie had described; amazing. The sun had been hidden behind a bank of cloud that stretched all the way across the horizon but it finally broke clear, dropping into the clear sky beneath. They sat on the cliff's edge, their legs hanging in thin air, Georgie sheltering in Ant's broad embrace, and watched the shimmering yellow orb as it sank into the sea, sending shards of red and orange in and around the darkening grey cloud that had been blocking its light until then.

Georgie and Ant didn't want the sun to sink, they wanted it to stay exactly where it was, so they could stay exactly where they were. But the sun was a dick about it. It continued to lower itself into the water, like a god easing into a hot bath.

They watched until it was just a glow of red above the water and then a fuzz of light in the sky above the horizon, and then nothing at all. They carried on watching, just in case it decided to pop back up again.

They were about to haul themselves to their feet when the moon stepped up behind them with an impromptu encore. It was low and red and did a decent impression of the sun. All that gave it away was its tell-tale drooping gait and its anguished face that peered out over the landscape.

Georgie and Ant knew their holiday was over. They had to get to work.

Chapter 36. Cabin fever

Georgie and Ant left the car at the clifftop and walked the half-mile to the cabin. The moon had lost its red tint as it climbed further into the sky and the white glow it cast was just enough for them to see their way; like nightlights that people put on their landings so their guests, too shy to turn on the light while creeping to the toilet in the small hours, wouldn't have to blunder around in the dark.

They each held a sawn-off shotgun, having decided that they would be best for close-up fighting. They also had their full-length rifles over their shoulders; giving them a total of four shots each before having to reload.

They were two-hundred yards from the cabin, which, as Georgie had explained to Ant, wasn't a cabin at all but a small, two-storey detached house. As expected, all the windows were dark, giving them no indication as to who or what might be inside. They were grateful that the surrounding fields were flat and empty because it meant they could rule out the possibility of mutants being concealed anywhere outside. All they had to worry about were the ones that might be lurking in the darkness of the cabin.

They stooped low and walked slowly for a few yards, then, as their road safety classes in primary school had taught them, they stopped, looked and listened. Seeing and hearing nothing untoward, they moved again.

They walked around the house slowly and carefully. They

looked through each of the ground floor windows but it was too dark to see inside. They reached the back door and Ant tried it. It was locked. They carried on walking. The front door was locked too. The house was intact; nothing had broken in. This was a good indication that no mutants were inside, but by no means a guarantee. From what Georgie and Ant had seen, the mutants' entry-procedure of choice tended to be to smash their way in, but the behaviour of both Farmer Mutant and Shy Mutant had suggested that there could be more in their locker. Georgie and Ant were taking no chances.

Georgie touched Ant's arm and pointed at the first-floor window above them. Ant retrieved a pebble from his pocket, one of several that he had taken from the clifftop. "You ready?" He whispered. He was close enough to Georgie to see that she was nodding. She raised her sawn-off and braced herself for action.

When they had been sitting on the clifftop they hadn't just been enjoying the view, they had been coming up with a plan. They had considered what Ant had called the Stealth/SWAT approach. This involved tiptoeing inside and checking each room by torchlight. If they saw any mutants, asleep or otherwise, they would shoot them, preferably at point-blank range. A downside to this plan was that as soon as the first shot had been fired, any other mutants in the building would come running to see what all the fuss was about. There was also the risk of itchy trigger fingers. Georgie and Ant didn't have elite military training and sneaking around in the dark is a nervy business; it wouldn't be out of the question for them to panic in the heat of the moment and inadvertently murder one or more of Georgie's family.

They had asked themselves why they were being quite so cautious. They had entered a lot of buildings on their travels and, whilst they had always been careful, they had pretty much just gone inside and hoped for the best. They had never given it as much thought as they were now. They were out in the sticks on the very edge of the country. Not many people had lived there before the end of the world, which meant not many people could have turned into mutants. It didn't seem a very likely spot for mutants to migrate to either; the sea was close but they couldn't picture mutants catching fish in those crashing waves.

So why, they had wondered, were they being so cagey now?

The plan they settled on was to make their way to the cabin under cover of darkness and break a window on the upstairs floor. If there were mutants inside they would make plenty of noise waking up, and Georgie and Ant would be ready to pick them off as they appeared at the front door. It wasn't just mutants that they were checking for; humans could be dangerous too. The window Georgie had chosen was in the master bedroom; the most likely place for her parents, or any other humans, to sleep. If anyone was inside they would react to their window being broken and Georgie and Ant would be ready.

Ant cast the first stone.

And missed. There was a loud *thwack* as it bounced off the plastic frame. Ant put his hand to his forehead, furious with himself.

They stood, silently waiting. They were in limbo; unsure if the noise from Ant's wayward throw was loud enough to wake anything inside. There was no sign of movement inside the cabin.

Georgie tapped Ant's arm and held out her hand, palm up. Ant pulled another pebble out of his pocket and handed it to her. He readied his gun and Georgie threw the stone.

The pebble sailed through the middle of the pane and

even though they were expecting it, the crunch of breaking glass made them both jump. They stood with their weapons at full attention, ready for violent chaos.

But nothing happened, for a few seconds at least. And then, a muted thump. It was barely audible but they both heard it. They stood, trying to hold in their panic, listening for a follow-up sound. There wasn't one and Ant took a few steps towards a ground floor window and peered inside.

A pair of yellow eyes stared back at him.

Ant lifted his gun and fired. A screech filled the air above the gunshot and the sound of shattering glass. Ant was about to fire again but Georgie's hand was on top of the barrel, pushing it down. "Stop. It's a cat. It's just a cat. Stop."

Georgie took Ant's hand and pulled him away, breaking into a run to the edge of the field. When they were a fair distance away she pulled Ant down onto the grass with her.

Georgie was breathing heavily. "There are no mutes in there, we'd know about it by now if there was."

"What about people?"

"I'm pretty sure there are no people either," said Georgie. "After all that racket we'd have seen some sort of movement."

"How did the cat get in then?"

"Did you not see the cat flap on the back door? It was there when we got the place, dad always said he'd get it closed off. He never did get around to it."

"What are we doing now, why are we lying here?"

"We're waiting to see if that gunshot of yours is going to attract all the mutes for miles around."

"I'm so sorry. Did I hit the cat?"

"No," said Georgie, "I have no idea how you managed to miss it, but I saw it jump away."

"I thought it was a mute."

Georgie was smiling in spite of their situation. "Yes, I

worked that out."

They lay on the grass and waited; both sets of shotguns to hand.

After half an hour Georgie raised herself up and stretched. "I think that's long enough. Let's go."

All the time she had been driving west, Georgie had told herself over and over that the chances of finding her parents were as good as non-existent. The 'evidence' they had found at her family home: the undamaged, open front door, the absence of her father's car, the word written on the reminder board, it was all circumstantial at best. And even if the evidence had been rock-solid, the chances of finding them alive in the cabin would still be remote. They could have found a *Dear Georgie* letter from her mother explaining that they had survived the Massacre of Loxwood Road and were heading for the cabin, and that still wouldn't mean they had survived the journey and avoided being killed since.

However logical this argument was, in reality it was just a self-protection mechanism; if Georgie had allowed her hopes to rise by even the tiniest amount then she would be running the risk of having them violently dashed on arrival, mimicking the fate of so many ships over the years on the unforgiving rocks that guarded the nearby coastline. Georgie didn't want to face that level of disappointment all at once, so she had done everything she could to accept in advance the idea that her family couldn't have made it. But her attempts had failed massively. Regardless of what she had told herself, her hopes had built up of their own accord until they had reached sky-high levels. She had tried to fight it. She had run through the cold hard facts in her mind, reminded herself of the reality of the situation. But she hadn't been able to stop herself from drifting into fantasy land, conjuring up rose-tinted daydreams of finding her parents and younger brother alive and well in the cabin, the tearful reunion, introducing them to Ant, sharing their stories, planning what they would do next.

Now - as they chipped away the remaining shards of glass in the window that Ant had fired through, climbed inside and walked from room to empty room - the bubbles holding the joyful scenes that had been swirling around Georgie's mind, stopped their swirling and burst, all at once, in a splat of disappointment.

There was no fairy-tale ending here. Georgie's family hadn't escaped to the cabin, unless they had been and gone, in which case they had shown an incredible lack of consideration by not leaving a note before they'd left. The one positive outcome for Georgie was that she had no evidence that proved categorically that her family were dead or had turned into mutants. Sadly, this didn't give her much comfort.

Georgie was reminded of a factoid she had once read in a museum. It had said that one of the guns in a firing squad almost always holds a blank so none of the shooters can know for sure that they fired a fatal shot. She had found this fascinating but always doubted how effective it could have been. Would it really have made the guys with the guns feel less guilty, either as they took aim at the bound and blindfolded target in front of them or relived the scene afterwards? The soldiers weren't stupid, they weren't going to absolve themselves of the responsibility, and any subsequent mental trauma, by clinging onto the faint chance that they had fired the empty round. Georgie knew the link to her situation was tenuous at best but she felt that the principle was the same. Sure, she could cling to a statistically possible but extremely implausible scenario because it was the one she preferred, but it was time to accept the most likely reality:

She was never going to see her parents again.

Chapter 37. Three's a crowd

I wish Anthony would stop talking about babies. I've told him it's a no from me and explained all the reasons why and he says he sees my point, but then the next day he'll just go and bring it up again.

It wouldn't be fair of us to have a baby. We're not going to live forever, so if we had a child we'd be as good as sentencing it to a life of loneliness after we've gone. The only way around that would be to risk our necks going out looking for other people or leave it up to the child to do that once we're in the ground. Finding other people is not an easy task, and there's no guarantee they'll be the sort of people we'd want to find. It's been eighteen months since the world ended and the longer time goes on, the more desperate the few remaining survivors will have become. The mutes will have got more desperate too.

We've got it as good as we could hope for here. I was crushed when we didn't find my parents, but one good thing that came out of it was that it brought us somewhere relatively safe. We've not seen a mute since we got here. Obviously that doesn't mean this area is mute-free; we have to assume that there are some around and that they could show up at any time, but it's kind of nice that we've not been attacked since we got here.

After drawing a blank at the cabin, I suggested we drive north to see if we could find Anthony's family. If nothing else I felt like I owed him that after he'd come all the way out here for me. But Ant wasn't interested. He said we'd done enough goose-chasing and should see if there was anywhere out here where we could take a time out. We didn't stay at the cabin, it's too exposed, anything could have sneaked up on us there. Instead we went house-hunting and struck gold about forty-minutes' drive away. It's on the south-east side of the chunk of Cornwall that sticks out into the sea, so it's protected against the wind from the west and it's still secluded. The nearest built-up area, if you can call it that, is a fishing village ten miles up the coast. It's definitely not the sort of place that anyone or anything is going to stumble across.

Our new residence can be described in one word: awesome. It's like a movie star's mansion in the Hollywood Hills. It's built on a slope that falls away onto its own private beach that's cut off from the rest of the coastline by sheer rocks on either side. The house is definitely someone's Grand Design, the four floors aren't stacked upwards, they're staggered, so they follow the line of the hill, making the place look like it's been carved into the rock of the hillside.

It gets better on the inside. The ultra-modern kitchen is a far cry from the rustic affair I'd always pictured myself in, but I can just about cope with the sleek lines, the quartz worksurfaces and the stunning views out to sea. The rest of the rooms are more of the same. We're living in somebody's dream home. And I've not even mentioned the best part yet. Actually, there's more than one best part.

The first best part is that the place is what the developers would have called an *eco-house*, which means it's basically covered in solar panels, and according to the brochures we found in the study, it's at least partly powered by the waves that we can see from every room. For some reason the brochures don't mention the old-fashioned gas that the cooker runs on, I imagine that's the place's dirty secret, but I'm not complaining.

The point is that we've got all the power we need.

Another best part is how secure this place is. Because it's landscaped into a narrow hillside, the only way to get into the property from land is by coming down the steep, purpose-built lane and through the automated garage door that's set into a very high, and very thick, concrete wall. It's nearly impossible for anyone to get in if they're not invited. I think that might have been a key part of the design brief. I wouldn't be surprised if a mafia-boss lived here before.

And that leads me smoothly on to the third best thing about this house: it doesn't contain the remains of its former owners. At least one person must have been here when the event happened because the garage door was open and a car was on the drive, but there's no trace of the car's owner or any passengers, just the clicker for the garage door in the coin-tray between the front seats. Not having to scrub out the stench of human remains when we arrived at the house was a huge bonus.

I could probably go on listing the best things about the place but I'll make this the last one. We've got a boat. And by that I don't mean a little rowing boat, I mean a proper boat with an engine and padded seats at the back, and a downstairs with more seats around a couple of little tables. It's even got a chemical toilet.

Actually, maybe a mafia-boss did live here.

The best thing about the boat, apart from it being really nice to have a boat, is that it means we can't get trapped here. If we get besieged by mutes then we can just stroll down to the jetty that sticks out of our private beach and disappear. Obviously we both hope that never happens, but it's good to know we have the option if it came to it. The other best thing about the boat, and yes, I realise I'm listing multiple best things again, is that we can use it to go fishing. The kingpin of the

West Country Crime-Syndicate was obviously a keen fisherman because there was plenty of fishing-gear on board, and Anthony and I have made very good use of it. Dad used to hire a boat and take us out whenever we'd stay at the cabin so I'm no slouch with a rod, and Anthony was delighted because I can tell him what we've caught. It's mostly mackerel but there's been plenty of cod and a few sea bass amongst other things. A high point for me, but not for Anthony, was when he caught a conger eel. It wasn't huge but it was plenty big enough. Watching Anthony trying to unhook the poor thing as it attempted to wrap itself around everything, including Anthony's arm, was hysterical.

We catch things from the beach too. Lots of crab and crayfish and even a few lobster. But it's not all *fruit de la mer*, we've planted vegetables in the fields at the top of the hill just outside of what we call our compound. The tomatoes were delicious and the first batch of potatoes weren't half-bad either. I have no idea why, but Anthony's decided to grow marrows. Neither of us likes marrows but he's doing it anyway. He says we can use them to make soup, even though neither of us has ever eaten - or expressed any interest in eating - marrow soup. I'm not sure why he's taken this mission on. I'd be interested to know what a psychiatrist might make of it. I can only assume it's a penis thing, but I'm just letting him get on with it.

We're not completely self-sufficient, we've had to make some trips outside. We mostly stick to isolated houses but we did take a risk and hit a retail park once, that's where we got all the seeds and planting gear from. There was a pharmacy there so I made sure Anthony got plenty of condoms, and I treated myself to cleansers and razors and all the things that men complain about women spending money on but soon notice when they don't. I know I don't have to pluck and scrub myself to please Anthony; I do it for me. I see it as a way of claiming my humanity back after everything we've been through. I won't pretend that Anthony's not satisfied with the result though.

We got ourselves some new clothes, too. It was definitely the nerviest shopping trip either of us had ever been on, but it turned out that the biggest worry we had was finding clothes that fit Anthony. Fortunately, one of the outlets had a *Big'n'Beefy* section. Ant loaded all of it into the trolley. It felt good when we got home, sitting in our luxury pad in our luxury chairs in clean, fresh clothes.

This was always meant to be a stopgap, somewhere to recharge our batteries while we decided what our long-term plans were. But to me, the longer this short-term break goes on, the more it feels like a long-term solution. When we arrived here just under a year ago we talked a lot about what we might do next. Crossing to Europe seemed to be the front runner, either by boat or through the tunnel. We were going to find other survivors, pitch in for the common goal, whatever that entailed. But none of that has come up for a while.

It feels like we're in a good place at the moment, both in terms of location and within ourselves. I still feel the pain of losing my family and everybody else I knew, and Anthony does too, but as I say, we've got it as good as we could hope for. I can see why Cornwall's answer to Tony Soprano chose to live here. Although judging from the pictures I've seen on the marble-topped sideboard, he looks more like an auditor than a gangster.

There might be one little fly in the ointment but it's probably nothing.

At the pharmacy, when I was stocking up on *women's things*, I got myself some tampons because I'd run out. That was six weeks ago. I've not had to use any of them yet.

Chapter 38.

I remember the list me and Georgie made just after she'd saved my arse that first time. All the questions we wanted answers to.

The first one. What the fuck happened? We still don't know the answer to that. We know that some sort of acid rain, poison rain, whatever, came down and it turned anyone it landed on into a raging cannibal, with lumpy purple skin and freaky eyes. But that's not the answer, that's a side-effect. What caused the poison rain? My guess is that we'll never find out.

We never found out about the electricity either. Did it just go off because there were no people around to keep it going or did someone switch it off?

I can't remember many of the other questions we wrote down. You'd think I would, wouldn't you? But I don't. It's weird because it feels like a really long time ago that Georgie was just a whisper on the other end of a walkie-talkie, but at the same time it feels like no time at all. One of the questions I do remember is the one about whether or not this thing has affected the whole world. We know the answer to that one now. It must have happened everywhere. For starters, we tried the radio every day, all channels, all frequencies and we never heard a word. And besides, if this wasn't a global thing then I'm certain some other country would have taken the opportunity to roll tanks into this green and pleasant land by now. Those of us who were left would have been easy pickings and I don't think the mutes would have put up much of a defence against a full-on invading army with guns and missiles and battle tactics.

That was going to be our next chapter, our next adventure. We were going to cross the channel into Europe and see what was going on there. It seems so simple when it's just chat, it seems like nothing at all. But the reality is something else entirely. I remember once going along with my mate Pete when he was thinking of buying a house. It was ridiculous, there was no way Pete was grown-up enough to buy a house, but I went along with him anyway because he was a mate. Jesus, I miss Pete. Anyway, the estate agent was a proper slimy bastard, like the exact caricature of a slimy bastard estate agent. I remember he wasn't wearing socks. He had long trousers on, and smart shoes, but no socks. It didn't seem right. Anyway, he was showing us round this overpriced shithole and when Pete pointed out that the lounge wasn't big enough to swing a slug in, Mr. Cock, Wank and Fuckarse didn't miss a beat. He said to Pete - and to me for some reason - "Well you can knock through into the kitchen, open up the space."

Okay, so I've never been in the building game but I'm pretty sure that knocking a wall down and making it all neat and tidy afterwards isn't the easiest thing in the world, but the way Billy No-Socks said it you'd think it was as easy as defrosting the fridge. And even if *knocking through* was the piece of piss the no-sock streak of piss was suggesting it was, it wouldn't have opened up any more space, it would have just made two small rooms into one medium sized room.

Buy some socks you twat.

I'm sure I was going somewhere with this. That was it, the difference between chat and reality. The Sockless Wonder was an extreme example, he was actively bullshitting us. Me and Pete told him so, but that's another story. The point is that we all do it, we all tell each other things that sound like we might actually do them, even though deep down we know there's no way in a billion years that we're going to.

Me and Georgie talked for ages about going to France. We talked about it like Ankle-Man had talked about knocking the wall down. We talked about it like taking a boat all the way from England to France was something we might do. I know the channel's not big when you compare it to the proper oceans in the world, but it's big enough. It's big enough to have tides and prevailing winds and all that malarkey. I wouldn't know the first thing about navigating to France. We'd probably end up in Scotland. But according to us, becoming intercontinental sailors wasn't the only option available to us, there was always the tunnel. That's right, we actually considered walking twenty-five miles through a pitch-black railway tunnel with Christ-knows-what waiting for us inside. We talked about it like we might do it.

Just knock the wall down. Just hop across to Europe. Jesus.

We weren't lying to each other. While the words were falling out of our mouths we believed every one of them. I'm sure there's something in that, something smart and profound about the human condition and the need sometimes to tell ourselves what we need to hear just so we can cling on to our dreams. Having the option of going to Europe meant that everything wasn't done with. It meant there was a chance of something else - the future wasn't closed.

When Georgie told me her news I knew she wasn't happy about it. She'd told me enough times what she thought about bringing a kid into this mess, but I couldn't stop smiling. I don't know how it had happened. I'd been careful just like she'd asked, honest! I said we should put it down to that old thing that people say, 'nature finds a way'. She didn't find that very funny. I told her that we'd find a way of making it work, just like the millions of couples who've found themselves in this position before, they found a way to make it work. We were no different, our situation was just a bit more… exaggerated.

To me, it was the best news in the world. Me and Georgie in our West Country retreat, as safe as we could hope to be, as comfortable as we could hope to be, bringing a new life into the world. I didn't want to sound too melodramatic but this was proper survival-of-the-species stuff. Our kid could have been the first step towards whatever comes next. Georgie didn't agree but I knew she'd come around. The mother's instinct was bound to kick in eventually.

But then the thing happened.

We'd kept telling ourselves not to get complacent, and again, while we were saying it we believed it, we thought we'd stick to it. But we let our guard down. Although, looking back on it, I'm not sure there was anything we could have done different, it happened so bloody fast.

Georgie was up top watering the plants. I'd have gone with her but I was going to give the boat a clean. The windscreen was filthy. The last few times I'd taken it out I'd had to stand up so I could see in front of me. I'd been waiting for a sunny day to go and sort it out, and there I was, in the garage, filling up a bucket with water.

And then it wasn't sunny anymore.

It started absolutely chucking it down. I couldn't believe it. It'd been totally clear before and now it was raining like I'd never seen. There was this smell in the air, like gunpowder. I've never actually smelled gunpowder but it was how I'd expect gunpowder to smell. But the scary thing wasn't the smell. Where the drops were hitting the concrete they were fizzing, like dollops of fat on a hot skillet.

I didn't realise straight away what was going on, I was just dealing with the here and now, and in the here and now there was toxic waste pissing from the sky and Georgie was out there, completely exposed, her perfect skin frazzling.

I didn't know what to do. I couldn't go out into that acid-monsoon, I knew I wouldn't last two seconds, so I just stood there like a total pussy, staying well clear of where the drops were splashing inside the open garage door. I was shouting Georgie's name, pathetically, over and over.

And after a few minutes the rain stopped.

I went outside. I could smell the soles of my trainers melting on the wet ground but I wasn't worried about my feet, I was worried about Georgie. I knew I wouldn't be able to see her until I reached the top where the ground levelled out, and it was driving me crazy that I hadn't got there yet. It was like one of those dreams where you're trying to run but your legs won't move. I stumbled and stuck out my right hand onto the slope in front of me to stop myself going over completely. I still have the burn marks on my knee and the palm of that hand.

That's when I heard Georgie's voice calling my name. I'd say it made me go faster but I was already going as fast as I could. I couldn't imagine she'd survived that chemical downpour so just hearing her voice was amazing news.

It took me a few seconds to realise that it wasn't amazing news at all, it was terrible news, the worst news.

It wasn't so much her voice, it was what she was saying. Actually she was singing.

"You say tomato, and I say tomarto, you say potato, and I say potarto."

We'd sang that song when we'd first dug the patch ready for planting, and it had become a thing. Every time either of us went up to do the gardening we'd start singing or humming that tune.

But Georgie had just been burned alive, she shouldn't have been singing anything. My doofus brain finally worked out what one plus one added up to.

Mute

I ran back down the slope and into the garage. I took the clicker from the shelf at the side and pressed the button. The garage door started to close. When it was half way down I pressed it again and it stopped. I went through to the open door to the house and waited in front of it.

I could hear Georgie getting closer, still singing that same line of the song over and over. It was like the creepiest horror movie ever. I saw her feet first, then her legs and the rest of her body through the half-closed garage door. Everything except her face. She stopped when she got to the door. She was wearing shorts and a vest top and the skin of her legs and arms looked like it had been barbecued.

She stooped under the door and came into the room.

All I could take in was her eyes. They were still that shocking, beautiful green but they'd inflated, nearly popping out of her scalded purple face.

I pressed the clicker and stepped back into the doorway into the house. Georgie took a step towards me. "You say tomato, Anthony. I say tomarto. You say potato. No-one says potarto."

The garage door clunked in place behind her and I stepped into the house and slammed the door.

I didn't have a plan, I just knew I couldn't shut her outside and leave her out there. It was hard enough to lock her in the garage. She's the love of my life and she's carrying my kid. This was the only thing I could think of in those few seconds that meant I could keep her close and keep her contained while I decided what to do. I sat on the kitchen floor with my back against the locked door, feeling it shake every time mutant Georgie pounded on the other side. I've never cried so hard.

Our first conversations through the door didn't go well. She stopped singing the tomato/potato song and started talking at least, but we didn't make much real progress. She just kept asking why she couldn't come in. "Why Anthony, why not?" It broke my heart.

I noticed from the glowing crack around the door that she'd worked out how to turn the light on, so at least she wasn't sitting in total darkness. I was chuffed about that. It took a while before I was able to feed her because I had to make sure she understood the procedure I'd come up with. We got there eventually. At mealtimes I'll knock on the door and she'll respond, then she'll go and stand at the opposite side of the room, and she'll keep talking so I can hear where she is, so I know she's not going to rush me when I open the door.

I give her whatever I've caught that day. She's easier to make dinner for now, I don't have to cook and I don't have to worry about cutting out the insides. She enjoys the crabs and lobster best because they're still alive when she gets them.

It's a shit life. I feel like a dungeon-keeper, throwing scraps of food to the poor bastards who'll never see daylight again, except this particular poor bastard is the most wonderful thing that ever happened to me.

I can't carry on like this.

I could leave, but I can't leave Georgie and I don't want to be on my own anyway. I've felt like taking the boat out where it's really deep and just jumping in. It's winter now, so I think the cold would get me before I'd need to worry about holding myself under long enough to drown. But again, I can't leave Georgie. And what about the baby? Georgie doesn't answer when I ask her if she can feel it inside her, but when I look in on her at mealtimes there's no doubting that everything's progressing on that score.

I miss her so much. The time we spent here before that fucking rainstorm already seems like paradise, we could have lived like that forever. But now we're living like this. I can't live without Georgie. And I can't live with her like this.

I've thought about it a lot. I've thought about nothing else for ages. I didn't have a plan before but I've got one now.

I'm going to spend as much time outside as I possibly can. I'll take a sleeping bag out there and as long as I can stay outside without freezing then I'm going to do it. If it does get too cold to spend the night out there then I'll sleep just inside the back door, and I'll leave the door open.

The next time it happens I'll be ready. The next time that rain comes down I'm going to go out, I'm going to let myself get absolutely soaking wet. Then I'll let Georgie out and we'll be together again, us and the baby, we'll be a family.

I hope it happens soon. It's really starting to smell in that garage now.

A.W. Wilson

FROM THE AUTHOR

I really hope you enjoyed it this book. If you did then please tell all your friends and leave a glowing review.

To check out other books I've written and to be updated on future releases then please go to my website and click on follow:

awwilson.com

If you want to get in touch, then please do:

contact@awwilson.com

Thanks!

Printed in Great Britain
by Amazon